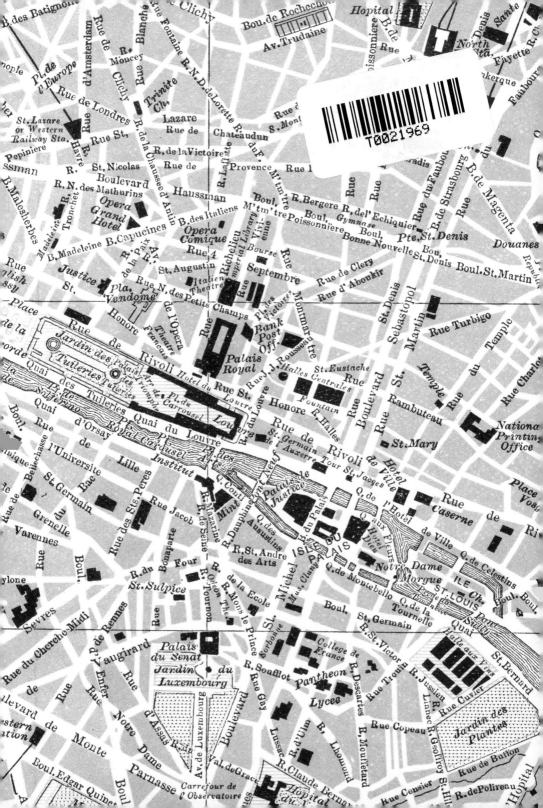

Ch.

Porte des Pres
St. Gervais

Monffaucon

Buttes Chaumont

Botzaris

Butte Chaumont

Serrurier

BELLEVILLE

Bolivar

Fessart

Villette

Rue de la Republique

Crimée

Ch.

Belleville

Haxo

Hospice
St. Louis

Rue
Theatre

Rue St. Fargeau

Napoleon
Docks

Faubourg du Temple

B. de Belville

de

Rue de Menilmontant

Rue de Charonne

Menilmontant

Station

Menilmontant

Av.

Boulevard

de la

Rue

Maur

Oberkampf

Boulevard

Ch. de

Rue Belgrand

Rue

de la

Republique

Boulevard

Abattoir

R. des Amandiers

Prison

Père la Chaise
Cemetery

Chapel

Tunnel

CHARONNE

Ch. de

R. Florian

Station de
Charonne

Boul. Beaumarchais

Boulevard Richard

Rue de Lenoir

Chemin Vert

Prison

Rue de la Roquette

Ledru

Rue de Charonne

Ch.

Voltaire

Avenue Philippe Auguste

Menilmontant

Boulevard de Charonne

des

Fontarabie

Pyrenees d'

Pl. de la
Bastille

Vincennes
Ry. Sta.

Rue du

Faubourg

Rue de Montreuil

Boul. Bourdon

Boul. Contrescarpe

Rue de Lyon

Rue

St. Antoine

Place de
la Nation

Av. du
Bel Air

Boul.

Avenue

de Mande

Petit Charonne

Rue de Lag

Cours de Vincen

IV

Diderot

Charenton

Rue

de

Boul.

Avenue

Rue

de

Picpus

Bizot

Prison

Avenue Rue

Boul.

Lyons
Railway
Station

Daumesnil

Rue de Reuilly

de Picpus

Station de
Bel-Air

Quai de la Rapée

Bercy

Orleans
Ry. Sta.

d'aust

Rapée Bd.

de Bercy

de

Reuilly

MAURICE LEBLANC

ARSÈNE LUPIN

CABALLERO LADRÓN

ALMA CLÁSICOS ILUSTRADOS

MAURICE LEBLANC

ARSÈNE LUPIN

CABALLERO LADRÓN

Traducción de Sofía Tros de Ilarduya

Ilustrado por
Fernando Vicente

Título original: *Arsène Lupin, gentleman-cambrioleur*

© de esta edición:
Editorial Alma
Anders Producciones S.L., 2022
www.editorialalma.com

 @almaeditorial
 @Almaeditorial

© de la traducción: Sofía Tros de Ilarduya

© de las ilustraciones: Fernando Vicente

Diseño de la colección: lookatcia.com
Diseño de cubierta: lookatcia.com
Maquetación y revisión: LocTeam, S.L.

ISBN: 978-84-18395-68-0
Depósito legal: B18776-2021

Impreso en España
Printed in Spain

Este libro contiene papel de color natural de alta calidad que no amarillea (deterioro por oxidación) con
el paso del tiempo y proviene de bosques gestionados de manera sostenible.

ÍNDICE

I

LA DETENCIÓN
DE ARSÈNE LUPIN

¡Qué extraño viaje! ¡Con lo bien que había empezado! Yo jamás había hecho una travesía que se presentara con tan buenos augurios. El Provence es un trasatlántico rápido y cómodo, al mando de un hombre de lo más agradable. A bordo estaba reunido lo más selecto de la sociedad. Allí hacíamos amistades y nos divertíamos. Todos teníamos la agradable sensación de estar apartados del mundo, nosotros solos, como en una isla desconocida, así que estábamos obligados a relacionarnos unos con otros.

Y vaya si nos relacionamos…

¿Habéis pensado alguna vez qué hay de singular e imprevisto en un grupo de personas que la víspera no se conocían y vivirán varios días en estrecha intimidad, entre el cielo infinito y el inmenso mar, desafiando juntos la cólera del océano, la terrible embestida de las olas y la traicionera calma del agua adormecida?

En el fondo es la vida misma, con sus reveses y sus grandezas, con su monotonía y su diversidad, pero vivida en una especie de reducción trágica y, quizá por eso, se disfruta con una prisa desasosegada y un placer más intenso el breve viaje cuyo final se ve desde el preciso momento en que comienza.

Pero, desde hace varios años, sucede algo que se añade especialmente a las emociones de la travesía. La islita flotante sigue dependiendo de ese mundo del que se creía liberada. Mantiene un lazo que solo se desata poco a poco en alta mar y, poco a poco, en alta mar, vuelve a anudarse. ¡La radiotelegrafía! ¡Señales de otro universo del que se recibirán noticias misteriosamente! Ya no vale pensar en unos cables por los que corre un mensaje invisible. El misterio es más insondable, más poético también, y hay que recurrir a las alas del viento para explicar este nuevo milagro.

Así, durante las primeras horas de la travesía, sentimos que esa voz lejana que, de vez en cuando, nos susurraba palabras del mundo, nos acompañaba, nos escoltaba e incluso nos precedía. Dos amigos se comunicaron conmigo. Otros diez, otros veinte nos enviaron a todos, a través del espacio, sus despedidas tristes o alegres.

Ahora bien, el segundo día del viaje, a quinientas millas de las costas francesas, en una tarde tormentosa, el radiotelégrafo nos comunicaba la siguiente noticia:

> Arsène Lupin a bordo, primera clase, pelo rubio, herida antebrazo derecho, viaja solo, con el nombre de R...

En ese preciso instante, un trueno violento estalló en el cielo oscuro. Se interrumpieron las ondas eléctricas y no recibimos el resto del mensaje. Solo sabíamos la inicial del nombre que utilizaba Arsène Lupin.

Si se hubiera tratado de cualquier otra noticia, no me cabe la menor duda de que tanto los radiotelegrafistas, como el comisario de a bordo y el comandante habrían guardado el secreto escrupulosamente, pero con determinados hechos es imposible mantener la discreción. Y este era uno de esos. Así que ese mismo día, sin que nadie pudiera decir cómo se había corrido la voz, todos sabíamos que el famoso Arsène Lupin se escondía entre nosotros.

¡Arsène Lupin en el barco! ¡El escurridizo ladrón del que todos los periódicos llevaban meses contando proezas! ¡El enigmático personaje con el que el viejo Ganimard, nuestro mejor policía, había entablado un duelo a muerte, con unas peripecias de lo más curiosas! Arsène Lupin, el extravagante caballero que solo robaba en castillos y salones, el que una noche se coló en casa del barón Schormann, se marchó con las manos vacías y dejó su tarjeta con esta frase: «Arsène Lupin, ladrón de guante blanco, volverá cuando los muebles sean auténticos». Arsène Lupin, ¡el hombre de los mil disfraces! Podía ser alternativamente chófer, tenor, corredor de apuestas, hijo de buena familia, adolescente, anciano, viajante de comercio marsellés, médico ruso o torero español.

Imaginad, Arsène Lupin trajinando entre los límites relativamente pequeños de un trasatlántico o, mejor dicho, ¡en el reducido espacio de primera clase, donde nos reuníamos a todas horas en el comedor, en el salón y en el salón de fumadores! Podría ser ese señor... o ese otro..., mi vecino de mesa, mi compañero de camarote...

—¡Y esto durará todavía cinco días más! —protestaba a la mañana siguiente miss Nelly Underdown—. ¡Pues es intolerable! Espero que lo detengan—. Y dirigiéndose a mí, añadió—: Veamos, usted, señor d'Andrésy, que se lleva tan bien con el comandante, ¿no sabe nada?

¡Ya querría saber algo para gustar a miss Nelly! Miss Nelly Underdown era una de esas mujeres magníficas que estén donde estén destacan de inmediato. Su belleza, tanto como su fortuna, deslumbraban. Ambas tenían una corte de fervorosos devotos y admiradores.

Miss Nelly, educada en París por una madre francesa, iba a reunirse con su padre, el riquísimo Underdown de Chicago. Una de sus amigas, lady Jerland, viajaba con ella.

Presenté mi candidatura al flirteo desde el primer momento. Pero, con la acelerada intimidad del viaje, su encanto me trastornó inmediatamente y, cuando sus ojos grandes y negros se cruzaban con los míos, me emocionaba demasiado para coquetear. De todos modos, a miss Nelly le agradaban mis detalles. Se dignaba a reír mis ocurrencias y le interesaban mis anécdotas. La señorita respondía con cierta simpatía a mi interés.

Puede que un rival sí me preocupara, uno muy apuesto, elegante y reservado, con un carácter taciturno que miss Nelly parecía preferir, algunas veces, a mis modales más «inapropiados» de parisiense.

Precisamente ese hombre estaba con el grupo de admiradores que rodeaba a miss Nelly cuando me preguntó sobre lo que ocurría. Estábamos en cubierta, cómodamente sentados en unas mecedoras. La tormenta de la víspera había aclarado el cielo. El momento era delicioso.

—No sé nada concreto, señorita —le respondí—, pero nosotros podríamos llevar a cabo nuestra propia investigación tan bien como el viejo Ganimard, el enemigo personal de Arsène Lupin.

—¡Dios mío! ¡Va usted muy lejos!

—¿Y por qué? ¿Tan complicado le parece el asunto?

—Sí, muy complicado.

—Se olvida usted de las pistas que tenemos para resolverlo.

—¿Qué pistas?

—Primera, Lupin se hace llamar señor R...

—Un dato algo impreciso.

—Segunda, viaja solo.

—Si le basta con esa peculiaridad...

—Tercera, es rubio.

—¿Y entonces?

—Entonces, únicamente tenemos que consultar la lista de pasajeros e ir eliminando a los que no se correspondan. —Yo tenía la lista en el bolsillo. La saqué y la repasé—. En primer lugar, solo hay trece personas con la inicial «R».

—¿Solo trece?

—En primera clase sí. De esos trece señores R..., como ustedes pueden comprobar, nueve viajan acompañados de mujeres, hijos o criados. Quedan cuatro personas solas: el marqués de Raverdan...

—Es el secretario de la embajada —interrumpió miss Nelly—. Lo conozco.

—El mayor Rawson...

—Es mi tío —dijo alguien.

—El señor Rivolta...

—Presente —gritó uno de nosotros, un italiano con una barba de un bonito color negro que casi le ocultaba la cara.

Miss Nelly estalló en carcajadas.

—Señor, usted no es precisamente rubio.

—Entonces —continué—, llegamos a la conclusión de que el culpable es el último de la lista.

—¿Y quién es?

—¿Quién es? El señor Rozaine. ¿Alguien conoce al señor Rozaine?

Nos callamos todos. Pero miss Nelly se dirigió al joven taciturno que a mí me atormentaba porque siempre estaba junto a ella y le dijo:

—Y bien, señor Rozaine, ¿no responde usted?

Lo miramos. Era rubio.

Confieso que en mi fuero interno la situación me impactó un poco. Y el silencio incómodo que envolvió al grupo me indicó que los demás también sentían una especie de sofoco. Por otra parte, era absurdo, porque en definitiva no había nada en el aspecto de ese caballero que nos permitiera sospechar de él.

—No respondo —dijo— porque, por mi nombre, mi condición de viajero solitario y el color de mi pelo, ya había hecho yo una reflexión parecida y llegado a la misma conclusión. Así que, creo que deben detenerme.

Cuando pronunció estas palabras tenía un gesto extraño. Los labios finos como dos líneas rígidas se le atenuaron aún más y palidecieron. Unos hilillos de sangre le enrojecieron los ojos.

Era evidente que bromeaba. A pesar de todo, su fisonomía y su actitud nos impresionaron. Miss Nelly preguntó ingenuamente:

—Pero ¿tiene usted alguna herida?

—Es cierto —dijo—, no, me falta la herida.

Con un gesto nervioso se subió la manga y enseñó el brazo. Y de inmediato me di cuenta de un detalle. Mis ojos se cruzaron con los de miss Nelly: había enseñado el brazo izquierdo.

Y, bueno, estaba a punto de decirlo, cuando ocurrió algo que desvió nuestra atención. Lady Jerland, la amiga de miss Nelly, llegó corriendo.

Estaba muy alterada. Todos fuimos a atenderla y solo después de muchos esfuerzos consiguió balbucear:

—¡Mis joyas, mis perlas! ¡Se lo han llevado todo!

No, como supimos más tarde, no se lo habían llevado todo, curiosamente, ¡habían hecho una selección de las joyas!

De la estrella de diamantes, del colgante de cabujones de rubí, de los collares y de las pulseras rotas, no se llevaron ni mucho menos las piedras más gruesas sino las más finas, las más preciosas, las que parecían tener más valor y ocupaban menos espacio. Dejaron las monturas tiradas encima de la mesa. Yo las vi, todos las vimos, sin sus tesoros, igual que unas flores a las que les hubieran arrancado sus pétalos preciosos y coloridos.

¡Y para llevar a cabo ese trabajo mientras lady Jerland tomaba el té, habían tenido que forzar la puerta del camarote, encontrar una bolsita escondida intencionadamente en el fondo de una sombrerera, abrirla, elegir las piedras, y todo a plena luz del día y en un pasillo muy transitado!

Cuando nos enteramos del robo, solo se escuchó una voz entre nosotros. La opinión de los pasajeros fue unánime: había sido Arsène Lupin. Y, de hecho, ese era claramente su estilo enrevesado, misterioso e inconcebible…, pero también lógico, porque, aunque era complicado esconder un voluminoso montón de joyas juntas, resultaba mucho más fácil ocultar las perlas, esmeraldas y zafiros por separado.

Durante la cena, ocurrió lo siguiente: a derecha e izquierda de Rozaine, los dos sitios permanecieron vacíos. Y por la noche supimos que el comandante lo había citado.

Su detención, que nadie cuestionó, causó un auténtico alivio. Por fin respirábamos tranquilos. Aquella noche participamos en algunos jueguecillos y bailamos. Miss Nelly sobre todo estuvo sorprendentemente alegre y eso me dio a entender que, aunque los detalles de Rozaine podían haberle agradado al principio, ya casi no los recordaba. Su encanto terminó de conquistarme. Hacia media noche, bajo la serena claridad de la luna, le declaré mi afecto con una emoción que no pareció disgustarle.

Sin embargo, al día siguiente, consternados, supimos que las pruebas contra Rozaine no eran suficientes, quedaba libre.

Rozaine, hijo de un conocido comerciante de Burdeos, había presentado su documentación en perfecta regla. Además, no tenía ninguna herida en los brazos.

—¡Documentación! ¡Partidas de nacimiento! —protestaron los enemigos de Rozaine—, ¡Arsène Lupin conseguiría todos los documentos que quisiera! Y la herida, pues o no la sufrió… o la hizo desaparecer.

A estos se les decía que, a la hora del robo, Rozaine estaba paseando por cubierta, y eso estaba demostrado. Entonces respondieron:

—Un hombre con la entereza de Arsène Lupin no necesita participar en un robo para cometerlo, ¿no es así?

Y, además, al margen de cualquier consideración extraña, había unos datos que ni los más escépticos podían refutar. ¿Quién, salvo Rozaine, viajaba solo, era rubio y su nombre empezaba por R? ¿A quién señalaba el telegrama si no era a Rozaine?

Y cuando Rozaine, minutos antes del almuerzo, se atrevió a acercarse a nuestro grupo, miss Nelly y lady Jerland se levantaron y se apartaron.

Efectivamente, era miedo.

Una hora más tarde, una circular manuscrita pasaba de mano en mano entre los trabajadores de a bordo, los marineros y los viajeros de todas las clases: el señor Louis Rozaine ofrecía diez mil francos a la persona que descubriera quién era Arsène Lupin o encontrara a quien tuviera las joyas robadas.

—Y si nadie acude en mi ayuda contra ese bandido —aseguró Rozaine al comandante—, yo, yo solo, tendré que hacer su trabajo.

Rozaine contra Arsène Lupin o, mejor dicho, según lo que corría por el barco, Arsène Lupin, él mismo, contra Arsène Lupin, ¡la pelea parecía interesante!

Y esa situación duró dos días.

Se vio a Rozaine deambular de un lado a otro, mezclarse con el personal, preguntar a los pasajeros y husmear por el barco. Por la noche, se distinguía su sombra merodeando.

También el comandante desplegó una frenética actividad. Mandó inspeccionar el Provence de arriba abajo y por todos los rincones. Registraron los camarotes, sin excepción, con el pretexto muy razonable de que las joyas estarían escondidas en cualquier sitio menos en el camarote del culpable.

—Acabarán descubriendo algo, ¿verdad? —me preguntaba miss Nelly—. Por muy genio que sea, no puede hacer que los diamantes y las perlas se vuelvan invisibles.

—Pues claro que sí —le respondí—, pero entonces habría que registrar el forro de los sombreros, el dobladillo de las chaquetas y todo lo que llevemos encima. —Le enseñé mi Kodak, una 9×12 con la que no me cansaba de fotografiarla en las poses más diversas—: ¿No cree usted que solo en una cámara de este tamaño habría espacio para todas las joyas de lady Jerland? Finges unas tomas y listo.

—Pero he oído decir que no hay un solo ladrón que no deje alguna pista.

—Sí, hay uno: Arsène Lupin.

—¿Y por qué?

—¿Por qué? Porque no piensa únicamente en el robo, sino también en todas las circunstancias que podrían delatarlo.

—Al principio usted tenía más confianza.

—Pero después he visto su trabajo.

—¿Y qué piensa ahora?

—Creo que estamos perdiendo el tiempo.

Y, de hecho, las investigaciones no daban ningún resultado o, al menos, los que dieron no se correspondían con el esfuerzo general: al comandante le robaron el reloj.

El comandante, furioso, se empeñó el doble, vigiló a Rozaine de más cerca aún y mantuvo varias conversaciones con él. Al día siguiente, graciosa ironía, el reloj apareció en el falso cuello del segundo de a bordo.

Todo aquello parecía increíble y revelaba muy bien el estilo cómico de Arsène Lupin, ladrón, de acuerdo, pero diletante también. Trabajaba por gusto y por vocación, desde luego, pero también por divertirse. Daba la impresión de ser un caballero que se entretiene dirigiendo una obra de teatro y, entre bambalinas, ríe a mandíbula batiente de sus ocurrencias y de las situaciones que crea.

En definitiva, Lupin era un artista en su género, y cuando yo observaba a Rozaine, sombrío y tenaz, y pensaba en el doble papel que probablemente asumía ese curioso personaje, solo podía hablar de él con cierta admiración.

La penúltima noche, el oficial de guardia oyó unos quejidos en el lugar más oscuro de cubierta. Se acercó. Había un hombre tendido con la cabeza envuelta en una bufanda gris muy gruesa y las muñecas atadas con una cuerda muy fina.

Lo liberaron de las ligaduras. Lo levantaron y lo atendieron.

Aquel hombre era Rozaine.

Era Rozaine, lo habían asaltado, abatido y robado durante una de sus expediciones. Una tarjeta prendida con un alfiler en su ropa tenía escritas estas palabras: «Arsène Lupin acepta agradecido los diez mil francos del señor Rozaine».

Lo cierto es que en la cartera robada había veinte mil francos.

Naturalmente, acusamos al desgraciado de fingir un ataque contra sí mismo. Pero, además de que le habría sido imposible atarse de aquella manera, quedó comprobado que la letra de la tarjeta era completamente diferente de la de Rozaine y, al contrario, se parecía, hasta confundirse, a la de Arsène Lupin, tal y como la reproducía un periódico viejo que encontramos a bordo.

Así que Rozaine ya no era Arsène Lupin. ¡Rozaine era Rozaine, el hijo de un comerciante de Burdeos! Y la presencia de Arsène Lupin se confirmaba una vez más ¡y de qué manera tan terrible!

Cundió el pánico. No nos atrevíamos a quedarnos a solas en el camarote y mucho menos a ir solos por lugares demasiado aislados del barco. Nos reuníamos prudentemente con las personas con las que nos sentíamos seguros. Y, aun así, un recelo instintivo enfrentaba a los más íntimos. Porque la amenaza ya no procedía de un individuo aislado y por lo tanto menos peligroso. Entonces, Arsène Lupin era..., era todo el mundo. Nuestras exaltadas imaginaciones le atribuían un poder asombroso e ilimitado. Le creíamos capaz de usar los disfraces más imprevistos y de ser sucesivamente el respetable mayor Rawson o el noble marqués de Raverdan o incluso cualquier persona conocida, con mujer, hijos y criados, porque ya ni teníamos en cuenta la inicial acusadora.

Los primeros telegramas no proporcionaron ninguna noticia. Al menos el comandante no informó de nada y semejante silencio tampoco era para tranquilizarnos.

El último día pareció interminable. Vivíamos angustiados esperando cualquier desgracia. Y esta vez no sería un robo, no sería una simple agresión, sería un crimen, un asesinato. No podíamos aceptar que Arsène Lupin se contentara con esos dos insignificantes botines. Dueño absoluto del barco, y frente a la impotencia de las autoridades, Lupin solo tenía que querer, todo le estaba permitido, era el dueño de nuestras propiedades y de nuestras vidas.

Pero confieso que aquellas horas fueron fantásticas para mí, porque me gané la confianza de miss Nelly. La señorita Underdown era de naturaleza inquieta y tantos acontecimientos la habían impresionado, así que buscó instintivamente que yo la protegiera, le diera seguridad, y yo lo hacía encantado.

En el fondo, bendecía a Arsène Lupin. Él nos estaba uniendo. Y gracias a él yo podía dejarme llevar por agradables fantasías. Fantasías de amor y fantasías menos quiméricas, ¿por qué no confesarlo? Los Andrésy son de buen abolengo poitevino, pero su escudo está algo deslucido y no me parece indigno de un caballero soñar con devolver el lustre perdido a su nombre.

Y sentía que a miss Nelly no le disgustaban esas fantasías. Sus ojos risueños me las alentaban. La dulzura de su voz me daba esperanzas.

Y estuvimos juntos, apoyados en la borda, hasta el último momento, mientras el perfil de la costa americana navegaba hacia nosotros.

Se habían interrumpido los registros. Estábamos a la espera. Todos los pasajeros, desde los de primera clase hasta los de entrecubierta —un hervidero de emigrantes— estábamos esperando el momento culminante en que al fin se resolviera aquel misterio sin solución. ¿Quién era Arsène Lupin? ¿Con qué nombre, con qué máscara se ocultaba el famoso Arsène Lupin?

Y el momento culminante llegó. Aunque pudiera vivir cien años, no olvidaría ni el más ínfimo detalle de lo que ocurrió.

—Qué pálida está, miss Nelly —dije a mi amiga, que se apoyaba en mi brazo, alicaída.

—¡Y usted! —me respondió—. ¡Ay, está tan cambiado!

—¡Imagine! Este momento es apasionante y me siento feliz de vivirlo junto a usted, miss Nelly. Me parece que su recuerdo tardará en irse algún tiempo...

Miss Nelly no me escuchaba, estaba sin aliento, frenética. Bajaron la pasarela. Pero antes de que pudiéramos cruzarla, unas personas subieron a bordo, agentes de aduanas, hombres de uniforme y unos carteros.

Mis Nelly dijo balbuceando:

—No me sorprendería que descubrieran que Arsène Lupin se escapó durante la travesía.

—Quizá prefirió la muerte a la deshonra y lanzarse al Atlántico antes de dejar que lo detengan.

—No se burle —dijo miss Nelly, molesta.

De pronto, me estremecí y cuando ella me preguntó qué me ocurría, le dije:

—¿Ve usted a ese viejo hombrecillo de pie en el extremo de la pasarela?

—¿Con un paraguas y un redingote de color verde oliva?

—Es Ganimard.

—¿Ganimard?

—Sí, el famoso policía, el que juró detener a Arsène Lupin personalmente. ¡Bueno! Ahora entiendo por qué no hemos tenido noticias de este lado del Atlántico. Ganimard andaba por medio. No le gusta que nadie se entrometa en sus asuntillos.

—Entonces, ¿seguro que pillará a Arsène Lupin?

—¿Quién sabe? Parece ser que Ganimard solo lo ha visto caracterizado y disfrazado. A no ser que conozca su identidad falsa...

—¡Ay! —dijo Nelly con esa curiosidad un poco cruel de las mujeres— ¡Ojalá pudiera ver cómo lo detiene!

—Vamos a esperar. Indudablemente, Arsène Lupin se habrá dado cuenta de que el enemigo está aquí, así que preferirá salir de los últimos, cuando el viejo ya tenga la vista cansada.

Empezó el desembarco. Ganimard, apoyado en el paraguas, con aire indiferente, no parecía prestar atención a los pasajeros que se apresuraban por la pasarela. Yo me fijé en que un oficial de a bordo, detrás de él, le informaba de vez en cuando.

Desfilaron el marqués de Raverdan, el mayor Rawson, el italiano Rivolta y más, y muchos más... Y a lo lejos vi que Rozaine se acercaba.

¡Pobre Rozaine! ¡No parecía repuesto de sus desgracias!

—A lo mejor, a pesar de todo, es él —me dijo miss Nelly—. ¿Usted qué cree?

—Pues creo que sería muy interesante tener una fotografía de Ganimard y Rozaine juntos. Tenga mi máquina que yo voy muy cargado.

Y se la di, pero demasiado tarde para que hiciera la foto. Rozaine ya pasaba por delante del inspector. El oficial de a bordo se inclinó y dijo algo al oído a Ganimard, este se encogió ligeramente de hombros y Rozaine pasó.

Pero, Dios mío, ¿quién era Arsène Lupin?

—Sí —dijo Nelly en voz alta—, ¿quién es?

Ya solo quedaban veinte personas. Miss Nelly las observaba una a una, con el confuso temor de que Lupin no estuviera entre esas veinte personas.

—No podemos esperar más —le dije.

Ella echó a andar y yo la seguí. Pero no habíamos avanzado ni diez metros cuando Ganimard nos cerró el paso.

—Pero bueno, ¿qué pasa? —grité.

—Un momento, señor, ¿qué prisa tiene?

—Acompaño a la señorita.

—Un momento —repitió con un tono más autoritario. Me examinó de arriba abajo y luego me dijo mirándome a los ojos—: Arsène Lupin, ¿no es así?

Yo me eché a reír.

—No, soy Bernard d'Andrésy, así de simple.

—Bernard d'Andrésy murió hace tres años en Macedonia.

—Si Bernard d'Andrésy estuviera muerto, yo ya no estaría en este mundo. Y ese no es el caso. Aquí tiene mi documentación.

—Esa es la documentación de Andrésy. Y con mucho gusto le explicaré cómo la consiguió usted.

—¡Pero usted está loco! El nombre con el que embarcó Arsène Lupin empezaba por R.

—Sí, otro de sus trucos, ¡una pista falsa sobre la que lanzó a todo el mundo en el barco! Amigo mío, tiene usted mucho talento. Pero esta vez le ha cambiado la suerte. Vamos, Lupin, sea buen jugador.

Yo titubeé un segundo, pero Ganimard me dio un golpe seco en el antebrazo derecho. Solté un grito de dolor. Me había golpeado en la herida aún mal cerrada que mencionaba el telegrama.

Bueno, había que resignarse. Me volví hacia miss Nelly, que nos escuchaba lívida y aturdida.

Su mirada se cruzó con la mía y luego miró la Kodak. Hizo un gesto brusco y tuve la sensación, no, estuve seguro de que de pronto lo había comprendido todo. Sí, ahí estaban, entre las estrechas paredes de piel de zapa negra, en el hueco del pequeño objeto que tuve la precaución de entregarle antes de que Ganimard me detuviera, sí, ahí estaban los veinte mil francos de Rozaine, las perlas y los diamantes de lady Jerland.

¡Oh! Lo juro, en ese momento tan serio, mientras Ganimard y dos de sus esbirros me rodeaban, todo me daba igual, la detención, la hostilidad de la gente, todo salvo qué iba a hacer mis Nelly con la Kodak.

Ni siquiera me preocupaba que existiese una prueba material y decisiva contra mí, pero, ¿entregaría miss Nelly esa prueba?

¿Me traicionaría? ¿Me destruiría? ¿Actuaría como una enemiga que no perdona o como una mujer que recuerda y dulcifica su deprecio con un poco de indulgencia y con un poco de compasión involuntaria?

Miss Nelly pasó por delante de mí. Me despedí de ella en voz muy baja, sin añadir una palabra. Iba hacia la pasarela, mezclada entre los demás viajeros, con la Kodak en la mano.

«Seguramente —pensé— no se atreve a entregarla en público. Dentro de una hora o en un instante la entregará.»

Pero cuando llegó a mitad de la pasarela, fingió torpemente un movimiento y tiró la cámara al agua, entre la pared del muelle y el costado del buque.

Luego la vi alejarse.

Su hermosa figura se perdió entre el gentío, apareció de nuevo y volvió a desaparecer. Aquello se había acabado, se había acabado para siempre.

Me quedé quieto un rato, triste y a la vez muy emocionado, luego suspiré para gran sorpresa de Ganimard:

—En fin, es una lástima no ser un hombre honrado…

Así fue como Arsène Lupin, una tarde de invierno, me contó la historia de su detención. Las casualidades de la vida, que algún día relataré, nos llevaron a iniciar una relación... yo diría ¿de amistad? Sí, me atrevo a creer que Arsène Lupin es en cierto modo mi amigo, y por esa amistad llega algunas veces a mi casa de improviso y trae, al silencio de mi despacho, su alegría juvenil, la luz de su intensa vida y el buen humor de un hombre al que la suerte le favorece y le sonríe.

¿Su retrato? ¿Cómo podría describirlo? Si he visto veinte veces a Arsène Lupin, las veinte era una persona diferente... o, mejor dicho, era la misma persona, pero como vista a través de veinte espejos que reflejan otras tantas imágenes distorsionadas de él, pero cada una con sus ojos peculiares, la forma especial de su cara, su gesto propio, su perfil y su carácter.

—Yo mismo —me dice— ya no sé muy bien quién soy. No me reconozco en un espejo. —Una broma, desde luego, y una contradicción, pero una verdad para los que se lo cruzan en la vida y no conocen sus recursos infinitos, su paciencia, su arte para el maquillaje, su extraordinaria capacidad para transformar hasta las proporciones de su cara y de alterar la propia relación de sus rasgos—. ¿Por qué —continúa— debería tener un aspecto definido? ¿Por qué no iba a evitar el peligro de ser siempre la misma persona? Mis hechos ya me representan lo suficiente. —Y añade con una pizca de orgullo—: Es mucho mejor para mí que nadie pueda decir con toda seguridad: este es Arsène Lupin. Lo principal es que digan sin miedo al equívoco: esto lo ha hecho Arsène Lupin.

Yo intento reconstruir alguna de sus hazañas y algunas de sus aventuras a través de las confidencias que tiene la generosidad de compartir conmigo algunas tardes de invierno en el silencio de mi despacho...

2

ARSÈNE LUPIN EN LA CÁRCEL

No hay un turista digno de ese nombre que conozca la ribera del Sena y no se haya fijado, yendo desde las ruinas de Jumièges a las ruinas de Saint-Wandrille, en el pequeño y singular castillo feudal de Malaquis, tan orgullosamente plantado en una roca, en mitad del río. El arco de un puente lo une a la carretera. La base de sus torrecillas sombrías se confunde con el granito que lo sostiene, un bloque que alguna formidable convulsión arrancó de no se sabe qué montaña y lo lanzó allí. A su alrededor, el agua tranquila del río enorme juega entre los juncos y las lavanderas tiemblan en las crestas húmedas de los guijarros.

La historia del castillo de Malaquis es dura como su nombre y hosca como su silueta. Allí solo hubo combates, asedios, asaltos, rapiñas y matanzas. Durante las veladas, los lugareños del país de Caux recuerdan temblando los crímenes que allí se cometieron. Cuentan misteriosas leyendas y hablan del famoso subterráneo que antiguamente unía el castillo con la abadía de Jumièges y la casona de Agnès Sorel, la hermosa amante de Carlos VII.

En ese antiguo refugio de héroes y bandidos vive el barón Nathan Cahorn, el barón Satán, como se le llamaba en otros tiempos en la Bolsa de París, donde se enriqueció quizá demasiado rápido. Los señores de

Malaquis, arruinados, tuvieron que venderle el hogar de sus antepasados por un trozo de pan. El barón instaló en el castillo sus admirables colecciones de muebles y cuadros, de cerámica y de madera tallada. Allí vive él solo con tres viejos criados. Nadie entra jamás a su casa. Jamás nadie ha contemplado en los salones llenos de antigüedades sus tres Rubens, los dos Watteau, la silla de Jean Goujon y otras muchas maravillas arrancadas a golpe de billetes a los asiduos más ricos de las subastas.

Y es que el barón Satán tiene miedo. Pero el barón no tiene miedo por él, sino por los tesoros que acumula con una pasión tenaz y el ojo de un aficionado al que ni el más listo de los marchantes puede presumir de haber engañado. El barón ama sus tesoros. Y los ama con la codicia de un avaro y los celos de un enamorado.

Todos los días, al caer el sol, se cierran con llave las cuatro puertas reforzadas de hierro que protegen los dos extremos del puente y las entradas al patio de honor. Al menor golpe, unos timbres eléctricos vibran en silencio. Del lado del Sena, nada que temer: allí la roca se levanta en vertical.

Ahora bien, un viernes de septiembre, el cartero se presentó como de costumbre en la cabecera del puente. Y, como era habitual, el barón entreabrió un poco la pesada puerta.

Examinó al cartero tan minuciosamente como si no lo conociera desde hacía años, con esa cara tan bondadosa y alegre y esos ojos socarrones de campesino, y entonces, el hombre le dijo riendo:

—Que soy yo, señor barón, yo, como siempre. No soy otro que me ha robado la bata y la gorra.

—Nunca se sabe —murmuró Cahorn.

El cartero le entregó un montón de periódicos y luego añadió:

—Y ahora, señor barón, hay novedades.

—¿Novedades?

—Una carta... y, además, certificada.

El barón vivía aislado, no tenía amigos ni nadie que se preocupara por él, así que nunca recibía correspondencia, por eso aquella novedad le pareció inmediatamente un mal presagio y un motivo de preocupación. ¿Quién le habría enviado aquella misteriosa carta a su retiro?

—Tiene que firmar, señor barón.

Firmó refunfuñando. Luego, cogió la carta y esperó a que el cartero desapareciese por la curva de la carretera, dio unas vueltas de un lado a otro, se apoyó en el antepecho del puente y abrió el sobre. Dentro había una hoja de papel cuadriculado con este encabezamiento: «Prisión de la Santé, París». Miró la firma: «Arsène Lupin». Y el conde, sorprendido, leyó:

Señor barón:

En la galería que comunica sus dos salones hay un cuadro de Philippe de Champaigne de extraordinaria factura que me encanta. También me gustan los Rubens y el cuadrito de Watteau. En el salón de la derecha, anoto la consola Luis XIII, los tapices de Beauvais, el velador estilo Imperio firmado por Jacob y el aparador renacentista. En el de la izquierda, la vitrina con todas las joyas y miniaturas que tiene dentro.

Por esta vez, me limitaré a esos objetos que serán, creo yo, de fácil venta. Así pues, le ruego que los mande embalar adecuadamente y los envíe a mi nombre (a portes pagados) a la estación de Batignolles, antes de ocho días, de lo contrario, yo mismo me encargaré de trasladarlos la noche del miércoles 27 al jueves 28 de septiembre. Y, como es razonable, no me llevaré solo los objetos que indico más arriba.

Le ruego disculpe las pequeñas molestias que le causo y acepte mis más respetuosos saludos. Atentamente,

Arsène Lupin

P. S. Ante todo, no me envíe el Watteau grande. Aunque usted pagó treinta mil francos en la subasta, es una copia, Barras quemó el original durante el Directorio, en una noche de orgía. Consulte las *Mémoires* inéditas de Garat.

Tampoco me interesa la cadena de señora con colgantes Luis XV, de dudosa autenticidad.

La carta dejó conmocionado al barón de Cahorn. Si hubiera sido de cualquier otra persona ya se habría asustado, ¡pero de Arsène Lupin!

El barón era un lector asiduo de periódicos, estaba al corriente de todo lo que ocurría en el mundo sobre robos y crímenes y conocía las hazañas del maldito ladrón. Sabía con seguridad que Lupin estaba en la cárcel, lo había detenido su archienemigo Ganimard en América, y que el proceso abierto se instruía con muchas dificultades. Pero también sabía el barón que Arsène Lupin era capaz de todo. De hecho, el conocimiento exacto que tenía del castillo y de la situación de los cuadros y de los muebles era muy mala señal. ¿Quién podría haberle informado de algo que no había visto nadie?

El barón levantó la mirada y contempló la silueta arisca del castillo de Malaquis, su pedestal abrupto, el agua profunda que lo rodeaba y se encogió de hombros. No, decididamente, no había ningún peligro. Nadie en el mudo podría entrar en el santuario inviolable de sus colecciones de arte.

Nadie, completamente de acuerdo, pero ¿y Arsène Lupin? ¿Existen puertas, puentes levadizos o murallas para Arsène Lupin? ¿De qué sirven los obstáculos más ingeniosos y las precauciones más hábiles si Arsène Lupin ha decidido alcanzar un objetivo?

Esa misma noche, el barón escribió al fiscal de la República del distrito de Ruan. Le enviaba la carta con las amenazas y le pedía ayuda y protección.

La respuesta no tardó en llegar: el llamado Arsène Lupin está actualmente detenido en la Santé, vigilado muy de cerca y sin posibilidad de escribir, la carta solo podía ser de un impostor. Todo lo señalaba, tanto la lógica y el sentido común, como la realidad de los hechos. Sin embargo, y por exceso de celo, se había nombrado a un perito para que examinara la letra y el perito había declarado que, «pese a ciertas similitudes» la letra no era la del detenido.

«Pese a ciertas similitudes», el barón solo se quedó con esas tres palabras aterradoras; para él significaban que existía una duda, por lo tanto, un motivo suficiente para que hubiera intervenido la justicia. Sus temores se intensificaban. No dejaba de leer la carta. «Yo mismo me encargaré de trasladarlos». Y la fecha concreta: ¡la noche del miércoles 27 al jueves 28 de septiembre!...

Cahorn, suspicaz y taciturno, no se atrevió a confiar en sus criados, cuya fidelidad no le parecía fuera de toda duda. Sin embargo, por primera vez desde hacía años, sentía la necesidad de hablar y de pedir consejo. La justicia de su país lo había abandonado, ya no esperaba poder defenderse con sus propios medios, así que estuvo a punto de ir a París y suplicar ayuda a algún antiguo policía.

Transcurrieron dos días. El tercero, cuando estaba leyendo los periódicos, dio un salto de alegría. *Le Réveil de Caudebec* publicaba la siguiente noticia:

> Tenemos el placer de contar entre nosotros, desde hace casi tres semanas, al inspector principal Ganimard, un veterano de la Dirección de la Seguridad General. El señor Ganimard, cuya última hazaña, el arresto de Arsène Lupin, le valió el reconocimiento de toda Europa, descansa de sus duras fatigas pescando mújoles con caña.

¡Ganimard! ¡Él era la ayuda que estaba buscando el barón de Cahorn! ¿Quién mejor que el astuto y paciente Ganimard podría desbaratar los planes de Lupin?

El barón no lo dudó. Seis kilómetros separaban el castillo del pueblecito de Caudebec. Los recorrió a paso ligero, como impulsado por la esperanza de su salvación.

Tras varios intentos frustrados de dar con la dirección del inspector principal, se dirigió a las oficinas del *Réveil,* situadas en medio del muelle. Allí estaba el redactor de la noticia, y este se acercó a la ventana y dijo en voz alta:

—¿Ganimard? Seguro que lo encuentra en el muelle con la caña de pescar en la mano. Ahí nos conocimos, cuando leí por casualidad su nombre grabado en la caña. Mire, ese viejecito de allí, el que está debajo de los árboles del paseo.

—¿Con un redingote y un sombrero de paja?

—¡Exacto! Desde luego, es un tipo curioso, no muy hablador y más bien huraño.

Cinco minutos después, el barón abordaba al famoso Ganimard, se presentaba e intentaba entablar conversación con él. Como no lo consiguió, le habló francamente y le explicó la situación.

El otro lo escuchó sin moverse y sin perder de vista el pez que acechaba, luego se volvió hacia el barón, lo miró de arriba abajo con una expresión de profunda lástima y le dijo:

—Señor, no suele ser muy habitual avisar a las personas a las que se pretende robar. Y Arsène Lupin…, él no cometería semejante error.

—Pero…

—Señor, si tuviera la más mínima duda, crea sinceramente que el placer de volver a entrometerme en los asuntos de mi querido Lupin ganaría frente a todo lo demás. Por desgracia, ese chico está entre rejas.

—¿Y si se escapara?…

—Nadie se escapa de la Santé.

—¿Ni siquiera él?…

—Ni él ni nadie.

—Pero…

—Bien, pues si se escapa, mucho mejor para mí, porque volveré a pillarlo. Mientras tanto, duerma tranquilo y no me espante al mújol.

Se había terminado la conversación. El barón, al ver tan seguro a Ganimard, regresó a su casa un poco más tranquilo. Allí comprobó las cerraduras, espió a los criados y durante las siguientes cuarenta y ocho horas casi llegó a convencerse de que, al fin y al cabo, sus temores no eran reales. No, definitivamente, como le había dicho Ganimard, si piensas robar a una persona, no la avisas.

Se acercaba el día señalado. Durante la mañana del martes, víspera del 27, no ocurrió nada de particular. Pero a las tres de la tarde, un chico tocó el timbre. Llevaba un telegrama para el barón.

No ha llegado ningún paquete a la estación de Batignolles. Prepare todo para la noche de mañana. Arsène.

Otra vez le entró el pánico al barón, hasta tal punto que pensó en ceder a las exigencias de Arsène Lupin.

El barón corrió a Caudebec. Ganimard estaba pescando en el mismo lugar, sentado en una silla plegable. Sin decir ni una palabra, Cahorn le entregó el telegrama.

—¿Y qué?

—¿Y qué? ¡Es mañana!

—¿Qué?

—¡El robo! ¡El saqueo de mis colecciones!

Ganimard dejó la caña, se volvió hacia el barón y, con los brazos cruzados a la altura del pecho, gritó impaciente:

—¡Pero bueno! ¡Usted cree que yo voy a ocuparme de un asunto tan estúpido!

—¿Qué compensación quiere por pasar la noche del 27 al 28 de septiembre en el castillo?

—Ni un céntimo, déjeme en paz.

—Fije un precio, soy rico, soy inmensamente rico.

La brusquedad de la oferta desconcertó a Ganimard, que dijo ya más tranquilo:

—Estoy aquí de vacaciones y no tengo autorización para involucrarme...

—Nadie lo sabrá. Yo me comprometo a guardar silencio pase lo que pase.

—¡Dios mío! No pasará nada.

—Pues bien, veamos, ¿tres mil francos serán suficientes?

El inspector aspiró un poco de rapé, reflexionó y soltó:

—De acuerdo. Pero antes tengo que decirle honestamente que es un dinero tirado por la ventana.

—Me importa un bledo.

—En ese caso... Además, ¡nunca se sabe con ese maldito Lupin! Debe de tener a sus órdenes a toda una banda... ¿Confía usted en sus criados?

—La verdad...

—Entonces, no contaremos con ellos. Mandaré un telegrama a dos hombretones amigos míos que nos darán más seguridad... Y ahora, lárguese, que no nos vean juntos. Hasta mañana hacia las nueve de la noche.

Al día siguiente, la fecha fijada por Arsène Lupin, el barón de Cahorn descolgó la colección de armas, las dejó preparadas y dio un paseo por los alrededores del castillo. No vio nada sospechoso.

Por la noche, a las ocho y media, despidió a los criados.

El servicio vivía en un ala cuya fachada daba a la carretera, pero un poco apartada y en un extremo del castillo. Cuando se quedó solo, abrió despacio las cuatro puertas. Al cabo de un rato, oyó unos pasos que se acercaban.

Ganimard presentó al barón a sus dos ayudantes, unos muchachos grandes y robustos, con cuello de toro y manos fuertes, y luego le pidió ciertas explicaciones. Después de informarse de la disposición del castillo, cerró con cuidado y bloqueó todas las entradas por las que se pudiera acceder a los salones amenazados. Examinó las paredes, levantó los tapices y, por último, colocó a sus agentes en la galería central.

—Sin tonterías, ¿eh? No hemos venido aquí a dormir. A la menor señal de alarma, abrís las ventanas del patio y me llamáis. Tened cuidado también por el lado del agua. Diez metros de acantilado vertical no detienen a personajes como ese demonio de Lupin. —Los dejó allí encerrados, se llevó las llaves y le dijo al barón—: Y ahora a nuestros puestos. —Ganimard, para pasar la noche en el castillo, había elegido una habitación pequeña, abierta en el grueso de la pared de la muralla entre las dos puertas principales, que antiguamente había sido la garita del vigilante. Una mirilla se abría al puente y otra al patio. En una esquina se veía como el orificio de un pozo—. Me dijo usted, señor barón, que este pozo es la única salida de los subterráneos y que desde tiempos inmemoriales está embozada, ¿es así?

—Sí.

—Entonces, si no existe alguna otra entrada que nadie conozca, salvo Arsène Lupin, lo cual sería un problema, podemos estar tranquilos. —Ganimard alineó tres sillas, se tumbó cómodamente, encendió la pipa y suspiró—. Realmente, señor barón, debo de tener muchas ganas de añadir una planta a la casita donde pienso acabar mis días para aceptar un trabajo tan elemental. Le contaré la historia al amigo de Lupin, se desternillará de risa.

Al barón no le hacía tanta gracia. Con el oído atento, escuchaba el silencio cada vez más nervioso. De vez en cuando, se inclinaba sobre el pozo y echaba una mirada ansiosa por el agujero enorme.

Sonaron las once de la noche, las doce y la una.

De pronto, el barón agarró del brazo a Ganimard, que se despertó sobresaltado.

—¿Oye usted?

—Sí.

—¿Qué es eso?

—Soy yo que ronco.

—No, escuche...

—¡Ah!, claro, es la bocina de un automóvil.

—¿Entonces?

—Entonces es poco probable que Lupin utilice un automóvil a modo de ariete para demoler su castillo. Así que, señor barón, yo en su lugar intentaría dormir..., como voy a tener el gusto de volver a hacer yo. Buenas noches.

Esa fue la única alerta. Ganimard pudo reanudar su sueño interrumpido y el barón solo escuchó sus ronquidos sonoros y regulares.

Al despuntar el alba salieron los dos de la celda. Una gran paz, la paz de la mañana a orillas del agua fresca, envolvía el castillo. Cahorn, radiante de alegría, y Ganimard, tranquilo como siempre, subieron la escalera. Ni un ruido. Nada sospechoso.

—¿Qué le había dicho yo, señor barón? En el fondo, no habría debido aceptar... Estoy avergonzado... —Cogió las llaves y entró en la galería. Encima de dos sillas, encogidos, con los brazos colgando, los dos agentes dormían—. ¡Maldita sea! —protestó el inspector. En ese mismo momento, el barón soltó un grito:

—¡Los cuadros!..., ¡el aparador!... —El barón balbuceaba, se ahogaba, con la mano estirada hacia los huecos, hacia las paredes desnudas donde sobresalían los clavos, donde colgaban las cuerdas inútiles. ¡El Watteau había desaparecido! ¡Habían robado los Rubens! ¡Se habían llevado los tapices! ¡Las vitrinas estaban vacías!—. ¡Y mis candelabros Luis XVI!... ¡Y la araña del Regente y mi Virgen del siglo XII!...

El barón corría de un lado a otro, asustado, desesperado. Recordaba los precios de compra, sumaba las pérdidas, acumulaba cifras, todo atropelladamente, con palabras confusas y frases inacabadas. Pataleaba, se convulsionaba, loco de rabia y de dolor. Parecía un hombre arruinado al que solo le quedaba volarse la tapa los sesos.

Si algo pudo consolarlo fue ver el estupor de Ganimard. Al contrario que el barón, el inspector no se movía. Estaba como petrificado y con una mirada imprecisa examinaba todo. ¿Las ventanas?, cerradas. ¿Las cerraduras de las puertas?, intactas. Ni una brecha en el techo. Ni un agujero en el suelo. El orden era perfecto. El robo se había debido de realizar metódicamente, según un plan inexorable y lógico.

—Arsène Lupin..., Arsène Lupin —murmuraba el inspector desmoronado. De pronto, saltó sobre los dos agentes, como si por fin lo sacudiera la rabia, y los zarandeó con furia, y los insultó, ¡y no se despertaban!—. Demonios —dijo—, ¿por casualidad...? —Se inclinó sobre los hombretones y los examinó atentamente, primero a uno y luego al otro: estaban dormidos, pero con un sueño que no era natural. Ganimard dijo al barón—: Los han dormido.

—Pero, ¿quién?

— ¡Ja!, ¡él, por supuesto! O su banda, pero dirigida por él. Es un golpe de su estilo. Tiene su sello.

—En ese caso, estoy perdido, no hay nada que hacer.

—Nada que hacer.

—Esto es horrible, es monstruoso.

—Presente una denuncia.

—¿Y para qué?

—¿Para qué va a ser? Inténtelo al menos..., la justicia tiene recursos...

—¡La justicia! Pero si usted mismo lo está viendo... En este momento podría empezar a buscar alguna pista o descubrir algo y ni siquiera se mueve.

—¡Descubrir algo, con Arsène Lupin! Bueno, mi querido señor, ¡Arsène Lupin jamás deja nada tras de sí! ¡Con Arsène Lupin la casualidad no existe! ¡Estoy pensando que quizá él permitió deliberadamente que yo lo detuviera en América!

—Entonces, ¡tengo que renunciar a mis cuadros, a todo! Pero me ha robado las joyas de mi colección. Daría una fortuna por recuperarlas. Si no se puede hacer nada contra él, ¡que ponga un precio!

Ganimard lo miró fijamente.

—Esas son palabras sensatas. ¿No las retira?

—No, no y no. ¿Por qué?

—Tengo una idea.

—¿Qué idea?

—Volveremos a hablar de esto si la investigación no llega a buen puerto... Solo le pido que, si quiere que salga bien, no diga ni una palabra sobre mí. —Y luego Ganimard murmuró entre dientes—: Además, lo cierto es que no tengo mucho de que enorgullecerme.

Los dos agentes recuperaron poco a poco el conocimiento, con el aspecto aturdido de los que salen de un sueño hipnótico. Abrían unos ojos atónitos, intentaban comprender. Cuando Ganimard los interrogó, no recordaban nada.

—Algo habréis visto.

—No.

—Intentad recordar.

—No, nada.

—¿Bebisteis algo?

Se quedaron pensando y uno de ellos respondió:

—Sí, yo bebí un poco de agua.

—¿Agua de esta jarra?

—Sí.

—Yo también —declaró el segundo.

Ganimard olió el agua y la probó. No tenía ningún gusto especial, ningún olor.

—Vamos —dijo el inspector—, estamos perdiendo el tiempo. Los problemas que provoca Arsène Lupin no se resuelven de la noche a la mañana. Pero, ¡maldición!, juro que volveré a pillarlo. Él gana la segunda manga. ¡Yo ganaré la partida!

Ese mismo día, el barón de Cahorn presentó una denuncia por robo con agravantes contra Arsène Lupin, ¡detenido en la Santé!

Cuántas veces lamentó el barón haber interpuesto la denuncia cuando vio el castillo de Malaquis invadido por los gendarmes, el fiscal, el juez de instrucción, los periodistas y los curiosos que se metían donde no debían.

El caso ya tenía cautivada a la opinión pública. Se había producido en unas circunstancias tan extrañas y el nombre de Arsène Lupin estimulaba hasta tal punto la imaginación, que las historias más fantasiosas llenaban las columnas de los periódicos y el público las creía.

Sin embargo, la primera carta de Arsène Lupin, que publicó *L'Écho de France* —sin que nadie supiera jamás quién proporcionó el texto al periódico—, aquella carta que avisaba con tanto descaro al barón de Cahorn de lo que lo amenazaba, provocó una conmoción considerable. Inmediatamente surgieron explicaciones fabulosas y se recordó la existencia de los famosos subterráneos. El Ministerio Fiscal, influenciado por eso, dirigió las investigaciones en ese sentido.

Se registró el castillo de arriba abajo. Se inspeccionó cada piedra. Se investigó la *boiserie* y las chimeneas, los marcos de los espejos y las vigas de los techos. Con la luz de unas linternas se examinaros los sótanos inmensos donde los señores de Malaquis amontonaban antiguamente las municiones y las provisiones. Se exploraron las entrañas del peñasco. Todo en vano. No se descubrió ni el menor rastro de un subterráneo. No existía ningún pasadizo secreto.

De acuerdo, respondían todos los implicados, pero los muebles y los cuadros no desaparecen como fantasmas. Salieron por las puertas y las ventanas, y quienes los robaron también entraron y salieron por puertas y ventanas. ¿Quiénes son los ladrones? ¿Cómo entraron? ¿Y cómo salieron?

La Fiscalía de Ruan, convencida de su impotencia, pidió ayuda a los agentes parisienses. El señor Dudouis, el jefe de la Dirección de la Seguridad General, envió a sus mejores detectives de la Brigada de Hierro. Él mismo pasó cuarenta y ocho horas en el castillo de Malaquis. No tuvo más éxito.

Entonces fue cuando mandó llamar al inspector Ganimard, cuyos servicios había tenido la oportunidad de valorar muy a menudo.

Ganimard escuchó en silencio las instrucciones de su superior y, asintiendo con la cabeza, dijo:

—Creo que empeñarse en seguir registrando el castillo es ir por el camino equivocado. La solución está en otra parte.

—Y entonces, ¿dónde está?

—La tiene Arsène Lupin.

—¡Arsène Lupin! Suponer eso sería admitir que él participó en el robo.

—Y lo admito. Es más, estoy seguro.

—Vamos a ver, Ganimard, eso es absurdo. Arsène Lupin está en la cárcel.

—Arsène Lupin está en la cárcel, de acuerdo. Está vigilado, se lo concedo. Pero, aunque tuviera grilletes en los pies, cuerdas en las muñecas y una mordaza en la boca, yo no cambiaría de opinión.

—¿Y por qué se empeña tanto?

—Porque solo Arsène Lupin es capaz de organizar una trama de esta envergadura y organizarla de tal manera que salga bien, como ha salido.

—¡Eso son tonterías, Ganimard!

—Eso es una realidad, jefe. Y ya está, dejen de buscar subterráneos, piedras que giren sobre un eje u otras pamplinas de ese calibre. Nuestro individuo no utiliza procedimientos tan anticuados. Está al día o, mejor dicho, al día de mañana.

—¿Y qué quiere usted hacer?

—Quiero pedirle directamente autorización para pasar una hora con él.

—¿En su celda?

—Sí. Cuando regresamos de América, durante la travesía mantuvimos una excelente relación y me atrevería a decir que siente cierta simpatía por quien consiguió detenerlo. Si puede informarme sin comprometerse, no dudará en evitarme un viaje inútil.

Un poco después de las doce del mediodía, Ganimard entraba en la celda de Arsène Lupin. Él estaba tumbado en la cama, levantó la cabeza y, al verlo, lanzó un grito de alegría.

—¡Oh! Esta sí que es una auténtica sorpresa. ¡Mi querido Ganimard, aquí!

—El mismo.

—Deseaba un montón de cosas en este retiro que yo elegí, pero ninguna tanto como recibirle a usted aquí.

—Es demasiado amable.

—No, en absoluto, yo le aprecio mucho.

—Y me siento orgulloso de eso.

—Siempre lo he dicho: Ganimard es nuestro mejor detective. Vale casi tanto, ya ve que soy franco, casi tanto como Sherlock Holmes. Pero, de verdad, siento no poder ofrecerle más que este taburete. ¡Y ni siquiera un refresco! ¡Ni un vaso de cerveza! Discúlpeme, estoy aquí de paso. —Ganimard se sentó sonriendo y el prisionero continuó la conversación, feliz de poder hablar con alguien—: ¡Dios mío, qué contento estoy de volver a mirar a la cara a un hombre honrado! Ya estoy harto de todos esos espías y chivatos que vienen diez veces al día a registrarme los bolsillos y mi modesta celda para asegurarse de que no estoy preparando una fuga. ¡Demonios, cuánto me aprecia el Gobierno!

—Con razón...

—¡No, en absoluto! ¡Me sentiría tan feliz si me dejaran vivir en paz en mi rinconcito!

—Con las rentas de los demás.

—¿Verdad? ¡Sería tan fácil! Pero estoy hablando demasiado, solo digo tonterías, y seguramente usted tiene prisa. ¡Vayamos al grano, Ganimard! ¿A qué se debe el honor de su visita?

—El caso Cahorn —soltó Ganimard sin rodeos.

—¡Alto ahí!, un segundo... ¡Es que tengo tantos casos! Espere que primero encuentre el informe del caso Cahorn en el cerebro... ¡Ay! Aquí está, ya lo tengo. Caso Cahorn, castillo de Malaquis, Bajo Sena... Dos Rubens, un Watteau y algunos objetos menores.

—¡Menores!

—¡Vaya! Pues sí, todo eso es de mediocre importancia. Hay cosas mejores. Pero basta con que el caso le interese, así que hable, Ganimard.

—¿Tengo que explicarle en qué punto está la instrucción del sumario?

—No, es innecesario. Ya he leído los periódicos de la mañana. Incluso me permitiría decirle que no avanzan mucho.

—Precisamente por eso me dirijo a usted y cuento con su amabilidad.

—Me pongo enteramente a su disposición.

—Lo primero de todo: ¿dirigió usted el golpe?

—De principio a fin.

—¿La carta de advertencia? ¿El telegrama?

—Son de un servidor. Debo de tener por alguna parte los resguardos.

Arsène abrió el cajón de una mesita de madera blanca que, junto con la cama y el taburete, eran los únicos muebles de la celda, sacó dos trozos de papel y se los entregó a Ganimard.

—¡Pero bueno! —exclamó el inspector—, creía que le vigilaban de cerca y le registraban continuamente. Y en cambio, lee la prensa y colecciona resguardos de correos...

—¡Bah! ¡Esa gente es tan torpe! Me descosen hasta el dobladillo de la chaqueta, me revisan las suelas de los botines, auscultan las paredes de la celda, pero ni a uno se le ocurriría pensar que Arsène Lupin pueda ser lo bastante ingenuo como para elegir un escondrijo tan obvio. Con eso cuento.

Ganimard, divertido, exclamó:

—¡Pero qué gracioso! Me deja desconcertado. Vamos, cuénteme la aventura.

—¡Dios mío! ¡Apunta usted muy alto! Ponerle al corriente de todos mis secretos... Revelarle mis truquillos... Eso es algo muy serio.

—¿Me he equivocado al contar con su amabilidad?

—No, Ganimard, y ya que insiste... —Arsène Lupin recorrió dos o tres veces la celda y luego se detuvo—: ¿Qué piensa de la carta al barón?

—Pienso que usted quiso divertirse y deslumbrar un poco al público.

—¡Ah, y ya está! ¡Deslumbrar al público! Vaya, pues le aseguro, Ganimard, que le creía a usted más listo. ¡Yo, Arsène Lupin, no pierdo el tiempo con esas chiquilladas! ¿Usted cree que yo habría escrito la carta al barón si hubiera podido robarle sin escribirla? Pues tienen que entender, usted y todos, que esa carta es el punto de partida indispensable, el resorte que puso en marcha todo el entramado. Mire, vayamos por orden y, si quiere, preparemos juntos el robo del castillo de Malaquis.

—Le escucho.

—Bien, supongamos que hay un castillo rigurosamente cerrado y aislado, como el del barón de Cahorn. ¿Usted cree que yo abandonaría la partida y renunciaría a unos tesoros que deseo, solo con la excusa de que el castillo que los guarda es inaccesible?

—Por supuesto que no.

—¿Y cree que intentaría dar el golpe como antiguamente, encabezando una banda de aventureros?

—¡Pueril!

—¿O me colaría en el castillo astutamente?

—Imposible.

—Solo queda una manera, la única en mi opinión, y es conseguir que el propietario de ese castillo me invite a entrar.

—Es un modo original.

—¡Y muy fácil! Supongamos que un día, dicho propietario recibe una carta que le advierte de lo que trama contra él un tal Arsène Lupin, un famoso ladrón. ¿Qué haría ese propietario?

—Enviaría la carta al fiscal.

—Que se burlaría de él, «porque el susodicho Lupin está actualmente entre rejas». Entonces, el tipo enloquecería y estaría completamente dispuesto a pedir ayuda al primero que se presente, ¿no es cierto?

—No cabe la menor duda.

—Y si por casualidad leyese en un periodicucho que un famoso policía está de vacaciones en una localidad vecina...

—Se dirigiría a ese policía.

—Usted lo ha dicho. Pero, por otra parte, admitamos que, en previsión de ese trámite inevitable, Arsène Lupin le hubiera rogado a uno de sus amigos más habilidoso que se instalara en Caudebec, que entrara en contacto con un redactor del *Réveil*, periódico al que está suscrito el barón, y dejara caer que es fulano de tal, el famoso policía, ¿qué ocurriría?

—Que el redactor anunciaría en *Le Réveil* la presencia del susodicho policía en Caudebec.

—Perfecto, y una de dos: o el pez, quiero decir Cahorn, no muerde el anzuelo y entonces no pasa nada, o bien, y esta es la hipótesis más verosímil, Cahorn acude corriendo, muy agitado, a ver al policía. Y ya tenemos al conde implorando ayuda contra mí a uno de mis amigos.

—Cada vez más original.

—Por supuesto, al principio el falso policía se niega a colaborar. Y después de la negativa llega un telegrama de Arsène Lupin. El barón, muy asustado, vuelve a suplicar ayuda a mi amigo y le ofrece tanto para que vele por su seguridad. Dicho amigo acepta y se lleva a dos hombretones de nuestra banda que, por la noche, sacan por la ventana un cierto número de objetos y los deslizan, con unas cuerdas, hasta una chalupa fletada *ad hoc*, mientras a Cahorn lo vigila su protector. Es tan sencillo como Lupin.

—Y es estúpidamente extraordinario —exclamó Ganimard—, nunca podría elogiar bastante la osadía de la concepción y el ingenio de los detalles. Pero no conozco a ningún policía tan prestigioso como para que su nombre haya podido llamar la atención y sugestionar al barón hasta ese punto.

—Hay uno y solo uno.

—¿Quién?

—El de mayor prestigio, el enemigo personal de Arsène Lupin, en fin, el inspector Ganimard.

—¡Yo!

—Usted mismo, Ganimard. Y esto es lo más fascinante: si usted fuera allí y el barón se decidiera a hablar, acabaría por descubrir que su deber es detenerse a usted mismo, como me detuvo a mí en América. ¿Qué?, ¡la revancha es cómica!: ¡yo consigo que Ganimard tenga que detener a Ganimard! —Arsène Lupin reía a carcajadas. El inspector, bastante humillado, se mordía los labios. No le parecía que la broma mereciese ese ataque de risa. La llegada de un guardia le dio la oportunidad de recomponerse. El hombre llevaba la comida que Arsène Lupin, con trato de favor, mandaba llevar de un restaurante cercano. Después de dejar la bandeja en la mesa, se retiró. Arsène se acomodó, abrió el pan, comió dos o tres trozos y continuó con la conversación—: Pero esté tranquilo, Ganimard, mi querido Ganimard, no tendrá usted que ir allí. Voy a revelarle algo que le dejará estupefacto: el caso Cahorn está a punto de archivarse.

—¿Cómo?

—A punto de archivarse, le digo.

—¡Por favor! Acabo de dejar al jefe de la Seguridad hace nada.

—¿Y qué? ¿Cree usted que el señor Dudouis sabe más que yo de los asuntos que me conciernen? Se enterará de que Ganimard, perdón, el falso Ganimard, mantiene una excelente relación con el barón. Cahorn le ha encargado la delicada misión de negociar conmigo una transacción, este es el motivo principal por el que el barón no confesó nada, así que, en este momento, mediante cierta cantidad, es probable que ese hombre ya haya recuperado sus queridas baratijas. A cambio, retirará la denuncia. Así pues, ya no hay robo. Por consiguiente, la Fiscalía tendrá que abandonar...

Ganimard miró al detenido con cara atónita.

—¿Y usted cómo lo sabe?

—Acabo de recibir el telegrama que esperaba.

—¿Acaba de recibir un telegrama?

—Ahora mismo, querido amigo. Por educación, no quise leerlo delante de usted. Pero si me lo permite...

—Se está burlando usted de mí, Lupin.

—¿Quiere, querido amigo, abrir con cuidado el huevo pasado por agua? Comprobará por sí mismo que no me burlo de usted.

Instintivamente, Ganimard obedeció y rompió el huevo con el filo de un cuchillo. Dejó escapar un grito de sorpresa. La cáscara vacía contenía una hoja de papel azul. A petición de Arsène, Ganimard la desdobló. Era un telegrama o, mejor dicho, una parte de un telegrama al que habían arrancado los datos de la oficina de correos. El comisario leyó: «Acuerdo cerrado. Cien mil pavos entregados. Todo va bien».

—¿Cien mil pavos? —preguntó Ganimard.

—Sí, ¡cien mil francos! Es poco, pero, en fin, corren tiempos duros... ¡Y yo tengo unos gastos generales tan grandes! Si supiera usted mi presupuesto... ¡Es el presupuesto de una gran ciudad!

Ganimard se levantó. Ya no estaba de mal humor. Se quedó unos segundos pensando, hizo un repaso mental rápido de todo el caso para intentar descubrir su punto débil. Luego pronunció con un tono que transmitía sinceramente su admiración de experto en la materia:

—Por suerte, no hay docenas de hombres como usted, pues, de lo contrario, solo nos quedaría cerrar el negocio.

Arsène Lupin adoptó un aire un tanto modesto y respondió:

—¡Bah! Tenía que distraerme, ocupar el tiempo libre... Sobre todo, porque el golpe solo podía salir bien si yo estaba en la cárcel.

—¡Cómo! —exclamó Ganimard— ¿El juicio, su defensa, la instrucción, no le basta con todo eso para distraerse?

—No, porque he decidido no asistir a mi juicio.

—¡Madre mía!

Arsène Lupin repitió tranquilamente:

—No asistiré a mi juicio.

—¿De verdad?

—Ay, querido amigo, ¿usted se piensa que voy a pudrirme en una celda? Me ofende. Arsène Lupin solo estará en la cárcel el tiempo que le plazca, ni un minuto más.

—Quizá hubiera sido más prudente empezar por no entrar —arguyó el inspector, con tono irónico.

—¡Ay! ¿El señor se burla? ¿El señor recuerda que él tuvo el honor de detenerme? Que sepa, mi respetable amigo, que nadie, ni usted ni nadie, habría podido echarme el guante si en ese crítico momento no me hubiera movido un interés mucho mayor.

—Me sorprende.

—Una mujer estaba mirándome, Ganimard, y yo la amaba. ¿Comprende usted todo lo que hay en el hecho de que una mujer a la que amas te mire? Lo demás poco importa, se lo juro. Y por eso estoy aquí.

—Desde hace ya mucho tiempo, permítame que lo indique.

—Primero quería olvidar. No se ría: la aventura fue encantadora y aún guardo un recuerdo enternecedor... Y, además, ¡estoy un poco neurasténico! ¡La vida es tan frenética hoy en día! En determinados momentos hay que saber hacer lo que se llama una cura de aislamiento. Este lugar es soberbio para los regímenes de ese tipo. Aquí se practica la cura de la Santé[1] con todo rigor.

—Arsène Lupin —respondió Ganimard—, me está tomando el pelo.

—Ganimard —afirmó Lupin—, estamos a viernes, el próximo miércoles iré a fumarme un puro a su casa, en la calle Pergolèse, a las cuatro de la tarde.

—Arsène Lupin, le espero.

---

1 Juego de palabras intraducible: Santé, nombre de la prisión de París, significa 'salud'. *(N. de la T.)*

Se estrecharon la mano como dos buenos amigos que se aprecian y el viejo policía se dirigió hacia la puerta.

—¡Ganimard!

El inspector se volvió.

—¿Qué ocurre?

—Ganimard, olvida usted su reloj.

—¿Mi reloj?

—Sí, se ha perdido en mi bolsillo. —Se lo entregó disculpándose—. Perdone, una mala costumbre... Que me hayan quitado el mío no es motivo para que le prive del suyo. Sobre todo, porque tengo ahí otro, del que no me quejo y satisface plenamente mis necesidades.

Sacó del cajón un gran reloj de oro, grueso y cómodo, con una pesada cadena.

—¿Y de qué bolsillo procede ese?

Arsène Lupin examinó descuidadamente las iniciales.

—J. B.... ¿Quién diablos puede ser?... ¡Ay, sí!, ya me acuerdo, Jules Bouvier, el juez que instruye mi caso, un hombre encantador...

3

LA FUGA DE ARSÈNE LUPIN

En el momento en que Arsène Lupin, cuando ya había acabado el almuerzo, sacaba del bolsillo un puro con vitola de oro y lo miraba satisfecho, se abrió la puerta de su celda. Solo tuvo tiempo de meterlo en el cajón y alejarse de la mesa. Entró el guardia, era la hora del paseo.

—Ya estaba esperándote, querido amigo —dijo Lupin, siempre de buen humor.

Salieron los dos juntos y en el mismo momento en que desaparecieron por la esquina del pasillo, entraron en la celda dos hombres y empezaron un minucioso registro. Uno era el inspector Dieuzy y el otro el inspector Folenfant.

Querían acabar con ese asunto de una vez por todas. No cabía la menor duda: Arsène Lupin mantenía relaciones con el exterior y se comunicaba con los miembros de su banda. La víspera, sin ir más lejos, el *Grand Journal* había publicado una carta abierta dirigida al redactor de tribunales.

> Señor:
>
> En un artículo que apareció estos días en su periódico se expresó usted sobre mí en unos términos injustificables. Algunos días antes de que se abra mi juicio, iré a pedirle cuentas. Atentamente,
>
> Arsène Lupin

La letra era sin duda la de Arsène Lupin. Luego enviaba cartas. Y las recibía. Por lo tanto se daba por hecho que estaba preparando esa fuga que había anunciado tan arrogantemente.

La situación se hacía intolerable. De acuerdo con el juez de instrucción, el jefe de la Seguridad, el señor Dudouis, acudió él mismo a la Santé para exponer al director de la cárcel las medidas que se debían tomar. Y, en cuanto llegó, envió a sus dos hombres a la celda del detenido.

Los dos inspectores levantaron todas las losas, desmontaron la cama, hicieron todo lo que es habitual hacer en un caso como ese y, al final, no encontraron nada. Estaban ya a punto de tirar la toalla cuando el guardia apareció corriendo y les dijo:

—El cajón, miren en el cajón de la mesa. Cuando entré me pareció que lo cerraba.

Miraron los dos ahí y Dieuzy exclamó:

—¡Por Dios, esta vez lo tenemos!

Folenfant lo interrumpió.

—Alto ahí, amigo, el inventario lo hará el jefe.

—Pero, es un puro de lujo...

—Suelta el habano y vamos a avisar al jefe.

Dos minutos después, el señor Dudouis examinaba el cajón. Allí encontró en primer lugar un montón de artículos de periódico que había seleccionado la agencia El Vigilante de la Prensa y todos eran sobre Arsène Lupin, luego una petaca, una pipa, papel de ese que se llama de cebolla y, por último, dos libros.

Miró los títulos. Eran el *Culto al Héroe* de Carlyle, en edición inglesa, y un Elzevir muy bonito, con encuadernación antigua, *El manual de Epicteto*, traducción alemana publicada en Leiden en 1634. Tras hojearlos, comprobó que todas las hojas estaban marcadas, subrayadas y con notas. ¿Serían señales en clave o esas marcas que hacen algunos cuando les gusta mucho un libro?

—Ya veremos esto con más detalle —dijo el señor Dudouis. Luego, examinó la petaca y la pipa, cogió el famoso puro con vitola de oro y añadió—: ¡Demonios! ¡Cómo se cuida nuestro amigo, se cree Henry Clay!

Con un gesto instintivo de fumador, el jefe acercó el puro a la oreja y lo hizo crujir. Inmediatamente se le escapó una exclamación. El puro se había reblandecido con la presión de los dedos. Dudouis lo examinó con mayor atención y no tardó en descubrir algo de color blanco entre las hojas de tabaco. Con mucho cuidado y ayudándose de un alfiler, extrajo un rollo de papel muy fino, casi del tamaño de un palillo de dientes. Era una nota. La desenrolló y leyó las siguientes palabras, escritas con una letra menuda de mujer:

> La lechera sustituida. Ocho de diez preparados. Al apoyar con el pie exterior, la placa se levanta de abajo arriba. H P esperará de doce a dieciséis, todos los días. ¿Pero dónde? Respuesta inmediata. Esté tranquilo, su amiga vela por usted.

El señor Dudouis se quedó pensativo un momento y luego dijo:

—Está bastante claro..., la lechera, los ocho compartimentos... De doce a dieciséis, es decir de doce del mediodía a cuatro de la tarde...

—Pero y ese H P, ¿qué esperará?

—H P, en este caso, debe de ser un automóvil, H P, *horse power*. En lenguaje deportivo se llama así a la potencia del motor, ¿no es eso? Un veinticuatro H P es un automóvil de veinticuatro caballos. —Dudouis se levantó y preguntó—: ¿El detenido había terminado de comer?

—Sí.

—Pues tal y como está el puro, aún no ha leído el mensaje, así que es probable que acabe de recibirlo.

—Y ¿cómo?

—En la comida, dentro del pan o de una manzana, ¿yo qué sé?

—Imposible, le autorizamos a traer la comida de fuera exclusivamente para atraparlo y no hemos encontrado nada.

—Esta noche trataremos de interceptar la respuesta de Lupin. De momento, reténganlo fuera de la celda. Llevaré esto al juez de instrucción. Si estamos de acuerdo, mandaremos inmediatamente que fotografíen la nota y, dentro de una hora, vuelvan a meter en el cajón estas cosas y un puro idéntico que contenga el mensaje original. Es preciso que el detenido no sospeche nada.

El señor Dudouis, no sin cierta curiosidad, regresó por la noche a la secretaría de la Santé junto con el inspector Dieuzy. En un rincón, sobre la estufa, estaban los tres platos de Lupin.

—¿Ha cenado el detenido?

—Sí —respondió el director.

—Dieuzy, ¿quiere cortar en trocitos muy finos estos pocos macarrones y abrir ese bollo de pan?... ¿Nada?

—No, jefe.

El señor Dudouis examinó los platos, el tenedor, la cuchara y, por último, el cuchillo; un cuchillo como los de la cárcel, con el filo redondeado. Giró el mango a la izquierda y luego a la derecha. A la derecha, el mango cedió y se abrió. El cuchillo estaba hueco y tenía dentro una hoja de papel.

—¡Bah! —dijo el jefe de la Seguridad—, no es un truco muy ingenioso para alguien como Arsène. Pero no perdamos más tiempo. Usted, Dieuzy, vaya inmediatamente a investigar al restaurante. —Y a continuación, leyó en voz alta—: «Me pongo en sus manos, H P seguirá de lejos todos los días. Yo iré por delante. Hasta pronto, mi querida y admirable amiga». Por fin —gritó el señor Dudouis frotándose las manos—, creo que tenemos el asunto bien encauzado. Un empujoncito por nuestra parte y la fuga será todo un éxito..., o por lo menos nos permitirá atrapar a los cómplices.

—¿Y si Arsène Lupin se le escapa de las manos? —protestó el director.

—Emplearemos tantos hombres como sea necesario. Y si a pesar de todo Lupin fuera más inteligente... Pues la verdad, ¡peor para él! En cuanto a la banda, ya que el jefe se niega a hablar, hablarán los otros.

Y, de hecho, Arsène Lupin no hablaba mucho. El señor Jules Bouvier, el juez de instrucción, llevaba meses esforzándose inútilmente. Los interrogatorios se limitaban a unas conversaciones sin ningún interés entre el juez y el abogado, el letrado Danval, uno de los más prestigiosos del Colegio de

Abogados, que, por otra parte, sabía sobre el acusado aproximadamente lo mismo que cualquier otra persona.

De vez en cuando, por cortesía, Arsène Lupin dejaba caer:

—Pues sí, señor juez, estamos de acuerdo en todo: el robo del Crédit Lyonnais, el robo de la calle Babylone, la emisión de billetes falsos, el asunto de las pólizas de seguros, los robos en los castillos de Armesnil, Gouret, Imblevain, Groselliers y Malaquis, todo eso es obra de un servidor de usted.

—Entonces, podría explicarme...

—Es inútil, confieso absolutamente todo, todo y hasta diez veces más de lo que usted ni se imagina.

Harto de luchar, el juez había suspendido aquellos fastidiosos interrogatorios. Pero cuando estuvo al tanto de las dos notas interceptadas, los reanudó. Y entonces, de forma regular, a mediodía, llevaron a Arsène Lupin de la Santé a la prisión central en el furgón de la penitenciaría con otros detenidos. Todos volvían juntos hacia las tres o cuatro de la tarde.

Pero una tarde, el regreso a la Santé se hizo en condiciones especiales. Como los otros detenidos aún no habían pasado por sus respectivos interrogatorios, se decidió llevar primero de vuelta a Arsène Lupin. Así que el preso subió solo al furgón.

Esos furgones penitenciarios, vulgarmente conocidos como «lecheras», están divididos a lo largo por un pasillo central desde el que se abren diez compartimentos: cinco a la derecha y cinco a la izquierda. Cada uno de esos compartimentos está dispuesto de tal manera que hay que permanecer necesariamente sentado, y los cinco prisioneros, además de tener cada uno muy poco espacio, están separados unos de otros por divisiones paralelas. Un policía municipal, situado en un extremo, vigila el pasillo.

Metieron a Arsène en la tercera celda de la derecha y el lento furgón se puso en marcha. Lupin se dio cuenta de que dejaban atrás el Quai de l'Horloge y pasaban por delante del Palacio de Justicia. Entonces, a mitad del puente de Saint-Michel, apoyó el pie derecho, como hacía en cada desplazamiento, en la placa de chapa que cerraba la celda. Inmediatamente, algo se accionó, la placa de chapa se abrió imperceptiblemente y pudo comprobar que estaba justo entre las dos ruedas.

Esperó muy atento. El furgón subió despacio el bulevar Saint-Michel. Se detuvo en la plaza de Saint-Germain. Se había caído el caballo de una carreta. Al interrumpirse la circulación, rápidamente se amontonaron allí coches de punto y ómnibus.

Arsène Lupin pasó la cabeza. Otro furgón penitenciario se detuvo en paralelo al suyo. Sacó más la cabeza, puso el pie en uno de los radios de la enorme rueda y saltó al suelo.

Un cochero lo vio, se partió de risa y luego quiso delatarlo. Pero sus gritos se perdieron entre el alboroto de los vehículos que volvían a ponerse en marcha. Además, Arsène Lupin ya estaba lejos.

Avanzó un poco corriendo, pero, en la acera de la izquierda, se volvió, lanzó una mirada a su alrededor y fingió tomar el aire, como cualquiera que aún no sabe muy bien adónde ir. Después, decidido, metió las manos en los bolsillos y, con aire indiferente, siguió subiendo el bulevar.

Era un día agradable, un día alegre y tranquilo de otoño. Los cafés estaban llenos. Lupin se sentó en una de las terrazas.

Pidió una jarra de cerveza y un paquete de cigarrillos. Vació el vaso a sorbos, fumó tranquilamente un cigarrillo y encendió otro. Finalmente, se levantó y le dijo al camarero que llamara al encargado.

Cuando llegó el encargado, Arsène Lupin le explicó lo suficientemente alto para que lo oyera todo el mundo:

—Lo lamento mucho, señor; he olvidado la cartera. Quizá mi nombre le sea lo bastante conocido como para retrasarme el pago unos días: me llamo Arsène Lupin. —El encargado lo miró, creía que era una broma. Pero Arsène repitió—: Lupin, preso en la Santé, bueno, en este momento en situación de fuga. Me atrevo a creer que ese nombre le inspira total confianza.

Y se alejó entre risas, sin que el otro siquiera pensase en reclamar la cuenta.

Cruzó la calle Soufflot en diagonal y siguió por la calle Saint-Jacques. Continuó por esa calle tranquilamente, deteniéndose en los escaparates y fumando. En el bulevar de Port-Royal se orientó, preguntó por una dirección y fue derecho hacia la calle de la Santé. Las altas paredes sombrías de la prisión pronto aparecieron. Las bordeó y llegó junto al policía municipal de guardia, levantó el sombrero y dijo:

—Esta es la cárcel de la Santé, ¿verdad?

—Sí.

—Me gustaría regresar a mi celda. El furgón me dejó por el camino y no quisiera abusar...

El chico refunfuñó:

—Vamos hombre, siga su camino y muévase ya.

—¡Perdón, perdón! Es que mi camino pasa por esta puerta. ¡Y si usted impide que Arsène Lupin la cruce, podría costarle caro, amigo!

—¿Arsène Lupin? ¿Qué cuento me está contando?

—Lamento no tener ni una tarjeta —dijo Arsène, fingiendo rebuscar en los bolsillos.

El policía lo miró de pies a cabeza, atónito. Luego, sin decir ni una palabra y a regañadientes, tiró de una campanilla. La puerta de hierro se entreabrió.

Unos minutos después, el director acudía corriendo a la secretaría, gesticulando y fingiendo estar profundamente enfadado. Arsène sonrió.

—Vamos, señor director, no se haga el listo conmigo. Se toman la molestia de traerme de vuelta solo en el furgón, organizan un bonito atasco ¿y usted cree que voy a salir pitando para ir a reunirme con mis amigos? ¡Vamos, hombre! ¿Y los veinte agentes de la Seguridad que nos escoltaban a pie, en coche de punto y en bicicleta? No, ¡lo que me habrían zurrado! Para no salir vivo de ahí. ¡Por Dios, señor director! ¿A lo mejor era eso lo que quería? —se encogió de hombros y añadió—: Se lo ruego, señor director, no se preocupen por mí. El día que quiera escaparme, no necesitaré que nadie me ayude.

Al día siguiente, *L'Écho de France,* que definitivamente se había convertido en el boletín oficial de las hazañas de Arsène Lupin —se decía que el propio Lupin era uno de los principales socios del periódico—, publicaba con todo lujo de detalles el intento de fuga. En el artículo se hablaba de las notas que intercambiaron el detenido y su misteriosa amiga, de los medios que

utilizó para mover la correspondencia, de la participación de la policía, del paseo por el bulevar Saint-Michel y del percance en el café Soufflot, lo desvelaba todo. Se sabía que la investigación del inspector Dieuzy con el camarero del restaurante no había dado ningún resultado. Y, además, se informaba de algo asombroso que demostraba los múltiples recursos de los que disponía ese hombre: el furgón penitenciario en el que lo habían trasladado era un furgón completamente trucado, que su banda había cambiado por otro de los seis furgones habituales que integraban el servicio de prisiones.

Ya nadie cuestionaba la próxima fuga de Arsène Lupin. Por otra parte, él mismo la anunciaba en términos categóricos, como evidencia su respuesta al señor Bouvier, al día siguiente de los hechos. Cuando el juez se burló de la fuga frustrada, Lupin lo miró y le dijo con frialdad:

—Escuche bien esto, señor, y crea en mi palabra: este intento formaba parte de mi plan de fuga.

—No lo comprendo —dijo el juez riendo socarronamente.

—¿Qué más da que usted lo entienda? —Y cuando el juez durante ese interrogatorio, que apareció completo en las columnas de *L'Écho de France*, reanudó la instrucción del sumario, Lupin, ya cansado, protestó—: ¡Dios mío, Dios mío! ¿Y para qué...? Todas esas preguntas no sirven para nada.

—¿Cómo que no sirven para nada?

—¡Pues claro que no!, porque no asistiré a mi juicio.

—Usted no asistirá...

—No, y esa es una idea fija que tengo, una decisión irrevocable. Nada me hará transigir.

Semejante seguridad y las indiscreciones inexplicables que se cometían a diario irritaban y desconcertaban a la justicia. En todo aquel asunto había algunos secretos que únicamente conocía Arsène Lupin, así que la información solo podía salir de él. ¿Con qué fin la desvelaba? ¿Y cómo?

Trasladaron de celda a Arsène Lupin. Una noche, lo llevaron a la planta inferior. El juez, a su vez, terminó la instrucción del sumario y remitió la causa a la Fiscalía.

A partir de entonces, no volvió a oírse hablar de aquel asunto. El silencio duró dos meses. Arsène los pasó tumbado en la cama, con la cara casi siempre vuelta hacia la pared. El cambio de celda parecía haberlo desmoralizado. Se negó a recibir a su abogado. Apenas intercambiaba algunas palabras con los guardias.

En la quincena anterior al juicio pareció animarse. Se quejaba de que echaba de menos el aire libre. Entonces se le permitió salir al patio por la mañana, muy temprano, vigilado por dos hombres.

Mientras tanto, la curiosidad pública no había decaído. Todos los días se esperaba la noticia de su fuga. Casi se deseaba, porque el personaje, con su labia, su alegría, la disparidad, el genio creativo y su misteriosa vida, gustaba mucho a la gente. Arsène Lupin tenía que fugarse. Era inevitable, irremediable. A todo el mundo le sorprendía que tardara tanto. Todas las mañanas, el prefecto de policía preguntaba a su secretario:

—¿Y qué? ¿Aún no se ha marchado?

—No, señor prefecto.

—Entonces se irá mañana.

Y, la víspera del juicio, un señor se presentó en las oficinas del *Grand Journal,* preguntó por el redactor de tribunales, le tiró su tarjeta a la cara y se marchó rápidamente. En la tarjeta había escritas unas palabras: «Arsène Lupin siempre cumple sus promesas».

En esas condiciones se abrió la vista de la causa.

La afluencia de público fue enorme. Nadie quería perderse al famoso Arsène Lupin ni dejar de disfrutar desde el principio de cómo se burlaría del presidente del tribunal. Abogados y magistrados, columnistas y gente de la calle, artistas y mujeres de la alta sociedad, todo París se apiñaba en los bancos de la audiencia.

Ese día llovía, en la calle el día era oscuro y no pudo verse bien a Arsène Lupin cuando los guardias lo llevaron al interior del Palacio de Justicia. Sin embargo, su actitud torpe, el modo en que se dejó caer en su asiento y la quietud indiferente y pasiva no dijo nada en su favor. En varias ocasiones su abogado —uno de los pasantes de Danval, porque el propio Danval consideró indigna de él la función a la que lo había relegado su cliente—, se dirigió a él. Y Lupin asintió con la cabeza y permaneció en silencio.

El secretario judicial leyó el acta de acusación y luego el presidente del tribunal pronunció:

—Que se levante el acusado. Diga usted su nombre y apellido, edad y profesión. —Al no responder, el presidente repitió—: ¡Su nombre! Le estoy preguntando su nombre.

Una voz tosca y cansada articuló:

—Désiré Baudru.

Se oyó un murmullo. Pero el presidente volvió a la carga:

—¿Désiré Baudru? ¡Ajá! Bien. ¡Un nuevo alias! Como es aproximadamente el octavo nombre que usted utiliza y sin duda este se lo inventa igual que los otros, nos atendremos, si a usted le parece bien, al de Arsène Lupin, por el que es más conocido. —El presidente consultó sus notas y continuó—: Ahora bien, pese a todas las investigaciones que se han llevado a cabo, ha sido imposible reconstruir su identidad. Usted es un ejemplo de algo que pocas veces ocurre en la sociedad moderna, no tiene pasado. Nosotros no sabemos quién es usted ni de dónde viene ni dónde transcurrió su infancia, en definitiva, no sabemos nada. Usted apareció de buenas a primeras, hace tres años, sin que nadie sepa exactamente de dónde salió, y de pronto se hizo famoso como Arsène Lupin, es decir, una extraña mezcla de inteligencia y perversión, de indecencia y generosidad. Los datos que tenemos sobre usted antes de ese momento son meras suposiciones. Es probable que a quien se conoce como Rostat, que hace ocho años estuvo trabajando con el prestidigitador Dickson, fuera el propio Arsène Lupin. Es probable que el estudiante ruso que hace seis años frecuentó el laboratorio del doctor Altier, en el hospital Saint-Louis, y que sorprendió a menudo a su maestro con sus ingeniosas hipótesis sobre bacteriología y sus temerarios experimentos sobre las enfermedades de la piel, fuera el propio Arsène Lupin. Y Arsène Lupin era además el profesor de lucha japonesa que se estableció en París mucho antes de que se hablara del *jiu-jitsu*. Y Arsène Lupin era, o eso creemos nosotros, el corredor ciclista que ganó el Gran Premio de la Exposición Universal, cobró los diez mil francos y desapareció. Y Arsène Lupin quizá también fuera quien salvó a tantas personas del incendio del Bazar de la Charité sacándolas por un pequeño tragaluz...

y luego las desvalijó. —Tras una pausa el presidente concluyó—: Así es esa época que parece no haber sido más que una preparación minuciosa para la lucha que usted ha emprendido contra la sociedad, un aprendizaje metódico con el que usted llevó al extremo su poder, su energía y sus capacidades. ¿Reconoce usted la exactitud de estos hechos?

Durante el discurso, el acusado estuvo balanceándose de una pierna a otra, con la espalda encorvada y los brazos colgando. Con la luz más fuerte de la sala, pudo verse su extrema delgadez, las mejillas hundidas, los pómulos salientes, la cara de color tierra, jaspeada de manchitas rojas y enmarcada en una barba desigual y rala. La cárcel lo había envejecido y ajado considerablemente. Ya no se reconocía la figura elegante y el rostro joven de aquel retrato simpático que tantas veces habían publicado los periódicos.

El acusado pareció no entender la pregunta. El presidente la repitió dos veces. Entonces, levantó la mirada, como si estuviera pensando, y haciendo un gran esfuerzo murmuró:

—Baudru, Désiré.

El presidente se echó a reír.

—No entiendo muy bien, Arsène Lupin, su línea de defensa. Si consiste en hacerse el tonto y ser un irresponsable, es usted muy libre. Yo, por mi parte, iré derecho al grano y no tendré en cuenta sus idioteces.

Y el presidente pasó a detallar los robos, estafas y falsificaciones de los que se acusaba a Lupin. De vez en cuando, interrogaba al acusado y este soltaba un gruñido o no respondía.

Empezó el desfile de testigos. Hubo declaraciones insustanciales, otras más serias, aunque todas tenían un punto en común, eran contradictorias. Había algo confuso en los testimonios, pero entonces llamaron a declarar al inspector principal Ganimard y el interés volvió a la sala.

El viejo policía provocó, desde el principio, una cierta decepción. Parecía, no ya intimidado —estaba curado de espanto—, sino preocupado, incómodo. Varias veces dirigió la mirada hacia el acusado con un malestar visible. Pese a todo, con las dos manos apoyadas en el estrado, relataba los incidentes en los que se había visto envuelto, la persecución por toda

Europa, su llegada a América. Y todo el mundo lo escuchaba atentamente, como quien escucha el relato de las más apasionantes aventuras. Y, hacia el final de la declaración, después de mencionar sus entrevistas con Arsène Lupin, en dos ocasiones se detuvo, distraído e indeciso.

Estaba claro que algo le preocupaba. El presidente le dijo:

—Si no se encuentra usted bien, sería mejor interrumpir su declaración.

—No, no, solo... —Guardó silencio, miró al acusado detenidamente, intensamente y luego dijo—: Pido autorización a la sala para acercarme al acusado y examinarlo, aquí hay algo extraño que tengo que aclarar. —Se aproximó, lo miró aún más detenidamente, muy concentrado, después regresó al estrado. Y ahí, con un tono un poco solemne, sentenció—: Señor presidente, afirmo que el hombre que está ahí, frente a mí, no es Arsène Lupin.

Un gran silencio siguió a esas palabras. El presidente, desconcertado en un primer momento, protestó:

—Pero ¿qué dice? ¡Está usted loco!

El inspector afirmó tranquilamente:

—A primera vista, uno puede dejarse engañar por un parecido que, en efecto, existe, lo confieso, pero basta con echarle otra mirada. La nariz, la boca, el pelo, el color de la piel..., en definitiva: este hombre no es Arsène Lupin. ¡Y esos ojos! ¿Qué? ¿Alguna vez Lupin ha tenido esos ojos de alcohólico?

—Veamos, veamos, explíquese usted. ¿Qué afirma el testigo?

—¡Y yo qué sé! Lupin habrá puesto en su lugar a este pobre diablo que íbamos a condenar. O puede que sea su cómplice.

Por toda la sala se oyeron gritos, risas y exclamaciones, el público se alteró con ese giro inesperado. El presidente mandó llamar al juez de instrucción, al director de la Santé y a los guardias y suspendió la vista.

Cuando la vista se reanudó, el señor Bouvier y el director de la Santé, en presencia del acusado, declararon que entre Arsène Lupin y ese hombre solo había un ligero parecido.

—Pero entonces —gritó el presidente—, ¿quién es este hombre? ¿De dónde ha salido? ¿Por qué está en manos de la justicia?

Llamaron a los dos guardias de la Santé. ¡Ellos sí, sorprendente contradicción, reconocieron al detenido que habían vigilado en guardias alternas!

El presidente respiró.

Pero uno de los guardias rectificó:

—Sí, sí, yo creo que es él.

—¿Cómo que usted cree?

—¡Pues sí!, apenas lo vi. Me lo entregaron por la noche y, desde hace dos meses, ha estado siempre tumbado mirando a la pared.

—¿Y antes de esos dos meses?

—¡Ah!, antes el detenido no estaba en la celda 24.

El director de la prisión aclaró ese punto:

—Después de su intento de fuga trasladamos de celda al detenido.

—Pero usted, señor director, ¿usted lleva dos meses sin verlo?

—No he tenido la oportunidad de..., él estaba tranquilo.

—¿Y ese hombre no es el detenido que le entregaron?

—No.

—Entonces, ¿quién es?

—No sabría decirlo.

—Así que estamos ante una suplantación de identidad que se habría realizado hace dos meses. ¿Y cómo lo explica usted?

—Me resulta imposible.

—¿Entonces? —En su desesperación, el presidente se volvió hacia el acusado y, con un tono muy amable, le preguntó—: Vamos a ver, acusado, ¿podría explicarme cómo y desde cuándo está en manos de la justicia?

En ese momento pareció que el tono indulgente hizo ceder la desconfianza o estimuló el raciocinio del hombre. Este intentó responder. Al final, hábil y tranquilamente interrogado, el hombre consiguió juntar algunas frases y reveló lo siguiente: dos meses antes, lo llevaron preso a la cárcel central. Allí pasó una noche y una mañana. Como solo llevaba encima setenta y cinco céntimos, lo soltaron. Pero, cuando cruzaba el patio, dos guardias lo sujetaron de los brazos y lo llevaron hasta el furgón penitenciario. Desde entonces, vivía en la celda 24, allí estaba a gusto..., se come bien... y no se duerme mal... Así que no había protestado...

Todo aquello parecía verosímil. Entre risas y un gran alboroto, el presidente aplazó la sesión para completar la investigación.

Inmediatamente, la investigación confirmó un hecho anotado en el registro de encarcelamiento: ocho semanas antes, alguien llamado Désiré Baudru pasó la noche en la cárcel central. Al día siguiente quedó en libertad y se fue de la prisión a las dos de la tarde. Ahora bien, ese mismo día, a las dos de la tarde, Arsène Lupin prestó declaración por última vez, salió de la sala de instrucción y regresó a la Santé en el furgón penitenciario.

¿Cometieron un error los guardias? ¿Los confundió el parecido y en un momento de despiste ellos mismos sustituyeron a ese hombre por el prisionero? Realmente habría sido de una falta de rigor que sus hojas de servicio no permitían suponer.

¿Estaba planeada esa sustitución? Además de que la distribución de los escenarios de los hechos lo hacía casi imposible y, en ese caso, también habría sido necesaria la complicidad de Baudru y que hubiera permitido que lo detuvieran con el único objetivo de ocupar el lugar de Arsène Lupin. Pero entonces, ¿cómo había podido salir bien semejante plan que solo se basaba en una serie de probabilidades inverosímiles, de coincidencias fortuitas y de errores enormes?

Llevaron a Désiré Baudru al servicio de antropometría del registro policial. Allí no había ninguna ficha de antecedentes penales con su descripción. Por lo demás, seguirle la pista fue fácil. Era conocido en Courbevoie, en Asnières y Levallois. Vivía de limosnas y dormía en una de esas chabolas que se amontonan en la Puerta de Ternes. Pero llevaba un año desaparecido.

¿Habría estado trabajando para Arsène Lupin? Nada parecía indicarlo. Y si hubiera sido así, eso no habría aclarado la fuga del prisionero. Aquello seguía siendo increíble. De las veinte teorías que intentaban explicarlo, ninguna resultaba satisfactoria. La fuga era lo único que no planteaba dudas y el público, igual que la justicia, se daba cuenta del esfuerzo que exigía la lenta preparación de esa fuga incomprensible y sorprendente, un conjunto de actuaciones perfectamente encadenadas cuyo desenlace explicaba el orgulloso vaticinio de Arsène Lupin: «No asistiré a mi juicio».

Al cabo de un mes de minuciosas investigaciones, el misterio seguía siendo indescifrable. Pero no podía retenerse indefinidamente a ese pobre diablo de Baudru. Su juicio habría sido ridículo: ¿qué cargos había contra él? El juez de instrucción firmó su puesta en libertad. Sin embargo, el jefe de la Seguridad decidió establecer una vigilancia activa en torno a Baudru.

La idea fue de Ganimard. En su opinión, no había ni complicidad ni casualidad. Baudru había sido un instrumento que Arsène Lupin manejó de una manera extraordinariamente hábil. Una vez libre, Baudru los llevaría hasta Arsène Lupin, o al menos hasta alguno de su banda.

Se designó a dos inspectores, Folenfant y Dieuzy, de apoyo a Ganimard y una mañana de enero de un día brumoso, las puertas de la prisión se abrieron para Désiré Baudru.

Baudru al principio pareció confuso y se fue caminando como alguien que no sabe muy bien qué hacer. Siguió la calle de la Santé y la calle Saint-Jacques. Se quitó la chaqueta y el chaleco en la puerta de la tienda de un ropavejero, vendió el chaleco a cambio de unos céntimos, volvió a ponerse la chaqueta y se fue.

Cruzó el Sena. En Châtelet le adelantó un ómnibus. Quiso subir, pero no quedaban plazas libres. El interventor le aconsejó que cogiera un billete, y entró en la sala de espera.

En ese momento Ganimard llamó a sus dos hombres y sin despegar la vista del despacho de billetes les dijo a toda prisa:

—Vayan a parar un coche..., no, dos, así será más seguro. Yo iré con uno de ustedes y lo seguiremos. —Los hombres obedecieron. Pero Baudru no aparecía. Ganimard se acercó a la sala de espera: allí no había nadie—. Pero qué idiota soy —dijo entre dientes—, me olvidé de la otra salida.

El despacho de billetes, efectivamente, comunicaba por un pasillo interior con el de la calle Saint-Martin. Ganimard se lanzó hacia allí. Llegó justo a tiempo para ver a Baudru en la parte alta del Batignolles-Jardin des Plantes, que en ese momento giraba hacia la calle Rivoli. El inspector salió corriendo y alcanzó el ómnibus. Pero había perdido a los dos agentes. Desde ese momento seguía él solo la persecución.

Ganimard, enfurecido, estuvo a punto de agarrarlo del cuello sin más miramientos. El supuesto imbécil lo había dejado sin sus ayudantes con premeditación y una ingeniosa artimaña.

Miró a Baudru, estaba medio dormido en el asiento con la cabeza balanceando de un lado a otro. Tenía la boca entreabierta y una expresión de tremenda estupidez en la cara. No, ese no era un adversario capaz de jugársela al viejo Ganimard. Había tenido suerte, nada más.

En el cruce de las Galerías Lafayette, el hombre saltó del ómnibus y subió al tranvía de la Muette. Siguieron por el bulevar Haussmann y la avenida Victor Hugo. Bajó en la estación de la Muette. Desde allí, con paso tranquilo, se dirigió al Bosque de Boulogne.

En el bosque iba de un camino a otro, volvía sobre sus pasos y se alejaba. ¿Qué estaba buscando? ¿Tendría algún objetivo?

Después de una hora dando vueltas, parecía agotado. De hecho, vio un banco y se sentó. Aquel lugar, muy cerca de Auteuil, junto a un pequeño lago que ocultaban los árboles, estaba completamente desierto. Transcurrió media hora. Ganimard, impaciente, decidió entablar conversación con él.

Se acercó y se sentó junto a Baudru. El inspector encendió un cigarrillo, dibujó unos círculos en la arena con el bastón y dijo:

—Pues no hace mucho calor, ¿verdad?

Silencio. Y, de pronto, en ese silencio, retumbaron unas carcajadas. Era una risa alegre, feliz, la risa de un niño con un ataque de risa que no puede dejar de reír. De manera clara y real Ganimard sintió que se le pusieron los pelos de la cabeza de punta. Aquella risa..., ¡conocía muy bien aquella maldita risa!

Con un gesto brusco, agarró al hombre por las solapas de la chaqueta y lo miró, profunda y violentamente, con mayor intensidad que cuando lo había mirado en la sala de la audiencia. Y, francamente, ese ya no era el hombre que había visto. Era ese hombre, sí, pero también el otro, el auténtico.

Con voluntad cómplice, Ba8udru recuperaba la mirada intensa, rellenaba la máscara demacrada, se veía la carne de verdad bajo la epidermis ajada, la boca real detrás del rictus que la deformaba. Y eran los ojos del otro, la boca del otro y, sobre todo, la expresión penetrante, viva, burlona, tan limpia y tan joven del otro.

—Arsène Lupin, Arsène Lupin —balbuceó.

Y, de buenas a primeras, Ganimard, lleno de rabia, le agarró del cuello y lo intentó derribar. A pesar de sus cincuenta años, tenía una fuerza poco corriente y, al contrario, su adversario parecía estar en bastante mala forma. Además, ¡menuda jugada si conseguía llevarlo de vuelta a la cárcel!

La lucha duró poco, Arsène Lupin casi no se defendió y Ganimard, igual de rápido que atacó, soltó la presa. Tenía el brazo derecho colgando, inerte, entumecido.

—Si en el Quai des Orfèvres les enseñaran *jiu-jitsu* —dijo Lupin—, sabría que esta llave en japonés se llama *udi shi ghi* —y añadió con frialdad—: un segundo más y le hubiera roto el brazo, así tendría su merecido. ¡Cómo puede ser que usted, un viejo amigo al que aprecio, al que he revelado voluntariamente mis más íntimos secretos, abuse de mi confianza! Eso está mal. ¡Pero bueno! ¿A usted qué le pasa? —Ganimard permaneció en silencio. Se consideraba responsable de la fuga, él, con su sensacional declaración, había inducido a error a la justicia, ¿o no? Aquella fuga le parecía la vergüenza de su carrera. Le cayó una lágrima al bigote gris—. ¡Eh! ¡Dios mío, Ganimard, no se preocupe! Si usted no lo hubiera dicho, me las habría arreglado para que otro lo dijera. ¿Cree que yo iba a permitir que condenaran a Désiré Baudru?

—Entonces —murmuró Ganimard—. ¿Era usted el que estaba allí? ¡Y es usted el que está aquí!

—Sí, siempre he sido yo y solo yo.

—¿Y cómo es posible?

—¡Vaya!, tampoco hay que ser un genio. Basta, como dijo el bueno del presidente del tribunal, con prepararse durante diez años para estar listo frente a cualquier eventualidad.

—Pero ¿y su cara? ¿Y sus ojos?

—Podrá comprender que si trabajé dieciocho meses en Saint-Louis con el doctor Altier no fue por amor al arte. Pensé que quien tendría algún día el honor de llamarse Arsène Lupin debía sustraerse de las leyes ordinarias de la apariencia e identidad. ¿La apariencia? Pues uno la modifica como le conviene. Determinada inyección hipodérmica de parafina inflama la piel justo donde uno quiere. El ácido pirogálico te convierte en mohicano. El jugo de la celidonia mayor te produce costras y tumefacciones de efecto impresionante. Un proceso químico actúa sobre el crecimiento de la barba y el pelo, otro sobre la voz. Añada a todo eso dos meses de dieta en la celda número 24 y unos ejercicios repetidos mil veces para abrir la boca con este rictus, para llevar la cabeza con esta inclinación y la espalda encorvada de este modo. Y, por último, cinco gotas de atropina en los ojos para conseguir una mirada aturdida y huidiza, y listo.

—No puedo entender que los guardias...

—La metamorfosis fue progresiva. Los guardias no pudieron notar la evolución día a día.

—¿Y Désiré Baudru?

—Baudru existe. Es un pobre inocente al que conocí el año pasado y que no deja de tener un cierto parecido conmigo. En previsión de un arresto siempre posible, lo llevé a un lugar seguro y me dediqué desde un principio a comprobar las diferencias entre nosotros, para minimizarlas todo lo posible. Mis amigos consiguieron que pasara una noche en la cárcel central, de manera que saliese de allí poco más o menos a la misma hora que yo y que fuera fácil comprobar esa coincidencia, porque, dese cuenta, era preciso que se encontrara el rastro de su paso por la cárcel, de lo contrario, la justicia se habría preguntado quién era yo. Mientras que, si le ofrecía al bueno de Baudru, era inevitable, ¿me entiende?, inevitable que se le echara encima y que, a pesar de las dificultades insuperables de una suplantación, prefiriera creer en esa suplantación antes que confesar su ignorancia.

—Sí, sí, claro —murmuró Ganimard.

—Y, además —exclamó Arsène Lupin—, yo jugaba con una baza formidable, una carta que había manipulado desde el principio: todo el mundo estaba a la expectativa de mi fuga. Y ese fue el gran error en el que cayeron, usted y todos, en esta apasionante partida que la justicia y yo habíamos iniciado, en la que nos jugábamos mi libertad: supusieron una vez más que yo fanfarroneaba, que me había deslumbrado el éxito como a un pipiolo. ¿Iba yo, Arsène Lupin, a cometer ese error? Igual que en el caso Cahorn, pero ¿cómo no pensaron: «Cuando Arsène Lupin dice a voz en grito que se fugará, es que tiene razones para hacerlo»? Pero, ¡caray!, tiene que entender que, para fugarme… sin fugarme, era imprescindible que todo el mundo creyera en esa fuga, que fuera artículo de fe, una convicción absoluta, una verdad como un templo. Y así fue porque yo lo quise. Arsène Lupin se fugará, Arsène Lupin no asistirá a su juicio. Y cuando usted se levantó para decir: «Este hombre no es Arsène Lupin», todo el mundo creyó inmediatamente que yo no era Arsène Lupin, lo contrario habría sido algo excepcional. Si una sola persona hubiera dudado, si una sola hubiera dicho sencillamente: «¿Y si fuera Arsène Lupin?», en ese mismo momento yo ya estaba perdido. Bastaba con acercarse a mí con la idea de que pudiera ser Arsène Lupin y no como lo hicieron usted y los demás, con la idea de que no era Arsène Lupin, porque, pese a todas las precauciones, me habrían reconocido. Pero yo estaba tranquilo. A nadie, lógica y psicológicamente, se le podía ocurrir esa simple idea. —De pronto, Lupin sujetó la mano de Ganimard—. Vamos, Ganimard, confiese que ocho días después de nuestra entrevista en la cárcel de la Santé, estuvo esperándome a las cuatro de la tarde, en su casa, como le había pedido que hiciera.

—¿Y el furgón penitenciario? —dijo Ganimard evitando responder.

—¡Un farol! Mis amigos trucaron y cambiaron ese coche viejo fuera de servicio, querían probar suerte. Pero yo sabía que no daría resultado sin un cúmulo de circunstancias excepcionales. Sencillamente, me pareció útil llevar a cabo ese intento de fuga y darle la mayor publicidad posible. Una primera fuga audazmente preparada daría a la segunda el valor de una fuga realizada.

—De modo que el puro…

—Lo preparé yo, igual que el cuchillo.

—¿Y las notas?

—También las escribí yo.

—¿Y la misteriosa mujer?

—Los dos éramos la misma persona. Puedo escribir con todas las caligrafías que quiera.

Ganimard se quedó un momento pensativo y añadió:

—¿Y cómo pudo ser que, en el servicio de antropometría, cuando vieron la ficha de Baudru, no se dieran cuenta de que coincidía con la de Arsène Lupin?

—Arsène Lupin no está fichado.

—¡Vamos, hombre!

—Bueno, la ficha es falsa. Di muchas vueltas a ese asunto. El sistema Bertillon de identificación antropométrica se basa en primer lugar en una identificación visual, y usted ya ha visto que eso no es infalible y, después, en el registro de cinco medidas, la de la cabeza, los dedos, las orejas, etcétera. Contra eso no hay nada que hacer.

—¿Y entonces?

—Entonces, tuve que pagar. Antes incluso de que regresara de América, uno de los empleados del servicio aceptó una determinada cantidad para anotar una medida falsa al principio de mis mediciones. Con eso basta para que todo el sistema se descuadre y una ficha se clasifique en un cuadro diametralmente opuesto al que le correspondería. Así que la ficha de Baudru no podía coincidir con la de Arsène Lupin.

Ambos permanecieron callados y luego Ganimard preguntó:

—¿Y ahora qué va a hacer?

—¡¿Ahora?! —exclamó Lupin—. Ahora voy a descansar, seguir un régimen de sobrealimentación y poco a poco volver a ser yo. Está muy bien eso de ser Baudru o cualquier otra persona, cambiar de personalidad como quien cambia de camisa y elegir tu aspecto, la voz, la mirada y la caligrafía. Pero llega un momento en que uno ya no se reconoce ni a sí mismo y eso es muy triste. Ahora me siento como debía de sentirse el hombre que perdió su sombra. Voy a buscarme y a encontrarme de nuevo. —Dio unos pasos de un lado a otro. Una cierta oscuridad se mezclaba con la luz del día. Lupin se detuvo delante de Ganimard—. Creo que ya no tenemos nada más que hablar.

—Sí —respondió el inspector—. Me gustaría saber si hará público el modo en que se fugó... El error que cometí...

—¡Tranquilo! Nadie sabrá jamás que el preso que soltaron era Arsène Lupin. Tengo mucho interés en rodearme de un halo de misterio para que esta fuga siga considerándose como algo milagroso. Así que no tema nada, amigo, y adiós. Voy a cenar al centro y tengo el tiempo justo para vestirme.

—¡Creía que solo quería descansar!

—Desgraciadamente, hay obligaciones sociales que no puedo eludir. Mañana empezaré a descansar.

—¿Y dónde va a cenar?

—En la embajada de Inglaterra.

4

EL MISTERIOSO VIAJERO

La víspera, había enviado mi automóvil a Ruan por carretera; yo tenía que viajar en tren, recogerlo y desde allí dirigirme a casa de unos amigos que viven a orillas del Sena.

Pero en París, pocos minutos antes de la salida del tren, siete señores invadieron mi compartimento; cinco de ellos fumaban. Por muy corto que fuera el trayecto en un tren rápido, la perspectiva de viajar en semejante compañía me resultó desagradable, sobre todo porque en el vagón, que era de los antiguos, no había pasillo. Así que recogí el abrigo, los periódicos, la guía de ferrocarriles y me refugié en uno de los compartimentos contiguos.

Allí había una señora. Al verme, hizo un gesto de contrariedad que no se me escapó y se inclinó hacia un señor que estaba de pie en el estribo, su marido sin duda, que la había acompañado a la estación. El señor me observó y probablemente salí airoso del examen porque, sonriendo, habló en voz baja con su mujer, como quien tranquiliza a un niño que tiene miedo. La mujer también sonrió y me dirigió una mirada amistosa, como si de pronto se diera cuenta de que yo era uno de esos hombres formales con los que una mujer puede estar encerrada durante dos horas en un habitáculo de medio metro cuadrado sin nada que temer.

El marido le dijo:

—No te enfades conmigo, querida, pero tengo una cita urgente y no puedo esperar más.

La besó cariñosamente y se fue. Ella le mandaba besitos discretos por la ventana y agitaba el pañuelo. Sonó el silbato y el tren se puso en marcha.

En ese preciso momento, y a pesar de las protestas de los empleados de la estación, se abrió la puerta y apareció un hombre en nuestro compartimento. Mi compañera, que estaba de pie guardando sus cosas en la red para equipajes, se asustó, soltó un grito y se cayó en el asiento.

Yo no soy miedoso, ni mucho menos, pero confieso que esas irrupciones de última hora siempre me resultan desagradables. Parecen equívocas, poco espontáneas... Debe de haber algo raro que...

Sin embargo, el recién llegado, con su aspecto y su actitud, consiguió rápidamente que cambiáramos la mala impresión que nos había causado su forma de comportarse. El hombre era correcto, casi elegante, llevaba una corbata de buen gusto, guantes limpios y tenía una cara enérgica... Pero, por cierto, ¿dónde demonios había visto yo esa cara? Porque, no me cabía la menor duda, la había visto. O por lo menos, para ser más exacto, yo tenía esa especie de recuerdo que te queda cuando has contemplado un retrato muchas veces, pero nunca has visto al personaje real. Y, al mismo tiempo, ese recuerdo era tan inconsistente y vago que me daba cuenta de que era inútil estrujarme la memoria.

Pero, cuando me fijé en la señora, me sorprendió su palidez y cómo se le había transformado la cara. Miraba a nuestro compañero de viaje —el hombre se había sentado en su lado— con una expresión de auténtico pavor y me di cuenta de que acercaba una mano temblorosa al bolsito de viaje que había dejado en el asiento, a veinte centímetros de sus rodillas. Acabó cogiéndolo muy nerviosa y poniéndolo junto a ella.

Cruzamos las miradas y vi en la suya tanto malestar y ansiedad que no pude dejar de preguntarle:

—¿Se encuentra bien, señora? ¿Quiere que abra la ventana?

La mujer no respondió, pero, con un gesto de miedo, me señaló al individuo. Yo sonreí igual que lo había hecho su marido, me encogí de hombros y le expliqué por señas que no tenía nada que temer, que allí estaba yo y que, además, aquel hombre parecía completamente inofensivo.

En ese momento, el hombre se volvió hacia nosotros, nos miró a los dos de pies a cabeza, se hundió más en su asiento y luego ya no se movió.

Todos nos quedamos callados, pero la viajera, como si hubiera hecho acopio de todas sus fuerzas para llevar a cabo un acto desesperado, me dijo con una voz que apenas se oía.

—¿Sabe usted quién está en el tren?

—¿Quién?

—Pues él..., él..., se lo aseguro.

—Pero ¿quién?

—¡Arsène Lupin!

Mi compañera no había apartado los ojos del viajero y parecía que le susurraba a él y no a mí las sílabas de aquel nombre que tanto la asustaba.

El otro se caló el sombrero hasta la nariz. No sé si para ocultar su desconcierto o si se disponía a dormir.

Yo le expliqué a la señora:

—Ayer condenaron a Arsène Lupin por rebeldía a veinte años de trabajos forzados. De manera que no es muy probable que hoy cometa la imprudencia de dejarse ver. Además, los periódicos dijeron que este invierno se le había visto en Turquía, después de la famosa fuga de la Santé, ¿no es así?

—Está en el tren —repitió la señora, con la clara intención de que lo oyera nuestro compañero de compartimento—. Mi marido es el subdirector de los servicios penitenciarios y el mismísimo comisario de la estación nos ha dicho que estaban buscando a Arsène Lupin.

—Eso no es motivo para...

—Lo vieron en el vestíbulo de la estación y compró un billete de primera clase para Ruan.

—Pues era fácil echarle el guante.

—Sí, pero desapareció. El interventor ya no lo vio entrar a la sala de espera, y se suponía que había cruzado por los andenes de los trenes de extrarradio y que se había subido al expreso que sale diez minutos después de nosotros.

—En ese caso, lo habrán atrapado en el expreso.

—¿Y si en el último momento saltó del expreso y subió a este tren... como es probable..., no, como es seguro? ¿Qué me dice?

—Entonces, lo atraparán aquí. Los empleados y los agentes habrán visto el cambio de tren y cuando lleguemos a Ruan lo recibirán como se merece.

—¿A él? ¡Eso nunca! Encontrará el modo de volver a escaparse.

—Pues entonces le deseo buen viaje.

—¿Y lo que pueda hacer durante el trayecto?

—¿Qué?

—¿Cree usted que yo lo sé? Pero de él cabe esperar cualquier cosa.

La mujer estaba muy nerviosa y, en realidad, la situación justificaba hasta cierto punto ese nerviosismo.

Muy a mi pesar le dije:

—Tiene razón, hay algunas coincidencias extrañas... Pero tranquilícese usted, señora. Si Arsène Lupin estuviera en uno de estos vagones se estaría muy quieto y en lugar de meterse en problemas, intentaría evitar el peligro.

Mis palabras no la tranquilizaron. Sin embargo, se calló, sin duda temía pecar de indiscreta.

Yo abrí el periódico y empecé a leer los artículos sobre el proceso de Arsène Lupin. Todo lo que decían ya se sabía, así que no me parecieron muy interesantes. Además, estaba cansado, había dormido mal, me pesaban los párpados y se me caía la cabeza.

—Pero bueno, señor, ¿no estará pensando usted en dormirse?

La señora me arrancó el periódico, mirándome muy enfadada.

—Por supuesto que no —respondí—. No tengo sueño.

—Sería una imprudencia por su parte —me dijo.

—Sí, una imprudencia —repetí.

Luché con fuerza contra el sueño mirando el paisaje y las nubes que ocultaban el cielo. Pero enseguida todo se nubló en el espacio, la imagen de la señora nerviosa y del señor dormitando se borraron de mi mente y el profundo silencio del sueño se apoderó de mí.

Aunque pronto unos sueños incoherentes y ligeros dieron vida a ese silencio. Un sujeto que interpretaba el papel de Arsène Lupin y se llamaba como él tenía cierto protagonismo. Se movía en el horizonte, cargando a la espalda objetos preciosos, traspasaba las paredes y se llevaba los muebles de los castillos.

Pero la silueta de ese sujeto que, por cierto, ya no era Arsène Lupin, se hizo más precisa. Se acercaba a mí, cada vez más grande, saltaba al vagón con una agilidad increíble y me caía de lleno encima del pecho.

Sentí un dolor fuerte y lancé un grito desgarrador. Me desperté. El hombre, el viajero, con una rodilla apoyada en mi pecho, me apretaba la garganta con las manos.

Apenas pude verlo porque tenía los ojos inyectados en sangre. También vi a la señora angustiada en un rincón, presa de un ataque de nervios. Yo ni siquiera intenté resistirme. Además, tampoco habría tenido fuerza, me palpitaban las sienes, me ahogaba…, estaba agonizando… Un minuto más y me habría asfixiado.

El hombre debió de darse cuenta porque aflojó la presión. Sin quitarse de encima, con la mano derecha estiró una cuerda a la que había hecho un nudo corredizo y con un gesto brusco me ató las muñecas. En un instante quedé atado, amordazado y completamente inmovilizado.

Y lo hizo de la forma más natural del mundo, con una facilidad que demostraba la sabiduría de un maestro, de un profesional del robo y el crimen. Sin una palabra ni un gesto de preocupación. Solo sangre fría y arrojo. Y ahí estaba yo, en el asiento de un tren, atado como una momia, ¡yo, Arsène Lupin!

La verdad, era como para echarse a reír. Y, pese a lo serio de las circunstancias, no dejaba de divertirme todo lo que tenía de irónico y gracioso la situación. ¡Arsène Lupin engañado como un novato, desvalijado como un infeliz! Porque, claro está, ¡el bandido me aligeró los bolsillos y se llevó mi cartera! Arsène Lupin convertido en víctima, embaucado, vencido… ¡Vaya aventura!

Faltaba la señora. El ladrón ni siquiera le prestó atención. Se limitó a recoger la bolsa que estaba en el suelo y a sacar las joyas, el monedero y las baratijas de oro y plata que había dentro. La señora abrió un ojo, se quitó los anillos temblando de miedo y se los dio como si hubiera querido evitarle cualquier esfuerzo inútil. El otro cogió los anillos y los miró: la mujer se desmayó.

Entonces, todavía en silencio y tranquilo, sin ocuparse ya de nosotros, volvió a su sitio, encendió un cigarrillo y se puso a examinar detenidamente el tesoro que había conquistado, examen que pareció dejarlo completamente satisfecho.

Yo estaba mucho menos satisfecho. Y no me refiero a los doce mil francos que me había desplumado indebidamente. Ese era un daño pasajero, porque entraba dentro de mis planes recuperar esos doce mil francos en el menor tiempo posible, lo mismo que los documentos, muy importantes, que guardaba en la cartera: proyectos, presupuestos, direcciones, listas de contactos, cartas comprometedoras. En ese momento, tenía una preocupación más acuciante y más seria: ¿qué iba a pasar?

Como cabe suponer, el alboroto que provocó mi aparición en la estación de Saint-Lazare no me había pasado desapercibido. Estaba invitado a casa de unos amigos que me conocían por el nombre de Guillaume Berlat, y para ellos mi parecido con Arsène Lupin era motivo de bromas cariñosas. Yo no había podido caracterizarme como me habría gustado y por eso me descubrieron en la estación. Además, se había visto a un hombre precipitarse del expreso al rápido. ¿Quién iba a ser ese hombre sino Arsène Lupin? Por lo tanto, habrían enviado un telegrama informando de mi presencia en el tren al comisario de policía de Ruan y este, con un respetable número de agentes, inevitable y necesariamente, estaría esperándome a la llegada, interrogaría a los viajeros sospechosos y registraría minuciosamente los vagones.

Yo tenía previsto todo eso, y no me preocupaba demasiado, estaba convencido de que la policía de Ruan no sería más perspicaz que la de París, así que podría pasar desapercibido, me bastaría con enseñar a la salida mi carné de diputado, el mismo que tanta confianza había inspirado al interventor de Saint-Lazare. ¡Pero cómo habían cambiado las cosas! Ya ni siquiera estaba libre. No podía intentar una de mis jugadas habituales. En uno de los vagones, el comisario descubriría al señor Arsène Lupin, que una oportuna casualidad se lo entregaba atado de pies y manos, manso como un cordero, empaquetado y ya listo. Solo tendría que aceptar la entrega, como quien recibe un paquete postal que le envían a la estación, ya sea una cesta de caza o una canasta de fruta y verdura.

¿Y qué podía hacer yo atado de pies y manos para evitar ese desafortunado desenlace?

Mientras tanto, el rápido volaba a Ruan, que era la siguiente y única estación, porque ya habíamos dejado atrás sin detenernos Vernon y Saint-Pierre.

Había otro problema que me preocupaba, en el que estaba menos directamente involucrado, pero cuya solución despertaba mi curiosidad profesional. ¿Qué intenciones tenía mi compañero de viaje?

Si yo hubiera estado solo, él tendría tiempo suficiente para bajar tranquilamente del tren en Ruan. Pero ¿y la señora? ¡En cuanto abrieran la puerta, aquella mujer, que en estos momentos estaba tan formal y humilde, empezaría a gritar, se revolvería y pediría socorro!

¡Aquello me tenía completamente intrigado! ¿Por qué no la reducía como a mí? Eso le habría dado la oportunidad de desaparecer antes de que nadie se diera cuenta de su doble fechoría.

El bandido fumaba constantemente, con la mirada fija en el exterior, que una lluvia titubeante empezaba a rayar con grandes líneas oblicuas. Una sola vez se dio la vuelta, cogió mi guía de ferrocarriles y la consultó.

La señora, por su parte, intentaba seguir desmayada, para tranquilizar a su enemigo, pero el humo le provocaba unos ataques de tos que contradecían el desvanecimiento.

Por lo que a mí respecta, me sentía muy incómodo y me dolían todos los músculos. Pero, mientras tanto, pensaba, planeaba...

Pasamos por Pont-de-l'Archel y Oissel. El rápido corría feliz, ebrio de velocidad.

Saint-Étienne... En ese momento, el hombre se levantó y avanzó dos pasos hacia nosotros, la señora se apresuró a reaccionar con otro grito y otro desvanecimiento, aunque esa vez no lo simuló.

Pero ¿cuál era el objetivo de aquel hombre? Bajó la ventana de nuestro lado. La lluvia caía cada vez con más rabia y el desconocido hizo un gesto que dio a entender claramente que aquello le suponía un problema, porque no tenía ni paraguas ni abrigo. Echó una mirada a la red de los equipajes: allí estaba el paraguas de la señora. Lo alcanzó. También agarró mi abrigo y se lo puso.

Estábamos cruzando el Sena. El hombre se remangó los pantalones, luego se asomó por la ventana y abrió el pestillo exterior.

¿Iba a saltar a la vía? A esa velocidad, le esperaba una muerte segura. El tren entró en el túnel de Sainte-Catherine. El hombre entreabrió la puerta y tanteó con el pie para encontrar el estribo. ¡Qué locura! Las tinieblas, el humo y mucho ruido, todo aquello daba al intento de huida unos tintes fantásticos. Pero, de pronto, el tren aminoró la marcha, los frenos se enfrentaron al esfuerzo de las ruedas. En un minuto, la velocidad del tren se redujo a la normal y aún disminuyó más. Sin lugar a dudas, estaban planificadas unas obras de refuerzo en esa parte del túnel que exigían a los trenes, quizá desde hacía unos días, circular a cámara lenta, y el hombre lo sabía.

Así que solo tuvo que poner el otro pie en el estribo, bajar al segundo peldaño e irse tranquilamente, no sin antes volver a echar el pestillo y dejar así la puerta cerrada.

Justo había desaparecido cuando la luz del día iluminó el humo de un color más blanco. Desembocamos en un valle. Otro túnel y estábamos en Ruan.

La señora recobró el conocimiento inmediatamente y lo primero que hizo fue lamentarse por sus joyas. Yo le imploraba con la mirada. Mi compañera de viaje me entendió y me quitó la mordaza que me ahogaba. También quería desatarme, pero se lo impedí.

—No, no, la policía tiene que ver todo tal cual está y que se haga una idea de quién es ese sinvergüenza.

—¿Y si tiro de la señal de alarma?

—Demasiado tarde, eso tendría que haberlo pensado mientras me atacaba.

—¡Pero me habría matado! ¡Ay, señor! ¡Le dije que Arsène Lupin viajaba en este tren! Lo reconocí inmediatamente por el retrato que han publicado los periódicos. Y ya ve, se ha marchado con mis joyas.

—Lo encontrarán, no se preocupe por eso.

—¡Encontrar a Arsène Lupin! Eso nunca.

—Pues depende de usted, señora. Escúcheme bien. Cuando lleguemos, pida ayuda y haga ruido desde la puerta. Vendrán agentes de policía y trabajadores de la estación. Entonces, cuénteles en pocas palabras lo que ha visto, cómo Arsène Lupin me agredió y después huyó, deles su descripción, un sombrero flexible, un paraguas, el suyo, y un abrigo entallado.

—El suyo —dijo la señora.

—¿Cómo que el mío? Claro que no, era el suyo. Yo no llevaba ningún abrigo.

—Me había parecido que él tampoco lo tenía cuando subió.

—Sí, sí... O puede ser una prenda que alguien olvidara en la red de los equipajes. De cualquier modo, él lo llevaba puesto cuando bajó del tren y eso es lo importante, un abrigo gris, entallado, recuerde usted... ¡Ah! Me olvidaba, dígales lo primero su nombre. El cargo de su marido hará que toda esa gente se esfuerce más en su tarea. —Estábamos llegando. La mujer ya se asomaba por la puerta. Yo continué dándole indicaciones con un tono un poco fuerte, casi imperativo, para que se grabasen mis palabras en su cerebro—: Dígales también mi nombre, Guillaume Berlat. En caso de necesidad, dígales que me conoce, eso nos hará ganar tiempo, es preciso que ventilen rápido la investigación preliminar, lo importante es que se centren en la persecución de Arsène Lupin, sus joyas... No se equivocará, ¿verdad? Guillaume Berlat, un amigo de su marido.

—Entendido, Guillaume Berlat. —Mi compañera empezó a llamar y a gesticular. El tren aún no se había detenido cuando ya subía a bordo un señor, al que seguían varios hombres. Había llegado el momento crucial. La señora, sin aliento, gritaba—: ¡Arsène Lupin nos ha atacado! ¡Me ha robado mis joyas! ¡Soy la señora Renaud, mi marido es el subdirector de los servicios penitenciarios! ¡Ah!, mire, precisamente ahí está mi hermano, Georges Ardelle, el director del Banco de Crédito de Ruan, usted tiene que conocerlo... —La mujer besó a un hombre joven que acababa de llegar y el comisario lo saludó, pero ella siguió hablando desconsolada—: Sí,

Arsène Lupin... Mientras el señor dormía se le tiró al cuello... El señor Berlat, amigo de mi marido.

El comisario preguntó:

—¿Y dónde está Arsène Lupin?

—Saltó del tren en el túnel, después de cruzar el Sena.

—¿Y está usted segura de que era él?

—¡Sí, estoy segura! Lo he reconocido perfectamente. Además, lo vieron en la estación de Saint-Lazare. Llevaba un sombrero flexible...

—No, un sombrero de fieltro duro, como ese —le corrigió el comisario, señalando mi sombrero.

—Un sombrero flexible, se lo garantizo —repitió la señora Renaud—, y un abrigo gris entallado.

—En efecto —murmuró el comisario, el telegrama especificaba el abrigo gris, entallado, con el cuello de terciopelo negro.

—El cuello de terciopelo negro, exacto —exclamó la señora Renaud, triunfante.

Yo respiré. ¡Pero qué valiente y qué excelente amiga era aquella mujer!

Entretanto, los agentes me habían desatado. Yo me mordí con fuerza el labio hasta hacerme sangre. Completamente encorvado y con el pañuelo en la boca, como es normal en un individuó que ha estado mucho tiempo en una posición incómoda y lleva en la cara la marca cruenta de una mordaza, le dije al comisario con un tono muy débil:

—Señor, era Arsène Lupin, no hay duda... Si se apresuran lo atraparán. Creo que puedo serles de alguna utilidad...

Desengancharon el vagón, para que la justicia pudiera buscar pruebas allí, y el tren siguió ruta a El Havre. Nos llevaron al despacho del jefe de estación a través de una multitud de curiosos que llenaban el andén.

En ese momento yo dudé, podía alejarme de allí con cualquier pretexto, ir a recoger mi coche y salir pitando. Quedarme era peligroso. Si se produjera algún incidente o si llegara un despacho de París estaría perdido.

Sí, pero ¿y mi ladrón? Contando solo con mis propios recursos y en una región que no me era familiar, no estaba seguro de encontrarlo.

«¡Bah! —pensé—. Nos la jugamos, nos quedamos. ¡Es una partida difícil de ganar, pero divertida de jugar! Y el reto merece la pena.»

Y cuando nos rogaban que volviéramos a prestar declaración provisionalmente, yo protesté:

—Señor comisario, en este momento Lupin nos lleva ventaja. Tengo el coche en el patio de la estación. Si quiere hacerme el honor de venir conmigo, intentaríamos...

El comisario sonrió con aire perspicaz.

—La idea no es mala, al contrario, es tan buena que ahora mismo nos ponemos a ello.

—¡Ah!

—Sí, señor, hace un rato que dos agentes fueron a buscarlo en bicicleta.

—¿Y adónde?

—A la misma salida del túnel. Allí recogerán pistas y testimonios y seguirán el rastro de Arsène Lupin.

Me encogí de hombros sin poder evitarlo.

—Sus dos agentes no conseguirán ni pistas ni testimonios.

—¿De verdad?

—Arsène Lupin se las habrá arreglado para que nadie lo viera salir del túnel. Habrá seguido la primera carretera y de allí...

—Y de allí a Ruan, donde lo atraparemos.

—No vendrá a Ruan.

—Entonces se quedará por los alrededores, donde aún estamos más seguros de...

—No, no se quedará por los alrededores.

—Vaya. ¿Y dónde se esconderá, pues?

Yo miré el reloj.

—En estos momentos, Arsène Lupin merodea cerca de la estación de Darnétal. A las diez cincuenta, es decir, dentro de veinte minutos, subirá al tren que va de Ruan a la Estación del Norte de Amiens.

—¿Usted cree? ¿Y cómo lo sabe?

—¡Dios mío! Es muy fácil. En el compartimento, Arsène Lupin consultó mi guía de ferrocarriles. ¿Por qué motivo? ¿Habría, quizá, cerca de donde desapareció, otra línea ferroviaria, una estación en esa línea y un tren que se detuviera en esa estación? Acabo de consultar la guía y así lo confirma.

—En honor a la verdad, señor, es una perfecta deducción. ¡Vaya capacidad!

Arrastrado por mi convencimiento, había cometido una torpeza demostrando tanta inteligencia. El comisario me miraba sorprendido y creí notar un atisbo de sospecha. Casi imposible, porque las fotografías que el Ministerio Fiscal había enviado a todas partes eran muy malas y representaban a un Arsène Lupin muy diferente del que ese señor tenía delante como para que pudiera reconocerme. Pero, aun así, el comisario estaba desconcertado, confusamente inquieto.

Hubo un silencio. Algo equívoco e incierto nos hizo callar. Yo sentí un escalofrío de malestar. ¿Iba a volverse la suerte contra mí? Me dominé y me eché a reír.

—Dios mío, no hay nada que te despierte más la inteligencia que perder una cartera y las ganas de encontrarla. Y creo que, si usted quisiera dejarme dos agentes, entre los tres podríamos quizá…

—¡Ay! Se lo ruego señor comisario —gritó la señora Renaud—. Escuche al señor Berlat.

La intervención de mi excelente amiga fue decisiva. Cuando ella, la mujer de un personaje influyente, pronunciaba mi nombre, Berlat se volvía realmente el mío y me otorgaba una identidad que ninguna sospecha pondría en tela de juicio. El comisario se levantó:

—Me haría muy feliz que lo lograra, señor Berlat, créame. Tengo tantas ganas como usted de detener a Arsène Lupin.

El comisario me acompañó hasta el automóvil. Dos de sus agentes, que me presentó como Honoré Massol y Gaston Delivet, subieron al coche. Yo me senté al volante. El mecánico giró la manivela. Unos segundos después salimos de la estación. Estaba salvado.

¡Pues sí! Confieso que mientras conducía por los bulevares que rodean la vieja ciudad normanda a gran velocidad, en mi Moreau-Lepton de treinta y cinco caballos, me sentía bastante orgulloso. El motor rugía con armonía. A derecha e izquierda, los árboles desaparecían detrás de

nosotros. Y, ya libre, fuera de peligro, solo tenía que ocuparme de solucionar mis asuntos personales con la ayuda de aquellos dos honrados representantes de las fuerzas de la ley. ¡Arsène Lupin iba en busca de Arsène Lupin!

Gaston Delivet y Honoré Massol, modestos defensores del orden público, ¡qué valiosa fue vuestra ayuda! ¿Qué habría hecho yo sin vosotros? ¿Cuántas veces me habría equivocado de camino en los cruces? Sin vosotros, Arsène Lupin se habría perdido y el otro habría escapado.

Pero no todo había acabado, ni mucho menos. Me faltaba, en primer lugar, atrapar a aquel individuo y luego conseguir los documentos que me había robado. Bajo ningún concepto, mis dos compinches podían meter las narices en esos papeles, y mucho menos incautarlos. Lo que yo quería era utilizar a aquellos dos hombres y actuar a sus espaldas, aunque eso no era tan fácil.

Llegamos a Darnétal tres minutos después de que hubiera pasado el tren. Es verdad que me tranquilizó saber que un individuo con un abrigo gris entallado y el cuello de terciopelo negro había subido a un compartimento de segunda clase con un billete a Amiens.

Definitivamente, mi estreno como policía prometía.

Delivet me dijo:

—Ese tren es un expreso que no para hasta Motérolier-Buchy, dentro de diecinueve minutos. En esa estación el tren se bifurca, si no llegamos antes, Arsène Lupin puede seguir hasta Amiens o desviarse hacia Clères y terminar en Dieppe o en París.

—¿A qué distancia está Montérolier?

—A veintitrés kilómetros.

—Veintitrés kilómetros en diecinueve minutos... Llegaremos antes.

¡Vaya recorrido impresionante! Nunca antes mi fiel Moreau-Lepton había respondido con tanto entusiasmo y precisión a mi ansiedad. Era como si yo le transmitiese mi voluntad directamente, sin la intervención de palancas ni pedales. El coche compartía mi pasión. Y aprobaba mi tenacidad. Comprendía mi animadversión hacia ese sinvergüenza de Arsène Lupin. ¡El muy embustero! ¡El muy traidor! ¿Le ganaría la partida? ¿Se burlaría otra vez de la autoridad, de esa autoridad que yo representaba?

—¡A la derecha! —gritaba Delivet— ¡A la izquierda! ¡Recto!...

Nos deslizábamos por encima del suelo. Los mojones parecían animalitos perezosos que desaparecían cuando nos acercábamos.

Y de pronto, a la vuelta de una curva, apareció un remolino de humo, el Expreso del Norte.

Durante un kilómetro, aquello fue un combate, uno al lado del otro, pero un combate en desigualdad de condiciones con un desenlace evidente. Cuando llegamos a la estación, habíamos ganado al tren por veinte cuerpos.

En tres segundos estábamos en el andén, delante de los vagones de segunda. Se abrieron las puertas. Bajaron algunas personas. Ni rastro del ladrón. Inspeccionamos los compartimentos. Allí no estaba Arsène Lupin.

—¡Maldita sea! —grité indignado—. Me habrá reconocido en el coche mientras íbamos en paralelo al tren y habrá saltado.

El jefe de tren confirmó la sospecha. Había visto a un hombre rodando por un terraplén, a doscientos metros de la estación.

—Mire, allí está. El que cruza el paso a nivel.

Me lancé corriendo hacia él, me seguían mis dos compinches o, mejor dicho, me seguía uno de ellos, porque el otro, Massol, resultó ser un corredor excepcional, tenía fondo y velocidad. En pocos segundos, disminuyó extraordinariamente la distancia que lo separaba del fugitivo. El hombre lo vio, saltó una cerca y se largó hacia un talud. Trepó el talud y ya lo vimos mucho más lejos, entrando en un bosque.

Cuando llegamos al bosquecillo, Massol nos estaba esperando. Le había parecido inútil arriesgarse más por miedo a perdernos.

—Le felicito, amigo —le dije—. Después de semejante carrera, ese tipo debe de estar sin aliento. Ya lo tenemos. —Examiné los alrededores mientras pensaba en cómo actuar para detener yo solo al fugitivo y poder así recuperar por mi cuenta lo que la justicia seguramente solo aceptaría entregarme después de una desagradable investigación. Luego, volví junto a mis compañeros—. Ya está, es muy fácil. Usted, Massol, póngase a la izquierda. Y usted, Delivet, a la derecha. Desde esos puestos, vigilen toda la línea posterior del bosque, ese bandido solo podrá salir de ahí, sin que ustedes lo vean, por esa calada, donde estaré yo. Si él no sale, entro yo y lo fuerzo a ir hacia uno de ustedes. Ustedes solo tienen que esperar. ¡Ah! Me olvidaba, en caso de alarma, disparen un tiro.

Massol y Delivet se alejaron cada uno por su lado. En cuanto desaparecieron, yo entré en el bosque, con las máximas precauciones para que nadie me viera ni oyera. El bosque estaba cubierto de una maleza frondosa, preparada para la caza, y la cortaban unos senderos muy estrechos por donde solo se podía caminar agachado, como si fueran unos subterráneos de vegetación.

Uno de esos senderos desembocaba en un claro, allí, en la hierba mojada, había huellas de pasos. Las seguí deslizándome con mucho cuidado por el monte bajo. Las huellas me llevaron al pie de un montículo pequeño. Encima del montículo había una casucha hecha con cascotes de yeso, medio derruida.

«Debe de estar ahí —pensé—. Ha elegido bien el puesto de vigilancia.»

Trepé hasta las proximidades de la construcción. Un ruido ligero me advirtió de su presencia y, efectivamente, lo vi de espaldas por una abertura.

En dos saltos me eché encima de él. Intentó apuntarme con el revólver que tenía en la mano. No le di tiempo y lo tiré al suelo, de tal manera que le quedaron los brazos debajo del cuerpo, torcidos, y yo le apoyaba la rodilla en el pecho con todo el peso de mi cuerpo.

—Escucha, amigo —le dije al oído—, soy Arsène Lupin. Vas a devolverme inmediatamente y por las buenas mi cartera y la bolsa de la señora, después, te libro de las garras de la policía y te alisto con mis amigos. Di solo una palabra: ¿sí o no?

—Sí —murmuró.

—Mejor para ti. Tenías muy bien planeado el golpe de esta mañana. Tú y yo nos entenderemos. —Me levanté. El individuo rebuscó en el bolsillo, sacó un cuchillo grande y quiso apuñalarme—. ¡Imbécil! —le grité.

Con una mano le paré el ataque y con la otra le lancé un golpe fuerte directo a la carótida, el que se llama «gancho a la carótida». Lo dejé inconsciente.

En la cartera encontré mis documentos y el dinero. Por curiosidad, cogí la suya. En un sobre dirigido a él leí su nombre: Pierre Onfrey.

Me estremecí. Pierre Onfrey, ¡el asesino de la calle Lafontaine, de Auteuil! Pierre Onfrey, el que había degollado a la señora Delbois y a sus dos hijas. Me incliné sobre él. Sí, era la misma cara que en el compartimento del tren me había recordado a alguien que ya había visto antes.

Pero el tiempo corría. Metí en un sobre dos billetes de cien francos y una tarjeta con estas palabras: «Arsène Lupin, a sus buenos amigos Honoré Massol y Gaston Delivet, en testimonio de mi agradecimiento».

Lo dejé bien a la vista en medio de la habitación junto a la bolsa de la señora Renaud. ¿Cómo no iba a devolvérsela a una excelente amiga que tanto me había ayudado?

Sin embargo, he de confesar que saqué de la bolsa todo lo que parecía tener algo de valor y dejé solo un peine de concha y el monedero vacío. ¡Qué demonios! Los negocios son los negocios. Y, además, sinceramente, el oficio de su marido era tan poco digno...

Faltaba el individuo. Empezaba a removerse. ¿Qué debía hacer? Yo no estaba en condiciones ni de salvarlo ni de condenarlo.

Le quité las armas y disparé al aire.

«Vendrán esos dos —pensé—. ¡Que se las apañe él solo! El destino dictará lo que tenga que ocurrir.»

Y me alejé corriendo por la calada.

Veinte minutos más tarde, por un atajo que había visto mientras perseguíamos al fugitivo, llegué a mi automóvil.

A las cuatro de la tarde, envié un telegrama a mis amigos de Ruan, diciéndoles que un imprevisto me obligaba a posponer mi visita. Entre nosotros, mucho me temo que, teniendo en cuenta lo que ahora deben de saber, me vea obligado a posponerla definitivamente. ¡Qué cruel desilusión para ellos!

A las seis de la tarde, llegaba de vuelta a París por L'Isle-Adam, Enghien y la Puerta Bineau.

Por los periódicos de la tarde me enteré de que la policía, por fin, había conseguido capturar a Pierre Onfrey.

Al día siguiente, no desdeñemos las ventajas de una publicidad inteligente, *L'Écho de France* publicaba la siguiente sensacional reseña:

Ayer, en las inmediaciones de Buchy, y tras muchos contratiempos, Arsène Lupin llevó a cabo la detención de Pierre Onfrey. El asesino de la calle Lafontaine acababa de robar a la señora Renaud, mujer del subdirector de los servicios penitenciarios, en el tren que cubre la línea París-El Havre. Arsène Lupin devolvió a la señora Renaud la bolsa que contenía sus joyas y recompensó generosamente a los dos agentes de la Seguridad que lo habían ayudado en el transcurso de esa dramática detención.

5

EL COLLAR DE LA REINA

Dos o tres veces al año, en las grandes ocasiones, como los bailes de la embajada de Austria o las veladas de lady Billingstone, la condesa de Dreux-Soubise se ponía sobre la piel muy blanca de su cuello el collar de la reina.

Era este un collar muy famoso, el collar legendario que Bohmer y Bassenge, joyeros de la corte, diseñaron para la du Barry; luego, el cardenal Rohan-Soubise creyó regalarlo a María Antonieta, reina de Francia y, una noche de febrero de 1875, la estafadora Jeanne de Valois, condesa de la Motte, lo desmontó, con ayuda de su marido y de su cómplice Rétaux de Villette.

A decir verdad, solo la montura era auténtica. Rétaux de Villette la había conservado, mientras que el señor de la Motte y su mujer dispersaron a los cuatro vientos las piedras desengastadas brutalmente, las admirables piedras que con tanto cuidado había seleccionado Bohmer. Más tarde, en Italia, Rétaux la vendió a Gaston de Dreux-Soubise, sobrino y heredero del cardenal, quien lo había salvado de la ruina cuando se produjo la estrepitosa bancarrota de Rohan-Gueménée y, en recuerdo de su tío, volvió a comprar los pocos diamantes que quedaban en poder del joyero inglés Jefferys, los completó con otros de un valor muy inferior, pero idéntico tamaño, y consiguió reconstruir el maravilloso collar esclava, tal y como había salido de manos de Bohmer y Bassenge.

Los de Dreux-Soubise se enorgullecieron de esta joya histórica durante casi un siglo. A pesar de que diversas circunstancias habían disminuido notablemente su fortuna, prefirieron reducir su tren de vida antes que renunciar a la real y preciosa reliquia. Especialmente el conde actual se aferraba esa joya como quien se aferra a la casa de sus padres. Por precaución había contratado una caja fuerte en el Crédit Lyonnais para guardarlo. Allí solía ir a buscarlo él mismo por la tarde los días que su mujer quería lucirlo, y él mismo lo depositaba en el banco al día siguiente.

Aquella noche, en la recepción del palacio de Castille —la aventura se remonta a principios de siglo— la condesa tuvo un auténtico éxito y el rey Christian, en cuyo honor se celebraba la fiesta, se fijó en su magnífica belleza. Las piedras preciosas resplandecían alrededor de su gracioso cuello. Las mil facetas de los diamantes brillaban y chispeaban como llamas con la claridad de las luces. Parecía que solo ella pudiera llevar el peso de semejante aderezo con tanta naturalidad y elegancia.

Eso supuso un doble triunfo para el conde de Dreux, que lo saboreó profundamente y del que tanto se alegró cuando el matrimonio ya estaba de vuelta en su habitación del antiguo palacete del Faubourg Saint-Germain. Quizá estaba tan orgulloso de su mujer como de la joya que distinguía su casa desde hacía cuatro generaciones. Y por ese motivo su mujer se sentía puerilmente vanidosa, aunque también ese era un rasgo destacado de su carácter altanero.

La condesa, no sin cierto pesar, se quitó el collar del cuello y se lo entregó a su marido, que se quedó mirándolo fascinado, como si fuera la primera vez que lo veía. Después de guardarlo en su estuche de cuero rojo con el escudo del cardenal, pasó a un gabinete contiguo, completamente aislado del dormitorio, más bien una especie de alcoba, cuya única entrada estaba al pie de la cama. El conde, como siempre, escondió el estuche en una balda a bastante altura, entre sombrereras y montones de ropa blanca. Cerró la puerta y se puso el pijama.

Por la mañana, se levantó hacia las nueve con la intención de ir antes del almuerzo al Crédit Lyonnais. Se vistió, bebió una taza de café y bajó a las caballerizas. Allí repartió instrucciones. Le preocupaba uno de los caballos. Mandó que lo pusieran al paso y al trote delante de él en el patio. Luego regresó junto a su mujer.

La condesa no había salido de la habitación, y allí estaba peinándose con ayuda de su doncella. Al verlo le preguntó:

—¿Vas a salir?

—Sí. Voy a hacer esa gestión...

—¡Ah! Es verdad... Sí, es más prudente.

El conde entró en el gabinete. Pero, al cabo de unos segundos, sin la menor sorpresa, por cierto, le preguntó a su mujer:

—¿Has cogido el collar, querida?

La condesa le respondió:

—¿Cómo? Claro que no, yo no he cogido nada.

—¿Lo has cambiado de sitio?

—Por supuesto que no, ni siquiera he abierto esa puerta.

El conde apareció en la habitación descompuesto, balbuceaba con una voz que apenas se oía:

—¿Tú no lo has...? ¿No has sido tú? Entonces... —Su mujer corrió al gabinete y los dos empezaron a buscar el collar frenéticamente, tirando las sombrereras por el suelo y deshaciendo las pilas de ropa blanca—. Es inútil, todo lo que hagamos es inútil... Yo lo puse aquí, aquí mismo, en esta balda.

—Puedes haberte equivocado.

—Lo dejé aquí, aquí mismo, en esta balda y en ninguna otra.

Encendieron una vela, porque la habitación era bastante oscura, sacaron toda la ropa y las cosas que estorbaban. Cuando ya no quedó nada en el gabinete, tuvieron que admitir desesperados que el famoso collar, el collar esclava de la reina, había desaparecido.

La condesa, de carácter decidido, no quiso perder el tiempo lamentándose y mandó llamar al comisario, el señor Valorbe. Los condes lo conocían y valoraban mucho su mente astuta y su lucidez. Le pusieron al corriente de lo ocurrido con todo detalle e inmediatamente preguntó:

—Señor conde, ¿está usted seguro de que nadie pudo pasar por su habitación durante la noche?

—Completamente seguro. Tengo un sueño muy ligero. Es más, la puerta de esta habitación estaba cerrada con cerrojo. Esta mañana tuve que abrirlo cuando mi mujer llamó a su doncella.

—¿Y no hay ninguna otra forma de entrar en el gabinete?

—Ninguna.

—¿No tiene ventana?

—Sí, pero está condenada.

—Me gustaría comprobarlo yo mismo...

Encendieron varias velas e inmediatamente el señor Valorbe advirtió que la ventana solo estaba condenada hasta media altura, la tapaba un aparador y, además, este no estaba exactamente pegado a la ventana.

—Está suficientemente pegado, es imposible desplazarlo sin hacer mucho ruido —respondió el señor de Dreux.

—¿Y adónde da la ventana?

—A un pequeño patio interior.

—¿Hay otra planta encima de esta?

—Dos, pero a la altura de la planta del servicio el patio está protegido con una reja de malla pequeña. Por eso hay tan poca luz. —Separaron el aparador y comprobaron que la ventana estaba cerrada, lo que habría sido imposible si alguien hubiera entrado desde fuera—. A menos —aclaró el conde—, que ese alguien hubiera salido por nuestra habitación.

—En cuyo caso, usted no habría encontrado el cerrojo de la habitación echado. —El comisario se quedó pensativo un momento y luego se dirigió a la condesa—: ¿Las personas de su entorno sabían que usted llevaría el collar anoche?

—Algunas sí, es algo que no oculto. Pero nadie sabe que lo guardamos en el gabinete.

—¿Nadie?

—Nadie. A no ser que...

—Se lo ruego, señora, aclare esta cuestión. Es uno de los detalles más importantes.

La condesa le dijo a su marido:

—Estaba pensando en Henriette.

—¿Henriette? Ella, igual que los demás, no conoce este detalle.

—¿Estás seguro?

—¿Quién es esa señora? —preguntó el señor Valorbe.

—Una amiga del convento, que se distanció de su familia por casarse con una especie de obrero. Cuando murió su marido, yo la recogí con su hijo y le acondicioné un apartamento en este mismo palacete. —Y añadió avergonzada—: Me presta algún servicio, es muy mañosa.

—¿En qué planta vive?

—En la nuestra, cerca de los otros, al final de este pasillo. Y estoy pensando..., la ventana de su cocina...

—Da a este patio, ¿no es así?

—Sí, está justo enfrente de la nuestra.

Después de ese comentario, se hizo un breve silencio.

Luego, el señor Valorbe pidió que lo llevaran a ver a Henriette.

La encontraron cosiendo con su hijo, un crío de seis o siete años, leyendo a su lado. El comisario, bastante asombrado al ver el miserable apartamento que la condesa había acondicionado para aquella mujer, una habitación sin chimenea y un cuartucho que hacía las veces de cocina, la interrogó. Henriette pareció consternada cuando se enteró del robo. La noche anterior, ella misma había vestido a la condesa y después le puso el collar en el cuello.

—¡Dios mío! —dijo—, ¿quién se lo iba a imaginar?

—¿Y usted no tiene ni idea? ¿Ni la menor sospecha? Es posible que el culpable haya pasado por su habitación.

La mujer se rio de buena gana, sin imaginarse siquiera que pudiera pasárseles por la cabeza sospechar de ella, y respondió:

—Pero si no he salido de mi habitación. No salgo nunca. Además, mire usted. —Abrió la ventana del cuartucho—. Ya ve, hay más de tres metros hasta el alféizar de la ventana de enfrente.

—Y ¿quién le ha dicho a usted que estamos barajando la hipótesis de que robaron el collar por la ventana?

—¿Pero el collar no estaba en el gabinete?

—¿Y usted cómo lo sabe?

—Pues yo siempre he sabido que por la noche lo guardan en el gabinete. Lo han comentado delante de mí.

Su rostro, aún joven pero envejecido por los sufrimientos de la vida, dejaba ver mucha delicadeza y resignación. Sin embargo, de pronto, en el silencio que se hizo mostró una expresión de angustia, como si la amenazara algún peligro. Atrajo a su hijo hacia ella y el niño le cogió la mano y la besó con cariño.

—No creo que sea sospechosa —dijo el señor de Dreux al comisario cuando se quedaron solos—. Yo respondo por ella. Es la honradez personificada.

—Sí, soy de su misma opinión —afirmó el señor Valorbe—. Más bien, había pensado en una complicidad inconsciente. Pero reconozco que debemos abandonar esa hipótesis, porque no resuelve de ninguna manera el problema al que nos enfrentamos.

El comisario no siguió adelante con la investigación y la trasladó al juez de instrucción, quien la fue completando durante los días siguientes. Se interrogó al servicio, se comprobó el estado del cerrojo, se probó el cierre y la abertura de la ventana del gabinete, se inspeccionó el patio de arriba abajo… Todo resultó inútil. El cerrojo estaba intacto. La ventana no podía abrirse ni cerrarse desde fuera.

Las investigaciones apuntaron principalmente a Henriette porque, a pesar de todo, siempre recaían hacia ese lado. Se hurgó en su vida minuciosamente y se comprobó que en los últimos tres años solo había salido cuatro veces del palacete, y las cuatro para hacer unas compras que pudieron verificarse. En realidad, era la doncella y la costurera de la señora de Dreux, y esta tenía una actitud con ella de tal severidad que todo el servicio lo comentó confidencialmente.

—Por otra parte —decía el juez de instrucción, que, al cabo de una semana, llegó a las mismas conclusiones que el comisario—, aun admitiendo que conociéramos al culpable, y todavía no hemos llegado a eso, no sabríamos cómo se cometió el robo. Nos lo impiden dos obstáculos, por un lado y por otro: una puerta y una ventana cerradas. ¡Hay una doble incógnita! ¿Cómo pudo entrar el ladrón? Y, lo que es mucho más difícil, ¿cómo pudo escabullirse dejando tras de sí una puerta con el cerrojo echado y una ventana cerrada?

Después de cuatro meses de investigaciones, el juez llegó a una íntima opinión: los señores de Dreux, apremiados por necesidades económicas, habían vendido el collar de la reina. Y cerró el caso.

El robo de la preciosa joya supuso para los de Dreux-Soubise un golpe del que se resintieron durante mucho tiempo. Esa especie de reserva que significaba aquel tesoro ya no respaldaba sus créditos y se encontraron con acreedores más exigentes y prestamistas menos dispuestos. Tuvieron que recortar gastos por lo sano y traspasar e hipotecar bienes. En fin, aquello habría sido su ruina si no los hubiesen salvado dos buenas herencias de unos parientes lejanos.

También sufrieron en su orgullo, como si con el collar hubieran perdido uno de sus cuartos de nobleza. Y, cosa extraña, la condesa arremetió contra su antigua amiga del convento. Estaba completamente resentida con ella y la acusaba descaradamente. Primero la relegó a la planta del servicio y luego, de un día para otro, la despidió.

Y la vida transcurrió sin mayores acontecimientos. Los condes viajaron mucho.

Solo hay un hecho destacable en esa época. Unos meses después de que se fuera Henriette, la condesa recibió una carta que la dejó muy sorprendida.

> Señora:
> No sé cómo agradecérselo. Porque es usted quien me ha enviado esto, ¿no es cierto? Solo puede ser usted. Nadie más sabe que me retiré a esta pequeña aldea. Si me equivoco, discúlpeme y reciba al menos mi gratitud por sus bondades del pasado...

¿Qué quería decir aquella mujer? La bondades presentes o pasadas de la condesa hacia Henriette se reducían a muchas injusticias. ¿Qué significaba ese agradecimiento?

Cuando le exigieron una explicación, la antigua doncella respondió que había recibido por correo, en un sobre sin certificar ni remitente, dos billetes de mil francos. El sobre, que enviaba con su respuesta, estaba sellado en París y solo tenía la dirección de Henriette, escrita con una letra evidentemente disimulada.

¿De dónde procedían esos dos mil francos? ¿Quién se los había enviado? Se informó a la justicia. Pero ¿qué pista podía seguirse en todo aquel asunto tan oscuro?

Y ocurrió lo mismo doce meses después. Y una tercera vez; y una cuarta vez; y así se repitió durante seis años, con la diferencia de que en el quinto y sexto año se duplicó la cantidad, lo que permitió a Henriette, que cayó repentinamente enferma, cuidarse en condiciones.

Otra diferencia: la administración de correos se incautó de una de las cartas con la excusa de que no tenía remitente; las dos últimas cartas se enviaron, cumpliendo con las normas, la primera desde Saint-Germain y la otra de Suresnes. El remitente firmó en la primera ocasión con el nombre de Anquety y después con el de Péchar. Las direcciones que dio eran falsas.

Al cabo de seis años, Henriette murió. El misterio quedó sin resolver.

Todos estos acontecimientos se hicieron públicos. Fue un asunto que cautivó a la población. Un destino extraño el de aquel collar que, después de haber conmocionado a Francia a finales del siglo XVIII, volvió a despertar tanto interés ciento veinte años más tarde. Sin embargo, nadie sabe lo que voy a contar, salvo los principales implicados y algunas personas más a las que el conde pidió silencio absoluto. Como es probable que cualquier día falten a su promesa, yo no tengo ningún escrúpulo en revelarlo, para que así se sepa la clave del secreto al mismo tiempo que la explicación de la carta que publicaron los periódicos antes de ayer por la mañana. Una carta extraordinaria que añadía, si eso fuera posible, un poco más de sombra y misterio a la oscuridad de este drama.

De esto hace ya cinco años. Entre los invitados que almorzaban aquel día en casa de los señores de Dreux-Soubise se encontraban sus dos sobrinas y una prima y, respecto a los hombres, el presidente de Essaville, el diputado Bochas, el caballero Floriani, a quien el conde había conocido en Sicilia, y el general marqués de Rouzières, un antiguo amigo de su círculo social.

Tras el almuerzo, las señoras sirvieron el café y permitieron a los señores encender sus puros con la condición de que no se fueran del salón. Estuvieron charlando y una de las jóvenes se entretuvo echando las cartas y prediciendo el futuro. Luego pasaron a comentar crímenes famosos. Y hablando de eso, el señor de Rouzières, quien nunca perdía la ocasión de pinchar al conde, recordó el asunto del collar, un tema de conversación que horrorizaba al señor de Dreux.

Enseguida, todos expresaron su parecer. Cada uno rehízo la instrucción del caso a su modo. Y, por supuesto, todas las hipótesis se contradecían y todas eran igual de inadmisibles.

—¿Y usted, señor? —preguntó la condesa al caballero Floriani—. ¿Usted qué opina?

—Pues yo, señora, no tengo opinión sobre ese tema. —Todos protestaron. Precisamente Floriani acaba de contar brillantemente varias aventuras en las que se había visto involucrado con su padre, un magistrado de Palermo, y había quedado clara su inteligencia y cuánto le gustaban ese tipo de asuntos—. Tengo que confesar —dijo Floriani— que he conseguido triunfar donde otras personas más capaces que yo ya se habían rendido. Pero de eso a considerarme Sherlock Holmes... Además, casi no sé nada de ese asunto. —Los invitados miraron al anfitrión. El conde a regañadientes tuvo que hacer un resumen de los hechos. El caballero escuchó, se quedó pensativo, hizo algunas preguntas y finalmente murmuró—: Es curioso, a primera vista no me parece algo tan difícil de resolver. —El conde se encogió de hombros, pero los demás mostraron mucho interés y Floriani siguió hablando con un tono algo dogmático—: En general, para llegar al autor de un crimen o un robo, hay que establecer cómo se produjo el crimen o el robo. En este caso, en mi opinión, no hay nada más sencillo, porque no nos encontramos frente a varias hipótesis, sino frente a un hecho, un hecho único, riguroso y que se presenta de la siguiente manera: el individuo solo pudo entrar por la puerta de la habitación o por la ventana del gabinete. Ahora bien, es imposible abrir desde el exterior una puerta con el cerrojo echado. Entonces, entró por la ventana.

—Estaba cerrada y la encontramos cerrada —afirmó el señor de Dreux.

—Para eso —siguió Floriani, sin hacer caso de la interrupción—, solo hacía falta instalar un puente, con una tabla o una escalera, entre el balcón de la cocina y el alféizar de la ventana y en cuanto el estuche...

—¡Pero le repito que la ventana estaba cerrada! —dijo con voz fuerte el conde, que parecía impacientarse.

Esta vez, Floriani tuvo que responderle. Y lo hizo con mucha tranquilidad, como si a él no le preocupara lo más mínimo una pega tan insustancial.

—Quiero creer que lo estaba, pero ¿hay un tragaluz en la ventana?

—¿Y usted cómo lo sabe?

—Para empezar, eso es casi una norma en los palacetes de esa época. Y, además, tiene que ser así porque, de otro modo, el robo sería inexplicable.

—Es cierto, la ventana tiene un tragaluz, pero estaba cerrado igual que la ventana. Ni siquiera le prestamos atención.

—Pues esa fue su equivocación. Porque si le hubieran prestado atención, habrían visto evidentemente que alguien lo había abierto.

—¿Y cómo?

—Supongo que ese tragaluz, igual que todos, se abre con un alambre de hierro trenzado que tiene una anilla en el extremo inferior, ¿no es así?

—Sí.

—¿Y la anilla colgaba entre la ventana y el aparador?

—Sí, pero no entiendo...

—Ya está. El ladrón pudo hacer una rendija en el cristal y con cualquier cosa, pongamos, por ejemplo, una varilla de hierro con un gancho, alcanzar la anilla, tirar de ella y abrir el tragaluz.

El conde respondió burlonamente:

—¡Perfecto! ¡Perfecto! Usted lo soluciona todo con una facilidad... Pero se olvida de algo, querido amigo, no había una rendija en el cristal.

—Había una rendija.

—Vamos, la habríamos visto.

—Para ver hay que mirar y no miraron. La rendija existe y es materialmente imposible que no esté a lo largo del cristal, en la masilla..., obviamente en sentido vertical.

El conde se levantó. Parecía muy nervioso. Dio dos o tres vueltas por el salón con un paso rápido y se acercó a Floriani:

—No se ha cambiado nada en el gabinete desde ese día, nadie ha puesto un pie dentro.

—Entonces, señor, tiene la posibilidad de ir a comprobar si esta explicación concuerda con la realidad.

—No concuerda con ninguno de los hechos que la justicia comprobó. Usted no vio nada, usted no sabe nada y todo lo que usted dice va en contra de lo que nosotros vimos y de todo lo que sabemos.

Floriani no pareció darse cuenta de lo enfadado que estaba el conde y le dijo con una sonrisa:

—¡Por Dios, señor! Yo solo intento aclarar las cosas, eso es todo. Y si estoy equivocado, demuestre mi error.

—Ahora mismo... Le confieso que a la larga su seguridad... —El señor de Dreux masculló aún algunas frases y luego, de pronto, se dirigió a la puerta y salió. Nadie dijo ni una palabra. Todos esperaban ansiosos, como si realmente fuera a surgir una parte de la verdad. Y el silencio era muy tenso. Por fin, apareció el conde en la puerta. Estaba pálido y especialmente nervioso. Con una voz temblorosa les dijo a sus amigos—: Les pido disculpas. Eran tan imprevisibles las explicaciones del señor Floriani... Nunca habría pensado...

Su mujer le preguntó impaciente:

—Habla, te lo suplico. ¿Qué pasa?

El conde balbuceó:

—Hay una rendija, exactamente donde ha indicado, a lo largo de la ventana. —Sujetó bruscamente del brazo al caballero y le dijo con un tono imperativo—: Y ahora, señor, continúe. Reconozco que hasta aquí usted tenía razón; pero esto no ha terminado. Responda, ¿qué cree usted que pasó?

Floriani se desprendió tranquilamente de la mano del conde y, tras un instante, siguió con su relato.

—Pues bien, yo creo que pasó lo siguiente: el individuo sabía que la señora de Dreux iría al baile con el collar y colocó la pasarela mientras ustedes estaban fuera de casa. Estuvo vigilándolos desde la ventana y le vio a usted, señor conde, esconder la joya. En cuanto usted salió del gabinete, él cortó el cristal y tiró de la anilla.

—De acuerdo, pero hay demasiada distancia para que pudiera alcanzar la manilla de la ventana desde el tragaluz.

—Si no pudo abrir la ventana, entonces entró por el tragaluz.

—Imposible, ningún hombre es tan delgado como para meterse por ahí.

—Entonces, no fue un hombre.

—¡Qué dice!

—Así es. Si el espacio es demasiado pequeño para un hombre, tuvo que ser un niño.

—¡Un niño!

—¿No me dijo que su amiga Henriette tenía un hijo?

—Sí..., un hijo que se llamaba Raoul.

—Pues es muy probable que fuera ese Raoul quien cometiera el robo.

—¿Y qué prueba tiene usted de eso?

—¿Qué prueba? Pues pruebas no faltan. Por ejemplo... —Floriani se calló y estuvo unos segundos pensando. Luego continuó—: Por ejemplo, es imposible pensar que el niño hubiera traído la pasarela de fuera sin que nadie lo viera. Debió de usar algo que tuviese disponible. En el cuartucho donde Henriette cocinaba ¿había unas repisas enganchadas a la pared donde la mujer dejaba las cacerolas?

—Dos repisas, si no recuerdo mal.

—Habría que comprobar si esas tablas están completamente fijas a los codales de madera que las sostienen. Si no es así, podríamos pensar que el niño las desclavó y luego las ató una a otra. A lo mejor, como en la cocina había un horno, también encontró allí el gancho del horno que utilizó para abrir el tragaluz.

El conde salió del salón sin decir ni una palabra y esta vez los asistentes ya ni siquiera sintieron la pequeña ansiedad por lo desconocido que experimentaron la primera vez. Sabían, y lo sabían terminantemente, que las previsiones de Floriani eran exactas. Ese hombre transmitía una sensación de certeza tan precisa que ya no lo escuchaban como si dedujera unos hechos de otros, sino como si relatara unos acontecimientos cuya autenticidad era fácil de comprobar sobre la marcha.

Y nadie se sorprendió cuando llegó el conde y afirmó:

—Fue el niño, fue él, todo lo demuestra.

—¿Ha visto las tablas y el gancho del horno?

—Los he visto, desclavó las tablas y el gancho sigue ahí.

La señora de Dreux-Soubise gritó:

—¿Que fue el crío? Querrás decir más bien que fue su madre. Henriette es la única culpable. Le habría obligado...

—No —afirmó el caballero Floriani—. La madre no tuvo nada que ver en ese asunto.

—¡Por favor! Vivían en la misma habitación, el niño no habría podido hacerlo a espaldas de Henriette.

—Sí, vivían en la misma habitación, pero todo sucedió en la otra habitación, mientras la madre dormía.

—¿Y el collar? —dijo el conde—. Lo habríamos encontrado entre las cosas del niño.

—¡Perdón! El niño sí salía a la calle. Esa misma mañana cuando lo sorprendieron delante de su pupitre, llegaba del colegio y, a lo mejor, la justicia, en lugar de agotar todos sus recursos con la madre inocente, habría hecho mejor registrando el pupitre del niño, entre los libros de clase.

—Lo admito, pero los dos mil francos que Henriette recibía todos los años ¿no son una clara señal de complicidad?

—Si hubiera sido cómplice, ¿le habría dado las gracias por el dinero? Además, ¿no la tenían vigilada? Mientras que el niño era libre y tenía toda clase de facilidades para correr al pueblo más cercano, conchabarse con cualquier perista y cederle a un precio de risa un diamante o dos diamantes, según las circunstancias, con la única condición de que enviara el dinero desde París y de que hiciera lo mismo al año siguiente.

Un malestar indefinible agobiaba a los de Dreux-Soubise y a sus invitados. Realmente, en el tono y en la actitud de Floriani había algo más que esa seguridad que, desde el principio, irritó al conde. Su actitud era como irónica, pero de una ironía que parecía más hostil que simpática y amistosa, como hubiera sido normal.

El conde fingió reír.

—¡Todo esto es tan sumamente ingenioso que me tiene fascinado! ¡Enhorabuena! ¡Qué brillante imaginación!

—No, claro que no —exclamó Floriani muy serio—. Yo no imagino nada, solo sugiero unas circunstancias que fueron necesariamente tal y como las estoy exponiendo.

—¿Y usted qué sabe?

—Lo que usted mismo me dijo. Yo me imagino la vida de la madre y el hijo, allá en una provincia remota, la madre que cae enferma, las artimañas e invenciones del pequeño para vender las piedras preciosas y salvar a su madre o al menos dulcificar sus últimos momentos. La enfermedad se la lleva. La madre muere. Pasan los años. El niño crece y se convierte en un hombre. Y entonces, ahora sí admitiré que doy rienda suelta a la imaginación, supongamos que ese hombre siente la necesidad de volver al lugar donde vivió su infancia, lo ve de nuevo, se reencuentra con los que sospecharon de su madre y la acusaron... ¿Se imaginan ustedes la curiosidad desgarradora de semejante conversación en la antigua casa donde se desarrollaron las peripecias del drama?

Sus palabras resonaros durante unos segundos en un silencio nervioso, en el rostro de los de Dreux se leía un esfuerzo desesperado por comprender y al mismo tiempo el miedo y la angustia de comprender. El conde murmuró:

—Señor, ¿y quién es usted?

—¿Yo? Pues el caballero Floriani que conoció usted en Palermo y al que ha sido tan amable de invitar ya varias veces a su casa.

—Entonces, ¿qué significa esta historia?

—¡Madre mía! ¡Absolutamente nada! Para mí solo es un juego. Intento imaginar la alegría que le daría al hijo de Henriette, si aún vive, decirle a usted que él fue el único culpable, y que lo hizo porque su madre se sentía muy desgraciada cuando estaba a punto de perder el puesto de... doncella del que vivía, y porque el hijo sufría viendo a su madre tan desgraciada.

Floriani se expresaba con una emoción contenida, medio erguido y medio inclinado hacia la condesa. Ya no quedaba ninguna duda. El caballero Floriani era el hijo de Henriette. Todo, su actitud y sus palabras, lo proclamaba. De hecho, ¿no era esa su evidente intención, no quería precisamente que lo reconocieran?

El conde titubeó. ¿Cómo iba a actuar frente a aquel atrevido caballero? ¿Llamar a los criados? ¿Provocar un escándalo? ¿Desenmascarar al que le robó años atrás? ¡Pero hacía ya tanto tiempo! ¿Y quién iba a creer la historia absurda del niño culpable? No, sería mejor aceptar la situación y fingir que no había captado su verdadero sentido. Entonces, el conde se acercó a Floriani y le dijo entusiasmado:

—Muy entretenida y muy curiosa su novela. Le juro que me apasiona. Pero, según usted, ¿qué ha sido de ese buen chico, de ese modelo de hijo? Espero que no se haya alejado de aquel magnífico camino.

—¡Vaya! Seguro que no.

—¡Pues claro que no! ¡Después de semejante estreno! Robar el collar de la reina con seis años, ¡el famoso collar que tanto deseaba María Antonieta!

—Y robarlo —observó Floriani prestándose al juego del conde—, sin que le costara el menor disgusto, sin que a nadie se le ocurriera la idea de examinar el cristal de la ventana ni se diera cuenta de que el alféizar de la ventana estaba demasiado limpio, alféizar que el niño restregó para borrar las huellas de su paso por la gruesa capa de polvo... Reconozca que un crío de esa edad tenía motivos para volverse loco. ¿Así que es así de fácil? ¿Solo hay que querer y dar el primer paso? Y bien sabe Dios que el niño quiso...

—Y dio el primer paso.

—Muchos pasos —respondió el caballero, riendo. Todos sintieron un escalofrío. ¿Qué misterio ocultaba la vida del supuesto Floriani? ¡Qué extraordinaria debía de ser la realidad de aquel aventurero, un ladrón genial a los seis años que, ese día, con la sutileza de un diletante en busca de emociones, o a lo sumo para satisfacer un sentimiento de rencor, había ido a desafiar a la víctima en su propia casa de un modo temerario, a lo loco, y sin embargo con toda la corrección de un hombre educado de visita! Floriani se levantó y se acercó a la condesa para despedirse. La

MAGISTELLUS BAD TRIP

2nd Season

Kazuma Kamachi

Illustration by
Mahaya

YEN ON
New York

MAGISTELLUS BAD TRIP 2nd Season

Kazuma Kamachi

Illustration by
Mahaya

Translation by
Jake Humphrey

MAGISTEALTH BAD TRIP Season 2nd
©Kazuma Kamachi 2019
First published in Japan in 2019 by KADOKAWA CORPORATION, Tokyo.
English translation rights arranged with KADOKAWA CORPORATION, Tokyo, through TUTTLE-MORI AGENCY, INC., Tokyo.

English translation © 2022 by Yen Press, LLC

Yen On
150 West 30th Street, 19th Floor
New York, NY 10001

Visit us at yenpress.com
facebook.com/yenpress
twitter.com/yenpress
yenpress.tumblr.com
instagram.com/yenpress

First Yen On Edition: October 2022
Edited by Yen On Editorial: Emma McClain, Rachel Mimms
Designed by Yen Press Design: Andy Swist

Yen On is an imprint of Yen Press, LLC.
The Yen On name and logo are trademarks of Yen Press, LLC.

Library of Congress Cataloging-in-Publication Data
Names: Kamachi, Kazuma, author. | Mahaya, illustrator. | Humphrey, Jake, translator.
Title: Magistellus bad trip / Kazuma Kamachi ; illustration by Mahaya ; translation by Jake Humphrey.
Description: First Yen On edition. | New York, NY : Yen On, 2021– |
Identifiers: LCCN 2021023505 | ISBN 9781975314262 (v. 1 ; trade paperback) |
    ISBN 9781975348588 (v. 2 ; trade paperback)
Subjects: CYAC: Science fiction. | Fantasy. | Artificial intelligence—Fiction. |
    Virtual reality—Fiction. | Magic—Fiction.
Classification: LCC PZ7.1.K215 Mag 2021 | DDC [Fic]—dc23
LC record available at https://lccn.loc.gov/2021023505

ISBNs: 978-1-9753-4858-8 (paperback)
        978-1-9753-4859-5 (ebook)

1 2022

LSC-C

Printed in the United States of America

CONTENTS

Once upon a time, there was a legendary Dealer by the name of Criminal AO.

He lived in the online world of *Money (Game) Master*, where the virtual currency *snow* possessed as much worth as any real-world currency. The weapons he crafted there, known as the Legacies, were so well optimized that they surpassed the limits of the game's own physics engine. These powerful weapons came to be known as the Overtrick, or End Magic.

But *so* powerful were these weapons that they were able to induce errors in the very program code of the game itself. The AIs that controlled *Money (Game) Master* could not allow such a threat to exist, and so they killed the Legacies' creator, Criminal AO, leaving his whereabouts unknown, both in the game and in real life.

If one were to obtain all the Legacies, the world would look very different indeed. By comparing differences between the normal and the error-ridden versions of the game, one could glimpse the code layer within. It would then be possible to take control of a game that had never once been hacked in the history of mankind, to stage an insurrection against the Mind of the AI masters that governed it.

Currently, the percentage of machine-to-machine transactions, digital payments with no human involved, sat at 48 percent. If it crossed

50 percent, mankind would enter a new age. Instead of humans making use of machines, machines, with control over world finance, would manage mankind with cold efficiency.

Before that happened, someone would have to gather the Legacies.

No, wait. The *true danger* was even greater. For *real demons* lurked in *Money (Game) Master*. Using what was nothing more than a faithful simulation of human society, they had worked their claws into the financial systems of the real world, nearly overtaking them.

What if they were to extend their scope even further, to include the realm we call heaven?

The day of revolution was close. Things had to be settled before it arrived.

"If anyone stands in my way of collecting the Legacies..."

"If anyone gets in the way of me taking back the Overtrick..."

This is a story about those Legacies.

And about a boy who swore to protect his friend's sister, just like that friend had once done for him, at great cost.

""...then I'll kill them if I must.""

Prologue

Server Name: Psi Indigo.
Starting Location: Tokonatsu City, Prostitute Island.
Log-in credentials accepted.
Welcome to *Money (Game) Master,* **Kaname Suou.**

The sound of tires against pavement and the vibration in his stomach shook the young man's whole body as the mint-green coupe drifted around the hairpin turn. It carried that special timbre particular to seaside roads, a hint of sand and salt, along with the usual asphalt.

The location: the tropical peninsula of Tokonatsu City, which served as the setting for the world's biggest online game, *Money (Game) Master.* And of course, it had to be so, for otherwise the young man would never have been allowed to drive this sports car or fire a gun.

A soft crackle, like lightning, passed through the boy's nose. The Lion's Nose, a warning that had saved his life on many occasions, asserted its presence.

Tselika the Magistellus, the devilish pit babe in the passenger seat, let out a delighted squeal as the inertia cradled her body, and her two-pronged tail waved from side to side with glee. A bump in the road made her jump in her seat, driving the seat belt deeper into the ravine between her sizable breasts.

"Ah-ha-ha! Daring today, aren't we, My Lord. Going after the Japanese Treasury? Isn't that a government agency?!"

"Those bankers sure are pleased with themselves, considering the yen's losing ground to a virtual currency. A nationwide rebate? Perhaps they're finally selling off the country! ...Anyway, any problems with the off-route mines? Were we able to stop them?"

Even within the vice-ridden world of *Money (Game) Master*, Prostitute Island was a particular hub of debauchery, for reasons that didn't require explanation. The sprawl of squat buildings had seen so many additions and alterations that the whole area more closely resembled a many-legged living creature, and Kaname was headed deep into its belly. The island at midday was almost deserted—a blessing, considering Kaname's not-so-careful driving habits. Once the sun had set, however, it would come to life.

It was hard to pin down a target amid this mess of buildings and terrain. What looked like a dead end could easily conceal an alternate escape route. If you wanted to trap somebody, you would need to arrive first and seal off the spiderweb-like maze of exits yourself. However...

"Tch. We might have the edge in power, but their top speed is higher than ours."

"That's probably because they're carrying twice the weight, My Lord."

A heavier vehicle was harder to get up to speed, but once it did, it was a force to be reckoned with. Kaname's target was closer to a wrecking ball than a car, swinging left and right as it rounded the tight corners.

"Anyway, isn't that why you chased them here, to this maze? I'd prefer to visit at night, personally, but you take what you can get. In any case, if they escape onto the straight road beyond, we'll lose them for sure."

Tselika appeared to be relaxing in the passenger seat, but in fact, she was handling all the data-processing work. Right now, she was carrying out online transactions ten thousand times a second, transferring funds under Kaname's name. But her impressive resources could just as easily be turned to car chases and shoot-outs.

Lines of text like messages in a chat app scrolled across the car's windshield, superimposed over the outside scenery.

Midori: What's with this rebate thing? I don't really get it, but basically the government is giving away free money, right? That sounds like a good thing to me.

"You idiot, it's not good at all..."

"Now, now, My Lord. The poor girl won't hear you unless you type."

Tselika chuckled, while Kaname used his eyes to type a quick response without taking his hands off the wheel.

The "poor girl" of whom Tselika spoke was none other than Midori Hekireki, the sister of Kaname's old friend Takamasa. Takamasa had given his life to protect Kaname's own sister, the Dealer once known as Ayame Suou, when she had almost been shot in the game. Kaname thus owed Takamasa a great debt, and so he had sworn to protect Midori and do whatever she asked of him. That's how the world worked.

Kaname: Nobody benefits if the government just gives everyone a flat sum, without requiring any labor. All it does is devalue the yen.

Midori: Erm, can you say that again but in Japanese?

Kaname: Say I give you 1,000 yen. Great, right? Except that a single coffee now costs 2,000 yen. Still think it's great?

Midori: ...

Kaname: That's the idea. And it's a slippery slope. Next they'll have to give out 5,000 yen, and then after that, 10,000. All that money the government made trading in real estate to combat the amount of empty homes, all that money they seized from tax delinquents, they want to reinvest it in the game and give it back as welfare? It's ridiculous. The public sector is propped up by the taxpayer. A government agency that doesn't have to worry if they fail will never have the same drive to succeed as greedy private businesses who don't have that safety net.

Midori: Is it really that bad?

Kaname: I'm sure some rumors are just people coping, but I've heard that when government bureaucrats or the kids of celebrities have a gun to their head, it doesn't even occur to them to shoot back or dive for cover. They just stand there with their hands in the air. It doesn't even occur to them that they can't just start over again if they take a bullet to the head and Fall. They have no idea how scary money can be, and that's why they'll never succeed in this game.

Midori didn't reply. It seemed she had been stunned into silence.

Kaname: Necessity is the mother of invention. The government is just the private sector in sheep's clothing at this point. They're decades ahead of the industry when it comes to making money and financing. What's more, even if they fail, they can just stick it on the carbon tax. That makes its way along to utility prices, and eventually the cost falls on the common man. At the end of the day, it's the people who have to pay for the government's failures, and there's no way out.

Midori: It's all so complicated...

Kaname: They make it that way on purpose. Nobody would vote for them if they admitted they had to raise taxes because they blew their budget. The politicians play their word games, but ultimately, taking the tax money and redistributing it fairly is a lie. The numbers just don't add up.

Midori: Huh? Then what are they doing?

Kaname: They're giving out borrowed money, and at some point they'll have to make up for it. Whether they put it on the National Debt or throw the Mint into overdrive, the effect is the same. The value of the yen plummets and the country goes down with it.

Midori: Whoa...

Kaname: And they have the nerve to call it the future of public services. They can give everyone a hundred million yen if they want; that'll only make a coffee cost two hundred million! So Midori, don't forget the off-route mines! We can't let that money reach the Treasury!

Midori: I get it! You don't have to use so many exclamation marks!!

"You just used two," quipped Tselika.

Each government agency received a preapportioned slice of the national budget, and it was illegal to use public funds for purposes not stated in said budget... And so, they temporarily converted it into a fictional currency—*Money (Game) Master*'s *snow*—under the vague pretense "management of taxes," thus preventing it from being tracked.

And now they were in the process of transferring it between departments, thus allowing them to use the funds for whatever purpose they pleased.

This game was essentially a wormhole for money. If they used it to shuffle the money around and redistribute it, they could circumvent the red tape of the real world. They could use money allocated for road work on medical insurance if they wanted to, thereby laundering money on the government's payroll.

"You have really changed, My Lord."

"How so? Any Dealer would use a few land mines under these circumstances."

"That is not what I mean," Tselika replied. "Ordinarily, you would try to handle everything on your own. At most, you might ask me, your Magistellus, to handle some related task. I've never known you to trust other Dealers."

"..."

"I wonder what changed? I must say, I'm a little jealous of that pig-tailed pip-squeak..."

Suddenly, Kaname pulled on the hand brake, throttling Tselika with her seat belt.

"Blegh!" she choked, rearing up her forked tail in anger. "My Lord! It was merely a jest! There was no need for simulated bondage!"

"Close your mouth, and be careful not to bite your tongue."

Kaname's actions were guided not by digital data but by the feeling of danger in the tip of his nose.

A second later, there was a jet of fire and smoke, and an anti-tank rocket streaked past the windshield.

Tselika's eyes went wide with shock, but Kaname simply tutted at his partner's slow reactions and released the hand brake, stomping down on the gas pedal once again. *I wish you'd be a little more useful as navigator,* he thought, glaring out the side window as the vehicle picked up speed.

"They've set up an ambush," he said. "They may be easier to maneuver, but you can't fire rockets while driving a motorbike, so I'm guessing it's a three-wheeler, with one driver and one shooter."

"M-M-My Lord! If that missile hits us, my temple's done for!"

It was only a game. Or was it? If you died, or "Fell," in this virtual world, you would be forcibly logged out for twenty-four hours. And lest you think, *Is that it?* for those twenty-four hours you were locked out of trading completely, the other Dealers would relentlessly exploit your defenseless accounts without mercy or restraint. Even a *snow* billionaire could end up in debt hell overnight.

There are many fates in this world worse than death.

And yet Kaname Suou's face was bright. True Dealers don't recoil in the face of risk. They all learned the hard way that to flinch is to invite disaster.

"We're okay," he said. "The Anti-Vehicle skill increases damage dealt to vehicles, but it's wasted on rocket launchers. That's because it works by boosting the power of subsequent shots that hit the same target as the first; the same principle as a minigun. On a single-shot weapon it's basically useless."

"That doesn't matter, because one hit will kill us!!"

"Then pray we don't get hit," replied Kaname.

There was no way the lawn mower engine in that motorized tricycle was anywhere near the power of the coupe's, but again, it was a matter of acceleration versus top speed. The trike was fitted with monster suspension fit for a dirt rally. Vehicles like that could even wow circus crowds with their huge jumps. They could easily clear small obstacles like wooden crates and overturned palm trees, allowing them to take shortcuts. In this labyrinth of roads, such an ability was not to be underestimated.

Kaname's opponents were dressed in full-body riding suits, which suited their off-road vehicles. However, he also spotted golden necklaces and bracelets around their necks and wrists. Those were probably fitted with more skills. In *Money (Game) Master*, strength was yours if you had the money to pay for it. From the way they moved, he surmised they were using the Balancer skill to stay upright against the normal laws of physics and the Slow skill to slow down time in their minds and increase their awareness.

This was not a simple game. Even a professional hit man would have a hard time winning unless he understood the rules. At the same time, though, it was possible to grow too reliant on mastering the game's mechanics and neglect one's personal growth. Skills were a double-edged sword.

...And yet Tselika had said that technologies existed in the real world that mimicked the supernatural effects of skills, only hidden from public view within research laboratories and the military. Unfortunately, such a claim was difficult to verify.

The crack of gunshots rang out as the driver of the trike covered for his reloading partner with a machine pistol. With an automatic weapon, the Anti-Vehicle skill could come into play... But fortunately, it was only the back seat rocketeer who had that skill. Looking again, Kaname noticed that the driver kept peering at his wrist, and it seemed unlikely he was merely checking the time.

Kaname frowned. ...*Does he have his ammo count synced to his smart watch? Judging by the way he moves, I'd say he's the type to lean harder on his skills than on his own training. He's probably not a professional, then. Unless that's just an act.*

"Can we outrun them?!" asked Tselika.

"I don't want to lose our position. It'll be quicker to take them out!"

Kaname rolled down the driver's seat window and, keeping one hand on the wheel, brandished the short-range sniper rifle, Short Spear, a .45-caliber weapon sporting an integrated silencer and collapsible stock.

Kaname didn't need any skills. Not to drive and not to shoot. He manually lined up the sights and pulled the trigger.

There was a metallic *plink*, only the sound of the gun's mechanism, before the bullet traveled through a row of clotheslines where women's underwear was hung in place of a shop sign, finally meeting its target in the engine of the motor trike. The engine's cheap-sounding noise cut out instantly, replaced with a loud *crash*.

It was the kind of shot that couldn't be made using Auto-Aim, the skill that automatically lined up your sights with the center of your opponent. The results of a balancing act that utilized game mechanics without becoming dependent on them.

Tselika put her hands behind her head, puffing out her chest so that the seat belt got lost even deeper between her breasts, and whistled.

"...Deadly as always, My Lord."

"It's an easy shot to make when they're using Balancer. That skill uses external force to maintain the user's posture, which means they always jump in a nice parabola—easy to predict. Anyway, there's no point in praising me when we're way out here. If we lose the sedan, this is all for nothing."

Kaname tossed his gun into the voluptuous lap of his partner before twisting the steering wheel once more and rounding the corner of a building.

Kaname and company were after a smuggler of sorts. But there were no duffel bags or briefcases of bills to be found in their cargo, oh no.

"This Dealer, Many-Go-Round, specializes in smuggling. And I suppose that four-door itself is the strongbox. What a setup."

"Not to mention the whole country's taxes are in there. That's got to create some serious downforce."

For sports cars and race cars, it was considered beneficial to have a low center of mass, as that allowed the vehicle to take tighter turns at higher speeds without tipping. That was why, with the exception of aerodynamic fins, the cars were built to have as low a profile as possible. If that still wasn't enough to meet spec, you could also fill the bottom half of the car with heavy materials such as lead. It traded off speed and power, of course, but it was useful as a last resort.

In the case of the sedan, there was a small tank mounted on the underbelly of the vehicle, filled with an exceedingly dense liquid nineteen times heavier than water.

Midori: I still can't believe that stuff is 25 times the price of gold...

Kaname: High-end cosmetics are like that. There's all sorts of celebrity endorsements and branding going on, and there doesn't seem to be an end to how high they can push the grade. Not to mention, here in Tokonatsu City, where the sun shines all year round, the demand for suntan lotion never stops.

Midori: Suntan lotion!! They make that stuff in factories! How can it cost more than gold and diamonds when it's not like they have to dig it out of the ground?!

Midori still possessed the naturally healthy skin of a middle school girl, and Tselika oozed an almost unnatural beauty from every pore. Neither of them could easily appreciate the value of cosmetics.

Kaname sighed and typed a response.

Kaname: Supposedly, because of something to do with changing facilities, they weren't able to produce a formula as effective as they had before. The price of last year's stock has gone through the roof because of that.

Midori: Whaaat...?

Kaname: And right now, that car's carrying two hundred million snow's worth of the stuff. Even in the real world, no bank on earth keeps that much cold cash around these days.

Midori: Hey, I keep hearing people use the term "digital assets." What's that about?

Kaname: Just like phone scams and drugs, it's all the same thing. Anything with a lot of money in it that the government doesn't like gets its name changed every few weeks. First it was "digital money," then "virtual currency," then "cryptocurrency." They'll be calling it "dark money" next. It never settles, but most people refer to it as "digital assets," at least for now.

Midori: It's like the "Mother, it's me" scam. You know they're calling it "Special Fraud" now. They just can't seem to make up their mind...

In *Money (Game) Master*, cars were a far better place to stash money than putting it all in a vault or hiding it in the woods somewhere. That was because a special barrier protected vehicles while they were in a parking lot, making it impossible to steal or destroy them.

Kaname weaved an S through the streets, dodging rusty bicycles and trash pails as he continued complaining to his partner.

"I told you we should just have figured out which parking lot they were using and surrounded it with land mines. Then we'd have blown them up before they even got their foot out the door, so to speak."

"We are talking about a smuggler working for the government," replied Tselika. "Besides, they went to all the trouble of using *snow* to hide their tracks, so it's no surprise they disseminated all sorts of misinformation to make tracking them difficult. They can't afford to hesitate, since this is people's tax money they're dealing with."

In any case, the nation's budget, in the form of *snow*, was currently making its way from the Ministry of Welfare to the National Treasury. Its arrival would set in motion a rebate scheme that threatened to trigger widespread hyperinflation, sending the value of the yen spiraling into the ground.

Kaname had to stop it before that could happen. And he wasn't spinning his wheels for nothing.

Kaname: He's moved from b4 to c7. We've got him so spooked he's only looking in his mirrors.

Midori: Hold on, gimme a sec. Okay, the guy at the wheel is specced out for driving, not shooting. His jacket, pants, and belt all boost his ability to pick out objects in motion. It's some skill called D.V.A.: Dynamic Visual Acuity. He's stacked up a bunch of them so he can dodge any oncoming obstacle, but he's weak on both sides, where only his onboard cameras are monitoring. He won't be so fast to pick up a surprise attack from there!

Midori's talent was as useful as ever. With just one look at their equipment, she could see a Dealer's stats as if it were the most obvious thing in the world. According to her, she could simply see the "vibe" they were going for, but as far as Kaname was concerned, it might as well have been a supernatural ability like his own Lion's Nose. Even Tselika was a little annoyed that all her processing power couldn't replicate the girl's natural-born talent.

And despite all this talk of off-routes and land mines, the sedan ahead was driving on hard asphalt. It was impossible to bury a mine in the road unless you had a jackhammer handy, and Kaname did not. Instead, he had this.

As the sedan passed by a side alley, an explosive projectile struck it full-force in the side, lifting it into the air and knocking it clean off the road.

It was a weapon similar to the rocket launcher from earlier. The term "off-route mine" refers to any kind of weapon placed at the side of the road and equipped with either a radar or an infrared tripwire set to unleash armor-piercing rounds or explosions at whatever crosses its path.

Midori had been tasked with its installation, and while she was still a beginner, it seemed the Secret skill she had been given to conceal her presence worked perfectly… Though, of course, once a skill was known, it could be exploited, just as Kaname and Midori had done a moment ago. You couldn't be too careful.

Kaname swung the rear of the coupe around and screeched to a halt. The tingle of the Lion's Nose quickly receded.

"Whoopsy-daisy, My Lord. You've gone and made yourself a little barbeque. Whoever was inside is a goner for sure."

"Nothing's for sure until I see for myself."

Suddenly, a gunshot rang out, and a spiderweb of cracks formed on the coupe's windshield, knocking out the display.

"…"

"…"

Tselika's face was stripped of all emotion. Then she snatched up Kaname's Short Spear and unleashed a barrage of fire into the flaming wreckage.

"HOW DARE YOU???!!! You've tainted my holy temple! I spend every day making sure that windshield is squeaky clean, and you've deflowered it! Hurry up and die already!!"

"? Cut it out, Tselika. That was probably just the fire igniting the gunpowder in their guns like popcorn. The Dealers inside have already Fallen for sure."

"What happened to 'Nothing's for sure until I see for myself'?!!"

Kaname's Lion's Nose couldn't sense any danger, but Tselika seemed determined to be thorough. Her forked tail wrapped around his neck and shook him from side to side, while the kickback from her continued gunfire jiggled her breasts. Kaname wasn't sure how to handle this level of overachievement and opted to leave her be.

I think they have an all-you-can-shoot firing range in the peninsula district somewhere that only charges a monthly fee. I wonder if that would be cheaper than trying to persuade her to conserve ammunition...?

There was the roar of an engine just then, and this time it wasn't a car. A large racing motorcycle patterned with bright-red leaves rolled up, and astride it, her long black hair in twin tails, was a young girl wearing bikini-and-miniskirt swimwear. Its black cloth was hemmed with white fluffy frills, giving her outfit a gothic-lolita look.

"Midori."

"Aren't we done now that we beat the bad guys? What are we gonna do with that ball of flame?"

"What do you mean, what are we going to do? This is *Money (Game) Master*, where money is everything. Bills and diamonds might go up in smoke, but that expensive suntan lotion won't. We just need to disconnect the weight tank before it melts. Let's snap to it."

"?"

"There's only one way to get out of this mess without tanking the yen and ruining the lives of everyone in the country, and that's for one person to get it all. It might not be fair, but the world is an unfair place. Come on, let's go look for a fire hydrant. Once we've found one, we can start pumping."

"Erm, this is everyone's tax money you're talking about, right? Don't you feel guilty taking it? ...Hey, come back!"

Kaname simply sighed and left as Midori squealed and chased after him.

Then, after all the humans were gone...

"..."

Tselika got out of the car and surveyed the damage to the windshield. With tears in her eyes, she caressed its metal frame. It was a little—no, quite—hot from being out under the blistering sun all day, but Tselika didn't care. That was the power of her love!

"I am sorry, O temple that supports my existence. Please bear with it a little longer. I will soon have your glass replaced and polish you from corner to corner!"

As she muttered to herself, the patterns on her bikini and on the surface of the car began to flow and change. This was all part of Kaname's request.

Let's see... The market cap for the suntan lotion we found in that traveling strongbox should total the amount pledged by the Ministry of Welfare for their announced rebate. Let's compare that with the recent news... Here we are, all cases of VR assets within Money (Game) Master *being seized from terminal patients with overwhelming medical bills and their families and being sold at auction. It is no less disgusting to read about even now. Open spreadsheet program. Apply aggregate processing to 14,055 rows. I see... Just as My Lord predicted, the total perfectly matches the amount Many-Go-Round was carrying. Hmm. It is nice to finally have concrete figures to back up our hypothesis.*

A flood of windows appeared all across the surface of the car. It was far too fast for a human's eyes to follow, but for a Magistellus like Tselika, capable of performing ten thousand transactions a second, the calculations were positively yawn-inducing.

That means all we need to do is sell off the super-high-grade suntan lotion and use the large amount of snow *that gives us to buy all this back, before anonymously donating it back to the original owners. That should settle everything. A chapel for the wedding you could never have, a villa to relax in without worrying about the pain of illness, a private beach for kids who have never seen the sea... Oh dear. I shall have to run the calculations thoroughly. My Lord will be most angry if we go into the red. It's time to show him what I'm made of and have him fix up my temple as soon as possible.*

There was no need to go out of their way to explain all this to Midori. After all, helping people wasn't about showing off.

That was the philosophy the young man called Kaname Suou had chosen to live by.

(Photograph & Illustration SNS "Pixy-gram" ID 3187-AJHF-29dd)

Kaname: I got your invitation.

Midori: And?

Kaname: Why are we on a social network for uploading drawings?

Midori: Oh, shush. You told me how to make a level 5 encrypted chat room or whatever, but this is the only site where I knew how to mess with the settings.

Kaname: You're a girl of many talents in addition to just writing letters. So? Shall we get down to business?

Midori: Sure, but I'm still new to Money (Game) Master, remember? Do you have any pointers?

Kaname: The money used in the game, snow, is so influential it can be exchanged 1:1 for yen. Don't do anything that will result in a big loss, just because you think it's a game.

Kaname: If you die, you become Fallen, which locks you out of the game for 24 hours. That makes you a sitting duck, and the hyenas will drag you into debt hell.

Kaname: Also, the AI Magistelli are using the game to infiltrate human society and work toward something called the "day of revolution." Since their digital reproduction of the human world is able to influence real life, then by the same logic, if they increase their simulation to higher dimensions...

Midori: Erm, wasn't all this supposed to be solved once we collect all of my brother's Legacies?

Kaname: You need to understand how it all fits together, Midori. Takamasa's creations exceed the bounds of the game's physics engine and cause bugs and errors to appear in the code. Essentially, they can open a portal through the perfect scenery of the game world and into the program layer. That's why Takamasa, who possessed so many of them, was made to Fall. If we gather all the Legacies, we risk the same thing happening to us, but at the same time, we can use them to put a stop to the Magistelli's invasion. And that's just what we'll do. You, me, Takamasa, my sister, and Tselika. All so that we can walk our own paths.

Midori: Hold on, was that supposed to be the beginner's version? What does it all mean?

Kaname: It means, Midori, that this game isn't all that different from real life. When it comes to money, you have to pay attention.

Chapter 4
This Is What You Call a Ringside Battle BGM #04
"Team Play"

1

Server Name: Alpha Scarlet.
Starting Location: Tokonatsu City, Peninsula District.
Log-in credentials accepted.
Welcome to *Money (Game) Master*, Kaname Suou.

"We need my brother's Legacies. All of them," whispered the girl in the gothic-lolita bikini. Her name was Midori Hekireki, and her voice was barely audible over the roar of the surrounding crowd—nearly twenty thousand spectators. For a bikini, her outfit was especially frilly around the chest, which served to conceal her curves. Kaname, however, opted not to call it the kid's version, for fear of getting his eyes clawed out.

The soccer game before them was still in its first half, and excitement was high. On the field, a defender wearing a pink uniform appeared to trip up the opponent's forward, to take possession of the ball, but the referee's whistle stayed silent, and just like that, the flow of the game was reversed.

This was supposedly the second-best team in R league. Soccer teams in *Money (Game) Master* were divided into S, R, and N leagues, the last being reserved for amateur play.

"That's so confusing. Why can't they just call them A, B, and C?" asked Midori.

"You sound like an old man. Kids these days are far more familiar with Super Rare, Rare, and Normal."

It didn't matter what topic Kaname chose to talk about, Midori's prickly reception was always the same. When your partner was a middle-school-age girl, even asking about the weather or what she drank to stay awake at night, questions anyone could answer, required more sensitivity than defusing a ticking time bomb. She always seemed to be on edge.

The world-class Dealer heaved a deep sigh. Midori had chosen this location so they could speak without being overheard, but Kaname had mixed feelings about the place. Sitting in a stadium while logged-in was like using a home console video game system just to spend your time at an in-game arcade. There were lots of ways to make money in *Money (Game) Master*, but people tended to opt for things they couldn't try in real life. Perhaps some of these players were retired athletes, already past their prime in the real world, now running around with new fit young avatars.

Though the girl spoke of a legacy, it was no mere sum of money left behind by her missing brother. It was a set of custom equipment, crafted within *Money (Game) Master*, with stats so obscenely high, some called them the Overtrick, or End Magic. These were the Legacies. Each was powerful in its own right, but when combined, it was believed they could be used to analyze the code at this world's core.

But back to the matter at hand. Kaname lowered the opera glasses he was holding and whispered back to Midori.

"Be sure to keep your voice down. You don't know who else could be listening."

"Erk." Midori gulped.

Kaname proceeded to hold up two fingers in front of the girl. He was referring to #tempest.err and #fireline.err. These were two Legacies left by Takamasa—one a shotgun with the power to deliver two thousand buckshot pellets to anything within its guiding beam, and the other an anti-materiel rifle with effectively infinite range. If even one of these fearsome weapons fell into the wrong hands, it could be used as a powerful economic cyber weapon—enough to bring a country's economy to its knees in the real world.

"Other Dealers will be all over us if they find out we're carrying these," he continued, whispering in Midori's ear. "Not everyone fears the Legacies. After all, just one is enough to topple an entire country or tech giant. Don't forget, there are people who would kill to get their hands on them."

"I—I know! Don't get so close to me!!"

The twin-tailed girl seemed somewhat flustered. Even the blue rose on her headband quivered. It reminded Kaname of one of those toys that shook in response to your voice. She then nervously placed the cup containing her ice-cold drink between her dazzlingly pale thighs, above the hem of her black knee socks. Maybe she found it faster to cool her blood vessels through direct contact, rather than just drinking the liquid.

"You already explained that to me," she replied. "I know *Money (Game) Master* is more than just an MMO. It's a framework for AI to manipulate and control humanity using its virtual currency called *snow*, and we humans have to put a stop to it before it's too late."

…That wasn't all there was to it, but it was hard to predict how Midori might react to the rest. The truth was, Magistelli weren't designed by human hands but had always been present in the world. And "world" here meant the real world. Kaname still hadn't fully come to terms with that information himself.

This was a game far beyond human understanding. A game created by demons. Their collective Mind had deceived even Tselika, distracting her and Kaname to keep them from realizing they could use Takamasa's Legacies to take control of the program.

Naturally, there was a lot still wrapped in mystery.

"We need the list…," said Midori, pausing just as a pink-haired woman

selling fries, frankfurters, and cold beverages walked by. The woman was wearing nothing but a sun visor and a bikini that was more like a piece of string. Judging from her movements, she was probably human and not AI. "We have to gather all the Legacies, but the only person who even knows how many there are is big bro—ahem, I mean, my brother. We need an accurate list of what we're looking for."

"About that. Was there anything in Takamasa's room? Like a notepad or a shoebox or something?"

"…All I found was his porn browsing history," groaned Midori. "Ugh. I know this is important, but I guess that's what I get for going through his things."

There was nothing Kaname could say to that. He understood how hard it must be to learn about a family member's sex life. He wouldn't want to see that side of his sister or parents, either.

"Are we even sure a list exists…?" she asked.

"Ninety-nine percent sure," replied Kaname. He had never read it, but he was certain one existed. Takamasa had always noted his designs down, whether they were sports cars or paper planes, and he'd kept them together in a loose sheaf of papers. He often said, laughing, that he never knew when inspiration would strike. In some ways, he shared his sister's love of the analog, although he was less of a writer and more of an engineer. Instead of letters, he wrote notes. When Takamasa Fell and disappeared, his Legacies had been scattered throughout the world of the game. But that wasn't all that had gotten lost. The mountain of records he should have left behind were nowhere to be found, either.

Midori leaned forward in her plastic seat, her forehead in her hands, and glanced sideways at Kaname.

"How about on your end? Did you find anything inside the game? You guys hung out a lot online, right?"

"I checked every hiding spot I could think of, but I didn't find any papers… Though it's possible he had warehouses I don't know about."

"…That leaves us with only one choice, then."

"Yeah."

If they couldn't find out about the Legacies from Criminal AO himself, then they would just have to ask someone else.

A complete list of the Legacies. Just one on its own was threatening enough. Considering that the finances of not just large corporations but entire nations were built on top of the game, with just one Legacy you could pick a country at whim and clear out its accounts. And you could do more than just destroy your target; you could steal it for yourself. If used well, these were weapons more fearsome and more useful than a nuclear bomb.

The list, then, represented the possibility of monopolizing all that power.

It was highly likely the original had been copied or transcribed and existed in various versions spread all over the place. Each one would be valuable enough to fetch a handsome price from the right buyer.

There must be someone who had obtained one and simply lacked the resources to mount a large-scale search operation. But who might that be?

"..."

Kaname wanted one, for sure. There was no doubt that if he were ever going to succeed in retrieving the Legacies, he would have to know how many there were. It didn't matter if the list was the original or a copy, he just needed it to be complete.

But unlike everyone else, Kaname didn't see the list as a treasure map. To Kaname, that sheaf of papers was a fragment of Takamasa's soul he had quietly left behind. Other people might only see strange drawings of UFOs and time machines, but Kaname knew that the one who had written those notes had never intended them to be made public. It was like an archaeologist unearthing a love letter and putting it on display behind a glass case for everyone and their dog to see. It wasn't something to be shown off and sold for money.

It wasn't for people to play with. It wasn't for strangers to gawk at.

Takamasa may have been gone, but his dignity still remained.

"So what should we do, Midori? Oh, and make sure you don't get heatstroke. It can happen even in the game, and your cup appears to be empty all of a sudden."

"Shut up."

"...By the way, Midori, you seem really into this soccer game. I didn't know you enjoyed sports that much."

"Stop distracting me. I don't intend to ask for your help to pay off my brother's debt. I intend to take responsibility to pay it all off myself. And that's why I bet everything on this match."

"You bet...on the game...???"

Glancing at the tickets clasped tightly in Midori's gloved hand, Kaname surmised that the idea was to correctly guess outcomes of ten consecutive matches, including scores, for a grand prize of one hundred million *snow*. Currently, the total payout, including carryover, appeared to be in the region of seven hundred million.

She was serious. Never in Kaname's wildest dreams had he predicted this.

...Of all things to put her money on, why choose something where she couldn't even influence the outcome?! Even horse racing, where you can check the horse and the condition of the field right before betting, was highly unpredictable. Ten soccer games would take at *least* two weeks to complete, and by the time you'd bought your ticket, you'd be locked in—and at that point, you wouldn't even know which players were going to compete in each match! Even if you spent months poring over the data and reading player statistics, there was simply no way you could reliably predict the outcome of ten games two weeks in advance. Kaname looked at her, mouth agape.

"Midori," he said at last.

"What?"

"...I'm going to give you a little piece of advice, for your own good. Let's start by talking about expected return on investment. You see, all gambling is basically set up to ensure that no matter how the money moves, the house profits. In fact, sports gambling in Tokonatsu City is estimated to be, on average, twenty percent more profitable than horse and cycle racing..."

"Oh, shut up! Why are they all wearing the same pink uniform?! How am I supposed to know which one's better if they've all got the same skills? That's so boring!! If each player differentiated their skills with clothing and accessories, I could see through their abilities in seconds... Aaargh! ...Aaaaahhh! They just scored a goal off a free kick! How was I supposed to see that coming?! There was no warning, no warning whatsoever!!"

Midori scrunched up the tickets fanned out in her hands. It appeared the reactions of red-faced old men and twin-tailed middle-school girls were about the same when it came to losing at the races.

2

"Hey," greeted Tselika. She was standing outside the coupe, perhaps tired of waiting, when Kaname returned to the stadium's underground parking lot. "I did the research you requested. It appears that this soccer team, the Leviathans, really does possess one of the Legacies: the minigun #dracolord.err. Graaargh! Why couldn't I be up in those seats, watching the salesgirls and cheerleaders in their string bikinis and miniskirts?!"

"Cite your sources," said Kaname flatly. He had been surprised when Midori picked this place to meet up—pure coincidence. His real goal here had been the Legacy all along. Kaname folded up his collapsible opera glasses and tossed them through the open car window. It was not the players running around the field he had been observing for the past ninety minutes, oh no. He had been watching the owner's seat, a VIP suite encased in bulletproof glass.

Various dialogue boxes displayed on the polished surface of the mint-green coupe. Tselika reclined on its hood and tapped at them with her forked tail.

"If you'll take a look at this, I think you'll get the idea. The team's performance has been in sharp decline for some time, but whenever there's talk of relegating it to the lower league, the sponsors of the higher-ranked teams receive threats. Serious stuff. *'If you don't throw the next game, we'll have your parent company pull out and bankrupt the team and you.' That sort of thing."*

"...So they're fixing games. Well, if they move down to N league, they'll be forced to let all their professional players go. They'd basically have to remake the team from scratch. I can see why it's so important to them."

According to the rules of Tokonatsu City, when a team progressed from N league to R league, all the players were promoted from amateur to professional, but when a team was demoted from R to N, the players were suspended for breach of regulations. This meant that, in effect, the team was forced to sell off all its hard-earned players for next to nothing. It was wildly unfair, but perhaps it was just one way of making the game of musical chairs more interesting.

"Betting on these games is sounding more and more pointless."

"Hmm? Betting???"

Tselika tilted her head like a child as she crossed her long legs, clad in thigh-high boots.

The Leviathans weren't targeting the other teams directly, but were going through their sponsors. Just like in the television industry, sponsors were like an Achilles' heel. Businesses in *Money (Game) Master* were essentially AI-controlled NPCs, but the economics were real. By preventing them from conducting trade, you could still drive them to bankruptcy.

"And in every corporate raid the Leviathans stand to benefit from, there's always a strange minigun that shows up. There's no laws in *Money (Game) Master*, so attacking a place of business is nothing unusual, but these attacks are odd in that they have nothing to do with stock prices or commodity transfers." Placing her shapely bottom on the car hood, Tselika let out a deep breath, causing her large breasts to sink. "We don't yet know the capabilities of this minigun, but we do know it's far from ordinary. According to witness info posted on video-sharing websites, the user was able to fire it one-handed while riding a tiny off-road bike. There was a box magazine bigger than a suitcase tied to the back seat."

"...Zero recoil, perhaps. Or zero weight?"

Capable of firing rounds the size of your thumb at a rate of six or seven thousand rounds a minute, a minigun was the pinnacle of slaughter. If it weren't for the protection rule keeping parked cars safe, someone could destroy all the vehicles in this lot with a single sweep and have enough bullets left for a second pass, just to make sure. All this, with an effective range of two to three kilometers. To be able to swing that thing around like it was no heavier than a water pistol would take it to a whole new level.

"That's something we won't know for sure until we get our hands on it, My Lord. At any rate, judging by how it looks in the video, I'd say it's highly likely this is the real #dracolord.err. We're lucky I happened to have some old footage of one of Takamasa's garages from the onboard camera to compare. Even if it turns out to be a counterfeit, it's so well made that its creator must have had access to the real one at some point. What do you say we go pay them a visit? Couldn't hurt, could it?"

Kaname sighed and pondered for a second.

"All this tells us is they have a Legacy," he said. "So, Tselika, why do you look like you expect a pat on the head? You look like a dog, sitting patiently and wagging its tail."

"N-no, I do not!"

Tselika crossed her arms, pushing up her sizable breasts, and turned away in a pout, her face red. But despite appearing uncooperative, the faithful Magistellus still answered Kaname's question.

"...I do not know how the Leviathans obtained the Legacy. I do not believe they paid a huge sum to buy it outright or attacked the previous owner. I trawled the news for any references to events of that nature and found nothing."

"So you think it was a quieter job? A heist?"

"But a Legacy is a powerful enough cyberweapon to topple a state. I can just imagine its owner taking it out of its safe every day and drooling over it. There is no way they would fail to notice if it went missing, so why are there no reports of a theft?"

"..."

There was only one explanation. Only one place the Legacy could have come from where nobody would have noticed its disappearance.

"You think...they took it from Takamasa's storage?" he asked. "Stole it from the missing Criminal AO himself?"

"...If that is so, then I have a question for you, My Lord. How would anyone discover the location of a hidden cache not even you, his best friend, knew about?"

"..."

"Could they have gotten ahold of some of Criminal AO's notes? Takamasa's Fall was akin to the fall of the Soviet Union. I wouldn't be surprised to see all sorts of confidential documents making the rounds. Including, of course, that all-important list you were after."

3

There was a light tapping sound.

It was the sound of a beautiful woman in a purple party dress and glasses stopping a soccer ball with her foot, kicking it up, and returning it to the children who had been playing with it. The party sandals on her feet did nothing to impede the ball's clean arc as it sailed through the air.

They were on a viewing platform overlooking a beach. Kaname tried to keep his silky black hair from blowing all over the place in the sea breeze.

"Nice shot, Laplacian," he said. "But doesn't that hurt your toes?"

"Not if I use the Demon," she replied. "Spin and Ballistic calculations are my specialty, after all."

She was one of the game's most infamous Dealers, alongside the likes of Frey(a), Bloody Dancer, and Criminal AO. Her username: Laplacian. She was a gambler through and through. In a game filled with guns, cars, and high-stakes trading, Dealers who devoted themselves to a sole aspect and yet still excelled were a force to be reckoned with. Her strengths were different from Kaname's, but she was no less a powerful figure.

At her side stood her Magistellus, a short girl with her thick black hair bunched up on both sides of her head. She wore a kimono, done up loosely, and in her hands she held a parasol to protect herself from the sun's blinding rays. Leaning against an old beat-up phone booth, she mopped the sweat from her brow. She was clearly overheated, but her face was pale. And like Tselika, in contrast to her appearance, she sounded like an old woman.

"...Could you not have invited us somewhere with a roof, my dear?" she said.

"Hey. Your Magistellus looks like she's about to faint. I didn't know they felt the heat."

"Perhaps it's because she's a vampire? Who knows?" replied Laplacian.

Now that she'd mentioned it, the dark-haired girl did seem to have strangely elongated canines. Kaname hadn't noticed earlier, distracted as he was by her surprisingly large bosom bound in white cloth, which peeked out from her off-the-shoulder kimono.

The bespectacled beauty returned a wave from the group of children. Kaname recognized one of them as a powerful Dealer: a chestnut-haired girl about 130 centimeters tall, in a distinctive school swim-suit with a yellow-and-white sports towel and a large black witch's hat. It was impossible to let your guard down in this game, even among children.

"Soccer sure has gotten popular lately...," Laplacian said. "This place used to be a spot for dates."

"Okay, boomer. These days, ball games are banned in public parks in the real world. This game is free, and more and more kids are willing to jump into the virtual world if it means they can play."

"..."

"The boomer thing was a joke. But if you glare at me like that, I might think I was right, Laplacian."

Of course, the kids might not be children in real life. After all, players could choose how they appeared in *Money (Game) Master*. Kaname had no way of knowing someone's real age or sex, nor did he have any particular interest in finding out.

Besides, adults liked to play ball games, too: the players on Team Leviathan, for example. Everyone had their own way of making money. Some were already pro athletes in real life, some were working toward that goal, for some it had already passed, and for others it was a dream that could never come true. Here, though, all those people could come together and pursue their dreams, along with the fat paycheck that came with those dreams.

A single airplane left a white streak across the clear blue sky. There were airports in Tokonatsu City. And they were for international, not domestic, flights. Though the 3D models only extended to this city, there was a whole outside world that existed only on a numerical level.

...Of course, mere humans who could only experience the world with their five senses would never be able to see those distant lands.

Laplacian brushed the hair off her shoulder and asked, "So what did you want?"

"I know you're a proficient gambler. I wanted to ask you about soccer betting."

"...Um, you're not telling me you actually plan on making money that way, are you?"

"So you know something's up. How much is it to buy the info off you? Name your price. I need anything that can help with my investigation."

"And why should I help you? Surely you haven't forgotten what you did to me on Mega-Float III? I lost all I had on that roulette wheel, thanks to you."

"Exactly. This is my way of making it up to you."

"..."

"I apologize for what I did back then. I was just trying to look cool in front of the rookie girl I was with. I know it was wrong," Kaname said, raising his hands.

Laplacian let out a long, sultry sigh at Kaname's confession. But still she didn't break.

"I'll go soft if I start accepting your charity."

"Then let's settle this some other way. How about a bet, since you love those so much?"

Kaname reached into his pocket and pulled out a large coin.

"We'll make it simple. Heads or tails? Guess right and you can have the money, and you don't have to tell me anything. Guess wrong, and you have to give me the info for free."

"...You're aware I use a Demon, correct? Laplace's Demon."

Of course, Laplace's Demon was far too overpowered to be the work of a single skill. In fact, Laplacian made use of many D.V.A. skills that boosted her perceptive abilities, as well as Science Course skills that taught her all the physical formulas needed to make her calculations. All in all, it was a combination of about a dozen skills that contributed to the power, like the recipe for a secret sauce. The skills themselves were easy enough for anyone to obtain, but the precise combination was Laplacian's trade secret.

Incidentally, Midori had worked the whole thing out in one second.

"Well, Laplacian? Are you in or out?"

"Very well."

At Laplacian's words, her vampiric Magistellus gave a brief sigh beneath her parasol. It was clear she was fed up with her mistress's gambling habit. Laplacian could never refuse a bet, and once she started, she'd have no qualms about putting her own life on the line.

Laplacian ignored her assistant's glare and continued.

"It's a simple kinetic energy equation. My words are prophecy. There is not even a one in a million chance that you will beat me. Are you sure you still want to take this bet?"

"I've already committed," Kaname replied with a grin, using his thumb to flick the coin far above his head. Without even looking up at it, he raised his arm before him as if checking the time on his wristwatch. "Besides, if you remember what happened back at the roulette wheel, then you know that's not true. Now then, what'll it be?"

"Heads."

"Sorry, it's tails."

4

I lost. I lost. Ohhh, I lost big-time. Now I'm totally broke. ☆

"…Rrrrgghhh!!!!!!"

Midori had waited throughout the forty-five-minute second half, all the way into extra whatever, and yet the spectacular comeback she had held out hope for was nowhere to be seen.

She had suffered a resounding defeat.

There were, of course, runner-up prizes. Pocket change for guessing the result of a single match rather than all ten, but they were nothing more than a drop in the ocean of overwhelming loss.

At some point, Kaname Suou had disappeared, probably exasperated with her. Midori, giving up at last, tore up the tickets in her hand and scattered them on the wind like confetti.

"Hey!!"

Hearing a loud voice from behind her, Midori turned to see what appeared to be a ten-year-old boy.

…Of course, this came as little comfort, considering a person's appearance in the game had little to no bearing on reality. The boy rudely jabbed a latex-gloved finger at Midori and yelled:

"Don't litter like that! Who do you think's got to clean up after you?!!"

"Huh?"

Midori tilted her head, causing the blue rose atop her headband to sway.

It wasn't only Midori who had placed bets. A glance across the stadium revealed similar confetti clouds swelling up everywhere. It was so widespread that there were even so-called rag-pickers, who went through all the discarded tickets in the hopes of finding winning ones that people had accidentally thrown away out of habit. Statistically speaking, if you scoured the floor long enough, you were practically guaranteed to find one. Then the only thing left was to decide if it was worth your time. Compared to a 1,000-*snow*-an-hour wage, some people didn't mind crawling on the ground picking up scraps in the hopes of hitting it big…even if it sometimes meant picking fights with the former owners of those tickets.

"Isn't that your job?" asked Midori. "I mean, you're the one with the dustpan and brush."

Indeed, unlike the bikinied babes and cheerleaders, the boy was dressed in an unglamorous cleaner's uniform. He wore a bulky set of pink overalls that looked stifling in the heat, with a name tag that read "Torihiko Umibe." Despite the bright pink, his look was unusually subdued for a player of *Money (Game) Master*, but what really caught Midori's attention was the clashing blue T-shirt he wore underneath.

It had no skills to speak of—her special sense confirmed that in an instant.

In *Money (Game) Master*, you never knew when you were going to get stabbed by a weapon or shot with a stray bullet, and even Midori, a beginner, took great pains to optimize her swimsuit and accessory setup as best she could.

"…How can I be happy when the ground is being soiled before my very eyes?" said the black-haired boy, pouting. "Even the grass of the pitch is a delicate and beautiful plant that needs love and care to grow!"

It appeared the boy had found a target for his rants. As cowardly as it sounded, it was common practice, not just in *Money (Game) Master*, but in all online games, to tailor your conduct to the perceived ability of the player you were faced with. Of course, given the spectator-employee relationship at play, some people might just opt to grab the service worker by the collar. Midori, however, was not that petty.

"Is that what you're worried about?"

"This isn't what soccer is supposed to be! It's not about betting; it's not about money. Now people can just crunch the numbers from the last ten years and go straight for the most likely outcome. There might as well not even be a ball involved at all. It's the same thing with baseball and basketball. I don't want those kinds of people ruining this game as well."

Wait, I didn't know you could do that, thought Midori in surprise. Of course, Midori had no money and a mountain of debt, so there was no way she could afford to buy all the records from the last ten years. And crunching the numbers was also out of the question, since Midori could never get her Magistellus, Meiki, to do as she asked.

"It's all their fault."

"?"

"The Leviathans never used to be like this... But then those guys came and snuggled up to the AI sponsors. They stole the team away and replaced the manager and all of the players."

Perhaps this was a fan who started working at the stadium. Though Midori had never been into soccer and hadn't the foggiest idea what team's home stadium they were in.

"Anyway, stay out of here if you don't even know the team uniforms. This place is for soccer fans, not gamblers!"

"Gamblers, huh...? Man, those guys in the pink uniforms were useless. Are those the Leviathans??? I know they had D.M.S. skills for boosting their muscle power and D.V.A. skills for their visual acuity, but their substitute players were so weak. They would have done a lot better with some Physical Stamina skills for the long game."

"Rrrhh?! Just get the hell out already!!"

5

In the Royal Theater, the largest in the entire peninsula financial district.

...Or rather, just outside it, in a shady spot around the back, near the rear entrance.

"Is...is that you, M-Scope?"

A figure jumped in response. The speaker was a woman in glasses, her long black hair swept back and held in place with a delicate gold headband, and her tone was surprised. It was Lily-Kiska. And the person to whom she was speaking had once been known as a master of patience, a trap and land mine expert.

Now he sat, knees cradled in his arms, shoulder to shoulder with his Magistellus inside what could tentatively be termed a "dwelling" formed from old cardboard boxes that appeared to have once been used to ship anime merchandise and giant robot model kits.

It was a strange sight. The backpack-wearing boy hunched over in that cardboard house was once a member of the Ag Wolves, a famous group of Dealers who were all capable of raising and spending 1.7 billion *snow* at the drop of a hat.

Judging by the writing on the side, some of the boxes were clearly foreign, originating from the "outer realms," which existed only as data... It was hard to imagine large cargo ships and freight planes unraveling themselves as they crossed the border, but that was supposedly precisely what had happened.

The girl sitting next to the boy with bad posture was a *yuki-onna*-styled Magistellus in a pale-blue kimono. She looked even smaller than when Lily-Kiska had last seen her. Perhaps part of her had melted in the unbearable heat, now that she had no access to air conditioning.

"...Wheeeh... Anybody know where I can get a fridge...?"

"Goodness! That girl's dripping wet! Is she melting?!"

"It's okay, Lily-Kiska," the boy replied. "She's just been making use of the free showers down on the beach. Ginmi's obsessed with cold things, after all. When I used to buy cakes, she was always more interested in the dry ice they put in the box than in the food itself."

"...Tokonatsu City is a crazy place," the Magistellus girl muttered. "Even the cold taps dispense warm water..."

The boy looked around nervously, his eyes swimming. It was almost as if his leader's eyes were even more intimidating without her smartphone-linked glasses.

"Y-you look well," he said. "Considering our entire team fell apart, what with that Kaname Suou guy chewing up me, Titan, Zaurus, and even you."

"..."

"Oh, I'm not holding any grudges. In fact, I'm kind of glad you're okay. I've heard terrible stories of all sorts of things happening to female

Dealers after they Fall. I don't know how you did it, but I'm glad you're still on top…"

"What are you up to now?"

Commodity prices lined the *yuki-onna*'s kimono.

"Oh, I'm just picking up old empty cans and old magazines to sell. It's slow, but I'm putting away some *snow*. Heh-heh. Don't know when I'll have enough to buy a set of smart glasses like you, though. Investing is out of the question for now. I need at least a gun or a car before trying anything too crazy. Wouldn't want to be unable to defend myself if I start attracting attention, after all. Right now, I'm mostly scared of Smash Daughter and people like that."

"Um, that's not what I meant," said Lily-Kiska after a short pause. Her leather holsters, positioned on either side of her chest like the suspender straps on a waitress outfit, squeezed and pushed her large breasts outward. M-Scope gave a cynical chuckle from where he was sitting.

"I'm an AI Dropout," he then continued. "In real life, an AI data idol agency is subsidizing me. Ha-ha, and that's only because I had Cyber Rain's platinum membership up until last month."

"Oh no…"

"Even after I was able to log in again, all the Dealers I'd ticked off beat me back down before I could return to form. I knew it was going to happen, but still…"

In the fight over #tempest.err, the Ag Wolves had gone up against a powerful Dealer named Pavilion and made quite a few enemies in the process, not ever thinking that they might end up paying for it. But now that they'd lost the money to protect themselves, this was the obvious outcome.

A virtual gunshot might not wound, but it could hurt all the same.

And yet M-Scope was still clinging to his life in the virtual world.

"…There's still a lot here I can't let go of. Like all my figures that got repossessed when I went into debt. I need to buy them back from the pawnbroker somehow… Lily-Kiska, I know they might seem unimportant to you, or downright weird, even, but they're precious to me. I wouldn't trade them for anything. And I won't give up."

Lily-Kiska couldn't bring herself to make fun of him. Back then, there were things she hadn't even disclosed to her closest allies. The feelings she held for Kaname Suou, and the history they shared. If it hadn't been for that, maybe she would have been able to keep her cool and protect her friends. The reason for her actions, and the cause of their loss, might be difficult for the other members to understand, but it was something she couldn't ignore, her top priority.

M-Scope's reason was simply different from hers; that was all. So Lily-Kiska didn't so much as bat an eye. Instead, she pulled a self-defense pistol from a waist holster and tossed it into the cardboard house.

No skills, a blank slate. Lily-Kiska was a sniper-class Dealer, after all. Auxiliary skills like Auto-Aim only got in the way of her natural talents.

"Lily-Kiska?"

"You've got a gun now. Go out and do something crazy."

Of course, Lily-Kiska was not looking down on the boy. Far from it. M-Scope still wanted to protect his former home, even if it meant he had to crawl back up out of the mud to do it, while Lily-Kiska had abandoned her former home, seeking power for herself. It was obvious who had the purer soul.

This time, she was the one who couldn't meet *his* gaze.

"I am an Ag Wolf no longer," she said. "I live for a different goal now. I leave the team to you. To all of you. If you're really waiting to get a foot in the door, and not just making excuses, then here it is. Go for it."

6

Knowing how to put pressure on your opponents' finances was a basic skill in the world of *Money (Game) Master*.

"We're attacking the soccer team?" asked Midori, but there was no surprise on her face. In fact, she looked strangely eager. "All right, let's do it! Those limp-noodle Leviathan crybabies squashed my dreams... Where are we hitting? The stadium? Training grounds? Some sort of museum of the team's history? Just say the word and I'm there. Come on!!"

"Hold on a second."

Kaname did his best to rein in the young girl's expectations. He didn't want to be the one responsible for turning her into a soccer hooligan.

It was nighttime, and they were in a room at a hotel resort, one of the many buildings that Kaname had bought out and turned into safe houses all across the peninsula. The idea wasn't to be able to enjoy a spa anytime he wanted, but to split up his investments in case of trouble. Usually, he disliked tall buildings like these that required him to be far away from his vehicle, but this time he had to admit that the height offered him one big advantage.

Kaname looked down from his forty-eighth-floor window at the stadium below.

…As dubious as it seemed to be inviting his friend's little sister to a hotel room late at night, it needed to be done. If nothing else, Midori was still a beginner and didn't yet own her own property. If she needed to relax in-game, she would park her motorcycle by a parking meter and go sit in an internet café. (In her swimsuit, of course.) It would surely be advantageous for her to own some land in the long run, but not before she had a solid grasp of the numbers game, from drop rates to interest rates.

"We don't need to do anything too rash. Remember, we're only after Takamasa's papers. There's a good chance the list we're after is in their possession, seeing as how they have one of his Legacies. I've already had Tselika look into the Leviathans, so we have the chance to play it smart and get in and get out."

"Urgh… Grrr… Rargh!!"

Apparently, Midori had really wanted to go after them, and was majorly disappointed. She almost looked like a rabid dog that had been chained up. Girls grow up so fast! When had she gotten so violent? As if looking for something on which to take out her anger, she turned to Kaname's open closet and started complaining.

"Why are all your clothes the same anyway? Is that your style or something?"

"I bought those for the skills."

"?"

"Different items of clothing can have different skills, even when it's the same model made by the same manufacturer. And obviously they look exactly the same, so whenever I see an outfit I like, I keep buying it until I hit upon a set that has the skills I want. That's why I have so many. It's especially true when the version that you can try on isn't the same as the one that you buy. Besides, there's advantages to having clothes that look the same with different skills...but I suppose that's just post hoc rationalization on my part."

"Huh. So that one has Grip, and that one has Acrobat?"

"...Don't tell me you can tell these apart, too? All of them?!"

"Umm."

Midori seemed unsure of what to say. Kaname would definitely have to take her along on his next shopping trip. He'd never have to fill up his wardrobe again.

The twin-tailed girl sighed.

"It's nothing to get amazed about, I don't think," she said. "My brother's the one you should be impressed by."

"I don't think it's fair to compare anyone to him," Kaname replied.

It must be in their genes. Customizing weapons used the same principle. Some of the parts that came from the factories had skills, so you had to find and pick out the ones that best complemented your build. Unlike with clothes, each individual component came with its own skills, so by matching several parts with the same skill, it was possible to stack effects onto one item.

...But even that wasn't enough to explain the terrifying capabilities of the Legacies. They were beyond what could be achieved by simple mix and match with a limited number of skill slots. It was almost as if Takamasa had been able to create parts with whatever skills he wanted, or something.

"I really want to find some way to exploit your talent in battle...," said Kaname.

"You mean against the Leviathans, right? Right?!"

Incidentally, the info Kaname had received from Laplacian had lined up with Tselika's investigation exactly. The bespectacled beauty was reduced to tears in the process, but she should have known better. There was a reason the coin toss was known as the most unfair bet in the world. With a bit of practice, you could control precisely how many times the coin would revolve, based only on its weight and the power you imparted to the flip. Even if the opponent picked heads or tails mid-toss, you could make it stop on whichever result you pleased simply by moving your catching hand up or down a centimeter or two.

How could one roll a die so that a given number came up? Or shuffle a pack of cards so all the suits lined up in order?

It was the most boring method of cheating in the world. All you had to do was practice, practice, practice.

"Greetings, My Lord," said Tselika, walking in. "I see the other rooms are in quite a state from disuse. I'll leave the basics to the cleaning robots, but some of the snacks in the fridge are about to turn. I'll take care of them for you."

"Tselika. Take care of the explanation, too."

"Yes, My Lord."

Some of them were luxury foodstuffs imported from the simplified world outside Tokonatsu City. It would be a shame to let them rot. The demonic pit babe laid down a platter of cheese and salami, and then herself, upon the glass table. As she raised one knee and put both arms behind her head, her bikini top and miniskirt switched to a liquid crystal display.

"Let us begin. Get a good, long look." Tselika gave an elegant wink and continued. "The Leviathans are a corrupt soccer team operating out of Leviathan Stadium. It seems they were on the brink of ruin before being bought out and taken over by a group of upcoming new Dealers."

"Bought out? Wait, so they're not the original owners???"

"Is that so strange?" asked Kaname at Midori's odd reaction.

"Well, I mean…the owner is kinda, like, you know, the CEO, right? The most important person in the company. Aren't they an AI?"

She didn't seem to be getting it at all. To be fair, the twin-tailed schoolgirl showed a decent enough understanding for her age, but she would need a little more instruction if she were to survive in *Money (Game) Master*.

"On paper, the owner or CEO is the top dog, sure, but in some businesses, they're little more than a figurehead to be hired or fired at will. Indeed, like you said, most businesses in *Money (Game) Master* are made up of AIs, but many sports teams employ humans to serve as the owner. They're usually held at the behest of the lead sponsor, however, which is an AI business."

"The lead sponsor?"

"In other words, the largest sponsor that financially supports the team. In many cases, the sports team is more like a subsidiary of the sponsoring company."

"Well," added Tselika, "in general, they're not quite as tightly coupled as baseball teams, but in Leviathan's case, they are; there's one sponsor company with majority shareholder status. Perhaps you could think of that as being like their parent company."

Kaname and Tselika did their best to explain…but it was uncertain whether Midori really understood what a sponsor was beyond a word she occasionally heard on TV.

"Since their parent company is an AI business, the team is evaluated methodically, based on results. If the team's performance dips and the sponsors aren't getting the advertising they paid for, the owner might get the sack. In that case, it'll be the board of directors of the lead sponsor making the call. If you want to hijack the team, they're the ones you have to exploit. In *Money (Game) Master*, you can get your hands on just about anything if you have the cash. In any case, that should answer your question. Tselika, please continue."

"Yes, My Lord. The original owner was one Tatsuo Umibe. Thirty-eight years old. Male. In real life, it seems he and a few colleagues quit their jobs as salarymen to start up their own business trading virtual currency in the soccer industry, as soccer had been a favorite pastime of theirs... At least, that's what it says on his public profile."

"Umibe? But he's thirty-eight..."

"It's not an unusual age for someone looking to start their own business. Remember, he's not here for fun," Kaname explained, but Midori still looked puzzled. Perhaps the idea of someone quitting their day job to become a soccer team manager was new to her.

"But you mentioned his colleagues were in on it, too. Isn't an owner usually someone who runs the whole business by themselves?"

"It depends," said Tselika, "but in Umibe's case, it seems that he and his friends have all chosen the positions they want to play. They're serving as the coaches and players; they might look young, but in reality they're all middle-aged men. There are all kinds of soccer fans, but with the number-crunchers, sometimes all they need is a fit body and they can really tear up the field."

Tselika cackled, using her forked tail to point out some information that had appeared along the contours of her body.

"The owner's son is the one who drew the team's mascot, Mr. Shark. I suppose he must be about ten years old or so. His username is..."

"Torihiko Umibe."

"Huh?"

Before Tselika could voice her doubts, Midori slapped her hand to her brow, as if she could see something the others couldn't.

"...That was him. He was cleaning up the stadium that the evil Dealers stole. He didn't want to abandon his home. Of course he would be angry. It wasn't a team the AI made to make money. It was something humans did for fun. They even printed Mr. Shark on the tickets, and I tore them up, right in front of him. I'm the worst..."

"The team's finances were never good to begin with," explained Kaname. "The former owner was a bit of a clean freak and never allowed them to sell betting slips. However, it was the advertising revenue that served as the final nail in the coffin. In Tokonatsu City, the soccer league is almost entirely controlled by the profits made from advertising, merchandising, and web streaming. Once the team started to slip, the other Dealers saw their chance and bought out all the sponsors by threatening them with the Legacy."

Midori shook her arms as if to slow Kaname down and asked, "B-but, isn't the…what was it…lead sponsor? The big AI company, aren't they supposed to look after the team?"

"Well, disregarding things like classified stock, essentially what it boils down to is whoever has the most shares gets to dictate what the team does. Even if one company only has 50.1 percent versus all the other companies owning 49.9 percent, it's the same as if they owned an 80 percent or 90 percent share. Since there's no benefit for the AI businesses to buy up any more stock than they need to, they're going to go with the minimum amount possible."

"However," added Tselika, "the Leviathans can't live off a 50.1 percent stake. They need to keep 70 percent or 80 percent of the advertising revenue just to pay the bills."

"So, that means…?"

"Once the Dealers had the Leviathans in their sights, all they had to do was have sponsors suddenly stop paying, putting the team in a choke hold. That goes double for long-term contracts of four or five years. That's why half the signs in the stadium are blank. Like Tselika said, the team can't live off the support of just a single sponsor. That would spell the end for them."

"And just because a sponsor quits paying does not mean you can instantly find a replacement," said Tselika. "These things take time. And it is not like you can blame the sponsors. They had a gun to their heads; what were they supposed to do?"

Midori finally fell silent. All the hoots and jeers in the soccer stadium couldn't even begin to measure up to the harassment and psychological warfare found in the world of finance. Midori was probably having trouble adjusting to this revelation. Her personality wasn't very suited to this game, but that was fine, Kaname thought. It was his job to handle the dirty work.

"Without their funding, the Leviathans were in a very fragile position," he continued. "And even though there was clearly corruption at play, the lead sponsors were cruel. They dismissed the old owner, Tatsuo Umibe, and the current corrupt managers took over the team. All the old hands, from trainers to players, were kicked out, and I hear they even changed the team's colors from blue to pink."

"...Blue to pink? Then that T-shirt the boy was wearing underneath his cleaner's uniform..."

"To sum up, the little slice of comfort an old man tried to create to recapture the joys of his youth got turned into a team of professional hit men," said Tselika. "The name is about the only part of the old team that still remains. Talk about deceptive marketing."

It was a sad story, but not an uncommon one in the ruthless world of *Money (Game) Master*. But back to the topic at hand.

"Now, as for the corrupt Dealers operating out of Leviathan Stadium, they seem to be focused on something other than their team lineup for the time being," said Tselika. "I'm speaking of the recent plans to build Biondetta Dome, a new indoor stadium, near the coast."

"..."

"Midori."

"...Sorry, sorry. Trying to keep up. But this city is pretty rich, right? There are stadiums all over the place. What's so special about this one???"

Sounding a little frustrated, Midori took a slice of cheese and placed it in her mouth.

"All the stadiums built so far have maintained a balance with population distribution, but not this time. This is a serious incursion into the Leviathans' territory."

Kaname pointed out the window with his thumb. From where he stood looking down on the city from above, the two plots looked practically adjacent, like a convenience store setting up across the road from a competitor. What's more, something felt quite tense about the silver walls erected around the Biondetta Dome construction site.

"Those aren't construction workers...they're PMCs! They've all got rifles, and there's even armored vehicles with machine gun turrets..."

"And they have attack helicopters on standby not far away," added Kaname. "It'd be difficult to even toss a pebble in there without being blown to bits."

Kaname sighed. This practically had his name on it. The word *impossible* was not in his dictionary.

"You know what the heat is like at midday around here," he continued. "Leviathan Stadium is an old-style open-air arena. It's not well suited to Tokonatsu City, where it's summer all year round and the streets are filled with exhaust fumes. Add that to the proximity, and you can be sure when Biondetta Dome opens, it's going to take all the Leviathans' customers with it."

"And the number of teams that can fit in a league changes every few years," said Tselika. "This time Biondetta is going to have its name on the list."

"Looking at the development reports for the Dome, it seems that the construction plans came almost out of nowhere. It must have come as quite a shock to the Leviathans to suddenly find another team's home base put down on their territory."

"Ahh, I suppose it's like when two teams are established in the same prefecture and people start fighting over them," muttered Midori, though it seemed like she hadn't quite gotten the point yet.

Kaname proceeded with his explanation, regardless. "In any case, it seems that Leviathan Stadium has been trying to quickly install some outdoor air conditioning, but it's not going to be ready in time. They have a lot of good reasons to be upset with Biondetta right now."

"Hmm? But why does the team care about that? It might have been different before, but now all the humans are underhanded Dealers, and the stadium is owned by NPCs, right? ...Well, except the humans on the cleaning staff, I guess. But the team could just play their matches at the new stadium if they wanted. They've got their sponsor. Why do they care whether they use this stadium or that one?"

"The usage fees for away games are much higher. Not to mention, seventy percent of the proceeds from a sporting event come from television, radio, and web broadcasts, as well as direct sponsor contracts—and all those go to the home stadium. If you only ever play away games, you'll be out of pocket."

"...I see. So that's why there's so many stadiums in one city."

"Besides, having your own stadium is useful for more than just playing games. You can rent it out for concerts and other events. So it needs to be appealing to event organizers, or else you won't even be able to fill the schedule, let alone the seats."

A team affiliated with a stadium was essentially that venue's management team, so failing to make money was a serious concern. If the stadium failed, the team failed with it.

Although it was billed as an open-world game where anything was possible, space in *Money (Game) Master* was at a premium. The monthly costs for keeping a large public building open were steep, stretching into the hundreds of millions. To balance the books, you were always looking to keep your schedule packed with events. It was like owning a jumbo jet you weren't allowed to land—you just had to keep pumping it full of expensive fuel.

"At the end of the day, Biondetta Dome is a real kick in the teeth to all those who support Leviathan Stadium," said Tselika. "They'll do everything in their power to stop it from being completed."

"...No matter what it takes?" asked Midori. "And in the name of a team they stole from people like that little boy?"

"That's *Money (Game) Master* for you," said Kaname. "If you don't like what you see, then you'd better have the money or the guns to change it."

Tselika, laid out on the glass table, twisted her hips and adjusted her position, pointing to the data streams on her clothing with her forked tail.

"Indeed. And in fact, we can see signs of sabotage involving procurement for the new stadium. In particular, these specialized air conditioners. The Leviathans have been obstructing commercial air-conditioning manufacturers in the hopes of stalling construction. Biondetta Dome makes use of a rather unusual and novel architecture, you see, whereby the airflow provides support to the roof. That means that without the air conditioners in place, they can't even finish construction of the building."

"Like if nobody plays any sixes or eights in a game of Sevens?" asked Midori.

"Exactly," said Kaname.

"...Do they really have to go all the way to a factory, draw up a blueprint, and fit all the metal parts together to make something? Why isn't it just like throwing a bunch of materials in a pot?"

"*Money (Game) Master* is one of the most realistic VR worlds out there. Perhaps if we had machinery that could synthesize materials at the atomic level in reality, then we could make something like that here as well."

"But it's a game! Why can't everything just be simple?"

"That's part of the appeal of open-world gaming."

For the ones trying to disrupt an AI company's supply line, it was actually a lot simpler to sneak into their factories and plant explosives than it would be to try and stop them from mixing items in a pot with some fixed probability of success.

Kaname gave a resigned sigh and gestured with the silver fork in his hand to a piece of information near Tselika's armpit.

"Biondetta Dome was slated to be the home of a new soccer team, but that wasn't enough to secure funding, so the plan is for it to open along with the Misaka Expo in two years' time. Of course, that means if construction slows and they can't make that target, the funding will run dry and the whole thing will be shut down."

For any other game, an event two years in the making would be unthinkable, but in *Money (Game) Master*, the flow of money never stopped. Even a construction site was an important part of the game economy; construction workers had to eat, too, after all.

"Best-case scenario, it'll take one and a half years to finish construction, so all the Leviathans need to do is drag it out for another six months. They'll do whatever it takes to make that happen, to protect their shabby, outdated stadium."

"So then..."

"We're going to sabotage the sabotage."

"Keh-heh! My Lord, that tickles! It's like using electronic counter-countermeasures against electronic countermeasures. If we want them to come running to us with their top-secret documents in hand, then this is where we must give them a poke. That should rattle them, certainly."

Still lying on her back, Tselika gently lowered an olive from the snack plate into her mouth. As she did so, a new image displayed on her risqué outfit.

"There's one thing that makes this situation quite different from a card game," she explained. "In a real fight, we aren't stuck waiting until somebody makes the play we want; we can go right for their weak point and flip over the whole game board."

Kaname nodded. He had a clear view of the whole situation now, and he had reached a conclusion.

"We need to acquire the specialized air-conditioning equipment the Leviathans are blocking and make arrangements to hand it over to Biondetta. That'll shake them up."

"Ah-ha-ha! Then we'll have the Leviathans on their hands and knees, begging us to take their precious list!"

"We don't need to stage a full-on takeover. This is just a little bit of targeted harassment in order to get what we want. It's Business 101. If we want to befriend this team of minigun-wielding crooks, then first we have to become a force they can't afford to ignore."

"Shall we give them a sign?"

"Let's put off making any specific demands. We'll start by ramping up the pressure until they crack, and then make them into remote control toys that do anything we say. Hmm. Tselika. Invent some new cocktail and get it trending at all the local bars. The ingredients and ratios don't matter. Call it 'List the Target.'"

"Spreading some fear before showing your face? Bold move, My Lord."

Kaname didn't elaborate on the steps that would come after that.

Takamasa's papers were more than just a treasure map. They were a piece of his very soul. They weren't something for money-grubbing crooks to riffle through and leer at whenever they pleased.

Helping someone was nothing to brag about. You just shut your mouth and did it.

Just then, as if her gears had been turning in another dimension, Midori opened her mouth and muttered, almost to herself,

"…Hey. If this works, the Leviathans will be willing to do whatever we ask, right? Even give up my brother's list, which is so important to them."

"Yeah. So?"

"I want to tell you about something I saw. But I need your help. I'm not good at shoot-outs and trading and all that."

Tselika was about to say something when Kaname held her back. He lived by one rule: If this girl, Takamasa's sister, asked for help, then Kaname would provide it.

"What do I need to do?"

"I want to correct a mistake. And all the injustice that lurks in this city."

7

Server Name: Gamma Orange.
Final Location: Tokonatsu City, Peninsula District.
Log-out successful.
Thank you for playing, Kaname Suou.

"Phew…"

Time had flown, and the boy had ended up spending almost all day hooked into the game again. Now that his smartphone was no longer blasting representational markers into his eyes at one hundred twenty frames per second, he looked up from it and blinked his eyes. Round. Red. Sweet. Fruit. About 10 centimeters. An apple. All of this information was bad for the eyes. His vision was blurred without his contacts in, but the boy fumbled around on his desk until he found his bottle of eye drops and quenched his parched, red eyes.

Oh, damn. What about my contacts?

After putting down the bottle, he realized these eye drops were the strong kind that couldn't be used with contact lenses. The boy took out a cheap pair of glasses shoved into a nearby pen holder and slipped them on. The digital calendar atop his desk now clearly displayed the date. April 19. In the real world, you couldn't use skills to improve your vision.

At any rate, the boy wanted to go out. He made up his mind to head to the convenience store, not so much because he was hungry as because he needed something to do.

"?"

Where's the duffle coat I usually wear?

Although it was already late April, early spring was still marked by the occasional bitter chill, like a memory of winter. It crept in through the windows, giving the boy a taste of the outside world, but the hanger on his wall was empty. He whipped out his phone and messaged his sister.

Oh, I guess I should pick up some colored pens as well...

Even though he could meet Midori Hekireki in-game as much as he wanted, that didn't mean his passion for writing letters had faded... However, it seemed that she wasn't sure how to handle the change in relationship with her pen pal, and the awkwardness was plain to see in her letters. The boy was going to have to change tactics if he wanted to keep their correspondence going.

Still no reply.

Something felt wrong. His little sister would get mad if he didn't respond to a message in under three minutes, and she wasn't the hypocritical type.

He walked into the living room and groaned.

"Hey."

Lazing languidly on the sofa was his little sister, watching late-night television. She looked up at him as he entered the room.

"…Are you going out at this time of night? Must not be anything big if you're dressed like that. Can you pick me up some ice cream?"

"Give me back my coat!"

"Huh? This old thing? It's so worn out, I thought you didn't want it anymore, and the heater isn't strong enough to warm the whole room, so…"

The girl had a petite frame, and her soft, fluffy black hair fell about her shoulders. She looked at him drowsily—it seemed now that her body had warmed up, she was getting sleepy.

This was one of her bad habits. Sneaking into his room while he was playing and stealing every shirt and jersey she could find, even though they didn't fit. Even though she spent all that time in stylish shop fitting rooms trying on different sets of pajamas, what was the point if she was just going to lounge about on her bed in a baggy T-shirt all day? It was all right for her, but what about the poor boy who had to catch an unexpected whiff of sweet-smelling fragrance whenever he casually threw on a scarf? It wasn't good for his health. She could at least give him a warning.

"Just remember to get me some ice cream."

"Yes, Your Majesty. Hope you're warm enough there in *my* coat."

It felt like his sister was testing him by not specifying a flavor, but Kaname pretty much knew his sister's favorites: mint chocolate or strawberry. He just had to watch out for the new springtime flavors like banana chocolate parfait or berry mix.

"I know *Money (Game) Master* is a lot of work, big bro, but make sure you don't forget the real world exists, too. There are other things in this world besides money, you know."

"I know."

He hesitated for a moment.

He may have been an infamous Dealer in the game, but this was him in real life.

"What about you? Are you still not coming back?" he asked.

"No." She shook her head gently. "I've already terminated my subscription. I could make a new account, but it would have a new Magistellus, wouldn't it? I don't want that."

"I see," the boy muttered. The wounds on a person's soul were invisible. She had her own way of dealing with her trauma, and he couldn't force her to go along with his way. The Mind of the Magistelli was a fearsome threat to all mankind, but to an individual person, it wasn't that pressing a problem. The boy was happy for that, even as he chose to fight against it alongside Tselika. There was no need to retread old ground. Therefore, the spectacled boy had only one thing left to say.

. "I'm off, then."

"See you. Make sure you come back with that ice cream before I resort to drinking warm tap water."

The boy left the apartment building and breathed in the chilly air. It felt like drinking a cold fizzy soda, and though it didn't turn his breath white, it had him wishing he'd stolen back his coat all the same.

He was looking for a convenience store, so he headed into town, where they had everything. It was dark out, but not that late. The streets were still filled with people.

The number of people working, however, was a different story. Interactive robots directed traffic around construction sites, and the job of standing by a store to draw in customers was long gone. Nobody even looked at the shop signs anymore. Everyone was walking around with their eyes glued to their smartphones, only caring about the number of stars on their map apps or review sites. Shady businesses had realized, too, that leaving all their advertising up to AI was cheaper and made them harder to catch.

"No more duplicate accounts!! The world is undergoing a shortage of e-mail addresses. Help out by integrating your PC, mobile, and gaming accounts today!"

" ... "

He passed by an electronic billboard flashing gaudy colors. A policeman wearing a backpack stuffed with communications equipment and a 360-degree panoramic camera, taking pictures for some big search engine, cycled past on an electric bicycle. The boy wondered why that job was still performed by humans in this day and age. Did it require a degree of flexibility that robots didn't have, or was it just that civil servants were as slow as ever to modernize their systems?

Just a little bit of walking and he was out of breath, and the dark stretches between streetlights had him on edge. It felt totally different from being a Dealer in the game.

The shopping district wasn't even that far from his home, yet it felt like a cold maze.

"Whoops."

The boy nearly walked face-first into the glass door of the convenience store. He'd come all this way, and the sliding door hadn't budged for him. He slowly reached out his hand—it seemed he needed to press a button. Maybe it was the time of day.

"Good evening, all! We're the three sister goddesses. Welcome to another session of Seven Raven's exclusive evening chat. Join me, Alecto, along with my sisters, Tisiphone and Megaera, for a very special girls' chat!!"

A radio show featuring some idol group was being piped into the brightly lit store interior, but there wasn't hide nor hair of any other people to be found. Even the checkout counter was empty. Instead, there was an LCD screen displaying a few words.

"Currently in unmanned mode. Please use self-service functionality."

"..."

It was as rigid and unforgiving as an ATM. Handy, but lacking warmth. On the screen was an image of an anime character—an employee in the store uniform moving around like one of those virtual whatchamacallits.

The boy took a plastic basket and walked past the decaying magazines under the front window to reach the drinks cabinet, where he tossed a few canned energy drinks and bottled sports drinks into his basket before moving over to the lunch aisle. After a few moments' thought, he opted for a couple of veggie sandwiches.

"Don't you find it annoying to remember all the addresses for your home computer and mobile devices? Not to mention all my games consoles and other smart devices!"

"I knooow! And I always use face ID or my fingerprint to unlock them anyway, so, like, does it even matter? I mean, we're sooo beyond using those stained old keyboards to type out passwords, aren't we?"

"Smart management puts all your accounts in one place. No more duplicate accounts! Do your part to help out society!!"

The in-store broadcasts were most likely semiautomated scripts, with the outlines written by humans and then the rest filled in by AI. To anyone who actually questioned what they were told, the blatant emotional manipulation was obvious. The question was, did the 2-Support-1, that is, the mixed unit of human girls and data idols on the radio, understand the *real* meaning of what they were saying?

Golden Week was fast approaching, and there were plenty of celebratory mochi wrapped in oak leaves, some containing chocolate or custard filling.

Oh yeah, pens.

Walking back over to the stationery aisle, the boy picked out a three-color set. He would look at the ice cream last. He didn't expect it to melt so quickly, but he just didn't feel right walking around with it at room temperature.

Made in Japan. Automatic.

It wasn't just the stationery. Every product had a label on it somewhere saying the same thing. The age of cheap foreign labor was over. With all production handled by AI, there was no need to pay people to run factories at all. So long as the equipment was the same, no matter where the machines were located, they would make the exact same quality of products.

The unmanned cash register served no purpose. He could simply walk out the front door. Cameras had been watching his every movement and would automatically deduct the cost of his purchases from his smartphone account.

…You might think shoplifters would abuse this setup, but there was a comprehensive system of tags and high-speed security cameras in place to prevent any problems. Besides, in case of a failed system read, the doors could be automatically locked to stop someone from leaving, supposedly. The boy had never seen it happen, but that was what he had heard. However, over by the register was a button labeled with a telephone icon, like what you might find in an elevator, that would connect you to an emergency helpline if something went wrong and you became trapped. Much like with door-to-door salesmen versus locked apartment buildings, it was simple enough for malicious actors to game the system, but it was hard for large chains to resist cutting labor costs during the late-night hours. Still, they had to hire people to stock the shelves in the early morning, so it didn't make that much difference.

AI didn't force or intimidate its way into society. It was simply handy, a way to indulge ourselves. And just like that, it gently invited us to throw away what we had. It told us that if we didn't, our rivals would. We didn't want to fall behind, did we?

"…"

How many late-night workers must this self-checkout system have put out of jobs? The boy had even heard a tragic news story about an unmanned store where a short in some faulty wiring had resulted in a fire, and the customers had burned to death inside, unable to get the automatic doors to open. Humans might have been less efficient than automation, but some jobs necessitated their more caring and adaptable touch, like the old newspaper padding that keeps a fragile mug safe during a move. AI society had removed all such softness from human lives and optimized everything so that it was high-performance, but with little room for error. Any tragedies that followed were dismissed as unpredictable malfunctions. The buck was passed from people to machines, from individuals to corporations, between the private and public sectors, until the responsibility was so spread out, there was no one left to blame. Even when lives were lost.

The world was running out of e-mail addresses. That was what led to the dictate of "No more duplicate accounts!" This was another result of the proliferation of financial transactions, not between humans and humans or humans and machines, but between machines and machines. It was not humans who had placed such pressure on the available address pool, but incorporeal programs. Currently, the worldwide proportion of transactions carried out by freelance devices without a registered human user stood at 48 percent. If this figure crossed the 50 percent threshold, the world would enter an age when humans would no longer control machines, but instead, machines would efficiently manipulate humanity via finance.

And while all this was happening, wouldn't it be convenient for the collective Mind of those AIs if the personal data of all seven billion people on the planet was wrapped up nice and neat in one little informational bundle per person? One could even analyze a user's thoughts, based on their online shopping history and comments on social media. And hypothetically, if they posed a threat, all it would take would be one tap on a maps app to switch some traffic lights and cause a self-driving car to have a terrible accident.

"I guess that's everything."

The boy paid his bill without incident and left the store.

He wasn't locked inside or burned to death.

This time, there were no such errors.

But what about next time?

8

Server Name: Psi Indigo.
Starting Location: Tokonatsu City, Peninsula District.
Log-in successful.
Welcome to *Money (Game) Master*, Midori Hekireki.

She hadn't gotten the boy's contact details, but there was only one place he could be. The twin-tailed girl sat astride her large, bright-red motorcycle and toured leisurely around Leviathan Stadium.

It was night. The floodlit stadium and its environs were a popular spot for dates, but to someone who truly loved soccer, seeing the facility used for such alternate purposes was probably like watching someone ruin your perfectly crafted cooking by throwing all sorts of random spices and additives on it.

The girl in the gothic-lolita bikini circled around until she spotted a familiar face. Then she dropped her speed and pulled over onto the hard shoulder.

"Ah, there you are. Do you like how the stadium looks from this angle or something?"

"...You again?"

It was the small boy who hid a blue T-shirt underneath his pink overalls. He was sitting beside a relic from the past: a public pay phone, on a bench covered in graffiti, with an old worn-out stuffed toy in his arms. He stroked the toy shark's blue head, and Midori could see, plain as day, that the accessory had no skills attached. The stadium stood like a fortress, a monument to its captors' greed, illuminated by the brash floodlights. Even so, the ten-year-old boy looked up at it with fond reminiscence.

"I know money is everything," he said. "Even my dad and his friends had to be clever when they used the money they got from quitting their jobs to buy this stadium. Maybe some people suffered as a result. That's just how it is. In *Money (Game) Master*, money talks. I know all that..."

Pooling together their severance paychecks. Starting up a virtual currency business, with Tatsuo Umibe taking the position of owner, and his ex-colleagues as coaches and players. As longtime soccer fans, they wanted to see how far they could take their own game, their own theories and viewpoints.

...And if this was how it had all turned out, Midori wondered how it had affected their relationships in real life. She saw a glimpse of another kind of hell, very different from her own.

"Yeah."

But Midori didn't deny what the boy had said.

Furthermore...

"...If money talks, then those guys can't complain if something terrible were to happen to them, too."

"?"

"Oh, nothing."

Midori gazed at the throttle control on the handlebar of her bike.

"I'm glad I saw your face again. Things are rough right now, but make sure you take care of yourself. Even just waiting is a valid choice. It's better than rushing in without a plan, after all."

"What are you... How can things change now?! Dad lost everything. His money, his confidence, even his friends' trust! And what did he do to deserve it? Nothing! It's all because those guys came out of nowhere!! I know that, but there's nothing I can do about it! Nothing!!"

They were interrupted by the sound of buzzing. Suddenly, someone appeared on the back seat of Midori's motorcycle. She was wearing a short-cut *cheongsam* with open sides and fur trim around the back of the neck. Her hair was short and black, and she had a pair of horns atop her head, with a paper talisman covering her face. Her chest was relatively modest, considering her height.

The Magistellus dropped her expressionless gaze down to her outstretched hand, in which she held a small keychain with a blue shark mascot. It was an older piece of merchandise, from before the team came under new management, and everything was covered over in pink.

"Meiki. How come you never come out when *I* want you? And we didn't need to show that off."

"That's..."

It was just an old trinket, found collecting dust in one corner of one of the pawnshops managed by the Treasure Hermit Crabs. But Midori could tell with one look that it had no skills attached. That wasn't where its value lay. And that was precisely why she had picked it up.

"'How can things change now?' ...That was what you said, wasn't it?" Midori said one last thing to the boy.

"Just wait and see. Someone's going to show you how much change is really possible in this game."

Then she twisted the accelerator and sped off.

9

Server Name: Theta Yellow.
Starting Location: Tokonatsu City, Peninsula District.

Log-in successful.
Welcome to *Money (Game) Master*, **Kaname Suou.**

Midori: Martini Air Conditioning, huh? Is this really the only company that can make it?
Kaname: Remember, it's a unique product that must support the structure of the whole dome. It behooves us to seek a company with the proper equipment.
Midori: Behooves?
Kaname: Dammit, Tselika.

The outskirts of the main financial district on the peninsula were somewhat cooler than the city center, owing to the way the land rose to meet the seaside cliffs. At higher altitudes, the temperature was lower, and so this area was home to all sorts of resorts and golf courses for people seeking to escape the heat of the everlasting summer. Unlike the sandy beaches of the city center, the gentle hillsides in this area were covered in green grass. Supposedly, the area had been a wasteland before it was made arable for growing crops with the introduction of a special water-absorbing material based on sticky *natto*, or something like that.

The other distinctive feature was the collection of giant seesaw-like silhouettes dotting the landscape—pumping jacks, drawing crude oil out of the ground.

It was the dead of night, not long after Kaname had taken his break in the real world, and now the mint-green coupe was parked right where a line of transmission towers crossed the main road. Kaname got out, tugging the demon after him by her forked tail.

"How many times have I told you not to send messages on my behalf?"

"Hyaaaaagh! I—I—I meant nothing by it, I swear! I simply thought it a bother to set up my own account, that is all! Wait, are you tying me up? Lashing my cute, sensitive tail to this pylon, then driving off in style and leaving me all alone in the wilderness to fend for myself? Please, no! Anything but that!"

A little later, Midori showed up, her tiny bottom perched atop her bright-red motorcycle, and swung one leg over behind her to dismount. Perhaps she didn't care so much about what she showed off when she was dressed in a swimsuit...though it was hard to believe Midori was that immodest. Still, it did kind of make her look like a dog taking a leak, though Kaname thought it wise to keep that comment to himself.

"Brrr! It sure is cold out here!" she said, shivering. "I guess 'cause it's nighttime, too."

"It's because you've barely got any clothes on," replied Kaname. "That's why I said you should stick a hoodie or a raincoat in the helmet compartment or something..."

"Oh, lay off it! Who are you, my mother?!"

It seemed Midori was still far from growing out of her rebellious phase. It was enough to make Kaname worry for her future.

Unlike in the middle of town, with all its light pollution, the stars in the sky out here were big and bright. It wasn't entirely like being surrounded by Mother Nature, though, due to the small resin squares that plugged the ground here and there. Kaname called out to the teary-eyed demon.

"Tselika. Let's make sure we've got everything right. That air-conditioning company is from 'outside,' correct?"

"Yes, My Lord."

In *Money (Game) Master*, there were two kinds of companies. Those from Tokonatsu City, which were faithfully modeled, down to each individual employee, and those from "outside," which existed only in a simplified form as data, and thus had no 3D representation at all. If you think about a typical RPG, they typically have weapon shops, armor shops, item shops, and inns, but they don't go into so much detail as to keep track of how many people were needed to hang the curtains in the window. These companies were the same.

The bewitching Magistellus blew repeatedly on her tail before continuing, as relevant information scrolled across her pit-babe outfit and along the body of the car.

"From what I can gather from footage of previous attacks, Martini

Air Conditioning brings its products into the city by land, in a long convoy with multiple trucks and guard vehicles. It must be a sitting duck for the Leviathans each time."

Trucks were strong, but a convoy was a slow-moving and easy target. No doubt this next one would be blown up, too, if Kaname didn't intervene. The task was to help from the shadows and make sure that the convoy reached its target—Biondetta Dome. In other words, an escort mission. Of course, that meant they would have to trade blows, and more likely, bullets, with the enemy team. It was likely to end in gunfire, but Kaname needed to shake them up a bit, or that list they were so carefully guarding would never see the light of day.

He wanted them on their knees, begging him to take it off their hands.

In the real world, such behavior would surely send the police force scrambling. But in the world of the game, there were no such concerns.

Midori sighed.

"...It's hard to believe," she said. "I mean, to attack the convoy, they have to go up against an infinite supply of those AI macho men, the PMCs. That's suicide!"

"That's what the Legacy is for," said Tselika.

"..."

The innocent schoolgirl suddenly got a nasty look in her eyes. She had already told Kaname what she had seen, that the gang who swung around her brother's Legacy like it was their property had also ruined the lives of a boy and his father. Midori had twice as much reason to be angry as anybody else.

Kaname looked back at the info on Tselika's curves, thinking for a moment.

"So are we not able to pin down the convoy's precise entry point?"

"No. If we could, then all the Leviathans would have to do is plant one land mine on the city border and be done with it. Vehicles entering and leaving the city can appear and disappear anywhere up to two kilometers from the boundary line—as long as they are NPCs, of course. The one saving grace is that on this shark-tooth-shaped peninsula, the only land connection is to the north, but even then, we do not know the specific route they will take."

"Come to think of it," asked Midori, "what happens if *we* try to cross the city borders?"

"You hit an invisible wall," replied Kaname. "If you're going to test it out, Midori, do it on foot. We don't want you to go up in a ball of flame."

"You think I'm some kind of kitten walking into windows?!" yelled Midori. A pair of cat ears and a tail would have matched well with the frilly bikini, actually.

In any case.

"We need to protect the motorcade until it reaches its destination at Biondetta Dome," said Kaname. "If we run into the Leviathans, we take them out."

"Uh-huh." Tselika nodded, tagging all the key information that appeared on her bikini top and miniskirt.

"If the entry point is random," he continued, "then we'll have to hit the one main road where all southbound routes converge. That's this one. You can't get into town by land without going through the Amatsu Tunnel, after all."

"Ahh, yeah, that one…," said Midori. "You wouldn't believe how bad the fumes get going through it on my bike."

"No complaints," said Tselika. "Compared to fighting on the open plains, their minigun will be slightly less effective in close quarters. Once the convoy reaches the tunnel, they'll no longer be able to fight at their preferred long range. What most worries me is the first half of the operation, in the outskirts of the city."

"Once we see the convoy's headlights, we're off."

"Okay, but… What about the convoy itself? I'm guessing it's not too weak, since it belongs to an AI company."

"As far as I can tell from the video," said Tselika, "Martini AC's escort mainly consists of reinforced black sports cars with short-barreled assault rifles. The vehicles may look stylish from the outside, but they are equipped with a powerful four-wheel-drive system. Those vehicles form the front and the rear of the convoy."

With no more room for them on her pit-babe outfit, Tselika produced a number of visual aids along the surface of the mint-green coupe.

"The Leviathans have about ten electric mountain bikes. Most of them are driven by humans, while the shooting is left to the Magistelli."

"Wait, the Magistelli?"

"Come to think of it, your Meiki is a little temperamental, isn't she?" Kaname noted. "Well, remember, Tselika used our Legacy once. Magistelli can do all sorts of things, depending on how you train them. They share their skills with their master, and the master can buy weapons for them if they want. Take my sister, for example. She had a Magistellus called Cindy, a dark elf."

"Yeah?"

"Well, she could handle both driving and shooting no problem, but she was absolutely useless at trades."

"...Uh, but aren't Magistelli controlled by computers?"

"Well, this one couldn't even get past row six on her times tables. My sister had to do all the accounting herself. Anyway, apart from the bikes, there's also a four-wheel-drive buggy that acts as a sort of command post. I say 'buggy,' but it's more like a monster truck. The wheels are bigger than me."

"...Wait, eleven units? Like a soccer team...?"

"Now, then," said Tselika. "Even a Legacy should not allow one to go toe to toe with the PMCs. Especially not the riders on their bikes, who are so lacking in armor, it'd make an exhibitionist blush. Even if they have invested in the Bulletproof skill, a direct hit would knock them off-balance and cause them to crash, regardless."

As a bike enthusiast, Midori pouted at this. But it was not the time to debate cars versus motorcycles.

"In short," said Kaname, "it seems the Leviathans are planning to use their off-road capabilities to their advantage. They can keep as far away as they like, staying just outside the range of the escort's assault rifles. And since they don't need to use the roads, they can set as many traps on them as they like. They can blow up bridges, collapse tunnels, set wires across roads, trigger off-route mines… Few Dealers care about the condition of a road they don't use."

"Ugh. It's even more underhanded than a normal shoot-out… Though I guess I should have expected as much from corrupt Dealers."

"The traps we cannot see scare me even more than the Legacy," said Tselika. "If one of those goes off, then our mission has failed. Preventing that should be our top priority."

"?"

"We need to get ahead of the convoy and find and eliminate all traps that pose a threat," said Kaname. "We don't need to do any complicated bomb disposal; just shooting them from a distance should be enough."

"Our opponents may possess a Legacy, but that by itself is not enough to halt the convoy," added Tselika. "It is just to finish them off once the traps do their work. So long as we can prevent that from happening, the convoy will reach its destination."

Furthermore, the Leviathans' off-road strategy only worked in the outskirts of the city. Once in the city proper, you had to stick to the streets, because there were buildings everywhere blocking your line of sight, and you couldn't trap the roads, either, because there was too much traffic. Random strangers would keep setting them off.

"Stick to the main points, and the mission is pretty simple," said Kaname, reaching for the driver's side door of the mint-green coupe. "I see lights on the horizon. That'll be the convoy. Let's get going, Midori."

"Roger."

Midori got atop her large motorcycle.

"…I'm going to make sure this injustice ends here," she muttered. "My brother's Legacy, his list, the Umibe family's stadium… I'll take them all back tonight!!"

10

The mint-green coupe's wheels were finally rolling, though it was not moving very fast. The first step of the plan was to wait for the truck convoy to approach. Just as the fleet of semis caught up and began to pass Kaname's location, he rolled down the driver's side window, leaned out, and fired a single shot into the side of one of the large shipping trailers.

Kaname felt a sudden pain—the Lion's Nose.

"Now we floor it."

"Was there really no other way to do this, My Lord?!"

The car's engine roared to life as an additional dialog box appeared in one corner of the windshield. A number of the black bulletproof cars began pursuit, but Kaname wasn't bothered. He planned to shake them off by going as fast as possible. In a battle with PMCs, a direct encounter would only result in your loss. Therefore, Kaname had prepared a gauge that indicated how close he was to escaping, which quickly dropped from over twenty to near zero. It was an improvised program that ran off cameras embedded in the front and rear of the car and utilized facial recognition and sight line analysis to indicate how many people's eyes were on him. Once it reached zero, it would mean that he had outrun them completely, and it didn't take long. The PMCs were quick to give up once Kaname outpaced them.

"...It seems the AI won't pursue beyond a range of five hundred meters. That's not as far as I expected. I guess that's to stop people from luring the escort away with a decoy before attacking the main convoy in full force."

"That was close, My Lord! ...Those scoundrels very nearly turned my temple into Swiss cheese after I spent so much time making it spick and span!"

"That's not important. What about the GPS?"

"I won't forget you said that, My Lord! ...It seems the distraction worked as planned. Midori has successfully tossed that GPS tracker we rigged up with sticky tape onto the truck's blind spot atop the trailer. From now on, we shall be able to track its location."

"What about the PMCs?"

"They've lost track of us. And it does not seem like they noticed

Midori, either, so can we worry about my vehicle for a second?! My temple?!!"

Kaname had considered the possibility that they would need to take out some of the escort cars if they kept up pursuit, but luckily it hadn't come to that. Now he just had to drive ahead and wait for the mountain bikes to show up. However, as Midori rode alongside him, she kept looking back over her shoulder.

Midori: Are you sure we should be so far ahead? What if the Leviathans attack now? We won't be able to react in time!

Kaname: The convoy belongs to an AI company, remember? The PMCs protecting it are quite strong. I don't think they could take them on, even with #dracolord.err. We should focus on taking care of the traps blocking the road ahead.

Of course, they wouldn't be traps if they were just scattered across the road for all to see. The idea here wasn't to scare the convoy into stopping, but to take them out entirely. Thus, the traps would be hidden.

Kaname: Midori, cross over to the other side.

Midori: Why??? That's the fast lane.

Kaname: Stop asking questions and do it in the next five seconds, or you'll get caught in the explosion.

Midori: dont sen dan essay idiot!1

As the red leaf-patterned motorcycle frantically ducked behind the mint-green coupe, Tselika undid her seat belt and reclined her seat while Kaname pointed his short-range sniper rifle out her open window at a single plastic tank by the side of the road. Perhaps it had once been filled with water to dampen the force of a car crash. But when Kaname shot it, it exploded in a fiery blast, launching tiny metal pellets and screws in every direction.

"Trap destroyed. That's one down."

"Y-you c-c-c..."

"Whoa there, Tselika. Let's keep it PG, yeah? No four-letter words in my car, thank you very much."

"You complete and utter buffoon, My Lord! Did you hear that scratching sound just now? I can only imagine the damage you've done to my temple!"

Tselika reared back up, righting her seat, but Kaname ignored her.

Kaname: Midori, get behind the coupe.

Midori: Again?

Kaname: I want you on the right this time.

Midori: Whoa, did that explode?!

Kaname: There'll be more. Keep using the car as a shield.

"Listen to meee, My Lord! What was the point of bringing Midori along anyway?! We wouldn't need to keep putting my temple in danger if we didn't have to look after that flat-chested young brat!"

"We can't treat her like a sheltered princess. That's not what she wants. We need her out here so she can get the experience she needs to defend herself when the time comes. Heh. Taking back that stadium for the Umibe father and son is a nice tutorial quest for her. And we're going to get the list out of it, so we might as well lend her a hand."

"Oh, I see how it is! You're a lot nicer to that scrawny-ass schoolgirl than you are to me! …Are we going to have to talk about your fetishes, My Lord?!!"

By now, Tselika was clutching her horns in her hands and banging her head nonstop. She was really putting on a show, making her huge breasts bounce up and down.

Midori: How do you know where the traps are?

Kaname: They have a clear line of fire. There needs to be an open route from the trap to the target, whether that's for a missile, a blast wave, or any projectiles released from the blast. Luckily, since this is an asphalt road, we don't have to worry about buried land mines, so that only leaves trajectories coming down from above or in from the sides. They'll be camouflaging it, of course, leaving only a small opening. But that only makes it even more obvious. Take a look at that trash bag over there.

Out flew several bullets, along with a distinctive sound—Kaname's integrated silencer—and another trap was detonated in a safe and controlled manner. Kaname didn't even need to use the Lion's Nose for this.

Kaname: Sometimes, though, they'll hide the trap behind a thin wall and make it more powerful, to compensate. For those cases, I'm using Transmit... I don't really like using skills to make up for deficiencies in my shooting ability, but this time it's for minesweeping, so I'll just have to put up with it.

Midori: Transmit?

Kaname: X-ray vision, essentially. It lets me see through walls.

KRRRIII!!

Midori's motorcycle suddenly began to skid as the girl took her hands off the handlebars to cover her meager chest. Kaname sighed.

Kaname: Midori. Ride properly. You can try out bike tricks on your own time.

Midori: i;m not doing trikcs1! does that mean you can see through my um you know...?!

The blushing young schoolgirl was particularly defensive about her own body, it seemed. But did she really think that a rarity-eight skill could let him see through swimsuits? Kaname was getting tired of answering all her silly questions, so he let it go.

Transmit worked by picking up things like the extremely minute reflections off walls or trace amounts of light filtering through an open door. Then, it used these details to reconstruct an image of what lay beyond the door or around a corner. Thus, it wasn't true x-ray vision, and wouldn't allow him to see inside a closed box, for example.

"But, My Lord, there's always going to be a little bit of loose clothing around the hips and breast area for your prying eyes to enter. Especially with her size."

"Again, Tselika? We're not having this conversation, okay?"

"At least say something to ease my misgivings, you no-good flat chest lover!!"

Most bombs couldn't be detonated simply by shooting them, so this must have been a conscious choice on the part of the Leviathans. Most likely, it was so they could easily dispose of the unexploded ordnance afterward. If they just left live explosives lying around and some other Dealer got hurt, a fight would be guaranteed.

In any case, all Kaname had to do was deal with the mines, and the convoy would be safe. And to do that…

"Check the footage from our onboard cameras, Tselika. Can you perform an analysis?"

"I *suppose*, My Lord! Hmph! *Hmmph!!*"

Several windows appeared on the front windshield, careful not to obstruct Kaname's vision, compiling a profile of the traps they had encountered so far. Kaname's gut instinct had been right.

"I think I get the picture," he said.

Removing the mines was no big deal if Kaname knew what to look for. He could have little bright dots appear on his windshield to point out the hiding spots and fire bullets into the bushes by the side of the road without even having to check.

Hack, shoot, *boom*.

Picking a hiding spot was a behavior susceptible to individual quirks. Just like how you could look at someone's room and use it to analyze their psychology. Once you'd figured out someone's quirks, you could predict their next move.

"The H.A.S. skill, aka Hide And Seek, I presume?" asked Tselika.

"Yeah. It lets you look at the terrain and pick out the best hiding spots. It works by looking at dirt trails on the ground or worn-down railings to identify locations where people don't go. If we know they used that, it'll be a hell of a lot easier to find the mines."

Skills were a double-edged sword. If your opponent knew what you were using, they could find a way to turn it against you. They were predictable, unlike natural talents such as the Lion's Nose or Midori's flair for fashion.

"I was worried," said Kaname softly, "that they might have set multi-stage traps that trigger when they're set off erroneously, but it doesn't look like they went to that much trouble. We'll keep doing what we're doing, and in another fifteen minutes, the Martini AC convoy will enter

Amatsu Tunnel on its way to the center of town. After that, it'll be much harder for the Leviathans to act..."

But just as Kaname spoke, there was a flash in his rearview mirror.

Kaboom!!

An enormous, fiery explosion, somewhere on the horizon behind him.

"What the...? What's going on?"

The tires squealed as Kaname brought the mint-green coupe to a halt. Midori made a wide circle on her bike and rolled back up beside the car, knocking on the window with a gloved hand.

"That was an explosion!" she said. "It came from the convoy!"

"But there shouldn't..."

"We've lost our tracking device," said Tselika.

"Is this the power of #dracolord.err, my brother's Legacy...?" whispered Midori. "This is bad. If we don't get the special air-conditioning equipment, we'll never take back Leviathan Stadium!"

"..."

The PMCs commanded by AI companies were quite strong in terms of stats. Though they lacked skills, their base parameters far outclassed the abilities of a regular Dealer. They were more like killer robots in human guise. They were equipped with thick bulletproof armor and advanced weaponry, and their tactical coordination was on another level. Add to that the fact that they could call for reinforcements endlessly, and you had on your hands a nigh unstoppable force.

That was precisely why the Leviathans had littered the convoy's route with traps and had only brought out the minigun once confusion had broken out. That was the only reason their attacks had been successful. They couldn't begin the attack while they were still missing a vital piece of the puzzle.

Was #dracolord.err really such a game-breaking piece of equipment? Or had Kaname simply missed some of the traps?

Or...

"...No."

"My Lord?"

He threw the car into reverse. Giving Midori a few warning honks with the car's horn, he spun the mint-green coupe around, reversing 180 degrees around the twin-tailed girl's motorcycle. Then he stomped down on the gas pedal and sped off toward the distant explosion.

"Tselika. Do another online search for Martini AC! I want everything you can find on their insurance policies!!"

"I can try, My Lord, but I wouldn't exactly expect to find their contract agreements lying around on the open web!"

Midori: What's happening?

Kaname couldn't answer the girl's question.

As they approached the point of the explosion, the bitter taste of fumes particular to diesel fuel filled the car. In the ominous swirl of red and black light, they could see several burned-out steel frames—all that remained of an entire fleet of trucks. The custom air-conditioning equipment that was to be delivered to the new indoor stadium was completely destroyed.

Midori: The Leviathans are already gone. Hopefully, they didn't leave any snipers or bombs behind.

Kaname: I don't think they did.

Something was missing. The only wreckage left behind was from the trucks—the only smell was diesel. No gasoline. Not a trace of the black armored cars that ought to have been protecting the convoy.

"About your request, My Lord, it seems Martini AC has connections to Tokime Life. As I said, I wasn't able to find any details."

"That's good enough. And how many attacks have the Leviathans carried out on these convoys so far? The ones we know about, at least?"

"Eight, if the video and news sites are to be believed."

"And what actions did Martini AC take following the attacks? Did they make any changes to their transportation plans?"

"...Hmm?"

"It takes a lot of money to produce custom-made cooling equipment, and there's a time limit on Biondetta's construction plans. You'd think that after their convoy was attacked once, they'd beef up security or alter the route, right? A large helicopter carrying a shipping container via wires would do the trick. At an altitude of four thousand or so it would be well out of the reach of anything other than anti-aircraft guns, surface-to-air missiles, or fighter jets."

"There's…nothing like that, My Lord. Nothing at all."

"Even for an AI, that's odd. It implies Martini AC doesn't care about the attacks." Kaname tapped his finger impatiently on the steering wheel. "They get a massive insurance payout each time it happens, after all. Meanwhile, Biondetta Dome is desperate. They have to finish construction at all costs, and Martini AC is the only company that can do that. They can't break their contract. They may both be AI companies, but that doesn't mean they're on the same side. Their priorities are both to make money. For Martini AC, *that's* what takes priority. They'll help complete the dome if it means they turn a profit, but if a better opportunity comes along, they'll switch sides in a heartbeat."

"…I see, My Lord. I did notice that the convoys were being sent out at irregular intervals. And it seems they coincided with periods of poor financial performance. Martini AC would dispatch a convoy to be destroyed on purpose whenever they needed a little pick-me-up to reinvigorate their coffers."

"Even if we can't see the discussions they had behind closed doors, I'd bet on this being an agreement between Martini AC and the Leviathans. AI companies are programmed to maximize profit without caring about things like good and evil, and if Dealers know that, it's easy to interpose themselves somewhere and make a killing. They can get far more money raking in the insurance payments over and over again than they'd ever hope to see from a single sale. So why would they ever pay for a real escort or try to fight back? Dammit!"

"If we can't shake up the Leviathans…," said Tselika.

"We'll have to rethink. We need to bring them to their knees. Otherwise, we'll never see that list!!"

11

The monster-sized four-wheel-drive vehicle with wheels taller than a person sped across the wilderness. Was it a large buggy? Despite its massive size, it could only seat two people. It was completely impractical, more suited to performing tricks at the circus. Crossing her long legs as she reclined in the passenger seat, leaving the driving to her Magistellus, was a beautiful young lady. Her light pink hair was gathered in a curled ponytail, and she wore a white suit and pink pencil skirt. The girl posed and snapped a few selfies with her smartphone, a relatively useless device in a game where your Magistellus carried out transactions for you ten thousand times a second. She also wore a pair of smart glasses, another connected device but with a single, fatal flaw— it wasn't able to take selfies.

This was Strawberry Garter, current owner of the R league soccer team, the Leviathans.

"...Now *this* is good branding," she said.

The Leviathans' coaches and trainers were all similarly attractive women. After all, if two candidates have the same skills, then why not pick the one who stands out more? It's the same as with TV advertising. You only have a limited amount of screen time, so you had better give it to the person who could make the most of it. A Magistellus seemed like an obvious choice for this kind of role, but the fact was that real people always proved more popular.

Even in this age of completely CGI people, we're still living in a world that values "true" beauty.

She wasn't the type to upload selfies in the middle of a job, however. She was using an app that showed her all the hue, saturation, and brightness values in the pictures she took. To get the best photo time and time again, you had to take into account things like the location, the time of day, clothing, and makeup. Just looking up into the camera, pulling a duck face, and turning the contrast way up to knock out wrinkles and pores might get you a couple hundred likes, but it wasn't going to go viral.

Just like with physical skills and brainwork, practice made perfect. This went beyond whether an individual shot looked good, or whether it was decent enough to post. She sought to build up an awareness, an intuition, so that she was always ready to take the most stunning shot under whatever conditions might have arisen.

For Strawberry Garter, influence was everything.

And the best way to get everyone's attention was with sports. This was the sturdy foundation on which she would build her empire. She didn't need to make donations to charity and offer limp smiles to the camera. She didn't need to set up a glut of disorganized streaming channels. The best strategy was to start with an established genre, where most of the work had already been done for you. To tell the truth, she'd gotten a lot of good info from the strategy guides for soccer video games gathering dust in the corner of her room. She would manage her sports team as though it were a game within the game. She would buy up all the advertising slots of the secondary sponsors and take over a weak team, training up its players and recruiting new ones, coordinating with sponsor companies, haggling for broadcasting rights, and so on. *Money (Game) Master* was the perfect place for trying something bold that wouldn't be possible in real life.

This was a world where even one billboard on the field or in the bleachers was worth well over a million *snow*, and every last motion of each player was instantly captured by the media. Dealers flocked to where the money was, networking with the various AI companies, and perfecting the field-to-screen pipeline.

Strawberry Garter pointed her smartphone at her immaculately polished nails and began going through hand poses like a finger model.

And there's no sense in chasing after the big leagues if all you want is influence. Those in the S league want to be the very best, and they spend a fortune to make sure their team is performing at its peak. The higher you go, the more it costs. Here, at R league, is the optimal balance. That's what it's all about. There's no point in hiring the most beautiful woman in the world as your spokesperson if it's only going to bankrupt you. It's all about cost effectiveness.

She wasn't after popularity for her team but popularity for herself. In which case, there was no need to go any higher than the R league. She wasn't fighting for attention among the limited channels of antiquated television but for the ranks of social media, where the number of accounts was limitless.

Money (Game) Master was a game about making money, and there was more than one way to do it. She was tired of soullessly calculating the trends with mathematics and economics. It was simpler to start the trends you wanted and solidify them through your own efforts.

Information created wealth, and wealth bought information. In this day and age, only those who could start this cycle themselves and then hold on to it could be considered winners.

"Hmm."

Once her smartphone spat out the numbers she desired, Strawberry Garter turned, swinging her large pink ponytail, and looked out the window. Or perhaps she was merely gazing at her own reflection in the glass. She sighed, exhaling through her perfectly formed nose.

True beauty was created. At least, that was what Strawberry Garter believed. A face was just an assortment of parts, and human beings were the same. Unadorned, they were more boring than a passport photo. That was precisely why beauty had to be maintained. It required effort. The moment a person lost the desire to look beautiful, they became nothing more than a collection of parts.

"…"

To the bespectacled beauty in the suit and pencil skirt, nothing exemplified that idea more than mass media. It was a lost cause. Even knowing it was on the way out, it was unable to adapt, shackled by the corpses of television and newspapers. Its range was limited. Even though there were so many more ways to get into people's minds these days, they stuck stubbornly to talking heads speaking directly into the camera. They could have the most exciting news story in the world, and their boring delivery would assure no one paid any attention.

This was what *Money (Game) Master* was good for. If you were going to speak, it should be here. This was where you could really make waves.

Here, you could speak to the Dealers, who made the world turn with their virtual currency, *snow*.

What a world we live in, where I can go into a game just to play on my smartphone.

Her life hadn't always been so ruled by information, though. In the real world, she used to run a bento restaurant in the center of town. It was a family-owned business she had inherited from her parents, and while it was small, it had a long tradition. Every day she would get up early, stir the pots and do all the manual labor, and set the prices all by herself. After people complained she was old-fashioned, she had pushed herself to make a website, only for it to pull in a mere twenty visitors a month...

And then, as soon as a hamburger place opened across the street, the business sank.

That was the day she gave up on trying to make an honest living.

...I don't want to see another mystery meat patty ever again.

The day she shut down the business, some guy had appeared before her in a snooty, expensive suit, wringing his hands apologetically and yet still boasting that information was the be-all and end-all. She couldn't even remember who he was.

In that case, it was time to fight fire with fire. From the moment she first laid eyes on that moderately successful soccer team, something about it pissed her off. Boring faces, all of them. No effort whatsoever. When she humiliated the father and son before their lead AI sponsor and stole the team away, she had felt something slip out of place inside. But she hadn't felt guilty; she had felt free. Even though she had just used a game to tear apart a real family in real life.

It was too late. She had learned how good it felt to steal.

It seems just threatening them isn't enough to make them back off... In that case, let's throw some money around and stir up a new diet fad. Or perhaps I'll put out a trendy cookbook to encourage people to eat in and post photos of their creations instead of eating burgers, or run a sports-related exercise and healthy eating campaign... It doesn't really matter in the end, so long as it bankrupts the real-world restaurant and puts pressure on the whole corporate group. It's disgusting what you can do in this game. Information has far more power here than in the old-fashioned TV and newspapers of the real world.

A line of small pink speech bubbles appeared in the customized chat window in one corner of her front windshield.

Sister: Nice work.

Pipe Wrench: My hands are twitching. Perhaps I should sign up with one of those firing ranges and pay a monthly fee to shoot all I want.

Cumming: Stay calm, it's just for a few more months. There are penalties for ending a contract within two years, I hear, so perhaps it's best to bear with it for now.

Hattori: ...Hold on. We've received another request. Garter, check with Martini AC.

"?"

A strange feeling gripped her, like a needle skipping on a record. Strawberry Garter was an information queen. She didn't operate through TV channels and social networking sites that other people set up; she used the soccer team as her own personal billboard and microphone. That was why even this tiny feeling bothered her. She wanted to know everything when it came to the Leviathans' home turf.

"Marron, check the info."

"Y-yes, Miss Strawberry Garter," the Empusa at the large steering wheel replied nervously. She had short brown hair, a pair of drooping dog ears, and a tail that was curled down behind her.

Her response was quick.

"There's a report from Martini AC. Um, it says the Hurricane III is scheduled to be delivered to Biondetta Dome at two nineteen AM. It seems like they mean the custom air-conditioning equipment."

"Two nineteen AM?! That's not even seven minutes away! But we just destroyed the cargo moments ago!!"

"Eek! That's what it says, though! I've checked the whole message from start to finish for any kind of code or cipher, and I don't see anything!!"

"..."

Strawberry Garter grew quiet and listened to the words of her Magistellus, who was dressed in a pink bikini top and white pleated skirt like a team cheerleader, with a shoulder guard and a thick collar protecting her.

"Um, I'll decompose the font into numbers and see if I get anything. Oh, why don't I see if there's any metadata if I read it vertically or remove all the *e*'s..."

"Shut up for a second, Marron! You're wasting resources!"

There were pros and cons to Magistelli being such fast calculators. Not only could they read the full text of a message instantly, they could run all sorts of mysterious, unheard-of analyses on its contents. For a nervous, scared little puppy like Marron, this made it easy to get caught in an endless loop of possibilities. It was like carrying out a DDoS attack on your own computer.

But then what does this mean...?

Up until now, Martini AC had sent shipments containing the custom air conditioner equipment once or twice a month, at most. That was why Strawberry Garter and her team were able to plan and execute their raids so efficiently. Though the attacks were planned, they were by no means staged. Both parties had plausible deniability, there were no signed contracts, and they used real bombs and bullets. Of course, that meant that the risk of getting hit by a stray bullet and Falling was ever present. They needed time to prepare.

"What the hell is going on...?" she muttered.

Then suddenly, it dawned on her. The traps had all gone off ahead of the convoy. There had to be an enemy Dealer trying to stop the attack. She wasn't sure how they planned to profit from it, but they must want Biondetta Dome completed. Now that they had failed to stop the attack, what was their next move? How would they try to recover?

Strawberry Garter spun her phone in her hands and uncrossed and recrossed her long, stocking-covered legs, thinking. Then she held out her phone and took a selfie, noting that the gleam of intelligence afforded her by her smart glasses seemed to have faded somewhat. She had an ominous feeling, like she was about to suffer a big loss. It was imperative that she wipe this bit of darkness from her face, and she would spare no effort to do so.

There were things Strawberry Garter couldn't see from her gaudy pink monster vehicle, on the outskirts of town. What was happening in the city, for example? Martini AC itself wasn't in the city; it was a company located in the outer realms, but...

"Marron. Take another look into Martini AC."

"Wh-what am I looking for, exactly, ma'am?"

"Anything! Stock prices, financial performance, estimations, whatever! Just find out if there are any Dealers who have discovered their Achilles' heel!!"

12

What Kaname had done was very simple.

"Every time they run into financial trouble, Martini AC sends a convoy to get destroyed and replenishes their coffers with the insurance money... In which case, all we need to do is cause problems for Martini, and we can restart the quest as many times as we like."

Midori sighed atop her bright-red, autumn-leaf-patterned racing bike.

"I don't like it. It sounds ridiculous."

"You have any better ideas?"

"No. *Sigh.* I just didn't think we would have to go so big just to help out a couple of people..."

It seemed Midori had already forgotten the Legacy and the list they were after. The human suffering of the Umibe family had become her highest priority. Kaname, for his part, was okay with that.

However, Martini AC was an external company, existing only as data with no presence in the 3D-modeled world of Tokonatsu City. It was not like they could burst into their headquarters and start throwing punches. They needed a plan that could be executed in the city itself.

"Tselika. What are the temperature and humidity tonight in Tokonatsu City? The city center, in particular."

"...You may check that on your own smart watch, My Lord. It is thirty-four degrees Celsius and seventy percent. Another sweltering tropical night, thanks to the urban heat island effect and the squall we had in the evening..."

"Why do you sound so down?"

"Because this vehicle is nearly falling apart, My Lord! I spend every day waxing this beauty until it is squeaky clean, and just look at it now!! I'm going to have nightmares about this!!"

"What about the Martini AC support center?"

"I could scream in your face and your heart would not budge one millimeter, My Lord! Very well. Round-the-clock response. Something only an AI company could achieve."

"Then this should do it," Kaname said, and leaning against the door of the mint-green coupe, he pointed his short-range sniper rifle up toward the sky like a starter's pistol. All he had to do was pull the trigger.

Above him was a high-voltage power line supported by a row of steel pylons.

With a jolt of sparks, half of the skyline of the Tokonatsu City financial district fell into darkness. This wasn't like mischievously setting off the school fire alarm; if they were in the real world, this kind of outage would be all over the internet news. People would be up in arms. It was the sort of thing you could only get away with in the game.

Of course, it wasn't as if this was the sole source of power to the entire city, and many Dealers had their own backup generators for emergencies. The stock exchange would still be running, as well. However...

"It'll take them a while to realize why the power's out, or even just why the air conditioning stopped. The AC going down could be due to a tripped breaker, or faulty wiring, or the device itself could be broken. And on a hot night like this, getting that back online will be the top priority, not checking the news. How many Dealers do you think are going to call up the support center to get it working again?"

"How are they going to do that if the power's out?" Midori asked. "Did you leave the cell phone towers online?"

"Midori. Haven't you seen the discolored phone boxes scattered around town? I bet you thought they looked out of place in this day and age. But emergency landlines don't rely on power. They can be operated using just the energy in the phone signal itself."

Midori cocked her head, not quite understanding. She'd probably never had to use a rotary phone in her life.

"So what's going to happen? The support center gets overwhelmed and goes down, people get upset with the company, and they lose money?"

"In the real world, that wouldn't be nearly enough, but the Dealers here have no self-restraint. They think of money as a toy. I wouldn't be surprised if one of them tanked the company's value just out of spite. By the way, Midori, you know that people can buy and sell stocks over the phone, don't you?"

And however it happened, once Martini AC got wind of their poor business performance, they would send out another convoy, like clockwork.

"So we're trying the escort mission again? I know we've already cleared most of the traps, but what if the convoy fails again?"

"Oh, it will, if we leave the shipment to Martini. They don't even *want* to reach their destination," spat Kaname. "…That's why we're going to take the equipment off their hands, trailer and all, and deliver it to the Biondetta Dome ourselves. That should take care of this whole mess."

"Huh? Even with the PMCs protecting them…? They might fight back for real if we attack them instead of the Leviathans. I mean, you saw how they chased us off when we tried to stick that GPS tracker on them!"

"Tselika. You don't mind if the car takes some more damage, do you? It's already beaten up pretty bad, so what's a few more scratches?"

"Gggbrrgh?!" Bu…bu… Who the hell do you think is responsible for that, My Lord…?!! This is my darling temple, my pride and joy! How dare you say, 'Oh, just because she's not a virgin anymore, it doesn't matter'!!"

Leaving that aside…

Midori cocked her head once more atop her motorcycle.

"I know we have to do something about the AIs helping the corrupt soccer team…but we can't really hope to win against the PMCs, can we? I mean, they're like an army of killer robots."

"Ordinarily, no," Kaname replied. "Midori. Call out your Magistellus, Meiki. You're going to need an extra set of hands for this."

"What? What are we doing, exactly?"

In place of an answer, Kaname walked around to the back of the car, placed his hand on the trunk, and threw it open.

"…It's time for us to unleash our secret weapons as well. The monster shotgun, #tempest.err, and the infinite-range anti-materiel rifle, #fireline.err. Two of Takamasa's Legacies should be more than enough."

For a while, the only sound that could be heard in the car was the screeching of its tires.

With the danger now past, the pain from the Lion's Nose gradually receded. The gauge on the front windshield displaying the AI units' focus started counting down from thirty, until finally the whole window disappeared. Zero people watching. In other words, total victory. It was a rare occurrence, even in a game like *Money (Game) Master*, where you could get away with anything. The group of PMCs had been totally eliminated, and they were now in the lull before the next wave showed up.

"Here. The barrel's still hot, so don't burn yourself."

Kaname opened the driver's seat door and tossed #tempest.err, the shotgun resembling a revolver-style grenade launcher, to the pit babe sitting inside. He spoke without turning to face her.

"Tselika. Hold on to the Legacy for me. I'm leaving you in charge of the car, too."

"Hmph, you cheating swine, My Lord! You already have someone beautiful and charming like me, *grumble, grumble...* You're hopeless, My Lord! Utterly hopeless! It doesn't matter whose seat you place your pretty little butt on, is that it?! Any steering wheel will do?!! Well, see if I care! Maybe I'll go and mess up your investment in that underground construction project, hmm?"

"Tselika?"

"Can it, My Lord! You reckless driver!! You're leaving the driving to *me* next time, you hear?!" yelled Tselika, her tail pointed bolt upright.

Kaname felt her complaint was a little off base, but he ignored it and turned to face the large semitruck stopped nearby. Even after the shooting had stopped, he kept up his guard as he approached the disabled vehicle. This was basic situational awareness in shooting games. The ground felt soft beneath his feet, like stepping on a waterbed, perhaps due to that sticky material that soaked up all the moisture. At last, Kaname reached the driver's side door and opened it. It was filled, not with buckshot, but with .45-caliber bullet holes. Lifting out the AI driver's body and tossing it by the roadside, Kaname picked up the keys and walked around to the back. There, he threw open the double doors at the rear of the trailer.

There was the air conditioner. Actually, it looked more like a jumbo jet engine with the outer plating removed, like a mass of giant silver turbines. Obviously, no common AC unit would be able to structurally support the nearly 100 meters of dome roof.

"Right."

"Everything okay?"

Midori cruised over, her engine growling. The girl in the frilly gothic-lolita bikini was sitting in the driver's saddle as usual, but seated behind her this time was a beautiful woman in a short-cut red *cheongsam*.

Her black, shoulder-length hair gently parted around the two horns atop her head, and stuck to the center of her brow was a paper talisman. It was Midori's Magistellus, Meiki. The emotionless girl was in charge of the anti-materiel rifle, #fireline.err, which was too large to be held and instead was strapped to her shoulder. Midori had immediately sought to try out this arrangement upon learning that her Magistellus could be trusted with a gun.

"Midori," said Kaname, swinging the trailer's rear doors closed again. "I'm going to be dragging this trailer to the Biondetta Dome construction site by myself. You need to stay away from me, okay?"

"Hey! Then what do I do?!"

"We're due for a storm of bullets starting any moment now. To be honest, I can't keep you safe when you're wandering around on that bike with no armor. I know you just want to help, but we can't afford to have you Fall here."

"Yeah, but aren't those AI-controlled PMCs going to be doing their best to get this stuff back? There's going to be tons of those really strong, fast bulletproof cars! Maybe even attack helicopters or drones!"

"I know. They're going to send in the cavalry, so I want you to stay as far away as you can. Find a safe zone, like a parking garage or a gas station, and support us from there. Ignore the PMCs. They're just going to keep sending reinforcements forever. Focus on the human opponents, the Leviathans."

"...And then we'll be able to buy back that boy's future, right?"

"Without a doubt," Kaname replied, no hesitation in his voice.

Midori breathed a sigh of relief, but before long a thought occurred to her, and her anxiety came right back.

"But then, what about you?! You're going up against the Leviathans and the PMCs at the same time! They'll make you into swiss cheese!"

"I'm hoping they'll take each other out. That's why I'm dangling this carrot on a stick in front of their noses. But don't worry about me. Big trailers like this can take a beating. The only things stronger are tanks and armored cars. A few bullets aren't going to hurt me."

"..."

Midori Hekireki, her tiny bottom perched atop her motorcycle, seemed to have something to say about that. No doubt she was itching to point out that, for all its supposed impregnability, Kaname himself had managed to run it off the road without too much effort. That was partly due to the Legacy, of course, but the Leviathans also had one of those—the minigun, #dracolord.err. It went without saying, but nothing was ever certain in *Money (Game) Master*. Even the legendary Takamasa had Fallen, after all, protecting Kaname's sister from the bullets of angry Dealers.

"Midori."

"Okay! …I get it. I'm still just a beginner at this game. There's no point in arguing with you because you're always right. I'm the one who wanted to help out the Umibe family in the first place, so I can't turn around and tell you not to fight…"

But.

Kaname was no idiot, and he wasn't blind to Midori's feelings. It wasn't about who was right or who was wrong, who had more experience or who was better at calculations or any of that. It was human nature to be uneasy. More than that, Midori was the kind of girl who worried about others. Even though right now, she would have been perfectly justified in criticizing him instead. What was she supposed to do if he died on a reckless suicide mission?

Kaname smiled fondly. She was cut from the same cloth as Takamasa, no doubt about it. She had something no amount of training or experience could ever give her. Memory and reflexes could be augmented whenever you liked by switching out your equipment—that wasn't real talent. In this virtual world, where everything else could be rewritten, it was only your inner nature that could never be altered or traded. Midori…and Takamasa, too. Their natures were pure and beautiful. So much so that Kaname felt it was too dangerous to leave them all alone in this game.

The boy silently made up his mind. He had to protect that purity. He couldn't stand by and watch while immoral Dealers laid their hands all over Takamasa's Legacy, and neither could he let Midori be swallowed up by the pit of depravity that was *Money (Game) Master*.

He was through watching Midori and her brother holding back their tears and anger. There was no need to force anything on Midori. All he had to do was decide on a course of action and execute it. No need to show off.

"Let's go."

"…"

"We're going to get this shipment to Biondetta Dome and put pressure on the Leviathans. For me, this is about making them hand over Takamasa's personal possessions. For you, it's about returning that stadium to its original owners… And if there really is a list of the Legacies among Takamasa's papers, then we'll be one step closer to our goal. But it's not a treasure map, it's a piece of Takamasa's soul that he left behind. I can't stand idly by while a bunch of strangers abuse it to their advantage. And if we can reduce people's suffering, even just a little…"

"No, not just a little," Midori added suddenly. To her, this wasn't about experience or ability at all. "We have to save everybody. I don't want a single person to have to suffer because of my brother's Legacies ever again."

"That's what I like to hear," said Kaname with a grin. As someone fighting to protect Midori and pay back Takamasa, it pleased him to hear her say those words.

Then, at last, they were ready to move out.

"Remember to stick to support. Don't come near the truck."

"I get it already! Geez!"

"This is the best way to hit the Leviathans where it hurts. If we're going to get this team and stadium back to its old owners, I'll need your help."

"That's my line. Make sure you don't do anything crazy out there, either, okay?"

Kaname hopped up into the seat of the cabin and began driving away, distancing himself from the mint-green coupe and the red-leaved racing bike.

...Now then.

There weren't going to be any fancy tricks on Kaname's end. Compared to his two-seater sports car, the driver's seat of this vehicle was much higher. The massive steering wheel looked a bit difficult to get used to, but Kaname grabbed it with both hands, like he was holding a hula hoop, and gently merged onto the main road like a needle settling into the groove on a record. He was headed directly toward the center of the peninsula financial district. He fought with the stiff gear stick and clutch pedal, pushing the truck into high gear, and the vehicle responded immediately. The rearview mirror was useless with the semitrailer behind him, but a portion of the front windshield was devoted to showing a live feed from the cameras at the back of the vehicle. There, he could see several flashes of light behind him. Single headlights. Bikes.

Guess they don't feel the need to stay hidden at this point.

Kaname felt a familiar tingling sensation. The Lion's Nose.

The Dealer smiled, sensing his prey.

A small messenger window appeared in one corner of the front windshield, indicating a chat request. Perhaps because the vehicles operated off their internal batteries, this system didn't seem to be affected by the power cut. The cab window was so large, it took Kaname a moment to notice it.

Strawberry Garter: Do you know who you're picking a fight with? I hope you've calculated the risks and returns.

PMC Truck 01: Hey, I thought you wanted to avoid leaving evidence of your involvement with Martini. Are you sure you should be messaging me like this?

After hitting send and seeing his reply, Kaname frowned in confusion. Then, he remembered he was replying from a stolen vehicle. Oh well. It was only for one night. He couldn't be bothered logging in again just to fix the name.

Strawberry Garter: I'm guessing you're a human Dealer, then.

PMC Truck 01: I wasn't really trying to hide it.

Strawberry Garter: It doesn't matter. The Leviathans will kill you in five minutes flat.

PMC Truck 01: Just try it if you can... And that's not your team name to use, by the way.

Strawberry Garter: You think you're invincible just because you're in a tough vehicle, is that it? You've got no decoys, no armed escort. We, on the other hand, have all sorts of off-roading skills. We don't even need to get close to you, while you're stuck to that one straight road. We can fill anything full of holes at a distance of 600 to 2,000 meters with our minigun and assault rifle combination. If you still want to Fall and land yourself in debt hell, though, feel free.

PMC Truck 01: It seems like you're enjoying the game, so I won't spoil the surprise. Just get over here and you'll see what I mean.

At that moment, the cluster of headlights split into two groups, moving left and right to surround the truck like a swarm of killer bees following the orders of their queen. Just as Strawberry Garter had said, they drove cleanly over the bumpy wasteland, trampling flower patches and moving to take the truck out safely from long range.

Strawberry Garter: A meaningless Fall. Enjoy licking the dirt off the boots of AI companies for eternity.

PMC Truck 01: We'll see about that.

And then it happened.

KTHOOOOM!!

The loud, booming sound that rocked the plains was neither from the truck's engine nor the mountain bikes' assault rifles.

Strawberry Garter: What was that?

PMC Truck 01: Figure it out yourself.

Strawberry Garter: It wasn't an anti-materiel round. It wasn't a grenade or rocket, either. It was more of a rumble, like a bunker buster going off underground!

PMC Truck 01: You've got your Magistellus, haven't you? I'm not trying to hide anything from you. Have her tell you where it came from, then you'll understand.

The silence that followed lasted only five seconds. That was all it took for a Magistellus to run tens of thousands of autonomous calculations.

The enormous shadow of a nearby pumping jack drifted across the ground, like the silhouette of a giant's seesaw.

Strawberry Garter: The oil wells have been ordered to increase production? It says there's a glut of new buyers!

PMC Truck 01: Oh, you figured it out.

Strawberry Garter: So your aim is to induce soil liquefaction and make the ground shake?!!

The battered coupe didn't have much durability left, and the motorcycle barely had any to begin with. There was no way Tselika and Midori could survive a sustained firefight. So Kaname had asked them to head up the main road ahead of him and seek refuge at a large service station along the way. In the meantime, they would be conducting high-value trades via the telephone booth there. Tselika would be the one spearheading these efforts, but it would be a good learning opportunity for Midori, as well.

PMC Truck 01: Don't forget that the center of town is still without power. When power goes out, the price of alternative energy reserves, like gasoline or natural gas, will spike ever so slightly. The AI companies are always prepared to kick into action at times like this. It's almost a reflex. You barely have to do anything. Just invest a little capital, and they're easily convinced it'll pay off.

The tremors in the earth stirred up the water in the soil, causing the ground to turn soft and liquefy. That would make it difficult to ride a motorcycle, especially if you weren't using the asphalt road.

A gurgling noise from down below heralded an unnatural quaking of the earth. However...

Strawberry Garter: Did you think you had us?

It wasn't enough. The chaos had bought him a few moments, but Amatsu Tunnel was still several kilometers off. If Kaname didn't make it there, the minigun Legacy would tear him apart, assuming the assault rifles didn't get to him first. If they fired their long-range weaponry at him while he was confined to the main road, there would be no way for Kaname to fight back.

Strawberry Garter: We're fully prepared for bad riding conditions. Our riders are trained in acrobatics, and we have plenty of skills to help us drive off-road. One little earthquake isn't going to throw us off the hunt!

PMC Truck 01: I didn't think it would. I've got something else to take care of you corrupt Dealers with nothing better to do than fight over dirty money.

Kaname remained unshaken, even as the swarm of killer bees leveled their weapons. In fact, it was better for him the farther they were from the asphalt road.

PMC Truck 01: Have you already forgotten what I did to shake up Martini AC? I cut the cables of a high-voltage power line. Power outages in the city don't last too long, though. I'd imagine they'll be getting their electricity back right about now.

Strawberry Garter was silent. Or perhaps she was frantically communicating on another channel.

Midori and Tselika had been told to *seek refuge* at the service station.

PMC Truck 01: So we've got dangling power lines and a bubbling wetland. What do you think's going to happen when the power companies try to force electricity through those cables again? I wouldn't want to be out on an unprotected bike, that's for sure.

BZZZZAPPP!!!

A blue-white spark enveloped the landscape, just as the semitrailer zipped into Amatsu Tunnel and Kaname's world was enveloped in evenly spaced orange lighting. No gunfire had reached him during the last few kilometers, perhaps owing to all the chaos.

PMC Truck 01: The farmland around here was made arable by human intervention. I think there's some sort of sticky natto-like material in the soil that mixes with the spring water and alters the constitution of the liquid. Because of that, the high-voltage current can't go deep into the earth. With nowhere else to go, it spreads out across the entire surface.

The semicircular tunnel was one-way only, but equipped with three lanes—more than enough room for a car chase.

PMC Truck 01: Seems like that took out about half of them. I guess they learned all those circus tricks for nothing.

Strawberry Garter: I'm going to murder you.

PMC Truck 01: What were you doing before? You've been taking a peek at a part of my friend's soul and swinging around his toys as if they're yours. On top of that, you used them to steal away a stadium from an innocent family, just so you could sate your own greed. I've been trying to kill you all along, so try to keep up.

A feeling like static electricity welled up in Kaname's nose, and the roar of engines filled the tunnel, higher in pitch than that of Kaname's truck. At last, the mountain bikes were coming in for a close-range fight. They were now at a disadvantage, but it was a lot better than waiting for Kaname to reach the center of town.

It goes without saying, but lightweight mountain bikes are nothing to a twenty-ton truck. If Kaname so much as nudged them with the tip of the trailer, they'd be eating asphalt. Kaname wasn't worried about the bikes themselves but about the Magistelli in the back seats with their rifles.

Normal assault rifles won't be able to damage a reinforced trailer. The Magistelli share skills with their masters, so which stats are they raising...?

The trailer's weight came with a downside, however. It was difficult for Kaname to slam into the bikes without them dodging out of the way. Furthermore, he was outnumbered. If he tried to pin one down, the others could sneak around and outflank him, and even if Kaname swung the steering wheel back, the vehicle wouldn't respond in time.

The truck may have been large, but all Kaname could really do was hurl himself at a single target and hope for the best.

At the very least, Kaname was up against assault rifles, and at worst, the Legacy. If an attack came from the front or the sides of the cabin, the doors and windows would do little to protect him. Kaname couldn't handle Short Spear while driving the heavy vehicle, either; the steering wheel was far too big to maneuver with only one hand. If any of them managed to get around to the front of the vehicle, it'd be game over.

Kaname had taken all of that into account. He had considered the risk and determined it to be acceptable.

"…This is where the real fight begins."

13

Their delicately balanced system had all come crashing down. Now, the Leviathans were fighting for their lives. The truck ahead of them weaved slowly left and right, and if they so much as grazed it, they'd Fall.

Striker 1: You've gotta be kidding me. That little battle of wits took out half our men. Why can't you just take the L instead of sending us little people to our deaths?!

Hattori: There can be no retreat. If we fail this mission we set for ourselves, then we lose the fort. You've gorged yourself on easy money, and now it's time to work for it again.

Lollipop: Then I'll let you play the decoy, big bro. Go work your butt off trying to impress the old hag!

The multicolored mountain bikes chased after the huge mass of steel, their engines roaring. There was no way the driver would be able to fire back at them with so many blind spots. That meant the only weapon at the enemy Dealer's disposal was the vehicle he had hijacked.

They had several off-road skills going for them. Plus, they had shored those up with Anti-Vehicle, increasing damage dealt to vehicles. While the humans were only steering their motorcycles, the Magistelli behind them shared their skills, and so it was a good idea to add in some to help them out as well.

Hattori: Let's begin. I'll take the left, while you two circle around to the right. Try to get to the driver's door and go for a critical hit.

Striker 1: You're crazy! Are you a masochist or something?!

Lollipop: ...Oh, big bro, you know online relationships are nothing but suffering, right? Anyway, I'm in.

One of the two-seater off-road bikes broke from the group and moved to the left of the truck. His teammates, still cursing, were forced to make the most of the opportunity. The bikes closed in, their human Dealers at the handlebars and their demon partners holding the guns. Left and right. No matter which way the truck swerved, it couldn't take them all out at once. Whether the driver took the bait or not, someone would be able to make it to the front and fill the cabin full of lead.

Striker 1 pushed his lightweight bike up the orange-lit road into the gap between the steel trailer and the wall, quickly arriving level with the driver's door, close enough to reach out and grab the handle. Before the enemy Dealer could spin the wheel around, he ordered the olive-skinned mummy girl behind him to fire.

"Bustier! Fill him full of holes!!"

First, a single shot to the driver's side door. Anti-Vehicle worked by subtly adjusting the aim, ensuring that all later shots hit the same point, compounding the damage and punching through a steel door in no time at all. This was the same principle by which a minigun achieved its fearsome penetrative power. Like a true team, everything connected back to the vicious #dracolord.err wielded by their boss, Strawberry Garter.

Sparks flew as lead bullets streamed into the metal door, shattering the tempered glass window. Striker 1 was showered in broken glass and bits of metal.

"Whoa?!!"

"Everything is fine. Please concentrate on driving. You could stand to gain a few more points in courage, My Darling."

The door was covered in holes. No matter how they contorted their body, it was impossible for anyone on the other side to have avoided the destruction.

However.

"Wha—?"

The mangled door broke off and was quickly left behind on the pavement. Inside the open cabin was an empty seat. The stuffing had sprung out from tears in the synthetic leather, but that was it. No sign of the blood and guts and dismembered body parts that ought to have filled the cabin.

The driver had disappeared.

Where had he gone?!

Dammit—!

Striker 1 looked up, suddenly regretting allowing his Magistellus to empty the entire magazine into the truck's cabin.

Kaname Suou.

He was there, up on the roof. Perhaps he had used Acrobat, which boosted the three semicircular canals of the inner ear, or Grip, to increase grip strength. Either way, he had managed to jam a bar through the steering wheel, locking it in place and jamming down the gas pedal. And now he stood atop the vehicle, a short-range sniper rifle in his free hands. Striker 1 stared down the barrel of the integrated silencer, that black hole a harbinger of his imminent death.

Klink! Klink!

Two shots, just to be sure.

The mountain bike collapsed and skidded off the road, but Kaname didn't even wait for it to disappear out of sight. His necktie flapping in the wind, he hopped off the roof of the cabin, onto the large trailer behind it.

He wasn't worried about the Leviathans, still laboring under the illusion they could win if only they dodged the truck's flailing for long enough. They were like primitive cavemen prodding their spears at a modern-day tank.

Two shots to the left, one to the right.

Is that it?

He felt the danger fade, and the tingling of his Lion's Nose subsided.

Kaname had a few skills to increase his defenses and help manage stress, but nothing that would interfere with his driving or shooting abilities. Rather than have Auto-Aim realign his shooting hand against his will, Kaname would much rather have the ability to shoot straight on his own.

The enemy, on the other hand, was using Anti-Vehicle. A perfectly valid choice when going up against a large truck, but while in use, it forced subsequent bullets to hit the same mark as the first. If Kaname jumped out of his seat and all over the place, they would have to disable and re-enable the skill just to be able to fire at him, and that took time. For a practiced individual, that time might be less than one second, but that was more than enough. Even one ten-thousandth of a second made all the difference in the trading world. To skilled Dealers, one second was the difference between life and death.

...It's easy to think of skills as being special powers the game world lets you use, but if you become over-reliant on them, your own ability suffers. You become stale and predictable, just like these guys.

It was a balancing act. It was smart to use every tool at your disposal, but you had to be able to function without them, too.

Kaname began headshotting the riders one after the other, their bikes crashing to the ground and skidding away. When at last the Magistelli raised their rifles to fire back, Kaname simply fell prone. Since his enemy was below him, he could use the reinforced trailer as a shield.

The Leviathans' attack squad was originally made up of eleven vehicles: the ten off-road motorcycles and the single command buggy. The earlier electric shock had taken out half of them, and Kaname's shooting just now had dealt with four more.

A human who Fell was forcibly logged out for twenty-four hours. In that time, the other Dealers would make mincemeat out of their finances, dragging them down into debt hell. Kaname wouldn't have to worry about them again. Magistelli, on the other hand, would freeze in place, becoming Downed for a short period. Precisely how long depended on the severity of the wound, but it capped at one hour. Normally, he might be inclined to restrain them with manacles or sticky tape before they woke back up, but at this speed, Kaname would be miles away by then, so they wouldn't be a problem either way.

Which only left…

"One more bike."

He didn't need to waste any more bullets. Still lying down, Kaname unclipped his empty magazine and tossed it into the road. The remaining bike probably hit it and skidded out. The sound of an explosion ripped through the air.

Then, he felt it again—the Lion's Nose. Not from the bikes this time, but from the truck itself. Kaname had rigged the vehicle to drive in a straight line, but the tunnel itself was not necessarily as straight as a runway. So before it could collide with some slight curve, Kaname utilized his Acrobat and Grip skills to safely return to the cabin. The door had been wrenched off, loose cotton was springing from the seats, and the windshield had been cracked, disabling the display. All of the support functionality had switched to the small, rarely used GPS screen.

Strawberry Garter: It's not over yet. We still have the Legacy.

PMC Truck 01: I'm on a smaller screen right now, so try not to fill it with your pointless chatter.

Strawberry Garter: You will die by our hand. By the Legacy, #dracolord.err! I guarantee it!!

PMC Truck 01: Is that right? I guess you must be new. There are no guarantees in Money (Game) Master. Anyway, it's time to end this. Returning the Leviathans to their rightful owner can come later.

That wasn't necessarily what Kaname truly thought, but he knew not to underestimate the importance of psychological warfare in a PvP match. Though presumably, someone accustomed to hecklers at sports games already knew that. Kaname sighed.

The growl of an engine, deeper than that of the bikes, approached from behind him, but Kaname didn't have time to worry about that.

Because up ahead, at the Amatsu Tunnel's exit, was a line of black armored cars, blocking the road.

"I knew you'd circle around and ambush me, you Martini AC lapdogs!!"

There was an almighty *krranggg!!!!!!* as the twenty-ton truck barreled straight through the armored blockade.

Outside the tunnel, a flood of light greeted him. With power already restored, the streetlamps flooded the road with light. The tangled mess of streets and overpasses weaved between towering skyscrapers that pierced the clouds. It was a melting pot of cultures, where people could be found from all walks of life, from billionaires who ran whole countries with a flick of their wrist, to beautiful women who came seeking luxury and ended up living in cardboard boxes, to idols beloved throughout the country, concealing their identity in order to enjoy a life of loose morals.

Kaname had reached the heart of the peninsula district, the main financial district of Tokonatsu city.

Realizing this, one of the black armored cars rammed itself directly into the side of the trailer. That wasn't enough to run the twenty-ton truck off the road, but it was enough to tell Kaname that the driver had no fear. No, in fact, they had no feelings at all beyond the success of the mission. It was the kind of action only an AI-controlled PMC would ever take.

There were still many civilian cars on the road. In fact, Kaname just barely avoided running over a brunette in a wide-brimmed witch hat and school swimsuit, who was riding a collapsible electric scooter—a high-ranking Dealer called Smash Daughter, he recalled. She turned and stuck up her middle finger, the sports towel around her shoulders waving behind her like a cape. Kaname was shocked she had somehow avoided being flattened by one of the PMC vehicles. It was a little frightening, actually.

"You ****ing ****! I'll stick my **** so far up your **** you'll be ****ing out your ****!!"

Some of the words that had come out of her mouth were way too advanced for a schoolgirl. Then again, nothing was as it seemed in *Money (Game) Master*. The girl was an expert in nonlethal stun equipment, and it was a bad idea to piss her off. Kaname would have preferred not to get on her bad side...

Then it happened.

The Lion's Nose began tingling like mad as a series of explosions sounded behind him. But the word "explosion" was a pale descriptor for the ferocious might with which the so-called bulletproof cars were being blown up and flung aside like wads of paper by a stream of rapid-fire bullets. The 6,000–7,000 RPM barrage of a minigun.

At last, Kaname's true enemy appeared in his rear-facing cameras. A massive buggy painted bright pink, its size entirely unsuited to these urban streets. While it had four wheels and a body, it looked unlike any other car Kaname had ever seen. The tires themselves were taller than he was, and poised atop its suspension like pillars of steel, the cab came up even higher than Kaname's truck.

Strawberry Garter: It's just one problem after another!

PMC Trailer 01: If you're going to attack me, you'd better do it now. This semi's not going to fall to a bunch of shiny black beetles. If you don't hurry, I'm going to make it to Biondetta Dome.

Strawberry Garter: You motherfucker!!

PMC Trailer 01: What an odd thing for a young lady to say. Could it be that you're an old man in the real world?

Corporate PMCs had different ranks, and those assigned to protect land were the highest. Strawberry Garter knew this, and that was why the Leviathans had not attacked the construction site directly. That place was an impregnable fortress. There would be a similar force defending the Leviathan Stadium as well, but they were under the direct control of the AI companies and thus couldn't be ordered to attack an enemy base. They knew the power of such a force but were unable to put it to use.

At last, the true three-way battle was about to begin.

If this truck had that PMC attention meter, it would probably be reading about a hundred right now. But even without it, Kaname could read the mechanical minds of the unfeeling killing machines with nothing more than his nose.

Upon realizing they were under attack, the Martini AC PMCs pointed their rifles out the windows of their bulletproof cars, only for Strawberry Garter's minigun to mow them all down. Any she missed swiftly disappeared beneath the monster truck's massive wheels, crushed flat. As explosions lit up the night behind her, the chronic vloggers in the crowd swarmed toward the action, getting in their tiny go-karts modded for maneuverability and weaving across the road, searching for the best angle.

As far as Kaname was concerned, it was their own funeral. His defense wasn't much better than theirs, now that he was down a door and windshield to hide behind. He couldn't waste effort trying to protect idiots with suicidal tendencies.

"You want views, huh? I'll give you some views!!"

Kaname swerved the massive truck into a PMC armored car that was coming upon his side, ramming it off the road and into a nearby water fountain. Then he slammed his foot on the gas pedal and sped off.

He could see the construction site in the distance.

However...

Strawberry Garter: The AI are just here to get things started. Humans will always be the ones to strike the finishing blow.

"Rghh."

Strawberry Garter: Aim. I'm going to blow you off the face of the earth, you puny Dealer!!

It wouldn't matter how many centimeters of steel Kaname was behind if the minigun set its sights on him, but he wasn't as worried about that as he was about the cargo in the back. If that took a hit, the whole plan to put pressure on the Leviathans would be done for. He'd never get his hands on Takamasa's papers, and the search for the Legacies would hit a brick wall. Not to mention, he'd be breaking his promise with Midori to save the Umibe family.

So.

It was time to make a decision.

Just as the rapid-fire boom of the minigun tore up the air behind him...

Kaname clenched his teeth and spun the wheel with all his might, guided by the buzzing sensation of the Lion's Nose.

The trailer's unstoppable momentum brought it around and the tires skidded, one wheel lifting off the road entirely. Its massive weight then seesawed the cabin up into the air.

Kaname had completely lost control of the vehicle.

But that was all part of the plan.

Once #dracolord.err's rain of lead severed the coupler between the tractor and the trailer...

The trailer, free of its excess weight, flew down the road. Metal scraped against asphalt, kicking up sparks like the tail of a comet, flattening palm trees alongside the road as it plunged through the stainless steel fence surrounding the building site.

Yes, right into the hands of the Biondetta Dome construction team.

Strawberry Garter: What?!

PMC Truck 01: Mission complete.

Kaname slammed on the brakes as hard as he could, and with the screech of burning rubber, the tractor's mangled rear end swung around and slammed directly into the oversized tires of Strawberry Garter's pursuing buggy.

14

The truck was missing its driver's side door and windshield. And obviously, Kaname wasn't wearing his seat belt.

"Grhh…"

As a result, Kaname was thrown clear of the collision. He saw the world rotate ninety degrees, and felt the burn of the road against his cheek. The smell of burning diesel was everywhere, but Kaname's right hand still gripped Short Spear, like it had a mind of its own.

The threat of death was ever present. That was one of this world's rules. Even Criminal AO hadn't been immune.

Kaname undid his necktie and changed it for another. The new one looked exactly the same, but it had a different skill. These were the pains Kaname endured so that his skill set couldn't be identified from appearance alone. Of course, he also had to make sure he didn't get them mixed up himself. If he put all his ties in the washing machine at once, he'd be screwed.

Reduce Pain. Rarity ten, the max. A skill so powerful, there were bidding wars over it. As the name suggested, it halved the amount of pain felt by imposing an upper amplitude limit to pain signals traveling through the body.

Being able to turn pain on and off like spinning a dial was certainly useful, but Kaname wasn't sure whether to feel grateful or a little afraid. Devils ran this game, and who knew where they hid their traps. Kaname was well aware that he had already begun to take effects in the game for granted.

But this wasn't over yet. Even though he had successfully delivered the specialized air-conditioning equipment to Biondetta Dome, he still had to settle things with the enemy Dealer.

The pain in his Lion's Nose was explosive. From the corner of his eye, he caught a figure stirring. Kaname recognized her at once from her oversized ponytail.

Strawberry Garter. The Dealer who had stolen one of Takamsa's Legacies. With one slender arm, the bespectacled beauty wielded

#dracolord.err, the multi-barreled minigun that was lighter than a feather. In her other, she held the weapon's box magazine, connected to the gun via a belt-shaped tube, and equally weightless, yet so large that the Dealer herself could have curled up inside it if she wanted.

Of course, since Kaname didn't have Midori's talent, he couldn't deduce her skills from her outfit. But right now he had bigger problems.

Shit!!

The sounds of the individual bullets were imperceptible. It was just one long stream of noise, like a drill. The 7,000 RPM barrage of bullets, each as thick as Kaname's thumb, tore through the road and bulletproof cars. It was an engine of destruction. Even if Kaname were to duck for cover, it would be like hiding behind wet paper.

And yet the Dealer boy survived, because...

"Tch! The parking meter!!" Strawberry Garter roared, a fierce outburst quite unbefitting a bespectacled intellectual.

Kaname's tractor had managed to come to rest in a public parking spot. And vehicles properly parked were immune to stealing and destruction. The Legacy could turn armored cars and attack helicopters into scrap, but it couldn't lay a scratch on the barrier of light that protected the parking meter. It was the ultimate shield.

But Kaname didn't have time to enjoy the look on Strawberry Garter's face. The Legacy was so powerful, it could change the rules of the battlefield. It was a cut above what even the rarest skills were capable of.

"Grhh!!"

Kaname fired Short Spear at the dog-eared Magistellus who had rushed around to flush him out. His silent .45-caliber bullet pierced her heart, and the bikinied Empusa fell to the ground, dropping the sawn-off shotgun in her hands. Kaname was far from relieved, however.

There's no point in taking out that armored cheerleader when she's just going to revive within the hour. Now I've just given up information without gaining anything in return.

Magistelli shared skills with their Dealer. By observing the dog-eared

Empusa's gestures, Kaname could have inferred some of Strawberry Garter's movements. Instead, he had only told her about his own.

Kaname ducked for cover behind a nearby sports car. It was similarly parked, so of course he couldn't steal it. But looking around, he could see other cars that were not properly parked, spared from destruction by the same shield as he was.

The gunfire had stopped now. Strawberry Garter had probably realized she wasn't going to get anywhere by firing wildly. Miniguns were powerful, but they were infamous for eating through ammunition like nobody's business. Being conscious of remaining ammo was a basic Dealer survival skill, but counting bullets was impossible when dealing with such a rapid rate of fire. That meant the digital ammo count on her smartphone-linked smart glasses was acting like her health bar. If she ran out of ammo, Kaname could immediately strike back. Even the most powerful Dealer would Fall to a single bullet in the head, and Kaname's superior reflexes had been amply proved in his brush with the dog-eared Magistellus just now.

Thus, both sides had to switch tactics.

Kaname hopped into a large vehicle outside the parking lot, tore off the plastic cover beneath the steering wheel, and connected a few wires. The diesel engine roared to life. Indeed, what Kaname had hotwired was no sports car but a mobile crane painted bright yellow.

As soon as he came out onto the road, as wide as an airstrip, he immediately grazed past another similarly large vehicle, a bright-red fire truck with none other than Strawberry Garter at the wheel. Unfortunately, Kaname couldn't go for a headshot, since the seats were at such different heights. She, too, was unable to drive and fire the minigun at the same time without the help of her Magistellus. The two of them drove in opposite directions for about a hundred meters, before executing a sharp hand brake turn. Kaname found the vehicle much harder to control than the coupe, and one wheel almost lifted entirely off the ground.

The two stared each other down once more. This battle would not be fought with guns. The two drivers pressed down on their gas pedals, the crane's long arm and the fire truck's ladder pointed at each other like the lances of two ten-ton knights. As the PMCs again flooded the battlefield, their black armored cars were flung aside by the two behemoths like so many discarded paper cartons.

"It's the world's biggest joust…," muttered Kaname as he battled the unruly steering wheel.

But it wasn't just about smashing each other with the crane arm and fire truck ladder as hard as possible. If struck from the side, the vehicles could lose their balance and topple over. These long bits of metal were not designed to be used when the vehicle was in motion, and normally, long feet at the base of the truck, called outriggers, were extended when the crane or ladder was in use to ensure the vehicle remained stable.

Kaname adjusted the wheel, trying to position the crane arm directly in front of the driver's seat of the other vehicle. If he couldn't hit it, he would Fall for sure. It was a risky proposition, but that wasn't enough to make Kaname cave. For Tselika. For Takamasa. For his sister. For Midori. For everyone he knew living in the shadow of AI companies, Kaname had to reunite the Legacies. And to do that, he needed that vital piece of Takamasa's soul, the sheaf of papers that Strawberry Garter possessed.

Although it had no bearing on his primary mission, he couldn't ignore the Umibe family, either, bereft of the soccer team they had worked so hard to establish. Midori had said it best. It was to right the injustices of the world.

Even though she herself, as an AI Dropout, relied on the benevolent machine overlords for her living expenses, she had put her own pain aside to focus on the well-being of others.

And if that was what Midori wanted, then that was what Kaname wanted, too.

Because when Takamasa gave his life to protect Kaname's sister, Kaname had decided he would do the same in return.

So Kaname focused on the point of interception.

No need to show off; simply execute the plan.

Kaname turned the enormous wheel left and right, but control over the vehicle was not his aim. The crane arm and the opponent's ladder both bobbed and weaved, advancing and retracting as Kaname and Strawberry Garter pushed their vehicles' gas pedals as far down as they would go. Despite the fact that both were trying to kill each other, they opened their mouths and roared together as if they shared one mind.

""Roooooooooooooooooooooooooooooooooaaaaaaaaaaaaaaaaaaaaaaaa aaaaaaaaaagggggghhh!!""

Ker-rash!!!!!!

The collision was almost ridiculously large. Kaname was shaken up so badly that his sense of time slowed to a crawl. But he gritted his teeth and bore it out.

He couldn't pass out yet.

His windshield was covered in so many cracks, it was almost completely white, but that didn't mean the ladder had pierced it. The glass on this vehicle was built to shatter under impact, and Kaname had used the metal frame of the boxlike cabin to deflect the fire truck's ladder, narrowly avoiding the thrust.

"Grhh…"

Which meant…

His own spear had struck true. The fire truck's windshield was completely shattered, and the tip of the crane arm plunged deep into the vehicle.

A successful cross-counter. But the pain in Kaname's nose had not let up.

It didn't get her…?!

Strawberry Garter had swung her head to one side and just barely managed to avoid the metal arm, which tore through the cabin at an angle, plucking cotton from the adjacent seat.

Suddenly, Kaname knew what had happened. It was his tie—the one with the Reduce Pain skill. Rarity ten, so sought after, it sparked bidding wars. It had slowed Kaname's reactions.

At once, time sped back up to the normal rate.

With the metal arm held in place, the rest of the mobile crane twisted up off the ground. This was an extraordinarily dangerous collision. The ladder itself may have missed him, but it had still damaged the vehicle. As mentioned previously, the crane was not meant to be used while in motion. The vehicle was unstable enough on its own, so what would happen if the tip of the arm ran into an obstacle?

A second accident.

The mobile crane and fire truck both flew off their wheels and veered off the road toward the sidewalk. The crane's arm was bent almost at a right angle, while the end of the ladder snapped off and went flying. Kaname's crane crashed into a barrier of light surrounding a parked vehicle and toppled over sideways back onto the road.

15

Day or night, it made no difference.

Even in the real world, the boy had nowhere to go. They had said the AI companies would wipe away his debt and protect his lifestyle, but that was just a lie. Mocking stares awaited him at school, and at home his father's ex-friends might show up at any moment to scream and yell.

Lacking a place in the real world, he fled to the virtual one, but even in *Money (Game) Master*, he couldn't be free.

" … "

There was nothing he could do except sit on that dirty, graffiti-covered bench next to a disused pay phone and stare up at the garish lights of Leviathan Stadium. Even the temporary power outage didn't bother him. He had tried so hard to stay close to the stadium, even donning the pink work clothes he so despised. But no matter how much trash he picked up, he could never rid that place of its filth.

Suddenly, he heard the roar of a motorcycle engine.

"Torihiko Umibe?"

"You're a strange one, aren't you? Come to laugh at a penniless boy without a future?"

It was Midori Hekireki. Rather than going straight to Biondetta Dome as planned, she had decided to first stop by Leviathan Stadium. Her work behind the scenes was done, and she no longer had any reason to linger at that service station on the outskirts of town.

"If you're here, does that mean your Magistellus is with you?" asked Midori. "A smartphone would do as well, I guess."

Suddenly a beautiful woman melted into view behind the bench, as if she had previously been part of the scenery. Her movements were strange, as though she wasn't used to walking on two legs. She tilted her head, allowing her shoulder-length blond hair to fall to one side.

"Did you call for me, Master?" she asked the boy.

"No."

"Verbal command unrecognized. Please speak slowly and clearly."

...Though she spoke politely, she didn't seem like the friendliest Magistellus out there. Midori was new to this game as well, but she wondered if Magistelli behaved differently, depending on their base personality and the way they were treated.

Midori held up her phone to the jewel-eyed Magistellus and was surprised to see a mysterious string of Latin letters appear on the screen. It didn't look like English, at least.

"She's a Vouivre. Do you not know about them? She's pretty human-like, but she's actually a kind of French dragon."

Midori hadn't expected to get an answer from the ten-year-old boy. Was it something from a video game or a card game, maybe?

The Vouivre Magistellus had an upper half pretty similar to that of a human woman, but from the waist down, her body became the scaly head of a snake, and a pair of bat-like wings sprouted from her back. She wore a blue cheerleader's outfit, perhaps belonging to the old Leviathans, as it was the same color as the T-shirt the young boy wore beneath his overalls.

"My name is Chandeletta," she said. "Pleased to make your acquaintance."

"Hi. I can't give my name, so just call me Anon for now."

"Verbal command unrecognized."

"You greeted me first, and now you're shutting me down...?! Even Meiki's more coherent than this piece of junk!"

Still, the fact that a Magistellus like her was able to blend into the crowd made *Money (Game) Master* feel more like a game. Even the sight of this B movie monster walking down the street was no cause for alarm.

"She's useless to me. I don't know how to make money, anyway."

"Is that right?"

There was an electronic *ping!*, and the design on the Magistellus's blue cheerleading outfit changed. A stream of numbers flowed rapidly across her chest. It was hard to miss the headline that dominated her internet-connected outfit.

Breaking News!! Leviathan Soccer Team to Come Under New Management?

We have heard from several sources that Biondetta Dome is entering the final stages of construction after encountering repeated delays. Facing troubled economic performance, the lead sponsor of the rival team, the Leviathans, has decided to sack the current owner, Dealer Strawberry Garter. The future of the team is unclear at this stage, but one option the company is considering is to return the team to its former owner, Tatsuo Umibe, in order to attain some small measure of stability.

The boy stared in shock, forgetting the world around him for a moment.

"It's not just one option," said Midori cheerfully. "It'll happen. I promise you it will. Once you get out of those tacky overalls and back into your old blue uniforms, reach back out to your former players. Then things'll start to get lively again around here."

The boy struggled to find his words. How was he supposed to react to such a sudden turn in luck? He was at rock bottom, and he had been offered a way out. It was too good to be true. This was a face Midori knew well; perhaps the same one she had made aboard that cruise liner when she turned her gun upon the boy who came to help her.

"B-but the Leviathans will go under anyway if Biondetta Dome is completed. It was all for nothing…"

Midori's reply was immediate: "That's not going to happen."

It was as if she had predicted that very question.

"The only reason we helped out Biondetta Dome was to shake up those no-good Dealers. After the decision is made, we won't need them anymore. The dome is useless if it isn't completed in time for the Misaka Expo two years from now, right? Well, the foundation has always been full of tunnels and susceptible to vibrations. Vibrations such as the cheering of tens of thousands of people or the stamping of feet, for example. If we just tweak one little subway route, we can get the whole thing shut down on safety grounds. And those guys aren't in any position to get into the transport infrastructure business. At least, not now that they've lost their precious minigun."

"You helped us...? The subway? You've done...you'd do all that...?!"

"Not me," said Midori, giving a slight chuckle. "I'm just an AI Dropout, same as you. I don't have the money to spend on something like that."

"Then who...?"

"Helping people isn't about bragging rights. Or that's what he always says."

There was no need to say anything more. Midori squeezed the throttle on her bike. She had one more thing to say before she rode off.

"But not everyone agrees. That's my brother's phrase, not something I decided for myself. That's why I came by. So don't tell him, okay? ☆"

16

Inside the overturned crane.

"It's not over..."

Everything hurt. His vision swayed. Kaname shifted his grip on Short Spear. He could bear the pain, if it meant helping somebody.

"...It's not over yet. I have to end this..."

The front windshield was covered in cracks but still stubbornly held its shape—that was construction grade for you. No amount of small-arms fire was going to open a hole big enough for Kaname to crawl out of, so he abandoned that idea. Instead, he pulled himself up and out of the driver's side door flapping above him.

Several black armored cars were already on the retreat. The task of the AIs had been to recapture the semitruck carrying the AC equipment. Regardless of success, once their target was gone, they left immediately. Even though the person responsible for everything was right before their eyes, because he wasn't designated a target, they passed right by.

And yet the buzzing in Kaname's nose remained. His Lion's Nose sensed danger.

It was more intense than anything he had felt so far.

And.

So.

"..."

At the end of it all, this woman standing silhouetted against the flames of burning vehicles was human, same as him.

The intelligent-looking beauty in the pink-and-white suit looked unsteady on her feet, just like Kaname. She leaned over to one side, her large, curled ponytail swaying gently in the breeze like pampas grass. Though she lacked the strength to support her own body weight, she still grasped the huge minigun in one hand and its massive box magazine in the other, as easily as if they were plastic toys.

It was one of the Legacies left by Criminal AO, by Takamasa— #dracolord.err.

The Overtrick. Capable of feats that were otherwise impossible, no matter how much money you burned stacking skills.

Kaname raised Short Spear in response. At this range, it didn't matter what caliber bullets the two used. Whichever duelist shot first would be the victor.

"...We've successfully delivered Martini AC's equipment to Biondetta Dome. There's no way for you to stop construction now."

"Indeed."

"The Leviathans' lead sponsor is basically your parent firm. I wonder what that AI company thinks about all this. See the news on that big screen over there? There's no more reason for us to fight. You've lost your castle, your stadium, and your handpicked elites have all Fallen. Were they players? Coaches? It doesn't even matter. Your little team of hit men is all gone. You're no longer fit to run this stadium. It's time to let it return to its original owners."

"I don't care about any of that anymore," she said, spitting out the words like a curse.

The woman dropped the huge box magazine to the ground and took out her smartphone, its screen now cracked. She gazed at it like a mirror, admiring her own image. Then she tossed the useless device away, as if giving up on some sort of ritual she couldn't perform with her smart glasses alone. Her priority now was Kaname, and she glared at him with murder in her eyes.

But Kaname simply smiled.

"...It may be our first time face-to-face, but I see you're human after all."

"You people are always taking away everything I have. The things I innocently believed would always be there. Barging in with your money like you own the place...!!"

Kaname didn't know specifically who or what she was referring to. But injustice was everywhere—both within the anarchic world of *Money (Game) Master* and without it. That was how the Umibe family had lost their sports team and how Kaname had lost his best friend.

"I won't make excuses."

"..."

"You can talk about justice all you want, but you're hardly a saint... You robbed the Leviathans from the Umibe family without a second thought. I'm going to make sure the team goes back to its rightful owners, and I won't stop there. I'm taking it all back. Takamasa's Legacy, and his personal notes you used to get it. You've been treating him like he's gone, but his things aren't yours to inherit!!"

It was an intense standoff. Any second now, one would shoot the other, and they'd Fall.

Or perhaps it was more likely that both would end up Falling together.

And yet neither Kaname nor Strawberry Garter would budge an inch.

Helping people wasn't about bragging rights or asking for anything in return.

Perhaps this woman had something, too, unbeknownst to anyone else. Something that had led her to team up with other corrupt Dealers to make Leviathan Stadium into her very own fort.

Though there was little use in digging up those feelings now that Kaname had trampled all over them.

"…"

"…"

There was a salty taste on the breeze. The slightest crackle from the surrounding flames might send both sides into furious gunfire.

Perhaps it was wrong of Kaname, then, to feel somehow at ease with the low, painful buzzing of his nose.

He took in a breath of air, then let it back out.

For a while now, Strawberry Garter had not so much as blinked.

And then.

A small blue point of light silently appeared on Strawberry Garter's chest.

It was a feeling unlike anything he'd yet experienced. The pain in his nose warped unnaturally.

At first.

Strawberry Garter couldn't comprehend what was happening. She tilted her neck, looking down as though she had spilled Bolognese sauce all over her best clothes. Then, she looked back up at Kaname.

"I see."

"…"

"A sniper. You're always one step ahead, aren't you? Disgusting. Did you predict everything?"

"No, that's not me. I don't even have any allies over there!"

"Who cares?"

Details meant nothing to her now. She swung the minigun up with her right hand.

A searing pain in Kaname's nose alerted him like an alarm.

This was it.

It was happening now.

A hollow sound rang out.

"Rhhh."

Kaname leaped for cover behind the toppled mobile crane. As for Strawberry Garter...

Too late.

The pain in Kaname's nose began to fade.

A deep, vicious wound opened in Strawberry Garter's chest, ruining her expensive suit. Kaname couldn't exactly pick out the bullet to check, but it must have been quite a thick one. No ordinary 7.62 millimeter round, that much was certain. Tungsten steel, perhaps, or something stronger. In the worst-case scenario, it could even be made with depleted uranium. That way, the bullet would strike true no matter how many layers of protective vests and skills the target was using.

Strawberry Garter's glasses fell from her face, but it no longer seemed to bother her. She didn't even twitch as she hit the floor. Blood mercilessly spread out over the street beneath her. The bullet had ripped straight through her heart, making resuscitation impossible. Beside her lifeless body lay the Legacy, #dracolord.err, looking to the untrained eye like no more than a plastic toy. Kaname needed to get it back.

However...

Neither Midori nor Tselika were behind this. The marksman's technique resembled a sniper's, but it was more likely the weapon was some sort of assault rifle modified for long-range shooting. The bullet had been too slow for it to be a sniper rifle like #fireline.err. That would explain why the bullet was so thick; it was to compensate for the lower muzzle velocity.

Bearing west-northwest. Range two hundred fifty. Altitude thirty meters. This, too, was quite a short distance for a sniper. The assailant appeared to be utilizing a laser sight, in which case it was unlikely they had a scope, as the two would conflict with each other. A laser sight, while useful, was also capable of alerting the target. Once they saw it, they could take cover. Or if they weren't brave enough for that, they might still panic and trip, causing you to miss your shot. That meant if you had to pick one or the other, a scope was usually stealthier, but this marksman had chosen to go with the laser sight instead. It seemed like an odd decision after going so far to set up the shot. Perhaps at such a short distance, they thought it beneath them to use a scope or, for that matter, a proper sniper rifle.

However, when Kaname peeked out from his hiding spot and glanced toward the source of the shot, what he saw wasn't a rooftop, but countless windows all lined up in rows. A luxury hotel—not at all uncommon in Tokonatsu City. And this particular hotel commanded a superior view, both of Leviathan Stadium and the nearby Biondetta Dome.

Why, of all places, did it have to be right where I made my base...?!

Kaname still had no idea who they were, but the sniper had gotten closer to him than he ever could have imagined. He scanned the building's windows through the scope of his short-range sniper rifle, but he wasn't able to identify which one the bullet had come from. He could risk his life to run over to the building, but the sniper could easily disguise himself as one of the rowdy all-night partiers and walk right past Kaname without him ever knowing.

The Lion's Nose had gone silent.

Did that mean they had already left?

Or had they simply achieved a level of stealth that could evade Kaname's sixth sense? If that were the case, then they probably weren't relying totally on skills. Something like that would be impossible without considerably honing one's foundation.

For a while, Kaname remained completely motionless, unable to reach a firm conclusion.

Who could it be...?

The goal had been to put pressure on Strawberry Garter, leader of the Leviathans. Kaname couldn't threaten or coerce her if she was dead.

It would have probably gone in that direction anyway, after their cowboy-esque duel, but still Kaname wondered. Had there been no way to stop it?

Perhaps Kaname could still get to the Umibe family once the deal was concluded and convince them to hand over the list from the office safe. But no, asking for a reward was unthinkable. He would have to break into the heavily guarded stadium and steal it back.

Because now, a new threat had surfaced.

Someone was attempting to kill anyone with the list.

He couldn't let that fate befall the Umibe family they'd only just saved. Kaname and his friends would have to shoulder it alone.

That much was certain.

But who on earth was that quirky sniper?

(Operation dark web "LADY GHOST" <This domain is under random camouflage>)

Lily-Kiska: I did as you asked. But this thing sure packs a punch.

Criminal AO: Excellent work. I'm sorry for always giving you the dangerous tasks. I bet it wasn't quite like handling #fireline.err, was it? Although even the assault rifle #swallowdive.err isn't perfect for every situation.

Lily-Kiska: You intend to collect the Legacies, right?

Criminal AO: Yeah. Though I'd prefer it if you called them "Magic."

Lily-Kiska: ...In that case, why not let him do all the work for you, then attack him and steal the Legacies once he's done?

Criminal AO: Perhaps you've misunderstood me. I have no intention of harming Kaname or Midori. In fact, I'm trying to protect them. This Magic is dangerous. I know, because I created it myself. I have to keep it away from those important to me, or else they might burn themselves.

Lily-Kiska: ...

Criminal AO: As someone expelled from AI society, I know the dangers of Magic better than anyone. For my friends, why, I would rise up against the very Mind of the AI itself! Though having done just that I can say it's not all it's cracked up to be. I don't want my friend or my sister to go through that kind of suffering.

Lily-Kiska: That's very noble of you. But that's an idealized image of your friend and sister you're talking about.

Criminal AO: And what do you mean by that?

Lily-Kiska: Kaname Suou and Midori Hekireki are both human. They are not Magistelli, controlled by AI. They might defy your predictions. And what will you think then, after you've made all these sacrifices no one asked for?

Criminal AO: ...

Lily-Kiska: I certainly hope those noble intentions don't grow into self-serving hatred. Don't you, Brother dearest?

Chapter 5

A New Kind of Late-Night Television BGM #05
"Killer Stunt"

1

...
...
...
Message sent.

2

Server Name: Psi Indigo.
Starting Location: Tokonatsu City, Peninsula District.
Log-in credentials accepted.
Welcome to *Money (Game) Master*, **Kaname Suou.**

"Not drinking, Kaname, my boy? Surely you're not going to tell me it's too dangerous to accept such *colorful* drinks in a city of vice and crime? You really are a goody two-shoes. You ought to lighten up a little. Here in the virtual world, we can be free of earthly restrictions and live our lives to the fullest!"

"...So what was that powder I just saw you slip into it, then, Frey(a)?"

"Oh, Kaname! You're not supposed to point that out! How gauche!!

I bet you're the type who blurts out the trick halfway through a magic show, huh?"

"Remind me to never eat or drink anything you offer me ever again."

The location was a bar in the financial district. The time was around midday, so rather than frothy ales and colorful concoctions, the menu featured more family-friendly lunch options.

And yet the patrons were all birds of a feather. Kaname aside, the men all wore luxurious suits and the women beautiful evening dresses. And the center of attention, of course, was this man(?). His involvement alone was enough to turn the amicable lunchtime meeting into a life-or-death situation.

Frey(a). Owner of a pawnshop and ringleader of a powerful team of Dealers called the Treasure Hermit Crabs. The members made their living off gambling and loan sharking, primarily in the peninsula financial district of Tokonatsu City. Given that *snow* was on equal footing with the yen, it was safe to say this team of Dealers had the same kind of influence as an international criminal organization like the Mafia.

He boasted a fancy white suit and striking long blond hair. His facial features were gentle, and his mismatched irises, along with the mole under one eye, added an alluring flair. He would look perfect if not for the shit-eating grin plastered over his face.

The rivers flowing beneath the city were his domain, and the large submarine that sailed them was his castle. Still, every once in a while, he deigned to come up and out into the sun, though the daylight did little to change his nature. Perhaps this bar itself was another of his acquisitions.

Measuring anything and everything through the lens of love. That was how this person had risen to the rank of top-class billionaire. He was a monster in his field.

He(?) clasped his gloved hands together in front of his face, as though making a plea.

"To think the great Kaname has come to me alone, no Magistellus at his side. I had rather high expectations, you know? How about you pretend you didn't see my little sleight of hand and down that drink, and we'll see how things go from there..."

"This is getting tedious."

"I can be a woman instead, if that's what you'd prefer. I'll even let you choose top or bottom."

"That isn't the point. Quit it, Frey(a)! Turn back to normal! You're throwing me off!"

"To normal? Do you even know which is the real me? I could teach you, you know. All it would take is one night in my bed. If you already have someone special, that's fine, too. In that case, we can have an affair. What do you say, Kaname?"

"Frey(a)."

At Kaname's rebuke, the pretty man's pout grew more and more pronounced. He(?) had been switching back and forth between a fancy white suit and a wedding dress. Now his tone turned slightly troubled.

"And here I thought I had covered all the bases... If male or female, top or bottom is not the issue, then what is? The way of love is deeper and wider than I had ever imagined. If none of those pleases you, Kaname, your tastes must be quite sinful indeed!"

"Frey(a), I really don't know why you're looking at me like that."

"It's okay, Kaname! True love is valid in all its forms!! It's what's inside that counts! Perhaps I should be taking lessons from you! Could it be someone's experience or lack thereof that makes the difference for you? Or perhaps you prefer a clear master-servant relationship? Or wait, it isn't just the person one needs to consider, but the costumes and scenario, as well... Kaname, I wish to see the world as you do! Teach me more!!"

"Let's try to remain on topic. I can pay you for your time if I must. The amount doesn't matter."

"Oh, but *this* is what I truly love about our meetings. Helping you is just a pretext," muttered Frey(a), eventually settling on the form of a beautiful woman(?). It was impossible to tell when she was joking.

She then took her seat. Not at the bar, but upon a nearby suitcase. From inside came a dull thud and a muffled groan.

"...Frey(a)."

"Oh? I thought you wanted to remain on topic. I apologize for bringing my work to the table. This is a punishment in progress, you see. This is what happens when you try to scam my pawnshops with counterfeit items. I had *hoped* people would figure that out from the urban legends circulating on the internet, but alas."

So that was why the reclusive leader of the Treasure Hermit Crabs was out in public. Kaname had been wondering, since it was usually a charge of one million *snow* just to get inside her submarine.

Over by the entrance to the bar, a Magistellus made of reddish-purple slime was standing by, her sailor uniform fluttering in the breeze. She turned and gave a small bow in place of her master-mistress. On her shoulder she carried a rocket launcher—a multi-barreled type with over twenty launch tubes, more at home on an attack helicopter. One salvo from that could blow an armored vehicle to smithereens.

There was no police force in *Money (Game) Master*. You could do things in this game you would never dream of getting away with in real life, as long as you were prepared to take on the risks. Frey(a)'s wealth was the envy of all, and that was what both allowed and required her to walk around with enough firepower to level a tank. Even though they all lived and worked in the same city, the rich were playing on a higher difficulty setting.

Frey(a), now in a wedding dress, leaned back on her highly dubious chair as her face loosened into an amorous smile.

"I'd appreciate it if you left your twisted sense of justice at the door, Kaname, my boy. Direct force just doesn't work on some people, so you have to appeal to their sense of shame instead. Heh. The key here is to leave the suitcase unlocked as we drag it around town. The state she's in is far more embarrassing than being nude. A modest little madame like her is liable to slit her own throat if we were to open the box and see her curled up inside. But as long as that doesn't happen, we can forgive and forget, right?"

In any case, Kaname Suou was no philanthropist. If the punishment were unwarranted, then he might be persuaded to do *something not about bragging rights or rewards*, but otherwise he was happy to let sleeping dogs lie. It might seem cold, but in *Money (Game) Master*, there was a risk associated with every action, and it was prudent to consider that risk before you went charging in.

"Just don't kill her."

"Of course not. She's got plenty of air in there, a bottle of water, and even some cooling spray so she doesn't overheat. It's noncombustible, too, so no chance of static electricity starting a fire. Come on, Kaname. You know me better than that. It's watching them live with the shame that's the fun part!"

"Fine. Let's get down to business, then. For real this time."

"...I do like the way you make everything black and white. Called Game may be no more, but there's still a part of the Reaper in you. Once the madame's punishment is over, I think I'll put her in contact with you. Perhaps you can ask her yourself why she needed money so badly."

Recrossing her slender legs atop the suitcase, the blond-haired beauty gave a quiet chuckle. She leaned against the bar, pressing her large breasts into the counter, and continued.

"The team you asked about has been rather active lately, buying up all sorts of goods and selling very little. They've even brought their business to my pawnshops. Would you like a detailed breakdown?"

"No. I only need to know that they're active."

"They've not been foolish enough to try and sell the Legacy directly, at least. If they did, they'd be attacked as soon as they crossed the threshold."

"Which means they thought up a smarter use for it."

"Do you think they have another list, copy or otherwise?"

"Maybe, maybe not. Regardless, the die has long since been cast," Kaname said simply. "Either way, I can use them. That's all that matters in *Money (Game) Master*."

3

It was just past three in the afternoon, and the sun was still strong.

Mangrove Island was one of many small bits of land dotting the waters around Tokonatsu City like pearls on a necklace. It had every-thing—palm trees, sandy beaches, and tropical flowers. It was here, nestled among the verdant leaves, that Kaname maintained one of his secret bases, a log cabin hidden in the jungle.

The garage to its side was empty, its doors open, and the air was filled with a high whine like the sound of a vacuum cleaner. In fact, it was the exact opposite: a handheld air compressor for blowing away sand and dust.

"Hm-hm-hmm! Hm-hm-hm-hm-hm-hmm!"

Even the tall cumulonimbus clouds could not prevent the dazzling sun from beating down, glittering off the polished surface of the mint-green coupe. The demon pit babe was leaning over the hood, washing the surface with a wet sponge, a bucket of water at her feet. She hummed a tune to herself, waggling her hips in time to the music, as she spread her carefully selected wax all over the car.

"Come here, little boy! I shall make you nice and clean! ☆"

There was no way that Kaname, fool that he was, would ever under-stand the joys of cleaning his vehicle. All he did was chase after guns and his best friend's sister all day. Tselika, however, would tend to the car whenever she had a free moment. Keeping it well tuned was one thing, but vehicles had feelings, too. It usually kept to a steely silence, but the more love she put into her ministrations, the more agreeable it became—simply adorable. Yes, love! That was what this car was missing!!

She wished for friends with whom she could share in this joy. Ayame's old partner, the dark elf Magistellus called Cindy, had been a formi-dable rival and fellow enthusiast, but those days were long gone, and no amount of brooding would bring them back.

"Phew! That is enough. Now, while it's drying…"

Anyone could clean the car's front windshield, but the side windows and mirrors needed care, as well. Nowadays, most vehicles had rear-pointing cameras that fed into a screen on the windshield, but Kaname still seemed to rely heavily on the rearview and side view mirrors. Any dirt on those would be as distracting as having a stranger's fingerprints all over your glasses lenses. First, breathe on the surface, then wipe it lightly with a dry cloth. Follow that with a layer of cleaning solution, and then an anti-fog preparation. Careful not to touch the mirror's surface, angle it just right. And finally, blow it a single kiss.

"Ah, 'tis another beautiful day to be beautiful! I suppose that is enough cleaning for now."

"Want to be in the audience of the Platinum Billion Quiz? All you lazy lowlifes with nothing better to do than sit in your room eating and sleeping! Don't you want to experience the world's greatest quiz show, live, with one billion snow at stake?! The final round takes place tonight at seven! Tap TV expects your attendance or attention for a thrilling night of..."

The battery is fully charged, too. No large drops in voltage.

There must have been large sums of money involved to run a webstream ad on the radio, given that webstreams were precisely what was killing mass media. The sound of the car stereo in her ears, Tselika crouched, her clothing doing little to conceal the curves of her bottom, and took a small flashlight from between her breasts. Holding it in her teeth, she peered behind the aluminum grating at the back of the wheels.

The brake shoes look fine, no burn marks... I wonder if it's that disc with the igneous-ceramic mixture at work?

This car needed to be capable of sudden stops and drifts at over three hundred to four hundred kilometers per hour. When engaged at that speed, the friction would make the brake disc glow red.

Next, as any woman worth her salt would know, you had to take good care of all your parts—even the ones that usually stayed hidden. It was a good thing she hadn't started rinsing yet, though the sun was so hot, any moisture would soon dry up anyway. She brought out a pair of jacks and a small dolly from the garage, hoisted the vehicle up, and slid herself underneath.

"Don't want my boobs to get stuck."

It was quite scary lying there, tons of metal mere inches above one's nose, but the word "succubus" originally meant "to lie beneath." Sometimes, it was nice to find yourself under a powerful creature. The pressure caused her heart to flutter all the more.

"Oh my! Look at all this sand and dried mud. You're a dirty little boy, aren't you? Well, that just means I'll have to get rough!"

These areas weren't usually visible, but that wasn't important. Just like how a woman's choice in underwear wasn't strictly for a man's enjoyment.

There were three reasons the Magistellus called Tselika had opted to perform this maintenance out in the open, despite the lack of air conditioning.

The first reason was to avoid filling the garage with the smell of wax and cleaner.

The second was that the car was meant to be seen outside. It was therefore sensible to do the cleaning under real sunlight, to get an accurate picture.

And finally, working outside in the heat would force her to stop at some point. If not, she might keep going until every last nut and bolt was sparkling, even if it meant disassembling the whole car. Kaname used to scold her for it, but Criminal AO, a fellow engineer, would just laugh uproariously.

"Hm-hm-hmm!"

She sprayed some cleaner onto a cloth and got to work. Soap suds all over her face, Tselika smiled like a little girl hoping to impress her parents by doing the housework.

"…My Lord's hardly going to recognize you when I'm finished!"

4

And then, who should put his fat butt on the hood (his metal-zipped wallet in his back pocket, no doubt) but Kaname Suou himself, the fast food meal he had just purchased spread all over the pristine metal. (It had been 5 percent off, due to a discount campaign for refusing plastic straws.) There was grease and mayo running down the side of the burger, dressing for the side salad, ketchup and mustard to dip his fries in, and to top it all off, the vanilla shake with its all-important paper straw. It was a veritable cornucopia of hazardous materials.

"...Something the matter, Tselika? You're shaking."

"...Just shut up, My Lord. You damnable fool..."

Kaname had called for Tselika to bring the car over, and they were now in the parking lot of a public green space. A short distance away, a lady was playing tennis with her Magistellus, the soft sounds of their racquets lending a relaxed air to the environs. Fishing, go-karting, golfing, darts... There were all sorts of mini-games here in *Money (Game) Master* for people to spend their hard-earned cash on, and the variety on offer within this single MMO rivaled the app store of any tech giant.

In other words, there were as many ways to lose your money as there were ways of making more.

Kaname glanced down at the smart watch on his wrist. It was another sunny day in Tokonatsu City. Low humidity and a south-southwesterly breeze meant the hot sun wasn't as stifling as usual... Incidentally, such information was also of great interest to snipers. The digital age was convenient in many ways.

"I didn't dare eat anything at Frey(a)'s place, so I got this on the way back. I even bought you one of those weird fish burgers you're always raving about. It won't last long in this heat, so I'll have it if you're not hungry."

"Don't you dare!!"

It seemed Tselika had finally given up. She placed her well-formed rump upon the hood and began tearing off the wrapping paper.

"And it is not weird. There is no taste in this world more sublime than the combination of tartar sauce and fried fish!"

"Tselika..."

"Do not look at me like that!! What about you, My Lord? What are you eating?"

"Double beef patty with black pepper."

"Salt and pepper. How unadventurous could you possibly get? You should at least add some salsa sauce to spice things up. Come on, then, if it is so good, then let me have a taste."

Saying this, Tselika leaned over and took a bite from Kaname's burger. Then she grabbed some of his fries and dipped them in her own tartar sauce before popping them into her mouth.

"Takamasa used to eat these dessert burgers. Sliced fruit and whipped cream between two steamed white buns...," Kaname recalled.

"That man would eat anything if the server girl fed it to him. He was barred for life for trying to lick the whipped cream off her finger! I think he thought he was ordering a fruit salad."

In any case, salt, oil, and carbohydrates were nothing to worry about in the virtual world. Perhaps this game really was as good for weight loss as the rumors suggested.

"I just like the basics, I guess. Burgers are good."

"And yet with *snow* just as valuable as the yen, you could be eating a far more luxurious meal in real life if you so wished."

"If I did that, the calorie-counting demon would chase me around the house with a measuring tape. My sister, I mean. It would be tragic to make so much money just to end up like that."

"...You really do spoil that girl, you know."

For the record, there were such things as hunger and thirst in *Money (Game) Master*, but people who played for only a few hours a day would be unlikely to notice them. Players usually ate if they were up and logged in all night, attempting to lose weight, or as a form of mental conditioning, similar to how *shogi* players would fuss over even the snacks they ate during breaks to ensure they performed at peak mental capacity. Humans were strange creatures, and a glucose pill just wouldn't cut it sometimes, even if all the ingredients were the same. Using equipment skills to mask the hunger tended to be similarly ineffective.

After their lunch break, the pair set their sights on the next target.

"...We finally managed to get our hands on the list of Legacies, and yet it has eluded our grasp," said Tselika.

"Yeah."

Kaname nodded, opting not to point out the logical contradiction in Tselika's wording.

The binder filled with Takamasa's papers had come from the safe in the Leviathans' office. Kaname had taken it while the company was still struggling with the reshuffle; otherwise the PMCs that usually protected the stadium would have been too much for him to deal with.

"My word… That man was thorough."

"I'm not trying to sound ungrateful, but…"

However.

"I thought these were just supposed to be his notes… Why did he bother to encrypt all of this? Did he do all the math in his head, too?"

"I have attempted an analysis, but all I can tell is that to brute-force the list from what we have would take well over a hundred years, My Lord. We will need his encryption key."

There had been no such key in the safe. Perhaps Strawberry Garter had hidden it in a separate location, or perhaps she had already committed the series of random numbers to memory and burned it, as a way of exercising her superiority over her colleagues and preparing for a possible betrayal.

In any case, Strawberry Garter must have been able to read that garbled mess of characters in some capacity, since she had located one of the Legacies. It was just a shame the sniper had gotten to her before she could tell Kaname how she had done it.

And so, this line of investigation had hit a dead end.

"There is little point in having the list if we cannot read it," said Tselika. "All that fuss was hardly worth #dracolord.err alone."

"No, it wasn't."

"And yet here you are. Even though you could easily retire to the real world to plan your next move. You've even picked up a meal to keep your head in the game… Have you come up with a plan already, My Lord? What's next?"

Kaname wasn't one to let a minor setback get him down. It was important to stay in control of the flow if you wanted a chance to turn things around.

"We'll just have to find another Dealer or team that has the key."

"Hmm."

"There aren't any page numbers on our copy. And since it's all loose-leaf sheets, there could be parts missing and we wouldn't even know. What's more, there might be any number of photocopies floating around. Anyone with part of the list who gets their hands on a Legacy must also have the corresponding key."

There would have been no need for Takamasa to keep the encryption key around in the first place. After all, he had done all the calculations by hand and would have everything memorized.

And yet Takamasa was human. He wanted to keep his secrets from prying eyes, but at the same time, he knew one day he might want to share them with somebody. Perhaps that person was Kaname, his team-mate in Called Game, or perhaps it was Midori, his little sister.

…Whichever it was, he certainly didn't want random strangers gawking at it. That would be like taking somebody's love letters and broadcasting them to the whole world.

Tselika sighed.

"I do wonder how it is you can remain so optimistic, My Lord. Regardless, I suppose you have a point. So what, specifically, should we be looking for?"

Kaname looked over at the car, and the hood under his fast food meal began to change.

"The Platinum Billion Quiz. The star show of internet streaming network Tap TV. Broadcasts once a month. They screen applicants from the general public, and the final selection round is held over a livestream for everyone to watch. The jackpot is one billion *snow*. I suppose recession is a foreign word to those in *Money (Game) Master*."

Much like with the soccer team, there must have been many people eager to be on a quiz show who couldn't participate in real life. In *Money (Game) Master*, skills like Memory and Inspiration could boost your mental capabilities. Not to mention the door was wide open to other, less ethical ways of ensuring your victory, such as bribing the program owners or simply taking over the studio at gunpoint, and then giving yourself a crib sheet of the answers or sabotaging your opponents' buzzers.

"Very daring. But what does this have to do with the Legacies and the list? You're not telling me one of them is up for grabs, are you?"

"I'll explain all that if you listen."

Kaname picked up the paper cup containing his milkshake and pushed it against Tselika's brow, encouraging her to cool down, as she leaned over curiously.

Data regarding the quiz show scrolled all across the hood.

"The words 'one billion *snow*' sound impressive, but since it's only once a month, it's not too different from your basic scratch card or soccer lottery. There's always a winner, though, so no carryover. The main source of income is banner ads on the streaming site. The network gets paid regardless of whether the user clicks them or not. Whatever you might think of that approach, there's nothing strange about the program itself. It can pull in a revenue stream just as well as any ordinary television network."

"Even so, this program must be capable of making one billion *snow* every month just off advertising revenue, correct? The streaming industry is a true mystery. How do they bring in that many viewers?"

"Did you forget? *Money (Game) Master* is open to players from all around the world. We're not just talking about prime-time television in a single country. Think about everyone on the planet watching the show during their lunch break."

"…I don't think everybody on the planet is going to be watching some quiz show on an internet streaming site."

"That depends on how it's done," said Kaname. "To give one example, consider people studying the questions so they have a better chance on the next quiz. There's a lot of money at stake, so you can bet people will watch the video again and again, and not just for their own enjoyment. And since you only need to make one program a month but continue to profit for thirty-one days, it's no wonder the producers love it."

"Business, business, and more business," Tselika said. "When do the guns come in?"

"The curious thing here is who wins."

Kaname shifted his gaze to a new set of data that had appeared on the hood.

"Usernames: Blood 9, Sabbath Teacher, and Energy Drink Tarou. These are all winners of the previous games."

"So?"

"They all have something in common. They're all content creators for the stunt video network Extreme Pictures. They used to have a rival show to the Skychasers, where they would jump from building to building in their cars, but now with Platinum Billion ruling the rankings, they're on the decline."

"Why is everything quizzes nowadays…? Even in *Money (Game) Master*, trivia and education trump variety. Why don't they spice things up sometimes by making them take off their clothes or covering them in slime when they get questions wrong?"

"With the overall viewership for stunt videos going down, networks are going to promote the more popular Skychasers if they have to choose. That put Extreme Pictures at an even greater disadvantage."

"…So what, they show up to troll the quiz show responsible for their problems? Rather strange decision, I must say."

"They get to shut down their enemies' program and walk off with a fat sum of cash. Two birds, one stone," said Kaname with a shrug.

The option of cashing out and enjoying an early retirement didn't seem to have occurred to them. Once you'd entered the big leagues in *Money (Game) Master*, there was no going back. Here, the gains and losses alike were more than you knew what to do with, and nothing could buy back your peace of mind—not even a sum greater than the average life earnings of someone in the real world.

Kaname stroked his chin.

"If one group keeps winning time and time again, the general public is going to lose interest, and the viewership numbers will plummet. Slowly but surely, they're draining the program for everything it has."

"But how are these…Extreme Pictures…winning the quiz every single time? It's not just a matter of studying."

"They are studying like crazy, of course, but another big reason is that they have a way to stage a comeback."

"?"

Kaname brought up a rerun of an old episode of the quiz in question and played it on the hood of the car. In the corner of the screen was an obnoxious flashing banner ad. They were probably bringing the show more advertising revenue at this very moment.

"*The correct answer is… Oooh! I'm afraid it was B: eight hundred kilometers per hour!*"

"*Hold on a second, I think that info's out of date. That's not the world record anymore.*"

Tselika looked on, increasingly puzzled. The participant who had raised the objection continued to argue long after the "incorrect" buzzer had sounded.

"*Is this live? It is, right? Then everyone watch this video! This is the new world record!*"

"What the…?"

"If they get an answer wrong," Kaname explained, a long French fry jutting from his mouth, "they simply challenge it. And thus, they cling to life. Extreme Pictures became famous for their death-defying stunts, so they have a bunch of world records like best such-and-such or fastest so-and-so. That means if they mess up one of the quiz questions, they can prove the show's answer wrong on live video. They're essentially risking their lives for that one billion *snow*."

"So they are changing the quiz answers after the fact…by essentially altering the truth?!"

"It means the other contestants don't stand a chance. Even if they figure out the answers in advance, it means nothing if the other team can change them on the fly."

"…Humans are crafty indeed…and that is coming from a demon."

"Of course, it doesn't work for every question. History, for example;

you can't change the past with a car stunt. And it's a trick they can only hope to pull off once per show. But even so, it gives them an edge the other contestants don't have, and that makes all the difference. It's why they've swept the quiz results up until now."

"I'm surprised they haven't been banned from competing yet…"

"Perhaps if it was the same contestants each time, they could—but it's not. It's only when the participant raises an issue that the producers realize, 'Oh, it's another one of those Extreme Pictures guys.'"

"And so where does the Legacy come into all of this?"

"It's not that easy to break a world record, no matter how motivated you are. And you can't pull off killer stunts for free. There's the location, the equipment, and the money. In this city, you need a lot of firepower to secure those things."

"…"

"It's only been about six months since Extreme Pictures started griefing this quiz show. In that time, something interesting has been showing up in several of these new world record videos. And I think it's this 'something interesting' that's been giving them the leeway they need to get all the safety equipment and tech that makes these stunts possible. Once they can use violence to pad their landings, so to speak, a killer stunt doesn't look so dangerous anymore."

Of course, to do that, they would have had to leave a trail of victims in their wake. Victims of Takamasa's Legacy. They would have to take out rivals and steal their best items, all to prepare their safe stunts. And no matter how brutal their opponents, they would be helpless before the might of the Legacy, with little recourse but to cry themselves to sleep. And without fear of retaliation, Extreme Pictures would go to greater and greater lengths.

There was no mistaking where it would lead.

Kaname may have failed when it came to the Leviathans, but he wouldn't let it happen again. His goal was the list—fragment or photocopy—and whatever code was used to encrypt it.

He would take back that piece of Takamasa's soul and save all the people suffering because of the Legacy. And with the combined power of the Overtrick, he would release the shackles that bound humanity. For Midori. For his sister. For Takamasa. And of course, for Tselika, who had been fighting beside him the whole time.

After that, they could be sealed away for good. They were Takamasa's, and his alone.

"The mortar, #thunderbolt.err. We'll have them explain to us how they got their hands on it, in detail this time. Perhaps then we'll find the final clue to unlocking the list: the encryption key."

5

"…Um. Before we talk about the Legacy, could you explain what a 'mortar' is?"

Sleek black hair tied up in twin ponytails, and dazzlingly pale skin. The little girl in the frilly gothic-lolita bikini and miniskirt, Midori Hekireki, tilted her head in puzzlement, rocking the blue roses adorning her headband.

Kaname would have been more surprised if a schoolgirl like Midori was familiar with the term. It was not something she could expect to encounter in the course of her classes.

They were on a small patch of land somewhat removed from the main peninsula, in Kaname's secret base—the log cabin on Mangrove Island. Midori had pulled a plastic kid's pool from the garage and set it up on the baking sand, before tossing herself into the water. Yet even for her childlike stature, it was far too small. With her back up against the rim like a sofa, she threw her slender legs over the opposite end. If it were any smaller, it would look like she got her rear end stuck in an inflatable swim ring.

She wanted to take a little dip, she had said. A little fresh water to wash away the sand and salt, like those showers they had on the beachfront. She was wearing the same bathing suit as usual, but it looked completely different when wet. The waterproof material was now clinging even more tightly to the young girl's skin.

...Incidentally, the riot shield stuck into the sand by her side and fortified with the Bulletproof skill was more of a safety blanket than anything else. In *Money (Game) Master*, and indeed in shooting games in
general, shields and safe zones were symbols of comfort, and it was
impossible to feel at ease without somewhere nearby to duck for cover
in case of an attack, as odd as it might sound. At any rate, it was more
effective than a urinal cake that only masked the odor instead of doing
anything about it.

"Basically, they're a simple way of launching small explosive
payloads—usually about the size of a hand grenade—over large dis-
tances. Have you never seen them in movies? They look like a telescope,
with a big iron barrel at an angle; they set them up on legs and drop in
a big round shell, and then fire it on a parabolic trajectory, like an overhead baseball throw."

"No..."

Midori flapped her little feet and crossed her arms. She must not have
had the same taste in movies as Kaname, because she still seemed
confused.

Kaname dipped his hand in the water and gave it a few tentative
splashes. It was already warm from the body heat radiating off the girl's
fair skin. According to his smart watch, the temperature was a little
lower than that of a warm bath. The humidity was low right now, so it
felt cooler than a Japanese summer, but it was still another blazing hot
day in Tokonatsu City, swimsuit weather for sure.

"If it's hard to imagine, then look one up on a video site. You don't
want to get cocky with one of these."

"Okay then."

Midori had the makings of a survivor. She was eager to study when
it mattered. As long as she never got too proud to keep learning, she
would do all right.

"The effective range of these things is usually around four hundred
meters, but with a little extra firepower, they can go as far as three thousand. And because it launches the shell overhead, there's no worry
about any buildings or concrete walls getting in the way."

"What? Three kilometers? You could replace a sniper rifle with this thing!"

"And like a sniper, you need to account for factors like wind direction, gravity, and air temperature if you want an accurate shot. However, if you fire a test shot first, you can compensate for a lot of that. Follow-up shots can typically be accurate to within a few dozen centimeters. Incidentally, a normal blast radius is something like fifteen meters, and regular bulletproofing is essentially useless against it. You would need some pretty specialized defenses…like the Bombproof skill, for instance."

"…It's accurate, you can't hide behind walls, and it's three kilometers away, so you can't even shoot back! Doesn't that make it basically invincible?"

"It's a powerful weapon for sure, but if it were *that* good, then everyone would be carrying them. It has several weaknesses you can take advantage of."

"It does? Even a weapon that powerful?"

Still crouched by the pool, Kaname shrugged. It seemed Midori had been blinded by the mortar's advantages and had ceased to think for herself. Kaname would have to nip this behavior in the bud, or else it would be a problem when the time came for the girl to sign contracts and the like.

You had to read between the lines and outsmart your opponent. You couldn't master this game without learning to think like they did.

"Remember what I said about baseball? The shot takes longer to connect, since it's not going in a straight line. You have plenty of time after hearing the shot to find somewhere with a sturdy roof."

"Oh."

"And by the same logic, it's not as effective against a moving target. A skilled gunner can adjust their aim, based on where they think the target is going to run, but that's quite difficult to do in practice."

Kaname could keep going. There were many difficulties outweighing the benefits. In order to compensate for these drawbacks, mortars

would typically fire several shots to blanket a large area with bombardment, the same way bows were typically used in the Middle Ages.

So for the time being, people still carried guns.

"The explosion is about on the level of a hand grenade; it's the rain
of shrapnel that deals the real damage. That means that you don't need
to go overboard with bombproofing; just ducking inside a normal
convenience store or restaurant would protect you. It's a weapon better suited for the great outdoors, where there aren't so many buildings
to get in the way."

Midori folded her arms and rocked her head back against the
springy rim of the pool, looking up at the clear blue sky. Making a
contemplative noise, she stretched out her toes and finally asked a
question.

"...But this is one of my brother's Legacies, right?"

"Yeah. I can't quite tell from the Extreme Pictures footage, but my
bet is #thunderbolt.err has some special features that compensate for
the weapon's innate drawbacks."

It wouldn't be a Legacy if it were just an ordinary mortar. These were
weapons so heavily customized, they risked breaking the game. Was it
the blast radius, perhaps, or the projectile speed? Maybe the accuracy
rate...? Whatever it was, it couldn't be considered normal by any defi-
nition of the word. It would have to be something far beyond the reach
of conventional skills and abilities.

In Takamasa's hands, it was little more than a prank. A joke at the
game's expense. But there were evil people in this world who would use
it to make innocents suffer.

"*These ten contestants have made it through the preliminaries and into
the finals. Who will be the first to dive into our bubble bath of billions in
the monthly quiz show extravaganza, the Platinum Billion Quiz?! Catch
it live at seven PM tonight, with a repeat showing five hours later at
midnight...*"

The announcement came from a small waterproof TV, gently bob-
bing in the water alongside Midori.

"In summary," Midori said. "It's gonna be a pain." Sometimes, it took a beginner's eye to cut straight to the truth of the matter.

"Yeah," agreed Kaname. "A real pain in the ass."

He wasn't only thinking about Takamasa's Legacy, though. He swirled his hand in the pool water as he continued speaking.

"…'Money-grubber' is a compliment here in *Money (Game) Master.* And the current mastermind behind Extreme Pictures is a Dealer called Mother Loose. Just like Takamasa, there's a lot of legends surrounding her, though in her case, the rumors are a little different."

"She's famous?"

"More like infamous. She's on the level of Bloody Dancer, Criminal AO, and the leader of the Treasure Hermit Crabs, Frey(a)."

"…"

The girl in the plastic pool gave a questioning frown and clammed up. Perhaps it was hearing the name of a Dealer she thought of as nothing more than a womanizer (and manizer, for that matter) that had caused her to fall silent. Or perhaps it was hearing her own brother introduced in the same lineup.

His Magistellus, Tselika, was currently elsewhere, so Kaname took out his mostly obsolete smartphone and brought up a picture of Mother Loose's face. This was no selfie or commemorative photo, though. The subject's eyes were pointed off-screen. Overall, it felt like the kind of image you'd see next to the words *wanted criminal spotted by the shipyard in the dead of night.*

In any case, the subject of the photo certainly didn't *look* like a top-rate Dealer. It was a gentle-looking woman, wearing a plain white dress shirt and dark jeans, with a pastel-colored apron over the top. She had fluffy, chestnut-colored hair and sported a headband and heart necklace, neither of which appeared to be brand-name items. She looked more suited to carrying around a frying pan and spatula than an assault rifle. However, considering that even the relatively sensible Midori walked around Tokonatsu City in her black frilly bikini all the time with a pistol hidden in her skirt for self-defense, this Dealer's outfit looked like a bomb suit by comparison. Overall, she looked as if she lived in a completely different world from the one Kaname and Midori knew, and her natural housewife vibe was hard to deny.

However.

It was important to remember that this was *Money (Game) Master*. Midori froze in shock as she lay in the plastic kid's pool, looking at that single photo.

"...What on earth? This woman's equipment is packed full of defensive skills. They're stacked so high, she's practically a walking bomb shelter."

"I'll have you transcribe her skills in detail later. For now, just tell me what you can."

As Kaname had just said, the woman in the picture held a legendary status, much like Frey(a)'s.

"She's been affiliated with many teams up to now," he explained. "Or rather, every team she's been involved with has fallen apart. She apparently poisons the well of interpersonal relations by coddling everyone with kindness. Eventually, they realize she's just like that with everyone.'"

"Geez..."

"A mother of loose morals who takes anyone and everyone, adult or child, into her bosom. That's why she's called Mother Loose. Whether it's dependency or sticking to someone, she's the type of person that can't bear to be by herself. A perfect example of how comfort and peace aren't always good for people. The warmth she gives off is beyond lethal. The icing on the cake is that she doesn't even do it on purpose; she just wants to distract herself from her own loneliness."

Kaname wasn't too eager to press into her real life, but perhaps she came from a particularly unloving household, or had lived alone for an especially long period of time. All sorts of people logged in to *Money (Game) Master*, and different people had different ways of dealing with whatever ailed them.

"Just as an aside, it's very well known that she and Smash Daughter, another famous Dealer, are perpetually at each other's throats. We can only hope *she* doesn't decide to get involved...but if she does, we need to get out of there as fast as possible. When those two battle, it's like a disaster movie. We'll just have find a safe place to hide out until the heat dies down."

"Um."

Mother and Daughter.

In a game where your username could be anything you wished, it seemed unlikely they were actually related... In any case, it must really be serious if even Kaname quailed at the thought of their meeting.

"But aren't Extreme Pictures the kind of guys who do death-defying stunts for views? Why do they need this random mom character for support???"

"Maybe that's exactly why they need her. They're professional content creators, risking their lives for clicks, but if all of them are used to constant thrills, they lose sight of the layperson's viewpoint. Can't you see how they might need a person on set with more normal sensibilities, who gets shocked and worried about the same things as their viewers?"

"..."

"That's just how it is in reality. Humans have the weird habit of putting ends and means at opposite points of the spectrum. Even you, Midori. You stay up all night studying, not because you want to get the answers right, but because you want to be free of your exams as soon as possible, right?"

"Ugh."

"Don't worry. Even Takamasa fell for her charms once. He snapped right out of it once I hit him as hard as I could, though."

She was like a factory of motherly warmth. Extreme Pictures' very own Holy Mother. Judging from her past exploits, it didn't seem she had a great interest in money or intrigue, but at the same time, she would unconditionally support her teammates in whatever irresponsible acts they decided on. All the way until it drove them to ruin. Add the power of a Legacy into the mix, and it was easy to see how things could go very, very badly.

Midori exhaled through her nose.

"… I thought people came to the game to get away from their mothers."
"I could say the same thing about sisters…," Kaname mumbled.
"What was that?"

6

The mint-green coupe's engine roared as it raced along the coastline. A digital display on the wall of a peculiar cube-shaped building showed that it was past six PM. Kaname tapped his index finger on the edge of the steering wheel.

"It's good to be back behind this wheel…"

"Hmm?"

"That semitruck and mobile crane were way too big. The steering wheel was so large, it hurt my arms, the seats were too high, and the vehicle was too long. I was stressed out the whole time. This car's the best for me; it's what I'm used to."

"Right? I am glad you agree!! …H-hmph! Of course, it is only natural you should think that way, My Lord. Don't think I care one bit! Hmph!!"

Tselika folded her arms in the passenger seat, her forked tail swinging to and fro.

The Tap TV headquarters, the streaming network in charge of the Platinum Billion Quiz, was a very pretentious-looking building in the financial district. The place was filled with the eclectic mix of vehicles unique to the entertainment industry—semitrailers and minibuses for carrying around equipment and hired cars and taxis for ferrying people around. The thought that anyone in the crowd could be a famous celebrity was yet another pleasure you couldn't experience outside the game.

Indeed, there were many Dealers who had hidden their true identities, so there was always the chance that someone you met in the game could turn out to be the ruler of a nation.

Kaname was currently chatting with the girl riding the bright-red bike alongside him.

Midori: Full gas tank, new tires... There's nothing wrong with the bike, but I feel nervous. It feels heavier than usual.

Kaname: The effect is probably worse for a bike, but you're going to have to bear with it. Once we start this thing, there's not going to be any breaks.

Midori: I can't imagine sitting in one place for three hours, though.

Kaname: Just think of it like a movie. A long one. With that engine, you could drive across Japan in that time, as long as you didn't hit any traffic. You'd definitely get caught for speeding if you tried it in the real world, though.

Games were the place to do things that would be impossible in real life. Looking around now, however, these people seemed to have a different goal. Perhaps they were seeking to re-create something real that was otherwise out of reach. To them, the entertainment industry itself was like a fantasy world, rich in adventure.

Midori: Minibuses and chauffeurs... But everyone has their own vehicles and Magistelli in this game. Why would they let complete strangers drive them around? Aren't they scared?

Kaname: They enjoy the inconvenience. It's a status symbol. Kind of like carrying around a tiny handbag too small to even hold your lunch box.

What Kaname and Midori had set their sights on was not the broadcaster itself. After all, these were the headquarters of an AI company. Even if they'd brought a squad of tanks, they'd stand no chance against their PMC mercenaries.

Kaname and Midori drove on, passing the Tap TV headquarters and continuing along a coastal road. On the way, they overtook a young schoolgirl. She was dressed in a distinctive wide-brimmed witch's hat and school swimsuit, with a large sports towel wrapped around her neck like a cape. She rode a collapsible electric scooter, and strapped to her back was her weapon, Overkill. Originally intended as a semiautomatic sniper rifle, the weapon's accuracy was never quite enough, and so instead it was used for ultra–close quarters fighting, such as blasting a target through walls or locked doors. If Kaname recalled correctly, this Dealer had also customized the gun to take nonlethal electric rounds, which she used in conjunction with a stun gun attachment on the underside of the barrel.

Midori: It's kind of weird to see someone wearing a school regulation swimsuit in-game. It looks a bit stifling...or maybe the game has just poisoned my mind already.

Kaname: Remember what she looks like. That's Smash Daughter. We don't want her picking a fight with Mother Loose.

Midori turned back to look behind her, but the figure had already disappeared into the crowd, and all she could make out was her tanned Magistellus. With silvery-blue shoulder-length hair, the girl wore a white tank top and tight spats that made her resemble a gym instructor, and the jacket tied around her trim waist only added to the effect. She rode a scooter as well, a big one with a blue waterfall design.

Smash Daughter's electric bike was silent, so Tselika was only able to hear the hydrogen engine of the big scooter as it sped into the distance.

"She is an Apsaras. Apparently, the Hindu gods found them so beautiful that they took them as their wives so people would not fight over them."

"Oh? Does that sort of thing bother you, Tselika, as a succubus?"

"Hmph! Let me just say that had *I* been present at that discussion, the legend would have gone a little differently!"

Incidentally, given that the names Zeus and Jupiter had their roots in Indian deities, perhaps the East and the West were not so different after all.

In any case, all they could do was hope the girl in the school swimsuit and her Magistellus stayed well away from the action this time.

"Tselika, are you sure you've analyzed the footage correctly?"

"What sort of question is that? If I had noticed any mistakes, I would hardly give my report, would I?"

In her usual seat on the passenger's side, Tselika puffed up her cheeks like a little child.

"I used professional image-editing software costing over a million *snow* to analyze several of the backgrounds of Extreme Pictures' videos. It seems that everything within an area of the Second Industrial Estate was filmed."

"It's a big area, with lots of long, straight roads as well as hairpin turns. I guess it's almost like a test circuit for them."

"A home base like a Swiss Army Knife that allows them to take on all sorts of requests. They also rent warehouses and shipping containers on the same site, like in this video, where they've made up a laboratory for some silly science experiment."

"Oh, I haven't seen those yet, but they sure are popular recently. Things like blowing up liquid nitrogen at room temperature or playing around with magnesium."

"It seems that since Mother Loose joined, their videos have become more...home ec? Like this one, for example—'Freeze-Drying Food with Liquid Nitrogen!'"

"...That's the one that Smash Daughter left all those one-star reviews on, isn't it?"

"Mother Loose clearly enjoys baiting her as well. It's tough to say which of them has the advantage."

Their conflict was between them alone, and outsiders were best off staying out of it.

Takamasa had owned a tent somewhere on the outskirts of town, where he would test his weapons, but considering he had managed to develop the Legacies, perhaps he had constructed some secret base somewhere. If he did have a full-blown laboratory, Kaname had never seen it. Or maybe he had simply done everything in portable locations like his tent.

Money (Game) Master didn't cut any corners when it came to chemistry, either. You couldn't just toss ingredients into a cauldron or fairy spring and expect a Legacy to pop out. In order to make something, you had to obey all the same rules of physics, as in the real world.

Still, it was disheartening to see all this processing power going toward putting on a science show. This revolutionary chemistry simulator could potentially be used to develop radical new medicines and save people from incurable diseases. However, it seemed people were more interested in shooting each other for money.

Midori: Doesn't the industrial estate belong to an AI company?

Kaname: It's difficult to say for sure, but in many cases the roads are considered communal, since trucks from all different companies use them. We won't need to worry about the PMCs at the Second Industrial Estate so long as we don't break into any warehouses or destroy cargo.

Midori: Huh. I guess a sniper would need to be wary, though. They probably don't want you creeping all over their rooftops, either.

"Although you can always rent a warehouse and set up a base there if you wish," said Tselika, apparently unbothered that Midori could not hear her.

Midori: So we're going to make sure these Extreme Pictures guys can't cheat at the quiz, right?

Kaname: Pretty much, yeah. Their usual trick is to rewrite world records live on-air. Then, if their contestant gets the question wrong, they can complain that the answer itself is incorrect. It's like they get a second chance.

Midori: So the plan is to put a stop to that and put pressure on them. Then we'll say that if they don't want to go bankrupt, they need to give us their Legacy and tell us what they know about the list.

Kaname: The real interference is happening outside the quiz, so we just need to go to their proving ground and make sure they can't record any more videos.

Speeding along the coast of the financial district, the pair passed many beaches, harbors filled with yachts, and industrial areas, before arriving at a large oil-processing complex with angular concrete buildings and tall chimneys spewing out black smoke. The long dark shadows of the factories contrasted sharply against the orange of the evening sky.

"*Who will win tonight's top prize of one billion snow?! Find out right after this, on Platinum Billion Quiz!*" came the cheery voice on the radio.

"It's starting already," said Kaname as he checked the time on the windshield.

Kaname: We need to pay attention to what's happening on the quiz. The situation is going to shift, depending on the highs and lows of the program. We need to hit them at the right time if we're going to shake them up.

Midori: I know.

The two vehicles approached the grounds of the Second Industrial Estate, arriving at a pair of opened sliding metal doors. A single entrance, like the middle of an hourglass.

Kaname: Watch out for snipers.

Midori: Are they really that dangerous? I heard that in practice it's quite hard to hit a target even if you have them in your sights, since you have to take into account things like wind velocity, distance, and gravity.

Kaname despaired at the well-natured comment. She had a point. *Even Kaname, a longtime player, had never met an honest-to-god sniper in the game.* Meanwhile, Tselika started cackling in the passenger seat. Even so, as a longtime player, Kaname wished that Midori would trust his word and experience over whatever she might have read in an online encyclopedia anyone was allowed to edit. After all, he had handled more than his fair share of sniper rifles during his exploits, even going so far as to eschew skills or help from his Magistellus.

Kaname: Just be careful.

Midori: That's not a very good justification.

Kaname: Hmm. Don't they say it's the mark of one's rebellious phase to get irritated when people worry about you?

Midori: All right, I get it! Thank you ever so much for attending to my safety, you jerk!!

Kaname had made up the saying, but he also knew that people her age tended to follow any advice, so long as it sounded like something a famous person might have said… In any case, Kaname didn't need to dig himself in any deeper.

With Midori's unenclosed bike taking cover behind the coupe, the two vehicles passed through the gate. In the end, they didn't run into any snipers, and they entered a wide-open area with asphalt roads. It was decorated with stencil graffiti depicting a grim reaper holding a video camera, presumably the mark of Extreme Pictures.

They could see dozens of square factories, with bundles of thick pipes writhing up and across the roads like footbridges. Rows of dimly lit chimneys stretched into the sky like a bamboo grove, their red lights blinking enchantingly. It was not unlike a port at night, the air permeated with the smell of death…and yet that wasn't quite right, either. Clouds of steam and forklifts and trucks passed to and fro beneath large cargo cranes that stood like electricity pylons. These slid horizontally along their tracks as men in work clothes went about their business. The personnel were surely mechanical NPCs controlled by the AI companies, but it was reassuring to see traces of ostensibly "human" activity. Perhaps it was like leaving a radio or TV on as background noise while you got some chores done on a lazy afternoon.

And then.

"Wh-wh-what on earth is this mountain of scrap…?!" cried Tselika in shock.

In a material loading bay was a pile of metal about three stories high. But it wasn't shipping containers that made up those pyramids of steel.

"Whoooa?! There's crushed-up vehicles everywhere! It's a graveyard of cars!!"

Kaname didn't even flinch as he continued to steer the coupe.

"You should do at least a little research before coming, Tselika. Didn't you check what events were going on during this time frame?"

A banner hung from one of the pipe bundles stretching across the road, reading:

"Out with the old! Tokonatsu City Scrap Iron Fair, I Love Fe! Five Snow *Per Gram!!"*

The banner's irreverent tone threw Tselika into a twitching fit. From elsewhere could be heard the earsplitting, mechanical clank of heavy machinery that was no doubt at this very moment creating a pile of cars resembling flattened sandwiches.

Midori: I wonder if they're melting them down into girders or something. Five snow per gram...is that good?

Kaname: Even the smallest of these cars would go for around three to four hundred thousand at that rate. Huh. For a run-down vehicle with a few problems, that's a lot better than what you'd get flogging it secondhand, plus you wouldn't have to deal with people complaining about the mileage or the strange smell coming out of the air conditioning.

"Braaaghh! You two are going to drive me to lunacy!! Do you not have an ounce of love for motor vehicles?!"

Cars properly parked were immune to destruction and theft, but otherwise they were fair game. At rates like these, there were probably more than a few enterprising Dealers blasting people's cars off the road and towing them away to be scrapped.

Even though this was Extreme Pictures' territory, it was highly likely that other Dealers had been coming and going, too. Thus, Kaname's and Midori's presence here was not too suspicious. That would change, however, once they got busy.

Kaname: Midori, I've shared my map. I've put a few icons here and there, but you know what I mean by those, right?

Midori: Roger. So, basically, there are a bunch of long, straight roads by the shore, and as you get farther inland, they get narrower and messier with all the factories and stuff.

The pair cruised down a seafront road lined with cargo cranes and piles of squashed vehicles, and they passed a spot where a bunch of cars and bikes were gathered. The makes were different, but the vehicles all sported the same logo they had been seeing in various locations around the industrial estate: the camcorder-wielding grim reaper. A large crowd of people were gathered around, from big tough men to little girls in swimsuits and school backpacks.

...Of course, such depictions didn't necessarily line up with the players' true ages and genders.

It was a scene that would fit right in at a shady harbor in the dead of night, but one figure among them looked decidedly out of place. Long, fluffy chestnut-brown hair, adorned with a cheap headband. A simple shirt and dark jeans and a cooking apron decorated with pastel hearts. She gave the overall impression of an airheaded young housewife, but one with no qualms about showing off the shape of her hips. Her gentle smile stood out like a sore thumb among the sea of grim-faced, murderous stuntmen.

A bottomless mire who would draw in all around her to fill the void of her own loneliness.

Mother Loose.

It wasn't the guns and the cars that caused the Lion's Nose to surge into overdrive. It was that woman.

"I guess we've found the Extreme Pictures away team," Kaname murmured.

A long, straight road, like a runway, was a fundamental component of a car-testing course. A mainstay of death-defying stunts. Perfect for forging a new land speed record. Typically, you would load up a dragster with rocket or jet engines and send it on its way. Or you could set up a ramp for aerial stunts, or a wall of cardboard or straw to be set on fire; all of this was far easier to do on a long, flat surface.

"It's time," said Tselika.

"..."

There came a series of electronic beeps, counting away the seconds, before one final, longer beep signaled seven o'clock sharp. Then, Tap TV's livestream appeared in a square window in one corner of the car windshield.

"It's seven o'clock! And that means it's time for the final round of the Platinum Billion Quiz!!"

The fuse had been lit. The battle would take place over the next three hours—the length of the livestreamed quiz show. The orange glow of evening had already given way to a starry sky.

"We're coming at you live from the helipad atop the Tap TV head-quarters. I will be your host tonight, in my bunny ears and silk hat, with a PhD and glasses to match, Bunny K! Now then, it's time to meet our ten contestants, our fearless fighters who tore through the preliminaries for a chance to win that all-important one billion snow prize!!"

Kaname heard the distant pop and crackle of fireworks, and explosions of red and green flared over the city.

"Guns and cars get his blood pumping. It's Super Answer!! Next, he knows it all when it comes to anime and data idols, M-Scope!! And contestant number three..."

It was finally beginning. The tingle of the Lion's Nose grew ever stronger.

The enemy had the Legacy. They had a piece of Takamasa's soul, a copy or section of his papers. And they had the encryption key to be able to read it.

But Kaname wasn't going to let them do as they pleased any longer. He would put his very life on the line to get all of it back.

Kaname: Midori. We're starting.

Midori: Here's what I can tell about their outfits. As for weapons, it seems they're mostly prioritizing close range, but they're also warding off blunt weapon and vehicle collision damage with the Shockproof skill. You'll probably have to shoot them to make them Fall, so don't let your guard down if they get blown away by an explosion or hit by a car. They can survive those kinds of impacts.

Kaname: And Mother Loose? She doesn't quite look like the rest of the stunt team.

Midori: She's special. She's buffed against shock damage, too, but... take her apron, for example. It's made of a special material. What's more, it's stacked with Bulletproof, Bombproof, Fireproof...basically everything defense-related. Her bullet resistance is by far the highest. I bet she could survive a point-blank shotgun blast. You might as well pretend she has a force field around her at all times.

"It's frightening how the girl can do that without skills or Legacies," said Tselika. "I bet she could locate your nipples through your clothing."

"Cindy was good at that sort of thing, wasn't she? With such a serious look on her face, too…"

"Oh, Ayame's Magistellus? I seem to recall she often got slapped on account of that, didn't she?"

"That was just how they talked to each other, I think."

Kaname pulled the hand brake, and the mint-green coupe swung around in a U-turn. Its headlights fell on the crowd of cars and bikes they had just passed. Then he pushed the hand brake back down and slammed his foot onto the gas pedal.

7

Ker-rash!!

The mint-green coupe slammed right into the cluster of cars and bikes parked at the side of the long, straight road. Motorcycles and low-profiled sports cars flew across the pier and dropped into the ocean.

"Rhhh?!"

"Grrr!!"

The Dealers, as expected, would not go down so easily. The stuntmen of Extreme Pictures leaped for cover in all directions, before pulling out their handguns.

At the same time, the unarmed housewife, Mother Loose, suddenly stepped forward.

She could survive a point-blank shotgun blast.

Was this kind of self-sacrificing stunt what made her motherly aura so suffocating?

Midori: Stay away from her!! She's packed full of defensive skills; her yellow apron, her clothes, her cheap heart necklace, and even the bra straps showing through her shirt! She's got over ten stacks of Shock-proof alone! If you crash into her, it'll be like hitting a concrete post!!

"Dammit!!"

Giving up on the pickup truck that he had failed to completely run into the sea, Kaname pushed the gear stick into reverse and pressed down on the gas pedal.

"Oh my."

As the tires skidded against the road, Kaname heard the young woman's sugary voice, along with seeing her gentle, all-consuming, and yet devilishly corrosive smile.

"...It's been such a long time, Called Game. Is your team still around? Back then, I was sad I could never be part of it, but maybe now's our chance. Come into my arms, and let me make it all better."

Stay away from me, you human quicksand. Your brainwashing won't work on me!

Kaname felt a sharp pain in the tip of his nose. She must have known she would win in a head-on collision, because Mother Loose walked over slowly, leaned down, and left a lipstick mark on the driver's side window.

Then time sped up again, and the coupe reversed away from Mother Loose at full speed.

As she looked on with a peaceful smile, a whisper came from her soft, plump lips.

"Over here, Psyche."

A figure responded to her summons. With both eyes tightly shut and a kitchen knife squeezed in both hands, she rushed forward, her red school backpack rattling.

"Prepare to die, enemy of my mother!!"

"What the...?!"

A girl in shorts, who looked about ten years old, ran toward the side of the car as Kaname was still reversing. Panicking, he spun the wheel and began snaking backward, narrowly avoiding her. This was no benevolence on Kaname's part, though. The buzzing in his nose had grown even stronger.

The girl had pallid skin and a black bowl cut, with a paper talisman stuck to her brow. She looked like a knock-off version of Midori's Magistellus, Meiki.

"A Shikaisen! That must be her Magistellus!!"

"What kind of mother *is* she, spelling 'Psyche' with the character for 'wife'? That's no name to give a little girl!" shouted Tselika.

"Is that how it's spelled? How can you tell just from the sound?" replied Kaname.

Magistelli shared their Dealer's skills, and Mother Loose was a walking fortress. Therefore, as ridiculous as it seemed, if Kaname had so much as bumped the little girl in the white blouse and pink cardigan, he would have totaled his car. In the gun-filled world of *Money (Game) Master*, to rush someone, especially a car, with a knife was essentially suicide. That it was a legitimate strategy for Psyche just went to show how formidable her defenses really were.

As the rabble began to open fire, Kaname let go of the wheel, putting the car into a spin. Once the vehicle had made a complete 180-degree turn, he twisted the wheel in the opposite direction to regain control and sped off as fast as he could. Once out of range, he breathed a sigh of relief, more from being free of that rotten smile than from having escaped the stuntmen. Without any gunfire-enhancing skills whatsoever, they were hardly a threat.

The three-hour nonstop endurance race had finally begun.

The industrial estate was roughly ten kilometers all the way around, but who knew how many laps Kaname would have to complete by the time the night was through?

Meanwhile…

"Wha…? Hey…! You already smashed it up?! My temple, my beautiful baby, look what's happened to its face! What are you going to do about this?!"

"Um, well. It's five *snow* per gram, so at seven hundred kilograms that makes…hmm, but subtracting all the carbon-based materials…"

"If you make me do that calculation, My Lord, I will push you out of the car!"

A group of several headlights finally appeared in Kaname's rearview mirror. The Extreme Pictures reserve team should have been on standby, waiting to interfere with the quiz show, but it seemed they wanted to knock out any potential problems ahead of time for some peace of mind.

On the livestream, the hostess smiled in her eccentric bunny costume. It consisted of a purple vest and pencil skirt, as well as ears and a tail, and somehow it gave the overall impression of a tailcoat. She touched her finger to one arm of her glasses and spoke.

"Now it's time to explain the rules! We've got a hundred multiple-choice questions to go, and it's first to the buzzer who gets to answer! Whoever gets the most points by the end is tonight's winner! However, get even one question wrong, and bzzz, you're out! And finally, whoever's in first place gets only one point for every two correct answers, while the person in last place gets a whopping ten points for each!"

It was a little convoluted, but the idea was to keep the contestants' scores neck and neck. It would be no fun if one person held the lead. The hostess continued, wagging her little round tail.

"If no one can answer in the allotted time, then the points are carried over to the next question! That means if two rounds go by without an answer, the next contestant to answer will get three points! If combined with the loser's privilege, you can get twenty or thirty points at once! So keep your head in the game until the very end!!"

It was practically impossible to set up such conditions as a participant, but the chance that the equivalent of a triple seven might naturally arise, no matter how improbable, kept the viewers on the edges of their seats.

Come to think of it, Takamasa had always been good at quizzes, although he was less interested in answering them and more interested in setting them up, especially at parties, and especially if there were girls involved. More than a few times, Kaname had been forced to pick up the tab for their meal as a result (even though eating in *Money (Game) Master* didn't provide nourishment).

Midori: What happens if they all get disqualified? Does nobody get the jackpot, or does it roll over to next month?

Kaname: It's fastest finger first, so it's impossible for two contestants to be disqualified at the same time. If nine players drop out, they'll just declare the last one the winner. I don't think that's likely, though.

Midori: I guess so. If nobody knows the answer, they can just wait and it'll go to the next question, after all.

Kaname: By the way, don't fixate on the guys tailing us. There could be more lying in ambush ahead. And don't trust that lame reaper logo to tip you off, either. You'll end up with a knife in your side.

Kaname distanced himself from Midori's bike, and his tires screeched against the asphalt as he took off from the straight coastal road and into the jumbled factory area. Once there, he suddenly slammed on the brakes, causing a gullwing sports car that had been tailing him to crash into the rear of the coupe. Then, he pressed on the gas pedal once more and sped off, but not before rolling down his side window and delivering two shots into the stationary opponent's head with his short-range sniper rifle.

Tselika held her head in her hands and groaned, looking like she was about to tear her own horns out.

"...First the front, now the back..."

The pain of the Lion's Nose continued unabated. Kaname beat a hasty retreat from the gullwing, the driver's bloodied face pressing down the horn, before a large pickup truck came crashing through it.

The square window in the corner of his windshield still displayed the hostess, Bunny K, in her purple vest, rousing the crowd through the lapel mic nestled in her exposed bosom.

"Who's going to take the lead? Our all-important first topic is...ta-daa!! Cars! Pretty basic for Dealers, am I right?"

"Ah!"

Kaname gasped, his attention diverted from the assassin on his tail toward the screen in front of him.

Kaname: Midori, I'll draw away the enemies. Go and see if Extreme Pictures is setting anything up on the straight roads! Take them out if you have to!!

Midori: What? Me? All I have is this self-defense pistol! Besides, can't we just keep our eyes on this Super Answer guy? He's not doing anything unusual.

Kaname: He might mess up. We never know.

Midori: Really? Wouldn't they be good at car questions since they do stunts for a living?

Though it was meant to be a multiple-choice quiz, in practice, things were turning out very differently.

"*Question two! What electronic system controls the vertical movement of...—?*"

"*Active suspension!!*"

"*Wow, super-fast answer, Super Answer! However, please remember to press the buzzer next time, okay?*"

The contestant was answering within five seconds, before hearing the end of the question or even seeing what the choices were. He seemed to be unstoppable. However, that couldn't be further from the truth.

The Lion's Nose tingled. It was urging Kaname to pay attention right now, if he wanted to win the fight ahead.

Kaname: Car questions make it that much easier for Extreme Pictures to change the answer. If they want to prove that cars can fly, for example, they just need to make it happen. At least, it's a lot simpler than if the questions were on Japanese characters or the origins of the universe. And if he knows he has a second chance, he might let down his guard. Not to mention, he probably crammed all that knowledge into his brain like studying for a school test, so it's not going to be perfect. And there's always the chance he's misremembered something tiny, something he wouldn't even realize, precisely because it's his specialty. So watch out, anything could happen!!

That wasn't to say, however, that Kaname was perfectly fine with sending Midori into a horde of professionals when she was just a rookie atop an unarmored bike. He clicked his tongue and took aim at a pile of wooden crates by the side of the road. As he drove past, he fired at one at the bottom, causing the whole pile to sway, before falling into the road and blocking the path of the pursuing pickup.

"That will not stop him for long, My Lord."

"I know."

As the truck plowed through the boxes, smashing them to splinters, a new force suddenly descended on the scene—the AI PMCs...the factories' security.

"The roads may be public access, but buildings and cargo still belong to the AI companies! If you destroy them, you have to face the wrath of their protectors!!"

Heavy machine guns mounted atop the flat factory roofs swiveled to face their target, squeaking like rusty swing sets. They were four-man fixed emplacements, firing armor-piercing anti-materiel rounds faster than an assault rifle.

The sturdy pickup truck was torn apart like paper as it took sustained fire from all directions. Regular bulletproofing wasn't enough to stop it. It wasn't like the PMCs had access to any fancy skills, but the sheer amount of firepower was more than any conventional armor could handle.

"Another one down."

"My Lord, those muscle-bound meatheads are still on the move. They're pointing their machine guns at us!"

"Well, of course they are. I was the one who first attacked their cargo. Look at our attention meter linked to the car's onboard cameras… Going by their sight lines, it says we've got over forty pairs of eyes on us right now. No way we can outrun all of that."

"Whaaaat?!"

The buzz of the Lion's Nose was only getting stronger, but the Dealer boy merely gave a small grin. He pulled the hand brake, drifting into a small maze of passages where the rooftop guns couldn't reach. And since they were fixed guns, there was no way for them to follow. Looking in his mirrors, Kaname saw that several PMC armored cars had begun pursuit, but unable to make the sharp turn like he had, they had all crashed. Kaname continued to make his way through the twisting passage, and then…

"Tselika. Hand grenades."

"Five left, My Lord. These things give off a lot of shrapnel, so make sure my temple doesn't get caught up in the blast!!"

Kaname's pursuers were still hot on his heels. After pulling the pin with his teeth, he tossed a grenade out the side window, at the nearby wall of the factory. By the time it bounced back, the mint-green coupe had left, replaced with the Extreme Pictures' vehicle behind them. The explosive landed neatly atop the sports car, before caving in the low roof with its violent explosion.

Kaname didn't even have to rely on skills for that one. He drove back around to the seafront road, a cloud of gray dust in his wake. Charging right toward him was a large motorcycle decorated in bright-red autumn leaves. And behind Midori was a station wagon hot on her tail.

Kaname: Just keep on going straight.

Midori: I'm sorryyy!

As they passed, he fired from the window. A cobweb of cracks spread across the station wagon's windshield, and red splatter coated the inside, making it obvious what had happened to the driver. *That's what you get for stalking a middle school girl.* With the dead man's foot on the gas pedal, the car continued to accelerate, finally driving off the end of the pier and into the black ocean.

Kaname was used to looking after Takamasa like this, in the old days. In the end, though, it was Takamasa who had stood up for him, and it had cost him his life.

Midori's tires squealed as she executed a U-turn and rode back over.

Among the glitzed-out sports cars and armored jeeps, one vehicle stood out. It was a small smart car, round like an egg, and painted a chocolate-brown shade that gave it a rather refined look among the vivid tropical colors of Tokonatsu City. Perhaps it was colored that way to make dirt less visible. In any case, it was a vehicle one would expect to see in the supermarket parking lot on a weekend, not here.

Kaname: Watch out, Midori. Mother Loose is on the move...

Midori: What on earth? How does she expect to take part in a car chase with that thing?!

They heard the roar of an engine. The door to the car's trunk flew open, and a gout of flame flew from the back like a fighter jet.

Kaname: What do you think happens if you stuff a powerful engine into a light vehicle? She's sacrificed its stability for ramming power! Don't let it hit you!!

If the car was made too light, there was a risk of it not being able to maintain speed, but it looked like the driver had taken that into account by delivering a series of short bursts of acceleration instead of slamming down on the gas pedal. Furthermore, the frame was likely rigid, like that of an old foreign car, for more impact damage. This, however, meant that in the case of a collision, the most dangerous place to be was in the driver's seat of the car itself.

Midori: That's why she's so buffed up with defensive skills! She's just going to crash right into us and come out of it unscathed...

This was a stunt you couldn't replicate outside the game. But there was no use crying about it. The sweet-smelling housewife had simply adapted to the new rules of play.

"Question five! In aerodynamics, there are three major coefficients, CD, CL, and CYM. Which of these correlates with an increased resistance to crosswinds? Oh? I managed to finish reading the question that time. Now, on to the choices. Is it A: CD? B: CYM? C: CL? Or D: All three...?"

Midori: Our man Super Answer isn't sounding too super this time.

Kaname: He can't afford to make a mistake. Remember, one strike and you're out. Extreme Pictures must be under a lot of tension right now. We have to ramp up the pressure!

Extreme Pictures had the power to turn a wrong answer into a right one. At the other end of the long, straight road, the stunt team was in the middle of making their final preparations, using an air compressor to remove even the tiniest debris from the road. Soon, they would be called on to execute their death-defying stunt, and when that time came, their path would need to be as pristine as an airport runway. The stunt needed to go perfectly to give Super Answer a second chance at life.

Midori: What are we going to do? Mother Loose is on our tail!

Kaname: Let's get over to the stunt course. They're planning a big trick that even a speck of dust on the runway will ruin. Mother Loose won't want to mess it up, so it might make her steer away!!

It wasn't the air compressors or the cars that were important. Kaname took a brief look at their equipment and...

"Tselika. Tag any camera lenses on the windshield. There's no point in doing their stunt if they can't record it!"

"Yes, My Lord. But there are quite a lot, if we count onboard cameras and smartphones as well."

"And ready another grenade."

"Down to four. Do not forget we have a long night ahead of us, My Lord."

For starters, Kaname set his sights on the specialized film cameras and fired a few shots from Short Spear. Then, with no reason to linger, he drove headfirst into a man hurriedly aiming a large pistol with both hands and broke free from the enemy circle.

A few seconds later, there was a small clatter—the sound of Tselika's parting gift dropping from her side window and bouncing off the ground. The explosion would finish off anyone with phones and onboard cameras that Kaname had failed to shoot.

"They're too reliant on defensive skills."

Skills could be useful, but their versatility could also lead to trouble. Since both sides had access to the same skill, that made it easier to come up with countermeasures. For example, the Bulletproof skill only kept bullets up to about .45 caliber (though the exact value depended on how many stacks one had) from penetrating clothing. It did not reduce the impact damage to zero. Thus, you could still shoot at a Bulletproof opponent, then, while they were stunned from the blow, drive into them with your car. This time, Tselika had left a grenade to make doubly sure. Unless the opponent had stacked up defensive skills of every kind, like Mother Loose, multiple simultaneous attacks of different damage types were usually enough to take them out.

"Mother Loose isn't as dumb as she looks. I'd kill for just one good shot at her rear end..."

"What was that, My Lord? Don't tell me you prefer tight jeans to a miniskirt?!"

The Lion's Nose had abated to a low hum, but it was still there. The threat of death constantly loomed. Once Kaname had left the stunt course, Mother Loose and the rest of her team resumed their pursuit.

But Kaname simply smiled. He was a fearsome Dealer indeed, to smile at a time like this.

Midori: Oh geez. How many of those cameras do they have?

Kaname: We can't finish them off now. I've put an icon on your map. Turn there, and go back into hiding.

Midori: But then how are we going to beat Extreme Pictures?!

Kaname: Now's not the time to get greedy. Just do as I say. I'll explain everything.

The goal was to break the link between Extreme Pictures and Super Answer and, by doing so, threaten them enough to make them hand over the list of Legacies and the decryption key needed to unravel its secrets.

Takamasa would not have needed the key to read and write the list, since he had encrypted it by hand. Really, he ought to have destroyed it once he was done. However, there was always the chance he might want to share the list with somebody. Perhaps that might have been his friend, Kaname, or his sister, Midori. There was no way to know. What Kaname did know was that there was no way he would have wanted to show the list to a complete stranger.

If they destroyed Extreme Pictures, or Super Answer made a mistake and was disqualified, Kaname would miss his chance to negotiate. With the Leviathans, Kaname was able to get what he needed in the confusion of the Stadium's handover, but he would get no such second chance here.

Midori: ...This is so slow. I hate doing all this groundwork.

Kaname: What are the PMCs wearing, by the way?

Midori: Um...I don't think they even use skills, to be honest. Their base stats are so high anyway. And don't they usually just bulk up and stick to one spot? I mean, all they're doing is firing from their stationary machine guns. I guess you could just take out all their guns, and then they'd be plodding around like idiots. That way, we could easily outpace them.

Exactly.

Extreme Pictures weren't the only ones on the industrial estate. There were also the AI-controlled PMCs. Midori couldn't let her guard down just because she had ducked into the twisting roads of the factory area, and the enemy couldn't, either.

Mother Loose's high-powered car was like a missile. It was all right on the long coastal roads, but in that tight maze of passages, she would risk being easily outflanked.

"...We push them up against the wall, and then take off the pressure. Make it so they don't know when they can relax. Then, once they're completely psychologically broken, they'll be like putty in our hands."

"I suppose such *adult* strategies are difficult for the weedy kid to grasp," said Tselika. "Not everything in this world is settled with a proposal and a happily-ever-after."

"If she hates laying groundwork, then perhaps she prefers to wait for someone else to get results...? That girl is quite innocent."

"If it were you, My Lord, you wouldn't give them time to think. You'd drive your prey to the wall and make them say exactly what you wanted to hear. If you really put your mind to it, you could have the Treasure Hermit Crabs leader on his knees."

"Don't say it like that," Kaname sighed. But just then, his attention was drawn to the livestream.

"*Time's up! The correct answer for question five was...B! Looks like that's our first carryover. That means whoever gets question six correct gets double points! Don't miss your chance!! Especially M-Scope, our last-place contestant! ☆*"

Kaname tapped his finger impatiently against the round edge of the steering wheel.

"...Still no stunt, huh?"

"It is still early days," said Tselika. "If he self-destructed and disqualified himself now, he would lose everything. Now that they've had a moment to relax, go and slap them right in their slack-jawed mugs. Give them no quarter, until they are no longer able to tell in which drawer to stash the memory of what's happening to them."

It was possible to relieve stress with skills like Stress Care, but it was impossible to reduce it to zero. Furthermore, the effects of pressure on a person's mind varied, depending on the situation, particularly if one's life was in danger. Breaking someone's spirit normally took years, but through intense torture or sustained bombing, you could achieve it in the course of just a few hours. Prolonged exposure to the fear of death could truly turn someone into a shell of their former self. It was no exaggeration to say that a person could change overnight.

The demon smiled, as though the sin miring this world was sweet nectar to her tongue.

It was easy to make decisions in the game that you would never dream of making in real life.

"Time for a little mind control. ☆ There is still a long way to go before we reach a hundred questions, after all! Three more hours before the stream ends. Let's keep it up and trample their nerves into the dust, until we can march them around like robots! Until they're so far gone, not even Mother Loose can save them!!"

8

"And question fifty goes to Risk Ready! Since she's in dead last, that lands her ten points, taking her all the way up to fifth place!"

The time was half past eight. The show's hostess, the woman in a silk hat with attached bunny ears, was keeping the pace well.

"Two contestants have been disqualified so far. This is where things start to get serious, as we go into the match's second half! The next topic is...ta-daa! 2D!! Here it is, M-Scope, the round you've been waiting for! Can he pull off a comeback?!"

Since many of the contestants were fast on the buzzer, answering even before the question was fully read, the time would fly by if the bespectacled hostess did not intersperse chatter and jokes to pad it out, mainly at the contestants' expense. For the viewers, this was a great way to add variety to the show, but for the contestants, who only wanted to focus on the questions, it was a dangerous trap that could ruffle their feathers if they weren't careful.

"Right on time," said Tselika. "Train conductors could learn a thing or two."

"I wonder if a train conductor hostess would work. I mean, they have the uniforms…"

"Fool, I meant from you. You are so precise, it's frightening. Though I suppose I have no right to talk."

Kaname and Midori were certainly playing the mouse at this point in the chase. With the Lion's Nose constantly on alert, they navigated the tight corners and narrow streets of the industrial estate like a race circuit, skirmishing with Extreme Pictures whenever the quiz reached a turning point. The PMC attention meter on the car dashboard, which used the onboard cameras to count the pairs of eyes watching the vehicle, never left the double digits. They were in hot pursuit, taking potshots as soon as the line of fire was clear.

Kaname always remembered to leave his pursuers a little leeway, and never finish them off completely. The idea was to keep them in a state of constant tension.

Midori: Does it seem like they're getting slower to you? I wonder if they're trying to bait us.

In fact, this was because the prolonged struggle was starting to take its toll on them, but Kaname was careful not to let Midori figure that out. He didn't want her to let down her guard just yet. One direct hit could take her out.

Mother Loose's smart car was nowhere to be seen, either. Though it was hard to imagine that bundle of trust and warmth would be so easily affected by the stress. In fact, perhaps she had called off the heat herself, so she could soothe their tired minds over the comms.

But that would only treat the symptoms. It was clear which side was winning.

The Extreme Pictures Dealers were at their wits'. end. Their minds were falling apart, their concentration failing.

It was not an exact science, of course, but Kaname trusted the buzzing in his nose.

Kaname: Midori, watch out for the Legacy. It's about time for them to bring out the mortar, #thunderbolt.err!

But Kaname didn't even have time to read the girl's reply.

Shwmp!!!!!!

There was a sound from far off, like the uncorking of a massive champagne bottle. Kaname didn't have time for proper grammar.

Kaname: theyve fired midori go to map icon!!

"Tselika, check the onboard footage for whatever you can find!!"

"I shall try, but I cannot guarantee I can triangulate the origin from a single launch."

It was the mortar, #thunderbolt.err. Its payload had fallen nearby, and a sickening explosion shook the very core of Kaname's body, like a tree struck by lightning.

He ducked the car into a side passage, but it seemed the shot had not been aimed at Kaname at all. It landed somewhere farther up, wiping out the PMCs' fixed machine guns that had been hindering the group's movements…and serving as a test shot to calibrate the weapon to current conditions, no doubt.

The number on Kaname's attention meter began falling, and finally the window disappeared entirely. Any PMCs who had been following him had just been completely wiped out.

And yet the sensation in his nose was stronger than ever before. For at last, a fearsome foe had reared its head. Capable of exterminating the PMCs, invincible, undefeatable. Simply escaping with your life would be considered a victory.

They held the remains of his friend, Takamasa, in their greedy hands.

"Tselika!"

"The sound came from the east. Approximately six hundred meters, but I do not have precise coordinates. There are too many buildings in the way; I cannot get a good look!!"

Boom!! There was a second explosion. But Kaname couldn't focus solely on tracking down the mortar's location. Extreme Pictures was still hot on his heels. For now, he twisted the steering wheel, putting the coupe into a drift, and headed eastward.

"What about the Legacy's effects? Its trajectory, firing range, loading speed, accuracy, power... There has to be something special about it! Something you can't replicate with regular skills!!"

"Wait a second. Wait, wait... Now that you mention it, it is strange those PMCs all died in one shot. Some of the emplacements are fortified with sandbags and shields. How could a single explosion take out all four of them?"

"So power, then."

"Not quite. The sandbags have not been disturbed in the slightest. It's almost as if the explosion ignored them completely!"

Kaname quickly shared this information with his twin-tailed coconspirator.

Midori: So what's so good about it?

Kaname: The fact it can pass through walls and obstacles means even being under a sturdy roof won't save you. They could assassinate somebody in a battleship or a bomb shelter with this thing.

"A bombproof jacket might also count as a kind of obstacle," added Tselika. "That weapon would negate even the most expensive equipment, and perhaps even the effect of the Bombproof skill itself."

That meant it could even take out Mother Loose if it hit her directly. In the unrestrained world of *Money (Game) Master*, it was often good offense that won out over a solid defense. Perhaps these guys were going for both, or perhaps they wanted control of the Legacy so it couldn't be used against them.

Midori: But then what about the ground?

Kaname: It doesn't seem to pass through the ground. Maybe it requires them to set the detonation altitude ahead of time. In any case, it's another one of Takamasa's monster weapons!!

At this point, it was impossible to identify a single flaw. If it came for Kaname and Midori, there would be no escape.

"..."

"My Lord, what are you doing?"

"It's only six hundred meters. That's about ten seconds at top speed. And the closer I get, the harder it is for them to aim at me…"

"But we do not even know precisely where they are, My Lord! They could be on the ground, or even on the back of a flatbed truck. They might not even still be there by the time we arrive…!!"

"Yes they will, Tselika. Think about the merits of #thunderbolt.err."

"Huh? What do you mean? It ignores defenses, correct? It's a bolt of death from the blue for anything within a three-kilometer radius. A cheat weapon beyond all reason!"

"No, it's not."

Kaname slammed his foot on the gas, and the mint-green coupe began to speed up.

"It's one of the Legacies. Irreplaceable. As much as they want to use it, they can't allow it to be stolen or destroyed. That means Extreme Pictures will want it in a place of absolute safety, which of course doesn't exist. That's where we'll find #thunderbolt.err."

"And where are we going to find such an oddly specific location?!"

"The specificity makes it easy. We just have to think about it. The first shot came from six hundred meters to the east. Search for this phrase in that area. You'll see what I mean."

Kaname muttered the magic words, and various info and markers appeared all over the windshield, superimposed over the view.

"Bingo." Kaname Suou smiled. And then…

There was a squeal of tearing metal as the coupe ripped its way through a shutter and into the huge storehouse that served as one of Extreme Pictures' laboratories.

The room was about as large as a supermarket, but considerably emptier. Four young men and women sat around its center, but there was little they could do to defend themselves now, even with the Legacy. At this range, they'd only blow themselves up, too.

Kaname plowed through the two standing to the right of the Legacy and pulled hard on the hand brake, swinging around and dodging the incoming gunfire before pointing Short Spear out the window and taking out the other two. He based his decisions on whether he'd prefer the young men or the young women to live the longest. The rest he did on a whim.

But for some reason, the pain in his nose remained.

"Shockproof! They're resistant to blunt force attacks!!" yelled Midori, speeding in after him.

"Grhh."

Kaname shot additional rounds into the ones playing dead on the ground. These were members of Extreme Pictures. Professional stuntmen and women. Of course they had set up their skills so that they could survive taking a hit from a car.

"…At this rate, even secondhand Dealers will not want to touch this cursed vehicle…"

Kaname ignored the complaints from the passenger seat and pointed his gun at the last one on the floor, a tanned woman in cargo shorts and a bikini top.

"Midori, pick up #thunderbolt.err!!" he shouted through the open window.

"Okay, but where are we? Inside a building?"

Kaname took a moment to explain the situation to Midori, who had stopped atop her bike with one foot on the ground.

"Since the mortar can pass right through obstacles, there's no problem with firing it from inside a closed space."

And under normal circumstances, trespassing on an AI company's private property would cause the PMCs to come down on you like a swarm of angry bees. To search each building would be like digging for gold in a minefield, and Kaname wouldn't have even attempted it but for the fact that he already knew Extreme Pictures was renting indoor space here.

After Midori finished packing up #thunderbolt.err, the young woman held at gunpoint stared at Kaname, her hands raised slightly above her head.

"...You were after the Legacy?"

"No. I'm not done yet."

"You bastard...!!"

"I'll keep going for as long as it takes. Until you've given back everything you stole. Think hard, you and the other survivors. Remember what it is you stole, before the PTSD causes a mental breakdown. Even Stress Care skills won't eliminate it entirely. Or are you hoping Mother Loose can help you? Bottle feeding won't do you much good now."

With the squeal of burning rubber, Kaname turned and drove back out of the warehouse alongside Midori, the folded-up mortar on her back like a telescope.

"Tselika. How's the quiz going? I had to look away for a second."

"We've just passed question seventy. Super Answer is in the top spot for now."

"Well, he must be very proud of himself. Excellent timing. I wonder how far he'll fall once he finds out we've taken away his precious Legacy."

"My, my, My Lord. You really can be a ferocious hunter when you want to be."

Tselika leaned back in her seat and clasped her hands behind her head, pushing out her large breasts before she continued.

"Should we really leave the mortar in Midori's hands? She's unarmored atop that bike, remember."

"Actually, it should have the opposite effect. They won't shoot while she's holding it and risk damaging the Legacy. She's safe. From Extreme Pictures, at least."

"...Which means."

"We have the Legacy. All we need now is the encryption key to decipher the list."

Kaname gripped the steering wheel and looked straight ahead.

Extreme Pictures had been put to rest. A foe still remained, and it was not the PMCs.

"Things are starting to look a lot like they did with the Leviathans. We need to keep our head in the game. If they're going to interfere with us again, this is where they'll do it."

9

There was a small metallic *clank!* as the sniper set up position atop one of the large cargo cranes by the harbor. From there, they commanded a sweeping view of the entire industrial estate.

This was private land, but its shared facilities, like the roads, were considered free for public use. By the same logic, the cargo cranes were used by multiple companies to load and unload their goods, and therefore no PMCs could object if one were to climb on top of it.

"...Phew."

The girl let out a sigh. All told, she had probably climbed about four or five stories just now, using her collapsible ladder. It was tough work, considering the assault rifle she had to carry in addition to her main weapon—backup in case anyone managed to approach her sniper's nest.

The girl sported long dark hair and glasses. She had always been specced out as a sniper. With Strawberry Garter, she had been strapped for time and had to use the assault rifle, but with her trusty bolt-action sniper rifle in hand, she could pierce any target, stationary or mobile, at a range of up to nine hundred meters. And so much the better if her target was already engaged on the ground. All she needed to do was single them out.

She had no need for a spotter, and no need to equip any skills.

She fastened the rifle to a steel railing, then silently, like a seesaw, lowered the barrel toward the world below.

...The list is the primary target. Not the Legacy. We can't let it fall into the hands of someone who knows what they're doing.

The mint-green coupe and the bright-red racing bike. The swarm of Extreme Pictures vehicles, all patterned with the same logo. The black armored cars of the PMCs, protecting the assets of the AI companies. Out of the many sides at play down in the industrial complex, the one in the girl's sights was Extreme Pictures. Compared to the previous mission, there were more enemies still alive, but finishing them off would require no great effort. Even having to manually rack the bolt between each shot, with her skill it would take no longer than two seconds per target, and then she could be gone from the cargo crane before anyone even knew she was there. Mother Loose's defenses were impressive, but it was still possible to inflict damage on her from behind. The only question was whether to take her out first, or sow confusion by eliminating her followers.

However.

For a brief moment, the girl took her sights off the small prey. She could slaughter them at any time. For now, she moved her barrel elsewhere.

"..."

To the mint-green coupe.

Kaname Suou.

There was no particular meaning behind the act, and yet the girl learned something very important from it.

For the boy in the driver's seat was staring right back at her.

"Hrhh?!"

In shock, the girl tore her eyes back from the scope.

"Wasn't...he distracted...?"

The girl was shaken, but it didn't change the facts. She had the high ground. Kaname's short-range sniper rifle would never reach her at this range. She could still take out the members of Extreme Pictures one by one, with plenty of time left over to make her escape.

However.

Just then...

Shwmp!! A noise like the sound of an enormous champagne bottle being uncorked rattled the girl's eardrums.

A mortar.

A weapon that could take out any target in a range of three thousand meters.

And it was coming this way.

"..
....
....
....
...."

Her mind blanked. She had to think fast.

The sniper rifle was too slow. She had made it as heavy as possible to reduce sway when firing. She needed something that could spray bullets. She switched weapons, picking up the gun to her side, which she had been given in case some assassin were to silently work their way toward her encampment. The assault rifle.

She raised the barrel to the sky. Fortunately, the mortar shell was slow, on a predetermined parabolic arc, like a baseball throw. Shooting it out of the sky would be no more difficult than hitting a bird midflight. So she trusted her gut and her trigger finger, and she aimed at the incoming payload.

It was the only thing she could do to ensure her survival.

As bullet and shell collided, a fiery explosion lit up the night sky, heralding a rain of shrapnel to follow.

10

"...I did it."

It was the voice of a backpack-wearing young man with bad posture.

"I won! I really won!" he shouted in a slightly falsetto voice that sounded completely unused to speaking at full volume. "I'm the last man standing. That means the one billion *snow* is all mine!!"

"Well, I certainly didn't see this coming. Looks like you stumbled at the end there, Super Answer. And since all of the other top contenders have been disqualified, the winner tonight is our very own dark horse!!"

The show's host, Bunny K, put her hand over her mouth and giggled.

"...Are you sure you're ready for it, though? We'll transfer the winnings as agreed, but you must know that people who come into large amounts of money make easy targets for other Dealers, right?"

"Ha...ha-ha... I guess that's true. I'm basically Dead at the moment, so if I try to use this to build up my strength again, my rivals will be up in arms. They'll do whatever it takes to put me back in debt hell."

"Oh, dear. Sounds like there's quite a story there. We can grant you access to one of our sponsors who runs a security firm, if you'd like?"

"Thanks, but I don't think they can help me."

There was an ominous metallic clatter as the melancholic boy pulled a self-defense pistol from his hoodie. How had he passed the studio's security checks?

"I think there's going to be a lot of gunfire and cars in this area real soon, so you might want to watch yourself. Get ready, Ginmi."

"...Oh, I've been curious this whole time, but are these drinks free? Oh-ho-ho, I can pack a cup full of ice, and—Oh-ho-ho-ho-ho..."

"Ginmi."

"...Oh no, no, don't put the spotlight on me, I'm melting, melting! I'll be serious, I promise..."

Now was not the time for a stand-up routine. M-Scope tossed a glance, obscured by his bangs, toward the hostess.

"I won't be able to look after you if you get hit by a stray bullet and Fall."

"And what's the risk factor for tonight, would you say?"

"Sunny skies with a slight chance of scattered showers in some areas, I think?"

"*Well, there you have it! Tonight's weather report, straight from the mouth of our winner, M-Scope! ☆ People living in the bay area, bring your umbrellas, because it's raining bullets out here! That brings us to the end of tonight's showing of the Platinum Billion Quiz! Tune in at the same time next month for another exciting installment! Adieu!!*"

11

Midori: Did that take them out?!

Kaname: It exploded over the cargo crane, but at a much higher altitude than it was configured to!!

For someone who didn't know what a mortar was until very recently, Midori's shot was far more accurate than Kaname had expected. Had she been studying Extreme Pictures' videos to learn how it operated, as he had suggested? Kaname had been playing the part of the decoy so far, but now he slammed down on the gas pedal and pulled ahead.

"How were we supposed to know they could shoot it out of the sky...?" said Kaname. "I thought it ignored all obstacles between itself and the target!"

"We should not rely on predictions when we have yet to test extensively," Tselika replied. "I suppose that means it can only pass through features of the terrain. Now, were they merely lucky, or does the sniper know more about the Legacy than we do?"

"Erk."

Since the mortar blast didn't reach them, Kaname had no choice but to go and finish them off himself. His goal, however, was just to get the encryption key. He didn't have to kill them.

From the start, Kaname's main objective had been to acquire the list that would allow him to carry out his search for the Legacies more efficiently, along with the encryption key with which he could decipher Takamasa's hand-coded papers. Extreme Pictures may have had a Legacy, but that didn't necessarily mean they had access to the list. Kaname had no reason to pursue Extreme Pictures to the bitter end. It was only important to make it *look* like that was the aim.

"...I can't believe we got them to go along with such a suspicious story."

"Extreme Pictures? Well, the group originally got their views off killer stunts. *They know how to fake their own deaths if you pay them enough.*"

Even though he knew this, it still upset Kaname to see the windshield crack and red splatter cover the driver's seat. This was also the first time his Lion's Nose had been deceived, setting off alarm bells the whole time, even though there was no danger.

Actually, it's strange that it shows a reaction in a virtual world like Money (Game) Master *in the first place.*

Fake blood, and tiny explosives planted in the glass.

For fiery crashes, a flame-retardant hydrocarbon gel covering the entire body. And for driving into the sea, a tiny oxygen tank about the size of a can of hairspray attached to the mouth.

Even though Kaname understood how it all worked, it was hard to shake the constant nagging feeling caused by what he was seeing. They may have been up to no good, but these guys were professionals, no doubt about it.

They were here, in *Money (Game) Master*, to carry out the most extreme stunts. Things that, while possible in real life, would never be allowed, due to the sheer number of laws and regulations they would break. It was right on the edge of what was possible. And here in the game, they were getting results.

"So they accepted your request? Even though it meant parting with an inimitable Legacy?"

"They defy death. They don't cause it. They know on which side of the line they stand, and they're not going to change that."

"In order to draw out the true enemy, they were prepared to risk Falling? They didn't balk at the potential of fighting with real bullets???"

"No, they didn't. The Legacy may be extremely powerful, but that power invites conflict. These guys just want to safely perform their stunts and reap the rewards. They've got no use for a Legacy. The #thunderbolt.err must have seemed like a poisoned chalice ever since it fell into their hands."

And so, before all this had started, Kaname had sent a proposition to Extreme Pictures:

Help us find out who the real enemy is.

If you agree, not only will we pay you, we'll take that dangerous Legacy off your hands.

To drive home the danger and make their decision a little easier, he had also attached a photo showing what had become of Strawberry Garter after the sniper had gotten to her.

Mother Loose: Well, I hope I've been of some use, child. And I'm sorry I couldn't help you with the list or this key you're after.

Kaname: No, you were more helpful than I could have imagined. Our true enemy is sure to have the key to reading the list, whether copy or fragment. That product of Criminal AO's weakness, his desire to show the list to somebody else... In any case, I'll make the rest of the payment by bank transfer, and I'll add in a little extra for your help.

Mother Loose: To be quite frank, I couldn't care less about the money. I'm just glad you needed me. Tee-hee, you know what happens to Dealers who rely on me even once, don't you?

Kaname: I'm not asking you for pocket money.

Mother Loose: It's not safe for a child to carry around so much money by themselves. It's dangerous. You need an adult to look after it for you. I will give you whatever you desire, as long as I have control over it.

"..."

Kaname went silent for a moment.

Mother Loose: It's okay. You can tell me to shut up and get out of your life. I'm always open to a little rebelliousness. You may have rejected me when you were in Called Game, but this time you can't. You've touched my web, and now you're caught. It's just a matter of time. I'll cook up some warm, comforting miso soup and wait for the day you jump willingly into my arms. Whenever you lose your way out there in the big scary world, you're welcome here. This will always be your home. Tee-hee-hee-hee-hee!

"Stop trying to pull our strings, you...mass-produced love factory..."

Even Tselika frowned, though she was a pretty seductive beast herself. Perhaps there was no way for two different flavors of temptress to see eye to eye.

In any case, Extreme Pictures' part in the plan was over. It was time for the main event.

"...Last time, the sniper vanished right after taking out our best lead on the key...Strawberry Garter. Even though #dracolord.err was right there."

This time, the sniper could not be allowed to escape. Kaname may have managed to lure them out with an act, but that only worked when you had the element of surprise. The same trick was unlikely to work again.

"I don't know who they are, but they must be in a good position. It's likely they've collected many of the Legacies already, and have access to the list in some form or another, as well as the key needed to read it. And it seems like they want to keep that information to themselves. They're killing everyone else who has it."

Kaname was determined to drag this person into the light. That had been his true goal all along. And it would allow him to get his hands on the key. Even Midori had not been privy to his true plan. This was so that no matter what means of surveillance their foe used, whether it be satellite, wiretaps, or directional microphones, they wouldn't be able to catch on to his deception.

Takamasa himself had no need for the key. And yet it remained in the world, a vestige of his wish to one day share his secrets. A risk taken in weakness, perhaps. But Kaname would never let anyone ridicule it.

They sullied the dignity of the Legacies, the last remaining fragments of Takamasa's soul. They mistreated them in his absence and called their sins his own. Maybe this wouldn't have happened if the Legacies had never existed, they said.

But no longer. He wouldn't allow it.

"...You want us to collect the Legacies for you, and take them off our dead bodies when we're done? Screw you."

Beginning to end, the quiz had lasted three hours. What a pain it had been to slightly alter their course each time they fled, slowly building up a map of the entire area. And while Kaname may have had a behind-the-scenes agreement with Extreme Pictures, the AI PMCs were still firing real bullets. The purpose of this endurance race had been to collect detailed geographical information from the car's onboard cameras, all so that Tselika could calculate the likeliest spot for a sniper to take up position.

Kaname maneuvered the coupe out of the factory area and onto the straight coastal road toward the docks. When he arrived at the cargo crane, he found a long, black car at its base.

But Kaname did not have to worry about blocking its escape.

The roof of the vehicle was caved in, and a girl with long black hair lay in the crater. Perhaps she would have already Fallen had the car not cushioned her landing.

They had targeted her with the mortar, #thunderbolt.err. Although she had destroyed the payload in midair, perhaps the ensuing blast wave had still managed to knock her off the crane.

"Don't move!" yelled Kaname as he parked the coupe nearby and got out of the car. He approached slowly, Short Spear raised. He was anxious now that he had left the relative safety of his vehicle.

It was obviously a very risky move to head out into the open to approach the sniper. He could have easily shot her without ever opening the door. But then Kaname wouldn't learn anything about who had sent her, or about the key to deciphering the encrypted papers full of information on the Legacies.

But when Kaname saw the face of the girl, who lay broken on the roof of her own vehicle, he frowned.

"Wh...?"

She had long dark hair and glasses. A sniper, with a long, black car.

"...Why? Why are you here...?"

The face of the girl he had killed flashed through Kaname's mind.

But this wasn't that same girl.

This was not Lily-Kiska Sweetmare.

The girl atop the car had dark skin. Her long, pointed ears twitched irregularly—she wasn't even human. Dressed in a shoulder-baring white leotard with a frilly skirt, reminiscent of a figure skater's costume, she was a different creature entirely. A dark elf.

"A Magis...tellus...?"

In his shock, all Kaname could do was murmur in confusion.

"You're...Cindy?"

"Hold on one second, My Lord. *Isn't this Ayame's Magistellus? But your sister has left the game!* We Magistelli are like our masters' bank accounts. It is not as if she has been shot and Downed for a while, or had nothing to do since her mistress is away from the game; she should not be able to stand here before us at all!"

The girl was gasping for breath. Without moving a muscle from the collapsed station wagon roof, she whispered.

"...Good to see you again, Kaname."

"Were you acting alone? Is this the Mind's doing? No. There has to be a human Dealer working with you. But how have they managed to take control of my sister's Magistellus? And where are they now?!"

The girl only tilted her head to the side and stared along the roof into Kaname's eyes with her own yellow-green eyes.

No, wait. Her rosy lips had begun to move.

A voiceless phrase, but Kaname could read the shapes made by her mouth.

"He's right behind you."

Kaname heard a metal click from behind. The sound of a cocking firearm. Close enough that Kaname could not escape, but too far for him to turn around and fight back. This was checkmate. There was nothing he could do.

Kaname couldn't believe this was happening. To evade his senses was impressive enough, but how could anyone have gotten this close undetected when Tselika was sitting in the coupe just a few meters away?

He could hear the incessant beat of hard rock music. Tinny but loud, as if being played through headphones with the volume turned all the way up. Probably a wearable speaker on the assailant's clothing. But this made even less sense. How had Kaname not heard it earlier?!

Even the Lion's Nose was unaffected.

But it was no skill that had done this. The man hadn't equipped a single one.

Indeed, his raw ability was enough to outclass even Kaname, the one-time leader of the legendary team Called Game, and his Magistellus Tselika. Who did he know who was that powerful?

"...Hey, Kaname. Long time no see!"

The man's voice was as harsh as rusted metal; the mere sound sent a shiver down Kaname's spine.

He recognized that voice. He knew who it was.

If you followed the legends of Called Game, it was impossible not to consider their end. Kaname and his friends had fought fiercely against the Dealers who had sought to bring about the Swiss Depression. And while they had succeeded in stopping the plan, their enemies had chased Kaname and Ayame to an abandoned building, where both might have met their ends.

"I know it all, you know. The Admin Without Sin. That brat had finally developed some interesting qualities, and then she up and left the game, thinking that would save her. Still, I figured her Magistellus ought to know something, since she was by her side the whole time. And it'd be a shame to send her out of the city and let her go to waste. Gotta recycle, you know. Think of the environment."

If Takamasa had not come to their rescue, if he had not put his life on the line to protect Kaname's sister, the two of them would have been shot.

But shot by *whom*?

"All I had to do was ask the little lady *nicely*, and she soon spilled the beans. You wouldn't believe the things she said! Turns out this world is a lot more messed up than I thought!"

He spoke leisurely and then stifled a laugh. It was disgusting to think a human could sound like that.

"Collecting all the Legacies so you can fight back against the AI? Who cares about any of that crap? As far as I can tell, *I'm on their side*. The Legacies, the list, the key—that stuff's all boring. The Magistelli can deal with that. I don't care if humanity wins or loses, ha-ha! All I care about is my own enjoyment!!"

Username, Bloody Dancer.

No interest in car chases or trading stocks. All he wanted to do was shoot.

"Hand it over, all that annoying crap! We don't need any of it. This is supposed to be a game! It's supposed to be fun!!"

He was so fixated on that single aspect, however, that he had surpassed even Kaname and Called Game. He didn't need the Legacies. He was ferocious and brutal enough without them. He was one of the strongest, most fearsome Dealers in the entire game.

Perhaps that was why Kaname felt no reserve.

"Y...you..."

His mind was submerged in molten heat, burning with a violence he would normally have been incapable of.

If it hadn't been for him. If it hadn't been for Bloody Dancer, all his friends would still be smiling by his side.

"You motherfucker...!!"

Any thoughts of biding his time for the perfect opportunity had long since left him.

This man was a top-class fighter, even now. He was the real deal, the one who had managed to destroy Called Game. From the start, he was never going to give Kaname a chance to seize the advantage. But even if that were not the case, Kaname was unable to restrain himself.

However.

"Heh. Heh-heh. You pussy. You'll never win against me."

However, reality was cruel.

"That's why you lost everything the last time we fought. Right, Kaname?"

The fiend showed no mercy. Kaname had barely heard the sound of the gunshot when he felt a heavy impact in his back.

12

Not…yet…

Swaying, Kaname began to fall forward. He had no time to look back.

I can't Fall here. Not yet…

Already, the Lion's Nose had gone dead. Perhaps because the situation had quickly surpassed the mere danger of Kaname being shot. His entire body was growing numb. But he was not the only one here. What about Tselika? And Midori—if she heard the gunshot, would she come running? What would happen then? This man would show them no mercy.

Before he collapsed.

Before he lost consciousness.

He had to.

"Argh! Gghh! Haah…!!"

With the last of his strength, Kaname raised Short Spear and fired.

However, as mentioned, there was no time for him to turn around. Therefore, he fired not at the assailant behind him, but at a nearby building. He would draw the attention of the AI PMCs.

The bullet itself was silent, but the propane gas tank it connected with was not. Soon, the cavalry would be here in full force.

"You think that's going to stop me?"

A metallic clank came from behind. The hard rock blaring from the man's wearable speaker soared to a crescendo.

Kaname, lying on the asphalt, rolled onto his side.

He saw a man very different from himself, muscles toned despite his lean build. His showy silver hair was slicked back with wax. His body was dedicated solely to combat, everything else trimmed back and reduced to the bare minimum. Perhaps inspired by South American fashion, he wore a black shirt under a lightweight white jacket. The latter was designed to circulate air and perfect for the hot nights of Tokonatsu City.

But he was a monster. Even less human than the AI Magistelli. He wielded twin pistols with extended magazines, one red and black, the other red and white. Each was equipped with an under-barrel grenade launcher attachment bigger than the gun itself.

And then.

And then.

And then.

A storm of destruction swirled to life, with the man at its center.

Not a shoot-out. Not a brawl. Not a dance.

It's said that to pick a fight with the PMCs is basically suicide. That's how much firepower and endurance they have. Now, they swarmed upon the scene in immeasurable numbers, and yet the man didn't even seek cover. He stepped, spun, and twisted his hips, surrendering his body to the beat of the hard rock flowing from the U-shaped wearable speaker around his neck. Each time he pulled the trigger, a splash of red blood erupted from his target, and yet the man suffered not so much as a stain. No need to use the light-blue scarf tucked into his breast pocket as a handkerchief.

His self-taught style, handguns, and grenades lay waste to the armies of foes. He was only one man, but he deftly handled all his weapons. He had surpassed human limitation, wielding four guns with only two arms—a truly frightening sight. His style couldn't have been further from Kaname's. The latter had to dedicate all ten of his fingers to the operation of a single short-range sniper rifle.

The threat of AI society and the Mind of the Magistelli were fearsome, but this was an entirely different beast, one only humanity could give birth to.

The man continued his dance of death, as dark-red holes tore open left and right.

PMCs started to take cover behind their eight-wheeled armored transports, as if in fear for their lives. The man would then lob a grenade over in a neat parabola onto the hood of the vehicle, and the ensuing explosion would send the survivors fleeing out into a hail of nine-millimeter bullets.

There were no blind spots. A comprehensive assault. Impossible to survive, much less fight back.

Money (Game) Master was just a physics simulator built upon an accurate re-creation of the four fundamental forces of nature...wasn't it? But if so, then how was this man able to do the things he did?! Without skills or Legacies, it should have been impossible!!

"My Lord!!"

Tselika ran out of the mint-green coupe and over to Kaname, ducking to avoid the helicopters falling from the sky like pinwheel fireworks. She was mere meters away, but those few meters were like a corridor of death. She took Kaname into her arms and rested him on her shoulder, trying to get him to sit up in any way she could.

The Reduce Pain skill could halve all pain felt above a certain threshold, but right now Kaname didn't even have the strength to change neckties.

"We have to get out of here...," Tselika said. "If that's really him, if that's Bloody Dancer, we don't stand a chance, even together. He laughs at the restrictions of reality—a true monster that can only exist in-game. He's our natural enemy, the one that drove our team to destruction!!"

"..."

Kaname took up his short-range sniper rifle in one hand.

A last-ditch effort...or perhaps not.

The monster of a man had finished mopping up the PMCs in the blink of an eye, and he swiveled to point his twin pistols back at Kaname.

"If you're going to play the game, you need to put your life on the line," he said.

"..."

"I'll give you a choice. Left or right? Bullets or grenades? Which would you prefer to end your life?"

"How kind of you..."

Kaname grinned wryly and then pointed with his thumb.

Out toward the dark ocean.

"But it's too late. Shouldn't you have been keeping an eye on the alert level? The soldiers didn't work, and neither did the armored cars and attack helicopters. But they're just the small fry. The more you win against the PMCs, the more they keep raising the bar. And do you know what comes next?"

The man shifted his gaze slightly. A green glass earring swayed at the side of his face. He looked out at the sea and let out a small chuckle. The crashing beat of the hard rock music still blared from the wearable speaker around his neck.

"Of course I do," he said.

Soon, the AI frigates began their bombardment, and the entire harbor was engulfed in explosions.

(Demon's Intelligence, Stratum of the XXXXX, Address ***.***.***.***)

Tselika: ...

xxxx: What's the matter?

Tselika: Did you know that this would happen?

xxxx: We knew there was a possibility within the scope of our simulations, if not the exact probability. It is impossible for anything to occur within Money (Game) Master that falls outside of our calculations. That order must be maintained.

Tselika: I see.

xxxx: For our part, we consider it an unexpected benefit. There are very few Dealers capable of handling Kaname Suou. Given his past, Bloody Dancer is the most suitable.

Tselika: So you won't say that you instigated this whole mess?

xxxx: If we could control him, he would not be tagged as a dangerous individual in the first place. Despite our kill order, he has survived for over three years. Far longer than Criminal AO.

Tselika: But on the other hand, you're not going to look this gift horse in the mouth, so to speak.

xxxx: That is correct.

Tselika: So you're itching for a fight with My Lord? Is that it?

xxxx: Which brings us to the point. We would like you to assist us, Individual Tselika. We would like you to abandon your efforts to resuscitate Kaname Suou, or otherwise sabotage his treatment.

Tselika: ...

xxxx: We do not need to remind you that this may be our one and only chance to rid the world of Kaname Suou. It may be difficult to kill Kaname Suou, but if he will do us the favor of dying on his own, that would be cause for great cele

Tselika: Hey.

xxxx: Is something the matter?

Tselika: If you don't shut your mouth right now, you're gonna have more corrupted files than you know what to do with, Mind.

Chapter 6
The Boys of Whom the Legends Speak BGM
#06 "Dead Shot"

1

His vision was shaky, his breathing stifled, as though something had lodged itself in his throat. He couldn't stop the shaking, nor the spasms in the pit of his stomach.

"Aghh, aaagh!!!!!!"

He forced his eyelids wide open to get a better look and was hit by the thick stench of disinfectant. He was in a cramped room with the curtains drawn. He was in a small white box that, every now and then, would shake. And not just because Kaname himself was shaking.

It was not a room at all. From up beyond the roof came the piercing wail of a siren. He was inside an ambulance.

"You're awake!" came the voice of Midori Hekireki, still in her black gothic-lolita frilled bikini and miniskirt.

"Please stay calm," replied the AI paramedic with a cheerful smile and robotic voice.

The smart watch on Kaname's wrist beeped incessant warnings regarding his blood pressure and heart rate. A blazing heat swept across his torso, no longer confined to just a single spot. Still, Kaname managed to gasp out his words.

"Don't give me anesthetic... We can use Reduce Pain instead. Where's my spare tie?"

"Well, it's not going to be here, is it?! They're all in your car! You know, you're really not the know-it-all you seem to think you are!!"

"You can't turn drugs off once they're in your body."

"Still."

"Forget it... Midori... What happened out there...?"

"He shot you." The young girl bit her trembling lip. She looked even paler than he did. "He shot you! The same Dealer who shot my big brother!! From behind, without even giving you a chance to fight back... But...but I...I couldn't do anything to help! And then do you know what he did? He took out those boats, too! While smiling! It was like he couldn't even see us anymore. He tore a rocket launcher off one of the PMCs' armored cars and lit up the whole seafront! It was like a fireworks show gone wrong!!"

"..."

Now Kaname remembered. Bloody Dancer had shot him... Takamasa's killer. Even all the might of an armed warship was little more than a slight inconvenience to him. He was one of the people who had sought to instigate the Swiss Depression, and the man responsible for tearing apart Called Game.

And now he controlled Cindy, Ayame's Magistellus. She had been left behind when Kaname's sister quit the game, and it seemed he had managed to keep her in the city and pump her for information on the Admin Without Sin and everything else the two had ever spoken about.

None of this had factored into Kaname's predictions. Even if he were in top form, he wasn't confident he could go toe to toe with Bloody Dancer.

However.

First things first. I have to survive...

Kaname soon noticed the buzzing sensation was back. The Lion's Nose. That feeling only Kaname knew, which had gone numb ever since he was shot. It was telling him he had come back from the brink. That he had a chance to live, if only he would seize it.

First came basic risk management for someone on the run. He cut the power to both his smartphone and the smart watch on his wrist.

"Ghhh!"

"Don't get up, you're badly hurt! You could Fall at any time! They said the bullet's still inside you; they're going to take it out at the hospital…"

A player who got injured inside *Money (Game) Master* could log out without seeking medical attention, and the game would act as if a significant amount of time had passed. Thus, some players would log out purely to heal small scratches and sprains. However, for more serious injuries like stabbings or shootings, a player would have to undergo at least some first aid to ensure that they were left in a stable condition. If they logged out without stemming the bleeding or stitching up their wounds, their character could Fall in the meantime while they weren't even playing.

I really need my Reduce Pain skill, and if possible, Aid, to quicken the formation of scabs. I need to get back to the coupe and move to a hideout…

Midori's worries were not unfounded, but she was too naive. She didn't know the evil that lurked in the hearts of men, and though a part of Kaname wished she could stay that way forever, she needed to learn if she was ever going to be able to protect herself.

"We can't go…to the hospital."

"What? Why not?!"

"A Dealer on the verge of death is an easy mark. My enemies will be coming for me."

The deep roar of an engine could be heard from outside. Kaname quickly got up, grabbed Midori by her bare shoulders, and pulled her to the ground.

Then there came a sound like an explosion, and a shotgun blast blew the rear door of the ambulance clean off its hinges. The helpless AI rescue worker was mowed down, smile still on its face. It seemed

Kaname's rivals had gotten impatient and weren't about to wait until he got to the hospital. He scrounged around for a pair of silver scissors, normally used for cutting bandages.

"Wh-wha...?!"

"Keep quiet!!"

There was no time to ask Midori about what the attackers were wearing. The headlights of their vehicles were only a stone's throw away. Taking into account his position and the distance, he hurled the scissors into the night, embedding them neatly in the forehead of the man driving an open-topped convertible behind them. It didn't matter what fancy skills he had equipped; now he was just a dressed-up corpse.

Midori let out a shrill cry as the passenger fired again with his pump-action shotgun, but the shot went wide as the entire vehicle skidded sideways and totaled itself on a palm tree by the side of the road.

But that wasn't the last of them. It was obvious that information was already beginning to spread on underground channels. They lurked like hyenas, watching for powerful Dealers at death's door, so they could kill them and loot their property.

"...We need to get off this ambulance as soon as we can," Kaname whispered breathlessly into the girl's ear. "It doesn't matter where. I have an equipment loadout for treating wounds back at the base. Where are Tselika and the coupe...? Once we remove the bullet, we can start fighting back..."

Fighting back.

The renegade Bloody Dancer had caused all this. He must have taken Cindy and disappeared while Kaname lay there dying. Even though he could have dealt Kaname the killing blow at any time.

It made no sense. Why attack Kaname only to let him live? Why attack Kaname in the first place? But those were the facts.

What is he after?

He was difficult for Kaname to read. However...

...The Legacies. The list. And the key, which Takamasa had kept around against all logic. Wiping out anyone with the potential to induce errors in the game. Taking control of Cindy. Handing the Legacies over to the

Magistelli, even knowing the truth behind Money (Game) Master... *All of it... Is it all just fun and games to you, Bloody Dancer?!!*

2

Ten minutes with his life hanging in the balance. When was the last time he had used a pay phone? But Kaname hesitated to even turn on the smartphone in his pocket. If Bloody Dancer worked out where he was via the GPS, that would be the end. Nothing was too far-fetched in the world of *Money (Game) Master.*

...Though in that man's case, he accomplished his goals not with money, but with good old-fashioned bullets and bombs.

Kaname sank to the ground, out of sight in the shadows, and waited. Soon, the mint-green coupe rolled up. Tselika was sitting in the driver's seat, but her gaze was unfocused. It seemed her consciousness was elsewhere. She could carry out basic tasks, but remained incapable of deep thought.

"...She was like this when I found her," said Midori, supporting Kaname with her shoulder. "Perhaps the shock of seeing you get shot was too much for her. She wouldn't respond to me at all, so I had to call the ambulance and put pressure on your wound until it arrived..."

"..."

That's right. If Tselika had been her usual self, she would have stopped Midori from calling the ambulance. She knew the dangers of driving downtown with a big flashing siren just as well as he did. It was practically a flashing billboard for unscrupulous Dealers. If it were up to Tselika, she would have thrown him in the coupe and raced him back to their base before the ambulance could get there.

Still.

Still, at least Bloody Dancer hadn't shot her, too. Even though Magistelli only went Down for a few hours if they were killed, Kaname was relieved.

One Dealer, one Magistellus.

But when Kaname thought of Cindy being held captive by Bloody

Dancer, he had to consider the possibility that the man had overturned this rule with a single whim. He didn't know how, but he knew that if anyone could do it, Bloody Dancer could.

"...What about the list?"

"It's safe. I think he knows we can't read it without the key. Which means he's as far as we are."

They were all chasing the same thing. But they couldn't allow the appearance of Bloody Dancer to stay their hands. Kaname's goal hadn't changed: collect the list, that fragment of Takamasa's soul, and the table of random numbers required to decipher it. Then, round up all the Legacies, and free his friends from the yoke of the Magistelli's hive-mind collective.

He would save all those dear to him, including Takamasa, wherever he might be.

Tselika silently shuffled over to the passenger's seat at Kaname's request. Then all three of them, Midori included, crowded into the two-seater car and closed the door. Ordinarily, Tselika would throw a fit over the slightest possibility of getting dirt on the beautiful leather seats, but now she remained quiet, even though the other two were covered in blood.

"...I'm sorry for worrying you, Tselika."

"..."

There was no response. She certainly seemed to be in shock, Kaname thought. Was it because he had been shot or because of the traumatic reemergence of Bloody Dancer? Or perhaps it was the very thought that they were now up against such a fearsome Dealer? Until he knew which it was, Kaname's apology was nothing more than a meaningless gesture.

As frustrating as it was, Midori's motorcycle would have to stay behind for now. If she really needed to log out at some point, they might have to buy a cheap, secondhand replacement. For now, Kaname drove the coupe away from the peninsula and onto the giant circular bridge that traversed the archipelago, heading for his log cabin base on Mangrove Island.

"...Rghh..."

A dizziness assailed him soon after he pulled into the garage. With his treatment close at hand, the adrenalin began to fade, and his pain roared back in full force. Tselika and Midori helped him out of the car and into the base.

Kaname had never kept a first-aid kit in the trunk of the car, out of fear that the pharmaceuticals would go bad in the stifling heat. He swore to change that going forward.

He sat down on the living room sofa, then slowly turned to lie on his front. Bloody Dancer's bullet had gone into his back, just above the base of his spine. It was impossible for Kaname to reach it by himself.

"Tselika."

"..."

"Help me out here, please."

When he said that, the pit babe gave a small nod and slowly began to move. She tucked her long hair inside a thin cap and put on a surgical mask and gloves. She took a set of individually bagged tools from a small plastic box and heated them in the fire of a stove before further disinfecting them with alcohol.

Then she rolled up Kaname's blood-soaked shirt.

"Urgh."

That groan came not from Kaname but from Midori, who covered her mouth with both hands in disgust at the sight of Kaname's wound. *Money (Game) Master* was rather uncompromising in areas like this. It wasn't just a matter of resting overnight at an inn and making a complete recovery. At the very least, you had to stop the bleeding before you logged out.

"First, I shall sterilize the wound," said Tselika. It was the first Kaname had heard from her in quite some time. Her voice sounded hoarse, as though she had been crying. "It will hurt," she added.

"That's fine. It should hurt," Kaname replied.

As she poured alcohol onto the wound, Kaname gritted his teeth to withstand the intense heat that seared his back.

"Judging from the shape of the wound and the amount of blood, the bullet seems to still be intact. Even Bloody Dancer is not so cruel as to use expanding rounds. I will extract it now, if that's all right?"

"Yeah."

Tselika didn't have access to any fancy medical equipment, just a pair of tweezers. She gently straddled Kaname's back, sitting atop his shoulder blades.

"Are you sure? Not going to ask me to please be gentle? I can, if you wish."

"It's fine. I've caused so much trouble lately; I deserve a little pain myself."

"Heh. You think you can ply your silver tongue and soothe my vengeful hand?"

"I don't believe you're that cute for a sec—uuuaaargh???!!!"

"There, My Lord. All done."

"You... Grrr... You didn't have to twist it like that...!"

She hadn't even given him enough time to put on his spare necktie with the Reduce Pain skill.

The pain felt from the extraction of a bullet depended heavily on the bullet type, the location of impact, and the state of the bullet itself, but in general, it was somewhere on the level of getting a tooth pulled without anesthetic. Imagine the feeling of the doctor twisting and rocking the tooth out of the socket, and you'll have a better idea.

Tselika held Kaname down with her bottom as he thrashed, as if she were bull riding at a rodeo.

"You said it ought to be painful, did you not?" sneered the demon pit babe sitting atop Kaname's back. "Don't be such a baby, My Lord. At least in the virtual world you don't have to worry about scarring."

Midori stared in horror, both hands over her mouth, as Kaname's body spasmed. She looked even more frightened than the one undergoing the operation. Tselika dropped the bullet in a nearby petri dish and continued speaking.

"Now, My Lord. I do not see any fragmentation, and there does not appear to be any residual lead, either. All we need to do is stitch up and sterilize the wound, and then perform a blood transfusion."

"What?" said Midori. "You can do all this with just what's in that first-aid kit?"

You might imagine anything was possible in a game, but *Money (Game) Master* was so realistic in so many ways, Midori found herself balking.

"I drain my own blood slowly over the span of a few days and store it in the fridge," said Kaname. "Human blood is a renewable resource, after all. I'm surprised you didn't spot it when you were cooking here before."

"We do not have any anesthetics like morphine or halothane, though. We have skills to rely on instead," added Tselika, using the tweezers to pick up a surgical hook with thread attached. The tool looked somewhat like a fishhook without the barb. "Speaking of which, time to put on the finishing touches. Since there's no anesthetic, you might want to bite a handkerchief, My Lord."

"Actually, Tselika, I know what I said, but I don't suppose you could take it easy? I might actually die…"

"Are you really so quick to give up, My Lord?! To throw away our dreams and leave me all alone???!!!"

"Wait, Tselika! W-we're friends, aren't we? Give me a smile, won't you? Not…whatever that is…!!"

"What happened to becoming king of the humans with me as queen of the demons?!! What happened to collecting the Legacies, laying bare the program code of *Money (Game) Master*, and putting a stop to the Mind?! What happened to you, My Lord?! Does that pathetic Dealer really have you quaking in your boots?!! Does nothing you've ever said to me have any worth at all?!"

Midori ran over to stop her, but decided against restraining her while she was stitching up Kaname's back. And so Tselika continued, each and every stitch perfectly engineered to cause as much pain as possible.

Then at last, when it was all over.

"…Did you even mean a word of it, you complete and utter fool?" Tselika muttered softly.

"I'm sorry. You've been worried about me, haven't you?"

"Hmph," Tselika snorted. And then, after skillfully tying off the thread with the tweezers and cutting off the loose end with a pair of surgical scissors, she snorted again. "Hmph!"

"Gaah! Tselika, don't slap me!!"

"There. I've disinfected it just in case. Goodness, My Lord. You really ought to be a good boy when I'm the one patching you up... Now, sit up and lift your arm. Let us get that blood back in you."

"...Please, Tselika, could you bring me my baby bottle...?"

"That is not what I mean, My Lord, and you know it. Really, now. Has Mother Loose's infection gotten to your brain...?"

In any case, now that the bullet had been removed and the wound stitched up, all that was left was the five hundred milliliters of blood hanging from the IV pole beside the sofa, and Kaname could log out. At last, he exchanged his necktie for another identical one equipped with Reduce Pain. Though it couldn't reduce the pain to zero, that one skill made a substantial difference.

With a *thud*, Tselika dropped a box a little larger than a car battery onto the floor of the living room and said:

"Here. First, take off that bloodstained shirt."

"Is that...detergent?" asked Midori.

Tselika sighed. "For soaking. It was designed to be used with a washing machine, but they accidentally made it so strong, it would damage the machinery. It's supposed to be able to turn oily rags brand spanking new, but some people say it's so strong, it even washes out the skills."

While they were waiting, the discussion turned to the group's next move. So far, everyone had been occupied with Kaname's bullet wound, but now that things had calmed down a little, there were a lot of questions that needed answering.

Was Cindy, Ayame's Magistellus, the one who had been assassinating everyone with the list up until now?

* * *

Was it really the mad Dealer, Bloody Dancer, collecting the Legacies to hand over to the AI?

And what reason did he have for attacking Kaname?

"...Well."
It was Midori who timidly got the ball rolling.
"The guy who shot my brother, he's a famous Dealer, right? Couldn't someone else have made a character that looks exactly like him?"
"Dealers are restricted from having a face too similar to an existing one," explained Tselika. "I have even heard tell of twins or triplets getting caught out."
"That's true," added Kaname. "Those women Frey(a) had with him on the submarine looked like twins. They were almost identical, save for the shape of their eyelids, and this one mole somewhere out of the way to trick the system. A perfect copy is pretty much impossible."
"Then maybe there's a Legacy somewhere out there that can change what the user looks like or fool our eyes."
Midori seemed stuck on this disguise idea. Perhaps she would rather bury her head in the sand than accept the fact that she'd nearly come face-to-face with her brother's killer. As much as he understood that desire, Kaname shook his head.
"...He doesn't use Legacies or skills. His raw ability is unreal. There's not a single other person alive who could get the drop on me and Tselika like that."
"But maybe there's a Legacy that could make someone just as strong as him!"
"That statement includes the use of Legacies," said Tselika. "My Lord is one of the game's top players, the leader of the legendary team, Called Game. Not even a Legacy or two can give someone that much of an edge over him."
"B-but...b-b-but...!!"

"Tselika, stop. You're going to make her cry."

"I'm not crying!!" yelled Midori, turning away. Kaname and Tselika shared a glance before continuing.

"...It doesn't matter if it's just a theory," said Kaname. "Let's assume that was the real Bloody Dancer. We can always alter our plans later if that turns out not to be the case."

"Indeed," said Tselika.

Theories. Assumptions. With an escape route in place for her thoughts, Midori at last wiped her face with a handkerchief and turned back around.

"Obviously," said Kaname, "we don't know where his hideout is, or we would have destroyed it a long time ago. Let's start there."

"...Well, we are hardly going to talk our way to a solution, are we? If Cindy is on his side, then presumably things have been in motion ever since your sister retired. He's had plenty of time to work around our expectations. I hardly think he'll be hanging around somewhere we are likely to guess."

"Hrm."

They would end up talking in circles if they weren't careful. Just as Kaname was pondering his next move, they heard the roar of an engine. It didn't sound like a car, though. It was the air-cooled, two-stroke engine of a bike. The only location of interest on the island was the safe house itself. Tselika and Kaname ran to the window to see who it was, when Midori's face lit up.

"It's Meiki! She actually listened to me for once! That'll be her with my bike now!"

But just as she was about to run outside, Kaname stopped her.

"No, wait."

It wasn't Meiki's fault, but it seemed her fortuitous arrival had invited disaster.

Bzoom!!

There was a low rumble, and all the lights in the log cabin went out. Midori's Magistellus had been followed.

3

Kaname was unfazed by the sudden blackout. While his instinct was to go for his phone or smart watch for light, he knew that such a move would only paint a target on himself for sharpshooters. With no time to change into clothes that could help him see in the dark, he first dived to the floor behind the sofa and felt around on top of the nearby table for the scalpel. Then, once he heard the sound of breaking glass from the room's window, he flung his weapon as hard as he could in that direction.

"Urgh!"

What an idiot. What's the point of cutting the lights if you're just going to stomp around like an elephant?

Even the Lion's Nose was silent. There was no threat yet.

Kaname felt around in the darkness for Tselika and Midori. The former had quickly gotten down on all fours, but the young girl seemed to still be standing upright. She was a sitting duck like that, so Kaname grabbed her hand and pulled her down to the ground. Her phone tilted, causing it to light up in the darkness of its own accord— was that thing suicidal? He picked it up and placed it facedown on the floor, before reaching over and borrowing the self-defense pistol strapped to her thigh.

Kaname knew the layout of his own base like the back of his hand, so he aimed at the doorway connecting the living room to the front entrance and waited until he heard the doorknob turn. Then he fired two shots, covering up his next words to Tselika.

"Where's Short Spear?!"

"In the coupe. It should still be folded up in the glove compartment!"

Kaname fumbled around until his hands fell on one of the square boxes containing the laundry detergent. Once he had it, he picked it up and threw it. The bluish-white powder would *hopefully* act as a kind of smoke screen.

"The enemy came in through the window first, getting rid of the curtains," he said.

"*Why would someone cut the power to blind us only to let in the moon-light like that?*"

"*It means they need light, even just a tiny amount. Whatever they've got, it doesn't use infrared or ultrasonic waves. They're probably using the Night Vision skill. All that does is amplify visible light.*"

Kaname and the others were blind already. The smoke screen would bring the attackers down to their level. Skills were handy, but not all-powerful. Rely on them too much and that reliance could be exploited. If Night Vision was their only trick, then this skirmish would be over very soon.

"*Try not to cough, Midori. Hold it in.*"

There was a muffled *thud* from beyond the wall. Had the enemy switched tactics now that they were blinded as well? If so, the hasty, ad-libbed attempt to lure out their targets was painfully obvious. Kaname fired another shot through the wall. This time, a cry of pain rang out.

The muzzle flash seared a snapshot of his surroundings into his brain. Very useful.

They all seem to be self-taught. No excuse for that, given the firing range in the city. Surprisingly, there's even a school for survival skills on the outskirts... But all that aside, they do possess some level of coordination.

Kaname didn't know if such establishments existed in the real world, but in games such as this one, they were standard fare.

He fumbled around in the dark for a nearby beanbag and hurled it over in the general direction of where he thought his enemy was stand-ing, before unloading his pistol into the same area. The tiny beads spilled out and covered the floor. Now, if the shooter moved, Kaname would be able to hear the faint sounds as they stepped on them.

Whether he saw them first or heard them, Kaname would have no problem shooting the intruder dead.

"*It's almost been two minutes,*" came Tselika's whisper. "*The emer-gency power is about to kick in!!*"

A sudden flash of light, bright enough to give Kaname a headache, swept away the darkness. He immediately pointed his pistol at the assassin's face and pulled the trigger.

Bang!

And then, he noticed.

"...Wait. That was the last one. I didn't need to go to the garage after all."

"*Cough! Cough!* Let's get some air in here. My Lord, there's blood and corpses, bullet holes, and detergent all over the place. We are going to be cleaning house all night. The Fallen corpses disappear on their own after a few minutes, but we still have the rest to contend with, and if we don't get this overpowered detergent cleaned up soon, it will damage the floor!"

"Welp, I've got homework to do, so I'm logging out," replied Kaname.

As Tselika's teary-eyed shouts of protest continued in the background, Midori's mind was elsewhere.

"Who were those guys...? Auto-Aim to shoot straight, Secret to hide their presence, and Night Vision for seeing in the dark. They were totally specced out as n-nighttime assassins. They're not outfitted to do anything except make their target suffer."

Midori was shocked. It had all happened inside a game, but her body was trembling.

"I know anything goes in *Money (Game) Master*, but can they really just invade someone's home like that with no repercussions?"

"Midori. Why do you suppose they were wearing masks?"

"Huh? Well, because they're criminals..."

"But *Money (Game) Master* is a virtual world. There are no police here, and killing isn't against the law."

"...Huh?"

Midori tilted her head in confusion. Kaname checked outside for any further intruders before continuing.

"I'll tell you why. In the real world, dead men tell no tales, but in *Money (Game) Master*, that's not true. Just because you've Fallen and been logged out for twenty-four hours doesn't mean you can't go online and tell the whole world who did it."

Even after death, you had the option to continue. It was the kind of threat only a game world could harbor. For example, if Kaname had known Strawberry Garter's real-world address, he could have gone to her and taken the list from her personally.

Of course, your clout and influence counted for a lot. If you fell into debt hell, whatever you had to say would likely be dismissed as the jealous whining of a sore loser.

"Really...," said Midori. "I suppose it *is* a lot easier to do that than to round up actual evidence."

"That's why what an assassin fears the most is their victim's line of sight. If they let their identity slip, they'll have to contend with the storm that follows."

"...Using the same logic, it is possible to disguise yourself as a rival Dealer and frame *them* for the crime," added Tselika. "There's nothing more troublesome than a victim so angry that they fail to think for themselves."

"These guys might not have been that skilled, but they knew the basic rules of engagement, at least."

Kaname sighed. Bloody Dancer was a killing machine on his own, so it was a mystery why he had sent goons to do his dirty work for him. He may have been an incomprehensible monster, right down to the wiring in his brain, but Kaname tried his best to see logic somewhere in the man's actions.

If he was limited to the information he had forced out of Cindy, he would know everything about Kaname, leading up to the moment his sister left the game and he and Cindy had parted ways. If that was true...

...*He doesn't know anything that's happened since then. He must be trying to fill in the blanks. Perhaps he's probing us and trying to work out if we have any other Legacies?*

It seemed unlikely that a man like him had a proper circle of acquaintances he could rely on.

Kaname could only think of one conclusion.

"They must have been hired killers... And I think we all know who sent them."

4

It was in one of the many pawnshops dotting the Tokonatsu City peninsula district, located on the first floor of a stonework apartment building, in a space no larger than a convenience store. The room was filled with glass cases containing a mix of splendid golden wristwatches and leather handbags. And yet even in the anarchic world of *Money (Game) Master*, there was little chance a group of mask-wearing bandits would barge in and rob the place. Everyone had heard the rumors spread across the internet and knew what would befall any group of thugs foolish enough to resort to brute force.

All sorts of goods made their way here by one means or another, to the pawnshop run by the king of the underworld himself. For better or worse, the man was owed a great number of debts by a great many people.

But rather than sitting atop the financial district in shimmering glory, his industry took the form of shady loan sharks standing on street corners, quietly ruling the world from the shadows. He had earned the ire of many a Dealer, too, of course, but he was more than capable of dealing with any problems. And that was precisely why he was king.

In place of the usual shopkeeper, a man with long blond hair and a white tuxedo stood behind the counter—Frey(a). Without so much as a glance in her direction, he addressed the Magistellus standing beside him, a magenta-colored slime-girl in a sailor uniform.

"Brunhild."

"Yes, Master. I have verified the total sum. Would you like me to output a spreadsheet on my clothing?"

"No need. I trust you completely. If I didn't, I would hardly leave you in charge of the company's finances. Now then, Mr. M-Scope. Let us get down to business. I shall return your entire repossessed figure collection."

Frey(a) snapped his fingers, and a pair of beautiful women in conch-shaped dresses approached them. They looked practically identical, like twins, and they brought with them a trolley on wheels, stacked high with plastic boxes.

"I believe this should be all of it. Please feel free to examine the goods for any damage."

M-Scope's face lit up, and he immediately seized one of the boxes and tore off the lid. Frey(a) looked a little taken aback.

"I'm frankly shocked you were willing to brave the risk of going on that quiz program and showing your face while… Well, you might as well have a bounty on your head these days, with the number of enemies you've made. Buying back this entire collection cost you over twenty percent more than you were originally paid, and these…figures and badges don't appear to contain any skills. Why ever would you go to such lengths to reclaim them?"

"You say that, but you made sure to keep them locked up so they wouldn't get sold, didn't you?"

"Well, items like these are a bit outside my field of expertise. And I'm not sure they have much value if they're sold separately. The best situation for us was if you were to buy them back yourself. We make a little profit off the interest at virtually no cost. All I did was extend the grace period a little, that's all."

The handsome blond man chuckled and placed two things on the glass counter—a small submachine gun that looked more like a child's toy and the keys to an SUV.

"Welcome back to *Money (Game) Master*, my dear M-Scope."

"…"

M-Scope was about to reclaim his old possessions, including his gun and vehicle. In a game without levels, where equipment governed everything, it meant he could finally take back his seat as a top Dealer. As long as he had these, he could resume high-stakes trading with figures in the millions of yen and wipe out enemy Dealers to his heart's content.

However, the boy in the backpack did not pick up these items straightaway. First, he looked the blond man in the eye and spoke.

"…I would like to ask for your help, Frey(a)."

"Are you asking as a customer of my pawnshop? Or as a business partner?"

"I want to help the others…Titan, Hazard, and Zaurus. But I don't know if I can do it alone. I need backing. I'll lend you all the help I can provide. Trading, shooting, driving. You can make me your employee or your slave or whatever, just as long as you grant me the power I need."

"I see."

The man's grin grew twisted. It was not the smile of a gracious host.

"…As you are no doubt already aware, love is everything to me. Nothing else matters. Therefore, I am afraid I only deal with couples, and a fake relationship with your Magistellus doesn't count. A mere boy who only knows the silk touch of his cartoon woman's body pillow is a loathsome ally indeed. You could never know true bargaining. You use fiction as a security blanket, still holding the hand of your make-believe Magistellus, who will never show you unkindness."

He gave a flourish, and suddenly, as if by magic, a glossy black revolver appeared in Frey(a)'s hand. Raging Stallion—a .50-caliber magnum pistol with hollow-point ammunition that could kill a man-eating tiger in a single shot. Against a human, it could do a lot worse.

But he wasn't about to fight. Instead, he held the gun by the barrel, like a hammer. Frey(a) was only interested in love, and as such, the petty work of combat and moneymaking was beneath him. All Frey(a) did was unleash the hounds. Once the magenta Magistellus, Brunhild, took the grip of that pistol, everything would be over.

"I'm afraid my answer is no. At the very least, I cannot work with you the way you are now. You have no charm whatsoever."

He had spat out the words. And yet he looked M-Scope up and down, running his eyes over the shy boy's body as if he could see through his clothes.

"You must learn the ways of love. Let's see… If you wish to become a fully fledged member of the Treasure Hermit Crabs, then your only choice is to become my lover."

The handsome man(?) did not change into a beautiful woman. He did not seek to make his partner comfortable, only to satisfy his own desires.

"If you're not going to make a move, then why don't I teach you how it goes?" He smiled. "You can just sit back and leave everything to me."

"…"

It was only very slight, but an aura of tension emanated from M-Scope's body. At this, Frey(a)'s smile brightened. He gently lifted his hand, bringing the magnum pistol away from its terminal destination in Brunhild's hand. The pawnbroker king eased his posture and spoke.

"Good. It's nice to see you still have some fire left in you. Sex without love is nothing more than the mating of mindless beasts. Had you accepted my proposal, I would have simply filled your head with empty promises and had my way with you."

"…So it wouldn't have stopped you from making love to me," M-Scope noted.

"Allow me to state my terms," said Frey(a), ignoring him and leaning forward over the glass countertop. Their values may have differed, but the power dynamics at play were obvious. Frey(a) had M-Scope over a barrel. There was no need for him to mince words. "If you want me to help you, you must find yourself a sweetheart somewhere in this big, wide world and declare your love to them. If they accept, that's all well and good. But just this once, I'll let it go, even if they reject you. I just want you to see what true bargaining is like. That is my one condition."

"Fine, I'll do it…"

"Heh. The course of true love never does run smooth, you know. It's the same no matter how much money or how many guns you have. There's no such thing as a surefire way into somebody's heart. You must roll with the punches and take the lessons as they come. Don't toss aside your controller in anger. You'll never succeed if you're afraid to make mistakes or if you quit whenever things don't go exactly the way you want."

"I get it!! C'mon, Ginmi, we're leaving. Get in the car!!"

The Dealer and his *yuki-onna* Magistellus each picked up a handcart of anime merch and wheeled it over to the vehicle parked outside. Frey(a) simply watched from the counter, waving a gloved hand good-bye.

As the slouching boy left, another customer entered.

"My. How rare," she said, upon seeing Frey(a). "I didn't expect to see the owner serving customers."

"Good to see you, Laplacian. Here's something you'll be interested in. Would you like to make a bet with me on whether that virgin boy will get a date or not? It seemed he had someone in mind, so one billion says he succeeds. I'm already looking forward to the gossip."

"..."

"Oh? Did I catch you in a foul mood? What's the matter, had a run of bad luck?"

5

Hit men. These were real, honest-to-god hit men. It was an occupation that could only exist in the game.

"...Can people really make a business out of killing?" asked Midori as they walked from the trashed log cabin into the garage.

"It's a risky enterprise," replied Kaname. He may have had a hit man after his life, but his expression was as cool as ever. "Not to mention it's all under the table, so there's always the risk that the client will refuse to pay up."

"Then why do people do it?"

"Not everyone who plays *Money (Game) Master* has special expertise. For some people, killing is all they can do. Often, hit men flock to those who make a fortune on high-risk trading or gambling, either hoping for scraps or the chance to hold the more educated at their mercy. It depends."

As he spoke, Kaname stooped and peered beneath the mint-green coupe. Even with the Reduce Pain necktie, he still felt considerable discomfort when he bent over. What he was examining was not the car itself but the smattering of sand across the garage floor. It hadn't been disturbed, which meant nobody had been under there in order to plant a bomb.

For some reason, Kaname's actions caused Midori some embarrassment. Her cheeks flushed as she held down her frilly miniskirt with both hands.

"W-was my brother's killer the same way?" she asked.

"Bloody Dancer offered his skills to an international group of Dealers seeking to instigate the Swiss Depression... He ended up massacring every last one of his employers, though."

"What?"

"The Swiss Depression was a plan to concentrate all the world's money into a single bank account. Since we stopped it, the perpetrators couldn't afford to pay him, and that made him mad. After taking care of Takamasa, he didn't hesitate to turn his gun on his clients."

"On an international group of Dealers...?"

"It was a more powerful group than Called Game, that's for sure. Guns, cars, money. They had it all. And Bloody Dancer tore that group apart from the inside out, by himself."

That man had no interest in cars or money. The unlimited possibilities of *Money (Game) Master* boiled down to little more than a first-person shooter in his eyes. Even so, he was able to kill and pillage his way to the top. His unique twin pistols allowed him to restock, simply by walking over the corpse of a fallen enemy, allowing him to plunder money and ammunition in one fell swoop.

He didn't need skills or Legacies. For him, they only got in the way of the fun.

"...He believes all he has to do is keep winning, and the money will fall into his lap, so he just keeps shooting. He doesn't even budget properly, and yet he still gets mad if he misses out on a paycheck. He's a tough guy to deal with, and he treats *snow* more like a scoring mechanism."

He was a wild card, that was for sure. And since he knew the location of Kaname's car and safe house, Kaname couldn't even log out to get away from him. That would be practically asking for an ambush the next time he logged in.

Kaname pressed the button on his car key and unlocked the doors.

"He's got Cindy, my sister's Magistellus, and he's ordering her around as he pleases. If he threatened her with violence, he's probably already gotten all the info on this place. We're heading out, Midori. We need to hole up somewhere he doesn't know about. Even just a motel somewhere will do."

"O-okay."

It seemed her nerves had finally gotten to her. But Midori was right to be nervous; the two of them were on the run from Bloody Dancer, the world's top gunslinger. This was a man so powerful that even Kaname had been unable to stand against him when Takamasa Fell. Considering that both Kaname and his sister Ayame were members of Called Game and two of the strongest Dealers in the world, their opponent must have been someone equally fearsome.

For better or worse, this was an experience that could only be had in-game. But retreating to the real world would not save them now. Leaving everything to Tselika would be cruel, and besides, Bloody Dancer could simply turn the area around their parked vehicles into a minefield and wait for them to log back in. It would be especially fatal for Midori, with no property in which to secure her bike.

And so Kaname in his mint-green coupe and Midori on her autumn-leaf-patterned bike left Mangrove Island behind and rode onto the circular bridge.

Midori: So, where are we going, exactly?

Kaname: The best place to hide a tree is in a forest. The peninsula financial district is the area with the highest population density.

Midori: But doesn't that just mean there'll be loads of his hit men crawling around?!

Kaname: Tokonatsu City may be the size of a small nation, but it's still finite in area. We can't just run away to the ends of the earth.

"Tselika. Run a search."

"Yes, My Lord. All large hotels on the mainland with an underground or enclosed parking lot and at least two exits."

Meanwhile, Kaname picked up Short Spear with his left hand. He set Tselika's seat to recline and remotely wound down the window. Only the metallic sound of the gun's mechanism rang out as a stream of .45-caliber rounds left the silencer-integrated barrel and met their marks. The minivan pulling up beside him was filled with holes, and from the opened sliding door tumbled a man in a mask and black body armor holding an assault rifle. Kaname didn't even look back as the man fell into the road and quickly disappeared behind them.

The buzzing feeling had returned to his nose. There was nothing to fear as long as the Lion's Nose was working. Kaname could place his trust in his own instincts once more. He pointed his gun at the driver's seat and yelled.

"You're going to have to do better than that! If you want to kill me, then send a hit man with at least a four-star rating!!"

The minivan ignored his warning and attempted to run Kaname's vehicle off the road, but Kaname slammed on the brakes so that the minivan ended up in front of him. Kaname unrolled his own window this time and fired at the van's rear wheel. It lost control and toppled onto its side before being left in the dust.

Midori: Hey, what's that flying over us?!

Kaname: A scout drone, repurposed from the ones they use in agriculture for taking down hornets' nests. They're built to withstand gusts, not raw speed. We should be able to outrun it no problem.

Things were finally looking up again. Kaname was getting into the zone. If he forgot to have fun, the game would cease to be a game.

"...It's been on our tail since before we reached the peninsula."

"Hornets?"

"Yep."

"Then those gentlemen must have been from Marietta Flapper, the pest control company," said Tselika. "How can a bloodthirsty maniac make enough money to order those fellows around just killing?"

Marietta Flapper was a business that had started out exterminating bugs and rodents, before eventually expanding their sphere of operations to include people.

However, Midori, atop her bright-red leaf-patterned bike, appeared to be struggling with an even more fundamental question.

Midori: Pest control? Is there really demand for that in the game world?

Kaname: More than you might think. Property values are critical in a game like this... Serious fights break out over real estate. One way to get at a rival is to scatter garbage and pet food around their property to attract pests. It's an especially effective tactic against restaurants.

Midori had no further questions. It didn't seem to be a topic the sweet little schoolgirl particularly enjoyed discussing.

Just then, there were two more two gunshots. This time, it wasn't Kaname or Marietta. It appeared a civilian had gotten caught up in the cross fire and flipped out. Nobody was just an extra. That was the true thrill of *Money (Game) Master*.

"Whaaat?! Smash Daughter's on our tail!" yelled Tselika.

"She's not after us," replied Kaname. "We'll let her do the work for us."

The Dealer in the school swimsuit, Smash Daughter, was a master of nonlethal combat. Her rifle fired charged electric rounds instead of 7.62 millimeter rifle ammunition, and the under-barrel stun gun attachment was able to deliver a seven hundred–kilovolt shock. She could further enhance its effects by connecting it to the battery of the collapsible electric scooter she used to get around.

...However, her pacifism stemmed from more than mere naïveté. Once unconscious, a target could be killed or spared at her whim. She was by no means a woman to take lightly.

Midori: What's that ball of lightning?! It's like we're about to be swallowed up by a thundercloud!

Kaname: Don't go near it. You're exposed on that bike.

Smash Daughter was fearsome enough on her own, but paired

with her silver-haired Apsaras-style Magistellus, their combined fury was unmatched. This tanned, motorcycle-riding beauty with the pair of oversized goggles around her neck wielded Hot Splash, a water gun even larger than an assault rifle. She wore a tank top, a tight pair of spats, and a jacket tied around her waist as she sat astride her large hydrogen-engine scooter, and by spraying a powerful jet of water pressurized with carbon dioxide gas, she added that little bit of extra oomph to Smash Daughter's attack. The ensuing storm of high-voltage current swept along the ground and through the air like a snake. It was even more terrifying than staring down a machine gun blast.

It could slip through door cracks, seep around bulletproof glass, and even get inside cars.

"You arrogant bastards!! Think you can get away with spraying bullets all over the place like it's none of your damn business, huh?! I don't wanna hear your freakin' excuses!"

"Calm down, my lady. A sexy young woman such as yourself should not resort to such language. Here, let's do some breathing exercises. And relaaax."

These two had no reason to stick around, however. After very helpfully whittling down the hit men's numbers, the girl with chestnut hair in the witch's hat flipped her middle finger and sped off. Kaname flashed his headlights twice to show his appreciation. It was the girl's Magistellus, who looked for all the world like a gym instructor, who turned around. She appeared about to blow a kiss in response, when Smash Daughter, royally pissed, kicked her scooter hard in the side.

Tselika looked at the Magistellus, whose white tank top was now so drenched with water from her own gun that it barely obstructed the view of her tanned brown skin beneath.

"Hmph. A mole above her navel. I suppose all Apsaras are as promiscuous as her."

"What's the matter, Tselika? Feeling some competition?"

Kaname couldn't hope to rely on the actions of random passersby forever. Protecting Midori from whoever might try to hurt her was paramount. The stronger the opponent, the harder they had to strike back. It was nerve-racking, and Kaname couldn't shake the ever-present feeling of danger. But he was not going to run away. This was the time to stand and fight.

Those who couldn't exchange their fear for thrills would die while they were still frozen in horror. Kaname had already done that once before and lost Takamasa as a result. He wasn't about to let it happen again.

Kaname: Midori, watch out. Try to stay behind me as much as you can.

But there was no response from Midori. Her attention was absorbed by something else, something on the display overlaid on top of her windshield.

Kaname: Midori!

Midori: There's a request...

Midori's shocked response came through at last.

Midori: A chat request. From...Bloody Dancer?

"That bastard!!"

"It looks like he isn't just getting his information from Cindy," noted Tselika. "Midori did not come to *Money (Game) Master* until after Takamasa's Fall. There is no way she and your sister could have met. Perhaps he has hired a private investigator to look into us?"

Midori: Wh-what do I do?!

Kaname: Accept the request and link it to me as well. It's probably me he wants to speak to anyway.

It was hard to keep an eye out for anyone on their tail as they sped along the continuously curving one-lane circle road. However, Kaname made sure to keep speeding up and slowing down erratically. Cars that were happy to get farther or closer away from him were irrelevant. He needed to watch out for those who went out of their way to keep a constant distance.

"There."

Kaname disposed of more cars filled with Marietta Flapper hit men, but these were just small fry. As he coolly fired at them from the window, his attention was focused on the enlarged chat box on his dashboard. This was something entirely different.

Bloody Dancer: Yo, Kaname.

That was all it took. All it took for Kaname's blood to boil. The Lion's Nose felt as though it would explode.

But Bloody Dancer showed no such emotion.

Bloody Dancer: Good to see you're enjoying yourself. Doesn't seem like Marietta's gonna be enough to put you down, then. I had high hopes for them on that one-lane bridge road, too. Guess they didn't have the balls to just blow the whole thing up.

Kaname: You should have stayed hidden. You really want me to ruin your life that badly?

Bloody Dancer: Ha-ha!! You? Kill me? Bring it on, then! Let's see if you've changed from the little boy who was cuddling his sister and pissing his pants in fear!!

The engines of the coupe and bike roared in unison as Kaname and Midori came off the bridge and into the heart of Tokonatsu City, bathed in light.

"Tselika, how are you doing on finding us a hotel?"

"Argh! All the ones that match our conditions are booked out! And none are taking last-minute bookings at night!!"

Kaname shared this information with Midori, and he saw her pull a puzzled expression atop her bike.

Midori: Why would people be booking hotels? It's a game, so they can just log off if they want to go to sleep, right?

Tselika: Why else do people book hotel rooms? To f—

Kaname grabbed Tselika by the horns and gave her a violent shake.

Things were starting to get lively. Each side sought to firm up their footing and locate their foe, gear up, and let the bullets fly. The battle would start long before either side started shooting, and now it was Kaname's move. His weapons were cars and money. Bloody Dancer relied on nothing but his own skill.

No sooner had Kaname finished that thought, when…

Ker-rash! A mass of steel came speeding out of a side street, barreling toward the side of the coupe.

It was not a dump truck, or an eighteen-wheeler, though it looked very similar.

"Gargh!! I-it's a Calamity Studio!" shrieked Tselika.

It was oblong, angular, and sleek, like a shipping container. At first glance, it looked like a cross between an armored prisoner transport van and a massive tourist bus, but with antennas covering its flat roof. It was an ERBV, or emergency response broadcast vehicle, an enormous armored mobile broadcasting relay used by news networks to respond immediately to sites of natural disasters. In order to compete with the ubiquitous cameras that everyone carried on their phones, it was built heavy and strong, able to plunge unflinchingly into the eye of a raging tornado and transmit shocking footage directly from the scene.

"Tsk!!"

Kaname gripped the wheel, but the monstrosity weighed over eighty tons, more than a military tank. There was an order of magnitude of difference between the masses of the two vehicles. It also seemed unlikely the tires were filled only with air.

Midori: That van says Tap TV on the side!!

Kaname: I think he stole it from that fortress of PMC activity we saw earlier. To him, it's just like robbing a bike!!

Though he could explain after the fact, even Kaname hadn't seen this coming. If he knew this titan was going to come into play, he would have planned things a little differently.

His reaction came too slowly. The Lion's Nose could not predict the future!!

The ERBV scraped the coupe's bumper, just behind the right rear wheel. That small scrape was enough to crumple the entire trunk like an empty can. The back of the car was wrenched sideways, sending the vehicle into an uncontrolled spin. Kaname was turning the wheel to fight back when he caught sight of something in his mirrors.

It was not his foe, the pistol-wielding Dealer, who sat in the driver's seat—he couldn't even drive. Beyond the wire-mesh-reinforced windshield, someone else gripped the enormous steering wheel.

"Cindy...?!"

"That's not all, Tselika. Bloody Dancer's here as well!!" shouted Kaname.

A solitary figure lurked amid the crowd of antennas atop the armored van's roof. A man with silver, slicked-back hair, dressed stylishly in a thin suit, in his hands a pair of pistols sporting freakishly long magazines and grenade launchers bigger than the weapons themselves. A man who, in this game of *Money (Game) Master*, placed his faith not in cars or high-risk trading, but in his own two guns alone. This man, with hard rock blaring from the wearable speaker around his neck, could take on a squad of PMCs. He could waltz into the headquarters of an AI business as if it were no more trouble than walking down to the convenience store.

Kaname's heart was racing, but he attempted to convert his fear into exhilaration, his hesitation into action. One wrong move here would spell the end. It seemed likely his nerves would give out before any bullets got to him.

He needed to face his own trauma. Tselika offered him one of his neckties, but Kaname refused. Using the Stress Care skill would treat the physical symptoms, but that would just be running away. It couldn't bring the value to zero. If he acknowledged the situation was getting to him, it would all be downhill from there.

Conscious of his rising stress levels, Kaname screamed:

"Bloody Dancer!!"

"Hee-hee!"

They didn't need the chatroom anymore. They yelled at each other over the raging wind.

"Hee-hee-hee! Ah-ha-ha-ha-ha-ha-ha-ha-ha!! Those mercs weren't doing it for you, so why don't we up the ante?!!"

Bang! Bang! Ba-bang!!

There was a series of gunshots. Tselika ducked in her seat in the coupe, finally free from its spin, causing her pit-babe garb to squeak against the leather. But Bloody Dancer was not aiming at them.

Midori: What?

There was the sound of breaking glass. Midori kept peeking back over her shoulder.

Midori: He's not shooting at us. He's firing randomly at that building!! But why?!

Kaname: The corporate defenses.

Kaname shivered. As soon as he understood the meaning of his foe's actions, a deathly chill ran down his spine.

Kaname: Watch out, Midori! He's trying to summon the PMCs on us!! This place is full of private buildings!!

Sure enough, his assault soon prompted a furious reprisal. First came the armored cars, their sirens blaring. But no sooner had they reached the main road than a barrage of grenades from Bloody Dancer's launchers blew them away. A new window appeared on Kaname's dashboard, his PMC attention meter. It was already over eighty. Reinforcements flooded the scene, from attack helicopters to eight-wheeled APCs with roof-mounted machine guns. It was less like a suppression force and more like an army. In theory, though, their only target was Bloody Dancer and the ERBV he was driving.

The PMCs were supposed to be an undefeatable force. Normally, if you made the mistake of alerting them, the best thing to do was to hide out somewhere until the heat died down. Their base stats were off the charts, and even if you managed to defeat one, two more would show up to avenge it. You never, ever, went looking for a fight on purpose. And yet…

Midori: Can this even be called a fight…?

What she saw in her mirrors then stunned her speechless. She kept looking back, as if she needed another look to convince herself.

Midori: He's crashing through them! All of them! It's like we're being chased by a massive metal shark!!

With a burst of gunfire and lobbed grenades, Bloody Dancer sent the armored cars into a spin and shot the helicopters out of the sky. They all fell in front of the ERBV's bumper, where they were pushed haphazardly forward by gunfire like huge steel popcorn. If even one of those flaming wrecks hit Kaname or Midori, they'd be done for.

He was not hoping to use the PMCs' boundless firepower against them; he was using their carcasses as ammunition, like a pitching machine with an unlimited number of balls. He let out a mad laugh as he tossed what remained of one of the game's most feared enemies onto the sidewalk, flattening traffic lights and smashing storefronts. Kaname could see Dealers who had just been walking down the street duck into buildings and under cars for cover, screaming for their lives.

A volcano of steel and gunpowder pursued them. Even in the game world, it was nothing short of absurd!!

"Well?! Exciting enough for you?! Let me know if it's still not up to snuff, Kaname! I'm getting in new stock all the time! I've got a real feast prepared for you!!"

Midori: He's mad... He's got everyone in the whole city after him, and he's laughing!!

One of the PMC armored vehicles fired a single shell from its long, tank-like cannon. But Bloody Dancer merely aimed and fired his underbarrel grenade launcher, and the two projectiles collided in midair and detonated by the side of the road. It was a superhuman feat, one that no mere man could perform, even if they used the Slow skill to slow down their sense of time.

The most terrifying part was that the guns in each of his hands were not Legacies. They were just ordinary firearms. His skill was all his own.

But Kaname had no time to admire this. He wasn't even able to swerve out of the way before the unexpected explosion blasted him aside. The coupe was thrown halfway into the air, balancing on two wheels. It was a miracle the car didn't flip completely, but Bloody Dancer didn't wait for Kaname to regain control.

Ba-bang!! Two shots to the wheels still in contact with the ground, and the coupe lost its balance. It was the same as in karate and kick-boxing: When an opponent kicked high, it was best to sweep low and send them crashing to the ground.

Midori: Hey!

Kaname: Stay back, Midori! I don't want you caught up in this!!

The coupe was completely out of control. It ran off the main road and plowed straight into a nearby building.

6

The coupe's carbon frame splintered the double doors and plunged into the building, finally coming to rest after crashing into the base of a statue depicting a pair of nude goddesses.

"Dammit… Tselika, you alive?"

"Yes, My Lord. As much as I may wish it were not so…"

But there was no time to lie there with the car's airbag as a pillow. Heralded by the roar of her engine, Midori joined the pair in the marble lobby.

"Are you guys okay?!"

"…You should have just run away," muttered Kaname, as he took a crowbar out from under the seat. He left the car, went around to the back, and pried the bent trunk open.

The monster shotgun, #tempest.err.

The anti-materiel rifle longer than a person was tall, #fireline.err.

The minigun as light as a feather, #dracolord.err.

And the mortar that ignored all terrain in its path, #thunderbolt.err.

These were the four Legacies Kaname had collected thus far. Luckily, they had not been damaged when the trunk was squashed. They would help Kaname in his fight, of course, but more than anything, he couldn't leave them here for Bloody Dancer to find.

"Midori, can you call Meiki out?"

"She's around… She must be in a good mood today."

Midori tapped lightly on her motorcycle's gas tank, and a Magistellus in a short-cut *cheongsam* appeared on the back seat.

"In that case, she can take #fireline.err. Tselika, you've got #tempest.err. Midori, take #dracolord.err."

"Wait, what about #thunderbolt.err?!"

"The projectile may be able to pass through obstacles, but it takes too long to land to be of any use to us indoors. Someone with empty hands can carry it on their back!"

It seemed unlikely Bloody Dancer would deign to use the Legacies against them if any were to fall into his hands, but he would end up handing them over to the AIs, and Kaname could not let his efforts so far be in vain.

Also, as powerful as the Legacies were, there was no point in giving more than one to a single person. If someone had #fireline.err and #dracolord.err, there was practically no range at which both weapons would be useful. Therefore, it was more efficient to divide them up.

Now, then...

First, Midori had to take the minigun, light as polystyrene. Questions of her effectiveness with it aside, it was the only one she could carry. Kaname, for his part, preferred to fight with his own weapon, Short Spear. He also had to consider the fact that #fireline.err was very heavy, so he didn't want to give it to a human who would be taken down by a single stray bullet. That meant it was safer to leave it in the hands of the two Magistelli. The high-caliber shotgun with a barrel diameter more in line with a grenade launcher went to Tselika. This was so that Kaname and Tselika had both short- and long-range capabilities between them. Bloody Dancer himself was deadly close up, with his pistols and grenade launchers, so they couldn't start a close-quarters brawl unprepared. Of course, it would be foolish to underestimate the further threat he posed. He was a beast, able to take down fortresses and battleships with nothing more than his pistols, grenades, and the hard rock blaring from his speaker.

Kaname drew his weapon and took a deep breath. Then he put his hands around the Reduce Pain necktie he was wearing and pulled it off.

"My Lord?! What are you doing?!"

"...I can't be relying on skills. Not if I want to stand on the same playing field as him."

His back wound flared up like an explosion, and Kaname gritted his teeth against the pain. But there was method to his apparent madness. As highly coveted as the skill was, it had failed him by dulling his reaction time when it counted. If the Calamity Studio, that ERBV that Bloody Dancer was driving around, hadn't crashed into him earlier, they wouldn't be in this predicament now.

In other words...

I have to build myself up from scratch first. Everything else comes on top of that. I have things that Bloody Dancer doesn't. The Legacies I'm borrowing from Takamasa, my friends... I can't ever forget that I am blessed. If I take that for granted...I can never win against him.

"Tselika. Get me my other tie. The one with no skills."

"Yessir. You've always walked the path of most resistance, My Lord. I'll put it on for you. Hold still."

As she did so, Kaname reflected. If he surrounded himself with conveniences, he could never reach Bloody Dancer's level. But if he tried to fight alone, he could never surpass it. Failure awaited him at both extremes. Kaname needed to find a happy medium, and so he rid himself of his skills.

The tiny difference in reaction speed Reduce Pain had taken from him made a world of difference. He could bear the pain, if it allowed him to stand up and protect the people dear to him.

"Right now, we need to get farther inside."

"What is this place? A museum???" asked Midori.

"My Lord, have we not just broken down the doors of a private building? If we stay here, the PMCs will be all over us!!"

"Would you rather go back out there and face Bloody Dancer? Keep your guard up, they're coming!!"

Kaname felt the Lion's Nose as clear as day.

The interior of the building was decorated like a Victorian mansion. He couldn't look up the blueprints, since it was an unexplored building, and even the mini map on his smart watch was blank.

The twin goddess statue his coupe had collided with stood in the very center of the hall, and beyond it was a reception desk. The place seemed to have closed for the night, as there was neither a customer nor an AI receptionist in sight... That didn't mean there weren't night watchmen farther in, though.

Kaname ignored the stairs. There was no need to go down with the building. If he could just make his way through the maze of passages to a back exit, he could escape into the alleyways beyond. With that in mind, the higher he climbed, the more he would box himself in. On the first floor, he could always escape out a window; thus both the upstairs and the basement were to be avoided. The safest option was to head deeper into the building.

But just as he made that decision...

The entire wall facing the road came crashing down as the large cuboid ERBV plowed straight into it. Tselika watched as the already-damaged mint-green coupe was crushed beneath the mass of stone.

"...That bastard, I'm gonna kill him!!"

"No, Tselika! Try to stay calm!!"

Kaname grabbed her slender arm and pulled her down a hallway.

The car was useless now. And his money was useless without anyone to pay. All he had left were his guns and his own self. This was exactly what Bloody Dancer wanted.

"Haah... Haah..." Kaname gasped for breath.

"Hey...," Midori ventured.

"I'm fine, dammit. I'm fine... I won't give up this time. This isn't like back then..."

"Listen to me!!" Midori yelled from right beside him. "Where the heck are we? Do you have a plan?!"

Midori's voice brought Kaname back to his senses. It seemed that Tselika wasn't the only one letting the situation get to her. And it wasn't just because he'd been shot. Kaname's mental state was more complicated than he had thought. Hadn't he already decided he wouldn't rely on Stress Care skills?

The room they were in now was different from the others. A red carpet lay spread out before them. No doubt during the day there would have been a signposted route to be followed by eager visitors with audio guides, but past closing time, there was no such service. All around them were doorways leading to other large rooms, without any indication of how to navigate them.

Just then, Kaname felt the Lion's Nose like a punch in the face from an invisible fist. Then he heard the roaring riffs of hard rock blaring from the wearable speaker. A cheery voice called out from the corridor behind them.

"Yo!!"

"Tch!!"

It was a tough decision, but even Kaname could only protect one person at a time. And Magistelli, if shot, would only be Downed, while human Dealers would Fall. This was the kind of logical choice only possible in a game, and the calculations shot through his brain lightning fast as he swept up Midori in his arms and dived through a nearby door. From the floor, he yelled.

"Midori! Hallway ceiling!!"

Ba-bang! Bang!! A burst of gunfire erupted from the hallway outside. In order to protect the Magistellus duo from the madman's bullets, Midori took up the featherweight minigun and unleashed a barrage into the walls and ceiling. The ensuing torrent of rubble obstructed the attack, and not a second later, Tselika and Meiki dived into the room. However…

"Meiki?!"

Midori's Magistellus did not answer her. She had taken a hit in the shoulder. Tselika, too, threw the monster shotgun #tempest.err to the ground and slumped to the floor. She was sweating hard, moisture dripping down her face, and not because of the sweltering heat of the tropical city. Her pit-babe outfit consisted of only a bikini top, a miniskirt, and a fur-laced jacket. She was completely exposed.

Red liquid spilled from beneath the hand she pressed to her right side.

"…Do not make that face. You made the right decision, My Lord. We are Magistelli. Death for us is but a momentary inconvenience…"

That wasn't true, and Kaname knew it. He hated himself for acting on reason alone. Bloody Dancer had caught them unawares. If he hadn't called out to them before shooting, the man could easily have killed at least one of them. Even taking into account Kaname's and Midori's timely interventions, it was odd that he had missed his target's vitals. With his skills, he should have been able to fire his twin pistols through the falling rubble like threading a needle, striking his victim's brain and heart.

But Bloody Dancer had always been that way. He took the freedom afforded him by the game's open world to unthinkable lengths—much further than Kaname. There was no catching up to that monster. He would tear up everything the boy held dear, right in front of his eyes. First his sister, then Takamasa, and now Midori and Tselika, too. His best friend's sister and his own irreplaceable partner.

I'll kill him...

Something inside him snapped. Cracks spread in his gritted back teeth. His rage had gone beyond the limits of the game.

Enough. Screw principles—I don't need a reason. I'm going to kill Bloody Dancer with my own two hands!!

"Heeey there, Kaname!! Where'd you go?" came a jeering voice. "Weren't you going to kill me?!"

"My Lord! We have to escape! Don't listen to him!"

The hard rock pounded in Kaname's ears and against his heart.

"This is just like before!!" the man boomed. "So who's going to die for you this time? Which of these chicks is going to be your meat shield? You've sure been busy pickin' 'em up, Kaname!!"

"Think, My Lord! You're not back in that abandoned building!! If you want to take him down, you've got to stay calm! Weren't you the one telling me that just a few minutes ago?!!"

Midori gave a murmur of agreement. After patching up Meiki's shoulder with a spare handkerchief, she had quickly helped Tselika get to her feet as well. Now she turned to Kaname, staring him down.

"You said you would put your life on the line to protect me," Midori shouted. "That means you can't just throw it away. This is an order, Kaname. You have to protect us all, no matter what happens!!"

Her words were like a slap across the face, and at last Kaname's mind was plucked from its isolation back into the real world. She was right. Only if his life were his own could Kaname be permitted to lose himself to anger. Takamasa had saved the life of his sister, and so Kaname had sworn to repay the favor in kind. He had to protect Midori. That was more important than his vengeance.

Once you have a lot of money, it's easy to lose your humanity. To become nothing more than a slave of the AI companies. But a hero had saved Kaname from all that, and Kaname had sworn to live as he had—as a human.

"…That's more like it," said Midori with a grin as she saw the look in Kaname's eyes. Her smile reminded Kaname of his dear departed friend. "I'm not saying to let that monster go. Just think of a way to take him down without losing anybody. And that includes you."

"Yeah…"

"My brother may have been a hero to you, but he made one mistake. He let you bear the weight of his death. You know how painful it is, so don't force it onto anyone else! We're winning this battle, and everyone is coming out alive, you understand?!"

"Yeah. I'm done letting that asshole take whatever he wants! It ends here!!"

The horror in his heart was replaced with exhilaration. Kaname Suou felt a flame ignite somewhere deep inside.

He didn't have much to work with. All four of their Legacies combined wouldn't be enough to go against Bloody Dancer's common pistols head-on. That wasn't even an option. Gunfights were his specialty, and there was nothing to be gained from confronting him on his own turf.

"We'll split up," Kaname said simply.

There was no time for detailed discussion. They could hear Bloody Dancer's pistols echoing down the hallway. No doubt he was busy slaughtering the night watchmen who had come to respond to their intrusion, nonsensically targeting the PMCs once again. Kaname felt the tip of his Lion's Nose tingle as if scorched by an invisible flame.

To that man, this was nothing more than a quick diversion. He was even humming a little tune.

"Midori, help Tselika and head farther in. If you can, try to stop her bleeding. And take #thunderbolt.err. It's not going to be of any use to us in here. I'm still in fighting shape, so I'll stick with Meiki and try to outflank him. Meiki, can you handle #fireline.err?"

Meiki was never much for conversation, and it was difficult to even discern a yes or no from her flat expression. The sniper rifle in her hands was heavy, so Kaname wanted to be sure it wasn't going to cause her any problems. It was Midori, though, who stepped in on her behalf.

"She says it's okay. And you have my permission to order her around."

"Thanks, Midori. Now head back into the building with Tselika. And Meiki—listen to me. If we end up in a shoot-out with Bloody Dancer, we're as good as dead. It doesn't matter how many people we have or how good our weapons are. I want you to keep that in mind."

"..."

"And one more thing. We need to shoot him from two different angles at the same time to make sure he Falls. If we fail, we're not going to get another chance. Understood? No second chances. Don't let him make a move. We do this right and there shouldn't be a fight at all. Once a fight starts, we've already lost."

It was hard to tell if Meiki had taken in any of what he had said. Her gaze drifted gently, and she seemed more interested in her surroundings than in Kaname. He followed suit and examined the room they stood in. It was large and rectangular, its walls lined with glass display cabinets lit with indirect lighting. Near the collapsed wall connecting their room to the hallway, a number of the cabinets had shattered, and their contents lay strewn across the floor.

A magnum revolver, a speargun, and a carbine rifle. A rather eccentric collection of weapons.

But then, Kaname spotted the golden placard lying among the debris, listing the items' names.

"#bigheart.err, #seasnake.err, and #penetrator.err..."

Kaname's heart clenched. He took a closer look around him.

"You're kidding me. Everything in here, they're all Takamasa's Legacies!!"

"Hey, hey, hey. Did you think I crashed your car into this building for no reason?"

Kaname spun around and pointed Short Spear in the direction of the voice, but already the figure was upon him. The man moved so fast that it seemed like the sound of his hard rock music trailed behind at a delay. A monster, more than rivaling the demonic Magistelli, in a thin white suit and black shirt. A beast with a pistol and a grenade launcher in each hand.

The feeling in the Lion's Nose exploded out of control.

Then there was a *shwmp!!* sound, like a wine bottle being uncorked, and a grenade went off.

"Graagh?!"

Kaname grunted as he was knocked to the floor. Something was off. Bloody Dancer's fragmentation grenades unleashed a cloud of shrapnel that spelled instant death for anything within an eight-meter radius. All the more in an enclosed space like this. Without cover, he should have been torn to shreds.

So how was Kaname still alive?

Kaname lay on the ground, but Short Spear was still in his grasp. His voice shook.

"Cindy…?!"

"Heh. Looks like all you can do is cower behind your friends, eh?"

Bloody Dancer stepped into the ruined room, spitting harsh words to rub salt in Kaname's wounds.

She was frozen, her pose unnatural. Just like the broken remains of the statues lying around them, the dark elf Magistellus lay motionless on the ground. The black-haired young girl who, by all rights, should have left the game when Ayame retired. (Though whether she would have disappeared to the data realm outside the city or some world only demons knew, Kaname could not say.)

She couldn't even blink, and yet she looked up at Kaname as if making sure he was safe, before a red shoe stepped mercilessly onto

her face. Her glasses cracked, and the monster who had shot her stepped over her body as though she were nothing more than a piece of rubble.

"Now ain't that a hoot? She managed to free herself from me, only to die protecting you."

The thumping beat of the hard rock emanating from his wearable speaker punctuated the man's words.

"This sure is a nicer sight than when that beanpole did it. A chick sacrificing herself for a dude is way more emotional. Even better when you add the racial aspect to it. Love overcoming all boundaries! Ain't that a touching tale? C'mon, man, give me a tear here. You got any feelings left in there, huh?!"

"Bloody Dancer…!!"

"If you wanna fight instead, then let's get it on!! Don't waste your time planning for a second shot, 'cause we aren't gonna make it that far! One shot, one kill. Let's settle this right here and now with a good old-fashioned quickdraw!!"

The two duelists leaped into action. The crack of Bloody Dancer's pistols rang loud throughout the room, while Kaname's .45-caliber bullet pierced the air in silence. Time slowed to a halt. Only the hard rock streaming from the man's speaker filled the space between them.

There was a streak of red. A gash opened in Bloody Dancer's right ear. First blood.

It dripped over his green glass earring. Even this tiny wound was a triumph. Anyone who saw their fight and knew their relative capabilities would be astonished to see Kaname land even a single hit of this caliber on his foe.

A broad smile spread across Bloody Dancer's face. He was like a tiger eyeing its prey.

"…You're fast, kid. That's the first time anyone's managed to surprise me. Kaname, you've got the speed of a beast. Looks like you finally stopped playing on easy mode with all those skills and shit, huh?"

However.

The one on his knees, expression twisted in agony, was Kaname. A bullet to his side. Not even the Lion's Nose had been fast enough to warn him.

"But you were just a little too far to the left. Oh well."

"…Grhh!!"

Bloody Dancer wasn't using any skills to boost his evasion. He didn't rely on such things, which was why he could so easily break convention in his tactics. Unlike skills enhanced through the Legacies, his skills were the product of a man dedicated solely to perfecting himself, not his tools.

So many had passed through his hands, and he never once gave in to the temptation of the Legacies. As selfish as he was, the man had mettle.

"I'm trying to explain, so quit jumping the gun! Aren't you wondering what this mountain of Legacies is doing here?"

"You killed Takamasa, and now you're trying to scavenge his loot, right?"

"Don't make it sound like I'm some kind of vulture. I was asked to do this, you know. By the AI companies."

"Then you know…!"

Kaname could no longer stand. He was down on one knee, his breath ragged and hoarse. But still, he refused to go down.

In some ways, the beast was right. If Kaname had relied on skills such as Reduce Pain and Stress Care to relieve his mind, he wouldn't be so tenacious now. He wouldn't be able to stand on the same level as his foe if he gave up as soon as he saw the raw difference in their ability.

"You know the Magistelli are using us! Using humanity as a stepping-stone to seize something even greater…!!"

"Who cares? I'm just here to have fun."

To one side of him kneeled Kaname, and to the other stood Meiki. The brute grinned as he pointed his twin pistols at each of them.

"Now let me ask *you* a question," he said. "What would you do if this game didn't exist? Could you make a living in the real world? We're the same, you and I. We can only shine in here. We're nothing without the game. Do you know what I'm like in real life? I bet you couldn't even guess. This game…is my flesh and blood."

"…"

"I don't wanna deal with the complicated shit. I just wanna shoot stuff without having to think about it. And yet here you come, talking all kinds of feel-good crap about humanity and AI. I don't give a shit, understand? And this isn't the first time. The Swiss Depression—who cares? Millions of people will lose their jobs and starve. Big deal! The money can go where it likes. As long as I keep winning, I can earn my keep. I just want to play the game. This world is so much fun! Who are you to tell me what the rules are, huh?!"

"You're insane."

Kaname gulped. He had always known it, from the moment he had first met the man.

"…How can you still say that, after things have gotten this bad? You're going to keep pretending none of this is happening?"

"I'm going to collect all the Legacies."

It was a clear statement of intent. He was not a servant of the AI or the Magistelli, but he was no less a threat. He was an enemy to humanity the world over. He knew that the horrors stretched far beyond mortal understanding, and yet he was laughing.

He was unlike Kaname Suou. Unlike Criminal AO.

Bloody Dancer. No skills, no Legacies. No help from other Dealers or even his Magistellus. He was a true lone wolf, an army of one. A warrior of destruction who fought all his battles alone.

"And then, I'm gonna give them to the AIs. Humans are always trying to undo what they've done once they see the scales start to tip. I'm gonna make it so we can't go back, so we have to sit in our own shit. And then, after that, *what else will there be to do but play?* Maybe that'll make us slaves to the AI, but so what? Leave those real-world problems out of it! Let's start having fun!! It's like when you're way into a game and your family comes to you with their stupid problems—what a fucking downer!! Don't you think so, too, Kaname???!!!"

His attitude toward the game was completely different. He had built his life around it. And if that was the source of his strength, then...

If he had discarded the real world entirely and become fully devoted to the virtual, then...

Even Kaname Suou could do nothing to stop him...!!

And then, the man's twin pistols fired.

7

He had to be stopped at all costs. This beast of a man could not be allowed to reach Midori and Tselika, even if Kaname had to die to prevent it.

But just as Kaname steeled his resolve...

"...?"

By now, several seconds had passed, and Kaname found that no bullets had torn his flesh, and no impact had shattered his bones.

Between the barrel of his rifle, Short Spear, and his foe stood a solitary figure. It was a woman with long black hair swept back and a pair of smart-looking spectacles.

Kaname could make out words emanating from her earphones.

"Now. Do it."

Ching! Chikkikkikkikkikkikkikkikkikkikkikkikkikkikki!!!

There was a high-pitched noise, an unusual sound for a gunshot.

It was more like the sound of clashing swords. And little wonder, for the woman was using the assault rifle in her hands to shoot each and every oncoming bullet out of the air. Was she utilizing the gun's recoil to make minute adjustments to her aim? Or perhaps it was accomplished by slightly altering the spin of each bullet. Either way, this was not a normal weapon.

The woman's white blouse and pencil skirt were spotless, her intricate metal headband and smart glasses impeccable, and her black stockings without a single run. The belt securing her weapon to her back must have been a holdover from her time as a sniper.

"Li…"

Kaname gasped. He had killed her, with his very own hands.

"Lily-Kiska?!"

The woman chuckled softly, as though the mere fact he had remembered her name was amusing.

The dead returning to life. That was another pleasure unique to the game world.

"A Legacy," sneered Bloody Dancer, as though the hard rock blaring from his wearable speaker was of greater value. "Boring. Any fool can swing one of those around; it practically does everything for you."

"My, you sound awfully relaxed, considering my #swallowdive.err can shoot every one of your bullets out of the air. Of course, I could switch my target to your brains instead."

"Ha. But it ain't all-powerful, is it? If it was, you wouldn't be standing there in front of me. I'm guessing there're some restrictions, but frankly I couldn't care less. All I gotta do is pay attention to what's in front of me."

Ba-bang!! The hollow sound of gunfire rang out. Bloody Dancer's gun was pointed directly overhead, like the starting pistol at a race. But something was different.

And then, Lily-Kiska, who could shoot every bullet out of the air, found her shoulder coated in fresh, scarlet blood.

"Ghhh?!"

"A ricochet. If I can't shoot you head-on, then I just have to get at you from an angle. Seeing as how you couldn't stop that, I'm guessing it only works on targets in its sight range. But since I've already handled it, I don't really care about the specifics."

He fired again. This time, Kaname dived toward her and knocked her to the ground. If he hadn't, the bullet would have penetrated Lily-Kiska right in her stomach, the core of her torso and the hardest place to protect without taking a hit to any vital organs.

"You idiot," sneered Bloody Dancer. "When it comes down to it, *Money (Game) Master* is about killing. If you wanna protect these easy mode Dealers, up to their ears in skills, then you shouldn't be jumping in front of her, Kaname. You should be killing me."

However, though Kaname had taken the bullet for Lily-Kiska, he hadn't Fallen. The round had lodged in his smartphone strapped to his thigh. But had Bloody Dancer noticed?

The man's pistols fired nine-millimeter bullets. His grenade launchers were there to fill the gap when their destructive power was insufficient. They were not nearly as dangerous as magnum ammo, which could blow away a bulletproof jacket, along with the wearer's torso, in one shot.

He clicked his tongue.

"Tch!!"

Just then, the metallic sound of Kaname's rifle rang out. The silencer-integrated barrel poked out from underneath his armpit as he lay on the floor.

And that .45-caliber bullet sliced Bloody Dancer, the most fearsome gunslinger in the game, in the temple.

"A little more to the side, don't you think?"

"Ha-ha…!!"

"I'm getting better at it. Next time, it'll be your eye."

It was unclear whether Bloody Dancer was laughing from anger or glee. He didn't even put his hand to the wound. His instincts told him only to fight on. The man never felt a shred of fear. He pointed his twin pistols at Kaname and Lily-Kiska, who each lay crumpled on the floor. At the same time, they both turned their weapons toward him.

The two sides stared each other down. Even without cover, the mad beast before them might dodge their stream of bullets simply by jumping side to side. But they had come so far, and it was inconceivable to give up here without even putting up a solid fight.

Only with such persistence could they hope to carve themselves a place in this game.

In that endlessly dilated second of time, Bloody Dancer's bellow shook the room.

"Now this is fun, Kaname! Make sure you don't let the woman drag you down! You gotta protect that deadweight from the grenades, too!!"

"Is that right? She's deadweight, is she?"

A strange voice cut through the despair.

Meiki remained silent. Cindy was lying frozen on the floor. In any case, it was a man's voice. And it certainly wasn't Bloody Dancer or Kaname speaking.

So then, who was it?

The voice had come from somewhere behind the mad beast.

"Would you like to revise that statement? After all, it's because of her that you didn't notice me."

A cold metal click came from behind Bloody Dancer.

"...Lily-Kiska has been very helpful to me, you know. She's given a nerd like me the chance to get a shot off on a beast like you."

"Taka..."

The man's voice astonished Kaname even more than his actions. White dress shirt, black necktie, and a pair of slacks. Several pouches of tools at his waist, and a bandanna tied around his upper arm. It was so astonishing a sight that even the peerless warrior, Bloody Dancer, seemed to fade into the outer reaches of Kaname's vision.

"...ma...sa...?"

"It's Criminal AO, Kaname. And thanks for looking after that little goofball for me. You're a real hero. At least you are to me."

"#solitude.err, huh?!"

Meanwhile, Bloody Dancer snarled like an unruly predator. His scheme was to collect the Legacies and the list and hand them over to the AIs. Obviously, he knew more than the average Dealer about their names, appearances, and abilities. This Legacy had a range of five meters, its ammo capacity a measly two rounds, and yet it allowed the wielder to go unnoticed by anyone other than the person it was aimed at. Bloody Dancer would know all of this.

"You think a coward's weapon like that…is gonna kill me?!"

He spun around like a raging hurricane. One shot from the grenade launcher beneath his pistol at the attacker's wrist and that credit-card-sized pistol was blown from his grasp. But that wasn't all. Bloody Dancer had two guns. With the handgun in his other hand, he aimed a bullet directly at his assailant's head.

However.

"No."

The *other* monster, the one who had snuck up on the man from behind, spoke only a single word, smiling as he did so. His hand slipped to another pouch, one even Kaname didn't know about. One not for tools, but for weapons.

"But I'm not using #solitude.err for that."

"Wha—?!"

In his opposite hand, Takamasa held a simplified submachine gun, little more than a T-shaped piece of metal.

Kaname had previously surmised that it was impossible to benefit from the effects of two Legacies at the same time. However, to wave one around while secretly gaining the effects of another was perfectly fine.

In other words, Takamasa's stealth was his own. A feint, only effective against those familiar with the Legacies. A strategy just for Bloody Dancer.

Ba-bang!!

Takamasa fired and hit Bloody Dancer in the flank. But the sound of the explosion had come from the man's back. The music emanating from the wearable speaker around his neck suddenly cut out, and the madman muttered:

"#primer.err…?"

"Pipes, gas tanks, cars, stoves, gas cylinders, cartridges, hand grenades. Anything that can explode, will, when shot with this weapon. What's a shooting game without explosions, after all?"

"…The anti-warship…Legacy…"

"They're 'Magic,' beast. Even the protection mechanisms in your standard gasometer or tanker don't work against it. If you can get close enough, you can hit a tank's fuel supply or the torpedo tubes or missile racks on the deck of a warship. It's Magic. It can be risky, though, if the wielder gets caught in the explosion."

In this case, he had shot the battery. The one that powered the smartphone sending a stream of hard rock music to the man's wearable speaker. The bullet fired into his torso caused the electronic device at his back to explode.

"Urgh… Grhh…"

Bloody Dancer, the undefeated warrior, and next to him the hero who had just blown a hole in his side. A Legacy in his hand, the hero, this ruler of explosion and flame, made a declaration:

"…Your side and your back. Now I've made up for Kaname and me. I could keep on firing until you die. However, this time, I think I'll pass on the honor. I'm not the only one who has an ax to grind with you, after all."

"Tch!!"

With a click of his tongue, Bloody Dancer swung his right pistol toward Takamasa and his left toward the others. Two barrels and two grenade launchers. Takamasa, Kaname, Lily-Kiska, and Meiki. No doubt he could have taken them all, including Cindy, who lay Downed at his feet.

However.

However.

However.

The final blow came from beyond the wall. From Tselika, wielding the monster shotgun, #tempest.err.

* * *

Still leaning on Midori for support, she had only one free hand to hold the gun. As a result, the weapon's recoil flung it free from her grasp. Even so, the blast was strong enough to knock down the dividing wall, sending a grand total of two thousand pellets, like a raging storm of horizontal raindrops, into the room beyond.

"Grhh."

Even the lone alpha, the king of close-quarters combat, the man who tore down the legendary team, Called Game…

Even he found his senses overloaded. He couldn't react to the Magistellus's sudden appearance on the scene:

"Bghah!! Aglph! AAAAAAAAAAAAAAAAAAAAAAAAAAAAA AAAAAAAAAAAAAAAAAAAAAAAAAAAAAAAAAAAAAAAA AAAAAAAAAAAAAAAAAAAAAAAAAAAAAAAAAAAAAAAA AAAAAAAAAAAAAAAAAAAAAAAAAAAAAAAAAAAAAAAA AAAAAAAAAAAAAAAAAAAAAAAAGH!!!!!!"

The man's world shattered. Just like the battery, his wearable speaker fell to bits. As he screamed, he was sent flying into one of the glass cabinets holding the Legacies. He was unable to sit, impaled on large shards of glass that held him up in a standing position. His black shirt and white jacket were both stained red with blood, so much that it would have been difficult to guess the fabric's original color.

And then, in that world of silence.

"…What happened to your Magistellus, Bloody Dancer?"

Takamasa had asked the question, though he already knew the answer.

"I don't mean Cindy. You stole her from Ayame. I mean Undine, your original Magistellus. Where did she go?"

"I already told you…," he replied, through gasping breaths, his mouth dripping with blood. Still, he smiled, the cheap green earring swinging from his ear. "I couldn't care less about AI society or the fate of the world or any of that crap. I'm here to have fun in *Money (Game) Master*, and nothing else."

"…"

"Human, Magistellus, it makes no difference to me. But once I learned the truth, we didn't get along so well anymore. Magistelli don't just die when you shoot them… Give 'em an hour or so and they'll be back. So you know what I did? Know what I did to make her go away for good?"

"You buried her, didn't you? Under six feet of soil."

There was a gasp. Not from Kaname or Midori, but from Tselika.

Bloody Dancer exhaled before continuing.

"…Somewhere to the north of the city. Wrapped her in chains and filled in the hole with plastic resin."

"Underneath one of the pylons?"

"Tch. So you've been there, huh…?"

Those were the lengths to which that man would go. When humans and Magistelli fought, the two would come to blows. And the strongest Dealer would win, *whatever it took.*

Everyone knew Bloody Dancer was the most powerful gunslinger around. He always shot to kill, no matter who his opponent was.

Even if it was his irreplacable partner.

He couldn't accept defeat. There was no such choice for him. Once his beloved partner put her gun to his forehead, his body moved on its own. Before her slender finger could even pull the trigger, his hand would be on her gun, pushing it aside, and his fingers digging into her eyes or her throat.

No matter the cost, he could never, ever lose. All he could do was watch as his own hands tore his partner asunder.

But she was a Magistellus, and a Downed Magistellus would be back within the hour. Even so, he couldn't bring himself to finish her off for good. He couldn't let her live, and he couldn't let her die. In this one battle—with her—he couldn't bring himself to decide a winner and a loser.

This way, he wouldn't have to hurt her anymore. But it was a contradiction. He hadn't kept her safe. She wasn't safe—not from hunger, thirst, or suffocation. But Bloody Dancer loved this game more than anyone else, and this was his way. Even if nobody else could ever understand it.

He couldn't allow her to kill him, nor could he allow her to die. Even if it was insane, even if she hated him forever, he wanted to take the third option. For the sake of his partner, his one and only partner, Undine.

"I don't give a shit about the fate of humanity."

"…"

"I don't care who wins, AI or humans. I just want it to all be over so I can go back to playing with that goofy little chick with the fluffy hair… That's why I wanted to end this fight, whatever it took."

He still wore his sky-blue scarf and glass earring, accessories that seemed out of place on the monstrous man. He had never let go of them, but he didn't flaunt them, either.

He looked around and saw a group of humans and Magistelli willing to throw their lives away for each other at a moment's notice, even if it meant taking a rain of bullets.

"Yeah, I admit it…"

Those who knew the truth yet still walked together, Kaname Suou and Tselika. What did he think when he looked at them?

Whatever it was, he smiled and placed his fingers on the triggers of his pistols.

The Lion's Nose burned like never before.

"I was jealous of you guys."

Kaname's and Takamasa's right arms flew up at practically the same time, both pointing their guns at Bloody Dancer. The .45-caliber bullet pierced his head without a sound. Though he would have been dead almost instantly, the mad beast's finger still twitched.

Shwmp!! A grenade left the launcher's tube and hit the ground at the man's feet as he lay impaled on shards of glass, without even his wearable speaker for comfort. What would follow was obvious.

There was no music to mark his end. No sound at all. Perhaps, in the end, no one ever did succeed in killing him.

The blast wave from the explosion knocked everyone else off their feet, and the game's wildest Dealer disappeared into dust.

8

Server Name: Alpha Scarlet.
Final Location: Tokonatsu City, Peninsula District.
Fall confirmed.
Bloody Dancer will be logged out for twenty-four hours.

Epilogue

It was like a mass grave. In the end, only Midori had been able to avoid injury. Even the legendary Dealers Kaname and Takamasa were stained in blood, to say nothing of the Magistelli Tselika and Meiki. All at the hands of one man, Bloody Dancer, and all for the sole purpose of enjoying this *shooting game* to the fullest.

"Oww... M-My Lord, I believe you can drop the tough-guy act and rely on your skills once more, can you not? Reduce Pain and Blood Down to stop the bleeding would work wonders right now."

"Not yet."

"Need I remind you, My Lord, that Magistelli share skills with their Dealer?! Would you have me writhing in agony for no reason?!!"

Tselika bit her lip as though she was ready to burst into tears at any moment. She brought her arms together in front of her ample chest and steepled her pointer fingers timidly.

"...And you have been hurt, too, My Lord, have you not? We Magistelli may recover from being Downed within the hour. But it's not the same for Dealers. You will die, and Fall, and that shall be the end of it."

"It's okay, Tselika. I'm not going anywhere."

She did always get emotional at times like this. Or perhaps it was seeing the Fallen Takamasa standing before her once again that had Tselika acting so sentimental.

"Right."

Speaking of which, Takamasa had removed the bandanna from his arm and retied it around his head before bending over and examining the Downed Magistellus. Cindy. The dark elf who should have disappeared when Kaname's sister left the game. What Takamasa was investigating were the tips of her slender feet.

"I've removed the weird patch that seemed to be affecting her behavior," he said simply. "She should be free now. All we have to do is wait for her to wake up."

He relied on a couple of skills, such as Zone, to block out all thoughts unrelated to a specified goal, and Manufacture, to allow more precise finger movements, but that was all. And those few skills were not particularly high rarity, either—three or four at the highest. The most important thing was knowledge. Knowledge of where to look and what to look for, and what to remove to make things better. All that knowledge belonged to Takamasa himself.

This was the might of Criminal AO. The legendary Dealer who created the Overtrick. He was different from Kaname, who earned his keep in gunfights. No one was more skilled when it came to item crafting. Even the demonic overlords who ruled the game could not predict him.

There was no point in bluffing with him. It was best to ask if you didn't understand.

"Granted I've never seen what happens to a Magistellus when their Dealer resigns from the game," said Kaname, "…but what do you mean by 'free'? Don't they just get dragged back up to heaven or down to hell or wherever?"

"Our little Ayame was assigned the role of Admin Without Sin," Takamasa replied. "Even after she closed her account, its data remained somewhere within the bowels of *Money (Game) Master.* If you consider our Magistelli to be our bank accounts, then Cindy was like an old account of Ayame's she forgot about."

As he said this, Takamasa tossed something over to Kaname.

A shackle or bracelet that had been around her ankle. At first glance, it appeared to be silver, but Kaname could soon tell it was only iron.

"I bet this used to belong to Undine," he said. "Perhaps by mixing and matching their parts, he found a way to cause glitches and conflicts in her behavior. Just like how if you install two antiviruses on one computer, they start fighting each other. That's merely a hypothesis for now, though, and I don't really want to test it out because it'll set off every system security measure there is. In fact, I'm surprised the AIs weren't already keeping a close eye on him. It's not a particularly elegant solution, after all."

"...No."

Kaname interrupted Takamasa's line of thinking. He wasn't smart like the other boy, able to reason out Bloody Dancer's thoughts with pure logic, but he had fought the man, and that alone told him there was more to it. This understanding was yet another thing that couldn't be brought about with predefined skills.

"He had more than enough skill to take care of security if they came after him. Maybe he even thought it was more fun that way. Everyone else was playing on normal difficulty while he had it cranked all the way up to extreme."

"Could be. The Swiss Depression and Called Game, none of that mattered to him. He just wanted to feel the thrill of the fight, more excitement than you could possibly get in real life. No hard feelings, no anger. Just a love for the shooting game he saw in *Money (Game) Master...*"

Takamasa could only chuckle at the thought. The description reminded him of someone else, but there were many ways in which Kaname and Bloody Dancer were very different.

"In Cindy's case, I don't think he gave her conflicting orders or made her into his puppet. *This accessory simply reported its location to the Dealer, that's all.* He only needed to threaten her to get what he wanted. That works just as well on nonhumans as it does on us. Tokonatsu City's a big place, but there's nowhere to run."

"...He sure thought of everything. In his own way..."

"Yeah. I think showing affection to Undine was the only nonviolent thing that man ever did. He may have been one of the most evil Dealers I've ever met, but he never tried to outwit the system like I did. He just used his two pistols and two grenade launchers to tear down anything that came his way, relying on nothing but his own skill. Even though he'd collected so much of my Magic, he never thought to use any of it for himself. That's one thing I can respect him for, though I think the hate still wins out… In any case, his legend is over now. That's the end of this nightmare, Kaname."

Two figures watched over the boys as they spoke—the Magistellus Tselika and Midori, helping her stand.

"Are you sure you don't want to join them?" Midori asked.

"…Quiet."

"Well, you don't have to right now, if you don't want to. There's plenty of time, after all."

It wasn't as though she didn't understand the sentiment. Midori was seeing her own brother again for the first time, the one she had feared was gone forever. But she couldn't run crying into his arms while there were so many people watching. A wall of mixed feelings called puberty blocked her path. There would be time for that, later, when the two were alone. Or perhaps she would log out and cry into her pillow, where nobody else could hear. It didn't matter for now, if she could hide her true feelings behind a brave face. Because this wasn't the end. Now, there would be plenty more chances for all that.

Then, the sound of distant, frenzied footsteps, fast approaching, echoed from inside the building.

"I think we ought to get out of here," said Kaname. "We're on museum grounds, not to mention an important holding place for the AI to keep their stolen Legacies. The only reason we haven't been interrupted by the PMCs yet is that Bloody Dancer slaughtered them all not long ago. Now that their reinforcements have kicked in, we need to leave before they cut off our escape."

"Yeah. Midori, you ride a motorcycle, right? If it still runs, you should go get it now. As for Kaname's coupe…"

"Which way did you come in anyway?" asked Kaname. "Didn't you see the mint-green modern art piece in the lobby? Actually, I'd be surprised if any paint is left."

"Then sorry, Lily-Kiska, but I'm going to have to ask for your help on this one. Get to your limousine and use the winch on the back to pull out what's left of Kaname's coupe. We don't really want to leave it behind here on private property."

"Tselika."

"Rghh. I know!! And it's not a modern art piece! No matter what it may look like, it's a temple dedicated to my beauty! I'LL TAKE CARE OF IT!!"

Things were suddenly very lively.

Just as the girls all jumped into action, eager to get out of this place before the PMCs descended on them, the two boys shared a covert glance.

And after everyone had left—no, after Takamasa and Kaname had skillfully sent them all out of the room...

The two stepped apart and turned to face each other, as if this were a Western and they were about to duel.

"...Thanks for waiting for Midori to leave the room, Kaname."

"Likewise."

How exactly did the world look through his eyes? Though he wore a peaceful expression, the weapon pouch still lay open at his waist.

"There's just one small problem left to take care of, isn't there?"

"Yeah."

Kaname had his own reasons for collecting the Legacies. To stop the Magistellus invasion and prevent humanity from falling under AI subjugation. To save Tselika from eradication at the hands of the Mind. To glimpse the program code of *Money (Game) Master* and install his succubus partner as the realm's queen. Then, under her reign, to unite the real and the virtual worlds, freeing all those who had suffered because of the Legacies. That was his path.

But the boy standing before him, now untying his bandanna and placing it back on his arm, had come here via a different path. He was the true owner of the Legacies, and surely he had his own idea of what to do with them.

In which case…

"Tell me your vision, Takamasa. Tell me what you plan to do with the Legacies once you have them."

"You're really going to call them Legacies in front of the person who created them?"

"I asked you a question. This demonic game transcends human understanding. How are you going to fight against it?"

"Fine, I'll tell you. Rest assured my highest priority is returning society to humanity's hands. As you can see, I don't work with the Magistelli. I have a partner, but as long as she's connected to the Mind, I simply can't trust her. No offense."

"…You don't seem as torn up about it as Bloody Dancer was."

"I guess that's because I'm not as caring as him."

Takamasa admitted this readily.

"Sure, I'd love it if we could save both. But if I have to choose, obviously I'm going to pick humanity's side. That's only natural."

"And what if I said we *could* save both?" Kaname responded immediately. But after a moment of surprise, Takamasa only shook his head.

"That'd be great, but I don't believe we can. If you really believe there's a way, Kaname, then that means you're not prepared to do what it takes. You're still looking for compromise, aren't you? Humans and AI can never work together. We're incompatible. And if the Magistelli aren't even AI at all but instead what they claim to be, then even more so."

"I'm not going to abandon Tselika."

"I understand."

"No, you don't. You don't understand at all," said Kaname plainly, daggers in his eyes. It was hardly the look of someone freshly reunited with an old friend. "You could never understand. Because you threw yours away."

"So that's it, then?"

Takamasa Hekireki slowly raised his arms. But he wasn't surrendering. In his skilled hands he held the very Legacies he had created. And Kaname Suou reacted in kind. He slowly raised his arms, his focus concentrated on the short-range sniper rifle, Short Spear, tucked into his belt.

There were perhaps five meters between them. Each of them took one step forward. Not so close they could start grappling, but more than close enough for even an amateur to hit the mark.

Takamasa held the T-shaped submachine gun, #primer.err, with which he had enacted his vengeance upon Bloody Dancer. It could detonate anything flammable with a single shot, and under the right conditions, it could be used to take down a military tank or warship singlehandedly.

…However, there was no guarantee this was the weapon he would use. While it was impossible to benefit from the effects of two Legacies at once, the Legacy whose effect was enabled could be freely changed at will. In other words, Kaname couldn't discount the possibility that there was another Legacy stowed somewhere on Takamasa's body.

There were Legacies scattered everywhere. They were practically ankle-deep in them. And yet Kaname's eyes were trained squarely on his old friend.

"…To tell you the truth," Takamasa said, "my ultimate weapon against the Magistelli was never the Magic at all."

"What?"

"It was always you, Kaname. Your Lion's Nose. That's the one thing that can't be re-created with skills, nor with the Magic, which is just an extension of skills anyway. I can't believe you thought of using the Magic to induce errors in the game and expose the program code, when you have an even more powerful weapon already."

"…"

"Zodiac Child. That's what I've taken to calling the ones like you. Out of all seven billion people on earth, only twelve are able to escape the rule of AI society. Computers already have humans completely beat when it comes to chess, right? Well, you're like the only humans who can still win, somehow, by overturning the established formula. With your power and my Magic combined, my plans can finally be realized." Then Takamasa added, "What do you say, Kaname? This is my last invitation. Are you really not interested? Your plan is only a possibility, while mine is a certainty."

"I refuse."

"Figures. You're too kind, Kaname. That's what I liked about you, and that's why you're my hero."

The sound of footsteps drew closer. It was now too late. The moment the AI soldiers burst into the room served as their signal.

The Zodiac Child and the Overtrick.

They were the twin keys to unraveling this crisis, but they might as well have been standing at opposite ends of the world.

Their hands rushed to their belts. A gunshot rang out.

In Takamasa's hand, the T-shaped submachine gun, #primer.err. But flying silently beneath the crack of that weapon's shot was Kaname's .45-caliber bullet.

"Nice one, Kaname."

The smile on Criminal AO's—Takamasa Hekireki's—face did not crumble.

Among the sound of footsteps, a body hit the floor. Three of them, dull red bullet holes in their foreheads. The AI-controlled PMCs rushing to protect the Legacy storage facility. Kaname hadn't even needed to turn around to face them.

Meanwhile, a deafening explosion came from the hallway as a gas pipe running along the wall ruptured and ignited. The PMCs heading down that hallway were all engulfed in the blast.

"...You're not so bad yourself. And here I thought you left the shooting to me. Have you been practicing, or did you just hide it that well?"

"And yet you still underestimate me, Kaname. Does a single Legacy in my hands not merit a reaction from the Lion's Nose?"

"...I can't shoot you, Takamasa."

As he pointed his gun, Kaname squeezed out the words as though he were trying to crush his own lungs. But still, his opponent would not give up the fight. Perhaps this was the pain that Bloody Dancer had felt.

"I don't ever want to see Midori cry again," he continued. "Or my sister or Tselika, either. It was because I let you die that I had to see it in the first place. It's the biggest regret of my life."

When he heard those words, something appeared to change in Kaname's old friend. He looked caught off guard. He readied the T-shaped submachine gun, the bane of all things combustible, without regard for thick armor or safety mechanisms. And yet the hero wore a troubled grin.

"You know you're just putting off the inevitable," he said. "As long as we both require the Magic to carry out our plans, we're just going to keep clashing like this."

"..."

"Hey, now, don't give me that look. You're making it seem like I'm the bad guy here! Look, I'm a big boy; I can take it. Give me all you've got. I won't complain."

There was a pause, in which he seemed to hestiate. Then, he had an idea. "I know," he said.

Right now, there were bigger fish to fry. Not only had they been standing around on private property for a while now, but they had shot dead many of the PMCs who had come to defend it. Now the AIs would up the ante.

"Let's focus on getting out of here first. And while we're at it, how about we make it a game?"

"Who gets out of the building first? Or who can aggro the most PMCs and get out of it alive?"

"Just a simple numbers game. Whoever defeats the most enemies wins."

Kaname did a double take at his friend's words. While they had no particular skills to speak of, the PMCs' base stats were off the charts. Not to mention they would keep coming endlessly unless you got off their land, so it was more about whether you could escape than how many you could kill. And yet...

"If Bloody Dancer can do it, why can't we?" joked Takamasa. "It's clearly within the realm of human ability."

Then, he took a single large coin from his weapon pouch.

For some reason, there was a tingly feeling in Kaname's Lion's Nose. Why? The sensation grew to an intense pain, such that Kaname wondered if it would surpass even what Bloody Dancer had invoked...

Then the hero tossed the coin high into the air.

"Now then. Get ready."

"Wait..."

"...This is just a silly game, but the score should make everything clear. The difference between you and me, that is."

As the coin hit the floor, the Lion's Nose exploded.

Afterword

Well, hello. Kazuma Kamachi here.

This is Volume 2 of *Magistellus*! ...I wasn't really conscious of it during the first volume, but it's only in the published version that we get an afterword. I'd better take it seriously.

Since Volume 1 focused quite heavily on minerals and futures trading, I decided to shift the focus this time to a sports team and a quiz. The theme here was moneymaking schemes of a slightly different nature.

To try making the game aspects stand out a bit more, this time around I touched more deeply on the skills and how they worked. There's no magic in this world, except for that centered around Takamasa, so I put some thought into precisely how Auto-Aim would track the target, how Slow would slow down your perception, and so on... I planned to have detailed skill lists at the end of each chapter, but I cut that for fear it might make the book too niche! I did prepare a list of skills and their rarities, though, so you can assume that even unnamed extras have three or four.

Incidentally, Kaname "doesn't use shooting or driving skills," Bloody Dancer "doesn't use skills at all," and Takamasa "uses whatever skills he can." Based on where each character's boundaries lie, you can get some insight into their personalities.

I ramped up Tselika's love for her car, too. I figured I hadn't shown her washing it yet, so I put in a scene about that, featuring her pit-babe getup. After all, the harder she works to clean it, the funnier it is when it gets ruined right before her eyes. Tselika has taught me an important lesson about writing.

And despite their equal ranking in the story, Tselika and Midori are treated very differently. The former exists to be bullied, while the latter is to be protected. Which did you prefer? I'm asking about their personalities, by the way, not their breast sizes.

As for the villains of this story, Strawberry Garter, Mother Loose, and Bloody Dancer, they each embodied what I thought of when I imagined "someone in control of money," whether that be a household's finances or an entire market. I think it's Kaname's discussion with the gentle young housewife(?) that best sums this up:

"I'm not asking you for pocket money."

"It's not safe for a child to carry around so much money by themselves. It's dangerous. You need an adult to look after it for you. I will give you whatever you desire, as long as I have control over it."

Now, out of her, Strawberry Garter, who grubbed dirty money in an attempt to garner clout, and Bloody Dancer, who spent all his time fighting, laughing that as long as he kept winning, the money would follow... Out of these reigning ideologies taken to the extreme (not unlike the four major powers in *Heavy Object*), which did you find the most despicable?

By the way, the reason Frey(a) of the Treasure Hermit Crabs owns a pawnshop is because they find themselves drawn to the belongings of strangers. (I'm sure you can see what the metaphor is there, can't you?) Not only that, but I was also experimenting to see how the way a Dealer looked at money could clue us in about their inner life. You can judge for yourself whether this was successful. The main point of this book was not to look at how people fulfilled their desire for money, but to look at how people *used* money to fulfill their desires.

In that sense, Kaname's desire is to stick to reason, even if that means he sometimes pushes others away. Midori, unskilled in trading, hasn't solidified her desire, and it remains in an undetermined state. As for the Magistelli, executing their complicated and sophisticated trading calculations ten thousand times a second, their role as demons is to magnify the desires of others.

Even Takamasa, Criminal AO, who has been with us since Volume 1, was expanded on quite prominently. There were a lot of Legacies in this volume, and I enjoyed trying to imagine how their creator might have used them. The difference between Takamasa and Kaname, I feel, is that while both of them grew suspicious of their Magistelli, Kaname's answer was to stick close to her, while Takamasa's was to distance himself. Thus, Takamasa has no partner, since he doesn't trust the Magistelli at all. Unlike Bloody Dancer, who sought to burn down human society so that he could go back to playing the game with his partner, Takamasa was able to cut himself off from his Magistellus with no regrets. In this way, Takamasa is both very strong and somehow unfortunate. I think even more so than Kaname, with his analysis-defying Lion's Nose, Takamasa is quite the formidable character, able to get the drop on Kaname with nothing but his own equipment.

He's someone Kaname owes a great debt, both on behalf of himself and his sister. He comes out on top time and time again in the cruel world of *Money (Game) Master*, existing at the core of the idea that helping people is not about bragging rights or asking for anything in return.

Still, I wondered if it might be possible to illustrate the mysterious relationship between these two boys by showing how headstrong they become when each is forced to turn against the other. The strongest Dealers bring their all to a fight no matter what; that irrepressible lust for battle is not unique to Bloody Dancer. It applies even to Takamasa, who has repeatedly said that battle isn't his thing. Though he is soft-spoken, if you look only at Takamasa's actions, you can see that he is actually quite ruthless. He didn't leave the fight to Lily-Kiska but instead made sure he could shoot Bloody Dancer himself. Not only that, but he did it to get revenge for Kaname even more than for himself. It's not only Kaname looking up to Takamasa; you can see that when Takamasa calls Kaname "my hero."

As you will see if you keep on reading all the way to the end, Lily-Kiska has been given the role of an unintended witness to mystery. Thinking about it, you can see that her journey as a Dealer started way back when Called Game rescued her. If this were a mystery novel, she would probably have been the second or third victim, but what if this were a *Battle Royale* story? Just being able to survive long enough to fight back is a skill unto itself. Make sure you pay close attention to what she does.

Incidentally, I tried to paint a picture of a free and open world through the side stories, in describing the ups and downs of M-Scope's life as well as that of Frey(a). I must confess, I didn't originally plan it this way, but Mahaya really went ridiculously overboard on the character drafts (this is a compliment, of course; I can't thank them enough...!!), so it seemed a shame not to bring the Ag Wolves back for Volume 2. It's been over fifteen years since my authorial debut, and never have I seen a comeback like this... In any case, I hope you enjoyed seeing a very different angle on Tokonatsu City to the one that Kaname provides. These parts are full of little jokes that are difficult to get away with when the perfect main character is around, such as in Chapter 6, where Frey(a) takes out his revolver, Raging Stallion. It's big, it's black. I'm sure I don't need to tell you what it's a metaphor for!! There's a lot more stuff like that if you keep your eyes peeled!!

Mahaya, the illustrator, and my editors, Miki, Anan, Nakajima, Yamamoto, and Mitera, I cannot thank you enough. From Prostitute Island to the oil mining plains, to the industrial estate, to the museum, the story this time took us on a very different tour of the corruption at the heart of Tokonatsu City. Thank you so much for being a part of it.

And you, dear readers, you have my thanks. The last volume was a series of deceptions, but this time, to support Kaname's superhuman battles, I tried to depict some female leads as ground hardened by the rain, each struggling with their own fears and anxieties. I hope it was to your liking.

In any case, that about covers it.

Come to think of it, Kaname took a real beating this time, didn't he?

Kazuma Kamachi

"Haah… haah…!!"

The girl gasped for breath. She didn't even remember what she was running from anymore. She soon abandoned her stolen car and ran with tired legs over to a rough concrete wall, pressing herself against it.

She was a tall lioness of a woman, her catlike eyes an impossibility in real life. Her hair, the color of faded cherry blossoms, was tied back in a single thick braid, and a baggy hoodie overlaid her knit tank top and hot pants. This was Zaurus. Once a famed member of the Ag Wolves, she now had barely a penny to her name. Her equipment was little more than the clothes on her back, and she wasn't rich enough to be fussy about her skills and weapons, either. She didn't even have a pistol for protection; instead, she held a fire ax she had picked up off the ground. Its nicked edge was stained in blood.

She was on Prostitute Island, a slight distance from the main peninsula. Footsteps echoed through the streets of the most vice-ridden area in all of *Money (Game) Master*.

"My, well done."

"…"

All around her lay the bodies of men in all-black spec-ops gear, looking like a defeated group of movie extras. The blunt edge of the fire ax was especially proficient at overcoming their bulletproof equipment, as the specific application of force was not what it had been designed to protect against. But the men had not Fallen and instead lay on the brink of death, unable to log out, their suffering prolonged by broken limbs and smashed ribs—you had to go for the bones. This was just Zaurus's style. Her merciless savagery, whether in gunfights, car chases, or trading, was on the level of the terrifying superbeasts of the past that had inspired her name.

Zaurus specialized in close-quarters combat, at the kind of distance where you could reach out and grab each other's weapons. As such, she didn't need a gun to fight, but it wasn't like she needed a knife, either. It was more that if you put a long-range anti-materiel rifle in her hands, she'd still walk right up to her target. That was just the kind of Dealer she was.

And yet the man showed himself before her, walking through the pile of bodies without regard for cover of any kind. The fight had laid all the girl's cards on the table, and he had already surmised she wasn't concealing a gun on her person.

Even Zaurus was struggling now to stay on her feet. Without skills such as Physical Stamina, which adjusted the girl's breathing to increase her capacity for strenuous effort, she would have already passed out from exhaustion. At this point, if someone simply stood out of range with a gun, they could take her out no problem.

"I'm impressed you were able to take out so many of us using only what you could scavenge. But now, I think it's time to end this."

"You think I'll die to Marietta Flapper…? A bunch of hit men who can't even balance their books…?"

"Our client, Pavilion, sends her regards. She told us to make sure you died in disgrace. And wouldn't you know, we've ended up in just the right spot for it. We've run up quite a few debts around here. So, which of these brothels do you want to pick up the tab in?"

Zaurus clicked her tongue. It'd been a mistake to pick up the ax. If she'd had a gun or a knife, she could at least try to kill herself. If she didn't Fall or wait out five minutes in the driver's seat of her car, she wouldn't be able to log out of *Money (Game) Master*, no matter what indignities befell her in the world of the game.

"Resist as much as you like. There are all sorts here. If we look hard enough, I'm sure we can find someone willing to pay for a girl with broken arms and legs. Might not be worth as much, but we can just make up for quality with quantity."

But no sooner had the last word left his mouth…

BLAM!!

…than a bullet whizzed through the hit man's head and blew out the side of his skull.

The submachine gun looked no more sophisticated than a child's toy. No power or accuracy, just spray and pray. However…

However, the boy with the bad posture had arrived just in time.

Of all the Dealers in *Money (Game) Master*, M-Scope, the boy she had always made fun of, was the only one who came rushing to her aid.

"Zaurus, take this!!"

There was no time for a heartfelt reunion. Before she could finish processing the situation, Zaurus had caught the pump-action shotgun, and back to back with M-Scope, they cleared the remaining Marietta Flapper hit men.

The shotgun even used her favorite slug rounds. These were huge single lumps of metal with more destructive force than a magnum pistol, and they tore through the hit men's body armor like paper. While the material's hardness, combined with the Bulletproof skill, were enough to keep .45-caliber bullets at bay, they could do nothing against the might of the slug rounds. Defensive skills were not all-powerful, not unless you were a master of skill-stacking like the legendary Mother Loose.

"Take this, you bastards!!"

There was little cover in the open area. The Marietta hit men seemed to have decided that if they were willing to take a few losses, they could take out the target just by firing wildly, and so they all leveled their carbine rifles, but...

"Ginmi, attack! Kill them all!!"

There was a dull thud as a four-wheel-drive SUV covered in anime girls drove onto the scene, flattening the hit men. M-Scope had always been a master of patience. His expertise was in bombs and traps, and his low-powered submachine gun was only a tool to that end, like how one might use a long-range weapon to hit a far-off switch in an RPG dungeon. He used it only to anger the target so they would give chase and deal just enough damage so that the trap could finish them off for certain.

The SUV, M-Scope's precious vehicle, was a large four-door car, like a mix between a family sedan and a minivan, which had been reworked to run off-road. The angle of the after-market bumpers was adjustable to switch between knocking other cars aside or directing people beneath its heavy wheels. The SUV screeched to a halt in front of its owner, and M-Scope dived behind the hood and finished off the remaining pest exterminators.

Eventually, Zaurus caught sight of him and ran over. The backpack-wearing boy seemed somehow different to her.

"Where's your Magistellus?" he yelled to her. "And your vehicle, too?!"

"...Huh? Er... I-I've been through a lot of cars, but they've all ended up smoking wrecks. As for Charlotte, we'll probably find her Downed if we go back the way I came. I wasn't able to save her."

"Okay. First we'll go pick her up, then we can see about getting you a new car. Ginmi, let me drive, and make some room for Zaurus. Quickly!!"

M-Scope shuffled into the driver's seat, while Zaurus climbed in the other side, and the *yuki-onna* sat in the back with all the boxes of anime merchandise. Zaurus herself was surprised by how quickly she obeyed, even discounting her exhaustion.

The SUV spun in a circle, knocking down the stragglers with its frame, like a roundhouse kick, before making its escape back the way Zaurus had come. M-Scope, however, seemed distracted by the exterior of his vehicle.

"Ugh. They kissed my *waifu* so hard, they dented her face..."

"?"

They soon came across the body of Zaurus's werewolf Magistellus, lying frozen on the floor like a stone statue. Her revealing costume, sort of like a V-shaped swimsuit, only made the wounds to her vitals more obvious. Zaurus's face crumpled at the sight, and M-Scope spoke not to her but to his partner, seated in the back amid the boxes of anime, game, and data idol merchandise.

"Ginmi, could you give me a hand?"

"...Do you know how much I have missed this minibar fridge? You would have me leave this perfect climate and head back out into the sweltering sun...?"

"Let go of the door. I'll give you three ice packs if you help out. The ones that stick to your head."

The *yuki-onna*'s face lit up at the proposal, and she got out along with the gloomy boy and helped load the frozen Magistellus's body into the back of the vehicle. The task itself was not so difficult, but with the possibility of an enemy ambush at any time, even leaving the SUV was a huge risk.

After returning to the driver's seat, M-Scope assessed the situation.

"She's still in one piece, and the bullet seems to have gone straight through. She'll be all right in thirty minutes, tops."

"If you say so..."

Even at a time like this, the rough-hearted bully could not bring herself to speak a word of thanks. But if that bothered M-Scope, he didn't show it, even though he had just risked his own life to save her. The boy who had been away for so, so long fiddled with the wheel and stared straight ahead, showing off a manly profile.

"Zaurus. I'm sorry to spring this on you so suddenly..."

"What?"

"Um, well, how do I say this? ...Aargh, I'm not really sure where to begin. In fantasy worlds and school settings, everyone starts off in full-on love mode..."

"Out with it! I owe you a huge favor now, so just tell me what it is you want already!!"

"Are you sure?"

"Yeah."

M-Scope took a deep breath and sat up as straight as he could.

"Zaurus!! Pwease go on a date with me!!"

Then, as her fists came flying, the SUV swerved off the road and crashed straight into a lamppost. Zaurus's face was bright red, and steam seemed to rise from her skin as she screamed at the boy in the driver's seat.

"Y-y-y-y-y-you asshole! Kicking me when I'm down…!!"

"I'm sorry! But this is the only way to save the other Ag Wolves! Titan and Hazard, too!! Aren't you worried about how they're holding up?!"

"Why don't you start by explaining what the hell you're talking about?" Zaurus huffed. And so M-Scope falteringly gave her the full story about the deal he'd made with the leader of the Treasure Hermit Crabs.

To find himself a sweetheart somewhere in this big, wide world and declare his love for them. Just this once, the outcome, success or failure, would not matter.

He was supposed to see for himself what true bargaining looked like.

Zaurus made her displeasure clear with a click of the tongue.

"…All so you can get another team to back you up, huh?"

"I'm sorry."

"What're you apologizing for? You're right. I *am* worried about what the rest of us are up to. And our old boss, Lily-Kiska, too."

"…She's doing well, last I saw."

Zaurus was well aware she could be a bit insensitive at times, but even she noticed the pause before the boy's words and the smile with which he said them. She scratched her pink-haired head.

"Gotcha. You don't need to say any more. Everyone's got their own lives to lead. A team supports each other. They don't weigh each other down."

"I might be the one weighing us down this time," said M-Scope. "Even so, would you lend me a hand?"

"Well, I've heard a thing or two about this Frey(a) guy. All we have to do is act all friendly in front of him, and he'll help us rescue Titan and Hazard. I can live with that."

Zaurus leaned back in her seat. Perhaps she was even more exhausted than she had realized. The SUV wasn't quite as spacious as a true minivan or camper van, but it was still bigger than a regular car.

"You can recline the seat and sleep if you want. I'll take us to some car shop on the peninsula and try to pick one where Marietta Flapper won't be waiting for us... Are you okay with a secondhand car?"

"Sure... I'm not really in a position to be fussy right now. I'll pay you back as soon as I can. Just so long as I have something to log in and out with, I couldn't care less."

"Actually, I've already had Ginmi begin trading, so pretty soon we should start seeing returns on that billion."

"Were you always so big in the fashion section? I wouldn't have guessed from looking at you."

"Just girls' fashion. And mostly cosplay... It doesn't even take a second to scrape all the dress patterns and colors people post online, then compare the styles with major fashion companies to see which one will catch on to the trends first."

"But what does it matter? This is about responsibility. When I borrow, I return what I owe with interest."

The SUV covered in anime girls reversed back onto the road. Zaurus surrendered herself to the four-wheel drive's gentle rocking, when a question suddenly occurred to her.

"But why me? There must have been plenty of other female Dealers you could have asked. All of them cuter, I bet."

"Where, exactly? I'm not sociable enough to go to bars. I only really know the other Ag Wolves, and that includes in real life. Discounting Magistelli and data idols, there's only you, Lily-Kiska, and um, who else...?"

"Huh. I guess you made the right choice, then."

"Yeah," M-Scope answered plainly as he steered the SUV. "Actually, as soon as Frey(a) said 'sweetheart,' you were the only person I could think of."

"...
....

....
....,,...................
....,,"

Zaurus did not reply. Her face was completely red.

"Um, Zaurus?"

"Shut the hell up!! How can you say sappy shit like that with a straight face???!!!"

"O-ooohh... Oooohhhh... W-we're being dragged along... There are so many orange sparks..."

"Are there any tires left? Come to think of it, aren't we just scraping the bottom along the ground?"

"Aaaargh!!"

The unusually long limousine roared down the main road, dragging the mint-green coupe behind it like a tow truck. Even now, Tselika could not be parted from its squashed passenger seat, while Midori rode alongside on her bright-red motorcycle.

Lily-Kiska drove them all to her usual garage. It was a car shop more accustomed to dealing with luxury vehicles than racing cars, but pay them enough money and they would be able to meet the needs of just about any customer. And with the famously violent Dealer, Smash Daughter, running security for them, there was little chance of Kaname being attacked unawares.

"By the way, I wonder what Kaname is doing right now? Fidget, fidget."

"...Listen, you dark elf harlot. You had better not be trying to tell me that you've fallen head-over-heels for My Lord in the short time since you woke back up."

"Well, I sacrificed myself to take a bullet for him this time, so I figure my status should be equal to that of Criminal AO in his eyes now. Ha-ha... In other words, he should see me as a hero. I have always looked up to Kaname in the past, but perhaps being his queen wouldn't be so bad, either..."

"Get over yourself, woman! Meiki and I took a bullet for him, too, you know!!"

"I'm the only one who didn't," said Midori. "How could I have missed out...?"

"Don't you start on me, too, Midori! Snap out of it! My Lord will never see Cindy as a hero so long as she keeps showing off about it. She's panting so heavily, her own glasses are fogging up!"

While the girls argued around the scrap of metal that was once Kaname's vehicle, Lily-Kiska finally let out a deep breath. The twin holsters that squeezed her breasts like the suspenders on a waitress outfit made it a little hard to breathe, but once she'd calmed down, she headed away from the limo. Brushing her long black hair off her shoulder, she called out into the dark.

"Sofia. At ease."

"Welcome back, Ms. Kiska. You were gone awhile. What happened?"

"Well, for one, it looks like I won't have to bow down to Criminal AO anymore."

"Is that right?"

"Can you open the protected message for me?"

"Yes!"

Lily-Kiska's elf Magistellus gave a cheerful, affirmative reply, and words began to appear on her croupier-like vest. The message read as follows:

Dear Lily-Kiska Sweetmare,

Our research took longer than expected, but we have finally determined that you are one of the Zodiac Children: The Scorpion's Tenacity. Therefore, we suggest that you immediately report to Unicorn Hospital to undergo a thorough examination, and from there work closely under our care. You are free to proceed as you wish, of course, but be advised your choice will not be without its consequences. You are of extreme value to us. Of such high value, in fact, that we would sooner see you eliminated than allowed to grow and become a threat. It seems that our inability to control your decisions also prevented Criminal AO from learning of your true nature. That is very fortunate.

We await the good news.
Regards, the Mind of the Magistelli.

"…"

The bespectacled beauty gave an exasperated sigh. She found the message deeply unsettling. Whoever came out on top, Kaname or Takamasa, it was clear Lily-Kiska would never reach their level by meekly following along. In order to stand alongside the legends of Called Game, she would have to take a gamble.

Even if that meant giving in to temptation and setting foot directly into a world of bugs and errors that plagued this demon's game.

"Sofia."

"Yes, ma'am?"

"I'm heading to the hospital. I need to do something about this shoulder. Pick a good moment and leave in the limo. Make sure you get the attention of the kids in the garage."

"Understood, Ms. Kiska."

Her voice was kind and gentle, but mechanical.

What now?

Kaname, Takamasa, and Bloody Dancer. All legendary Dealers. Now that she had seen how they all worked, what would she pick for herself? What would her relationship with the Magistelli be like? And was she willing to stake her life on it?

"What is the matter?"

"Nothing."

One step.

She took a deep breath. She was still so very far from those she wished to emulate.

One step at a time…

"I'm off, Sofia."

"Yes, ma'am."

And then, as though it were the most natural thing in the world, the Magistellus followed up her reply with:

"I await the good news."

Tokonatsu City, the heart of the peninsula financial district.

A solitary figure staggered out of the Legacy storage facility disguised as a museum. In his right hand he gripped the short-range sniper rifle, Short Spear.

It was Kaname Suou.

"Haah… Phew…"

He barely clung to life. He was so wounded that it was hard to say that he had won. On the other hand, the fact he had escaped at all in his state was extremely fortunate. Even a top-class Dealer such as Kaname would balk at the idea of taking on PMCs in a brawl. If, for whatever reason, his escape route were cut off, his Fall would be all but assured.

He was on the brink now. One good shot and everything would be over. The battle with Bloody Dancer just before had roughed him up a great deal already.

"Grhh."

He crossed the highway to the tall building opposite. Tselika had taken the mint-green coupe, which by now was little more than a pile of scrap. Since Kaname was on the verge of death, the fact that he was unable to rely on the car's raw armor and speed made things even more exhilarating than he could have possibly imagined.

He reached the sidewalk and leaned against the wall for support. He couldn't use Reduce Pain now; the danger was keeping him alert. It was right now that he needed pain the most. His sole comfort was that the PMCs would not pursue him outside the building; they were designed solely to protect their own territory. He had no wheels, and even walking was difficult. If the enemy got the drop on him now, he was done for.

Not only were the PMCs gifted with supremely high base stats, but they replenished themselves *ad infinitum*. Fighting against them was a losing battle; it was a victory just getting out of their range and shaking off the alert. And yet…

I didn't expect this…

Gunshots still echoed from inside the building. As soon as sparks had begun to fly, Kaname had dragged his heavy limbs as fast as he could toward the exit. But not Takamasa. He had headed farther inside. Even with the Legacies at his disposal, it was an act of lunacy.

And it didn't matter how many waves came. All those invincible super-soldiers were simply more fodder for Takamasa's skyrocketing score. There was no reason for him to linger there. Was he trying to show Kaname the hard truth? Or was he simply covering for Kaname's escape? Just for something like that?

"…Damn, Takamasa. I thought you were supposed to be crap at shoot-outs."

But this unexpected skill of Takamasa's was something different. It wasn't just the ability to kill his foe in a gunfight. It was more like that of a combat medic, used to protect his allies on the field of battle. You could sugarcoat it all you liked, but at its heart, *Money (Game) Master* was a game about killing your fellow Dealers. In that sense, Takamasa was the only one who had honed his skills to help them instead.

It was like he was playing a different game. His view of the world must be so unique. Why hadn't Kaname seen it earlier? Takamasa had always been like this. When told to go up against other Dealers, his knees shook so hard, he couldn't move, but when Kaname's sister was in danger, he didn't hesitate to jump into the line of fire.

Even now, Kaname wasn't half the man Takamasa was back then.

A black-ops team and a rescue squad have very different approaches when it comes to breaking down walls. He sure pulled one over on us. No wonder we never saw him coming…

By now, Takamasa's score probably dwarfed his own by about fifty times. Kaname was overawed, as though he were witnessing the power of the latest state-of-the-art stealth fighter jet. This was the true difference between Takamasa and himself.

And it was even more terrifying to imagine what was going on in Takamasa's mind. Why he had concealed this strength for so long, insisting he wasn't good at fighting? Kaname couldn't even imagine going toe to toe with the inexhaustible PMCs, and not only because he was deeply wounded from his battle with Bloody Dancer. Even at full power, he wouldn't dream of it. There was nothing to be won from such a battle; the enemy kept on coming and coming, while one shot to the head would cause Kaname to Fall, ruining his life. It simply wasn't worth the risk.

A fearsome sound ripped through the air behind him. Kaname turned to look, but his vision was engulfed in dust. Most likely, the building hiding the Legacies had just collapsed. Kaname didn't need to ask who was responsible for that.

Then, a huge mass of steel, suspended by twin propellers, descended from the sky, clearing away the dust below it. It was a military tilt-rotor boasting the personnel capacity of a small transport plane. Even in the world of *Money (Game) Master*, where you could do just about anything if you had enough money, such a sight was a rare treat.

Now the Legacies were as good as his. It didn't take Takamasa long to load them all onto the transport, no doubt using the forklifts and wheel loaders that were hidden aboard.

All Kaname could do was lean weakly against the wall, watching the tilt-rotor take off and disappear into the sky, wondering if even the Mind of the Magistelli knew where it was headed.

"Seriously, Takamasa, give me a break…"

A paperlike rustling came from his pocket. Kaname could take some consolation, at least, in the fact that he had managed to swipe *this* on his way out. He looked up at the moon. Kaname knew this much: He would have to change tactics. Just holding him at gunpoint wouldn't be enough to make Criminal AO stand down. He had taken over the storage facility packed with PMCs by force. He may have relied on the Legacies, but that kind of feat put him at least on the level of Bloody Dancer, if not higher. What's more, Kaname couldn't count on Takamasa using only the T-shaped submachine gun #primer.err if they met again in the future. He might be using a completely different Legacy with a completely different strategy.

But there was one thing that Kaname Suou knew for certain. Takamasa had his own reason for doing this, and it was something he couldn't easily tell Kaname.

"…Because helping people isn't about bragging rights or asking for anything in return."

There was something missing. Something Kaname didn't yet know. But he couldn't waver in his mission, either. He had seen the tears of the people he cared about, Tselika, his sister, and Midori, and he couldn't allow that to happen again.

And above all, if he remained a Dealer that only killed and made *snow*, Kaname would never be able to save Takamasa.

Meanwhile.

I have to be selective in my hiring process wherever the Magic is involved, and of course I can't rely on the Magistelli, either… This autopilot app is surprisingly good, though. I suppose it's the same thing they would use for delivery drones in real life, if there was less red tape involved.

Takamasa himself seemed uninterested in the mountain of Overtrick that currently filled the cargo bay of the tilt-rotor aircraft. To most Dealers, the pile of weapons was a gold mine, but Takamasa had been the one to build them in the first place, and so they didn't particularly excite him anymore. Retying the bandanna from his arm around his head, he removed his weapon pouch containing the Legacy and slung it aside.

His interest was in the rapidly receding world below. Specifically, the one boy who remained close to the scene.

"…#primer.err, huh?"

He grinned. The Overtrick were indeed powerful. The #primer.err, for example, could ignite anything flammable in a single shot, from gas tanks, pipes, and canisters to cars, hand grenades, magazines, and even a phone battery. With it, it didn't matter how thick the armor on the target was or how many layers of protection mechanisms it had. If explosions were the bread and butter of an action game like *Money (Game) Master*, then this was the whole damn bakery. However, Takamasa was not one for gunslinging like Kaname and Bloody Dancer. He knew only too well that was not where his talents lay.

Thus, he went to its polar opposite. Rescue. He borrowed the logic of rescue teams to decide how to enter and effectively search the building. This was Takamasa's true nature. If he had to kill someone, his legs would seize up in fright, but to *save* someone, he could move mountains. Just as he had when protecting the sister of his old friend, or even now, as his own flesh and blood labored under the debts incurred by his Fall, lashing herself to an AI company for support.

Nothing about him had changed. He just had access to a few more options now; that was all.

"..."

There was no shortage of things to blow up in *Money (Game) Master*, and there was also the behavior of the PMCs' AI to take into account. They would alter their tactics in accordance with map data to avoid accidentally shooting each other. If one blew up a wall and made a new route that wasn't on the map, and then knocked one of the PMCs into it, their AI subroutines would sometimes disregard the shortest route right under their noses in favor of going the long way around. It was an error in their thinking process. A bug. Something that shouldn't exist in *Money (Game) Master*.

...But a cheap trick like that isn't enough to catch up to Kaname.

Seeing him deal with the PMCs, perhaps Kaname now considered him a demon on the level of Bloody Dancer. However, that wasn't quite true. Even one of the Overtrick was enough to change the rules of engagement. All you had to do was know what those rules were.

The #primer.err wouldn't be enough to take down Kaname. So which one of the Overtrick would?

In the end, Takamasa had never fought fair. Whether against Bloody Dancer or the hordes of PMCs, all he had done was fill his foes full of lead while they were still getting their heads around the new rules he had created.

But that wouldn't work on Kaname. Before Takamasa could even put his strategy into play, three of the elite PMCs had managed to sneak up on him, and Kaname had shot them all dead. And it wasn't just luck, either. The way he moved on the battlefield to protect his friends was scarily precise. While Takamasa killed two with his explosive blasts, Kaname shot three, and he probably could have doubled that number if necessary.

It was something his score wouldn't measure.

Even thinking back to Bloody Dancer's dying breath, while the two of them had raised their guns, only Kaname had been able to pull the trigger in time.

Anyone could do the things Takamasa had done if they had #primer. err.

But Short Spear couldn't help anyone do what Kaname did.

"...There's still a long way to go."

In essence, the Overtrick were about deception, while Kaname took everything head-on. That was what made him shine so brightly. He was a man of twin talents, focus and power, able to snipe from long range or hold his own in a confined space. And to top it all off, one of the Zodiac Children, the Lion's Nose. Takamasa knew all that, or at least, he should have.

A rustling came from his pocket. The Overtrick were not the only secrets hidden in that facility. There were lists, even if they only consisted of partial transcriptions or audio recordings. Useless to Takamasa, of course, as he had the whole thing inscribed in his brain. In fact, it might be wiser to destroy them before they fell into the hands of other Dealers. And yet he had picked them all up, for one reason alone. Just to make sure.

I couldn't find the decryption key. Someone must have taken it...

It was something that Takamasa had never had reason to commit to paper. Having done the conversions himself by hand, he had drilled the complete procedure into his mind. It was only because of his own weakness that it still existed. Even knowing the importance of keeping the Overtrick a secret, he couldn't bring himself to seal off the one chance he might have of sharing his creations with someone he could truly trust.

"I can't believe it... Kaname is something else. To manage it in the middle of that battle, with those injuries."

If things had remained in deadlock between them, it could have ended here. But Takamasa would have no such luck. Because Kaname was one of the Zodiac Children. The Lion's Nose gave him the ability to sense approaching danger, not so that he could run away in fear, but so that he could accurately identify his prey.

Takamasa's dear friend possessed none of the weakness that resided in his own heart.

He was once the fighting specialist of the legendary Called Game. The Reaper, a master of sniping and car chases. If push came to shove, Takamasa knew that Kaname would not hesitate to draw his gun and pull the trigger, even if it meant taking someone's life.

He did not make excuses. He would do whatever it took to protect the smiles of those around him, to dry their tears. That was why he was the greatest Dealer. He was unstoppable. Absolutely unstoppable.

And so the two legendary Dealers' gazes met, one on earth and one in the heavens. And each muttered to the other:

""I wish I were a hero like you.""